P9-AOH-746

IMAGE COMICS, INC.

Robert Kirkman: Chief Operating Officer / Erik Larsen: Chief Financial Officer / Todd McFarlane: President / Marc Silvestri: Chief Executive Officer / Jim Valentino: Vice President / Eric Stephenson: Publisher / Corey Murphy: Director of Sales / Jeff Boison: Director of Publishing Planning & Book Trade Sales / Chris Ross: Director of Digital Sales / Jeff Stang: Director of Specialty Sales / Kat Salazar: Director of PR & Marketing / Branwyn Bigglestone: Controller / Kali Dugan: Senior Accounting Manager / Sue Korpela: Accounting & HR Manager / Drew Gill: Art Director / Heather Doornink: Production Director / Leigh Thomas: Print Manager / Tricia Ramos: Traffic Manager / Briah Skelly: Publicist / Aly Hoffman: Events & Conventions Coordinator / Sasha Head: Sales & Marketing Production Designer / David Brothers: Branding Manager / Melissa Gifford: Content Manager / Drew Fitzgerald: Publicity Assistant / Vincent Kukua: Production Artist / Erika Schnatz: Production Artist / Ryan Brewer: Production Artist / Shanna Matuszak: Production Artist / Carey Hall: Production Artist / Esther Kim: Direct Market Sales Representative / Emilio Bautista: Digital Sales Representative / Leanna Caunter: Accounting Analyst / Chloe Ramos-Peterson: Library Market Sales Representative / Marla Eizik: Administrative Assistant
IMAGECOMICS.COM

RADICAL PUBLISHING

President & Publisher - Jesse Berger
Chief Financial Officer - Mark Kaufman
General Counsel - Matthew Berger
Director of Sales - Teddy Cabugos
Art Director - Jeremy Berger
Social Media Director - Josh Berger

RADICALPUBLISHING.COM

GIANT GENERATOR

COLLECTION DESIGN BY **JEFF POWELL**

ISBN 978-1-5343-0437-6

THE LAST DAYS OF AMERICAN CRIME. First Edition. September 2017. Published by Image Comics, Inc. Office of publication: 2701 NW Vaughn Street, Suite 780, Portland, Oregon 97210. Copyright © 2017 Rick Remender and Radical Publishing, Inc. All rights reserved. Originally published in single magazine form as The Last Days of American Crime #1-3. The Last Days of American Crime™ (including all prominent characters featured herein), its logo and all character likenesses are trademarks of Rick Remender & Radical Publishing, Inc. unless otherwise noted. Image Comics® and its logos are registered trademarks of Image Comics, Inc. Radical Publishing, Inc. and its logos are registered trademarks of Radical Studios, Inc. No part of this publication may be reproduced or transmitted, in any form or by any means (except for short excerpts for review purposes) without the express written permission of Radical Publishing, Inc. All names, characters, events and locales in this publication are entirely fictional. Any resemblance to actual persons (living or dead), events or places, without satiric intent, is coincidental. PRINTED IN THE U.S.A. For information regarding the CPSIA on this printed material call: 203-595-3636 and provide reference # RICH – 761221. For international rights inquiries, contact: foreignlicensing@imagecomics.com.

THE LAST DAYS OF AMERICAN CRIME

WRITTEN BY
RICK REMENDER

ILLUSTRATED BY
GREG TOCCHINI

LETTERED BY
RUS WOOTON

ORIGINAL SERIES EDITOR
LUIS REYES

COLLECTION EDITOR
SEBASTIAN GIRNER

COVER ART
GREG TOCCHINI

CREATED BY
RICK REMENDER AND **GREG TOCCHINI**

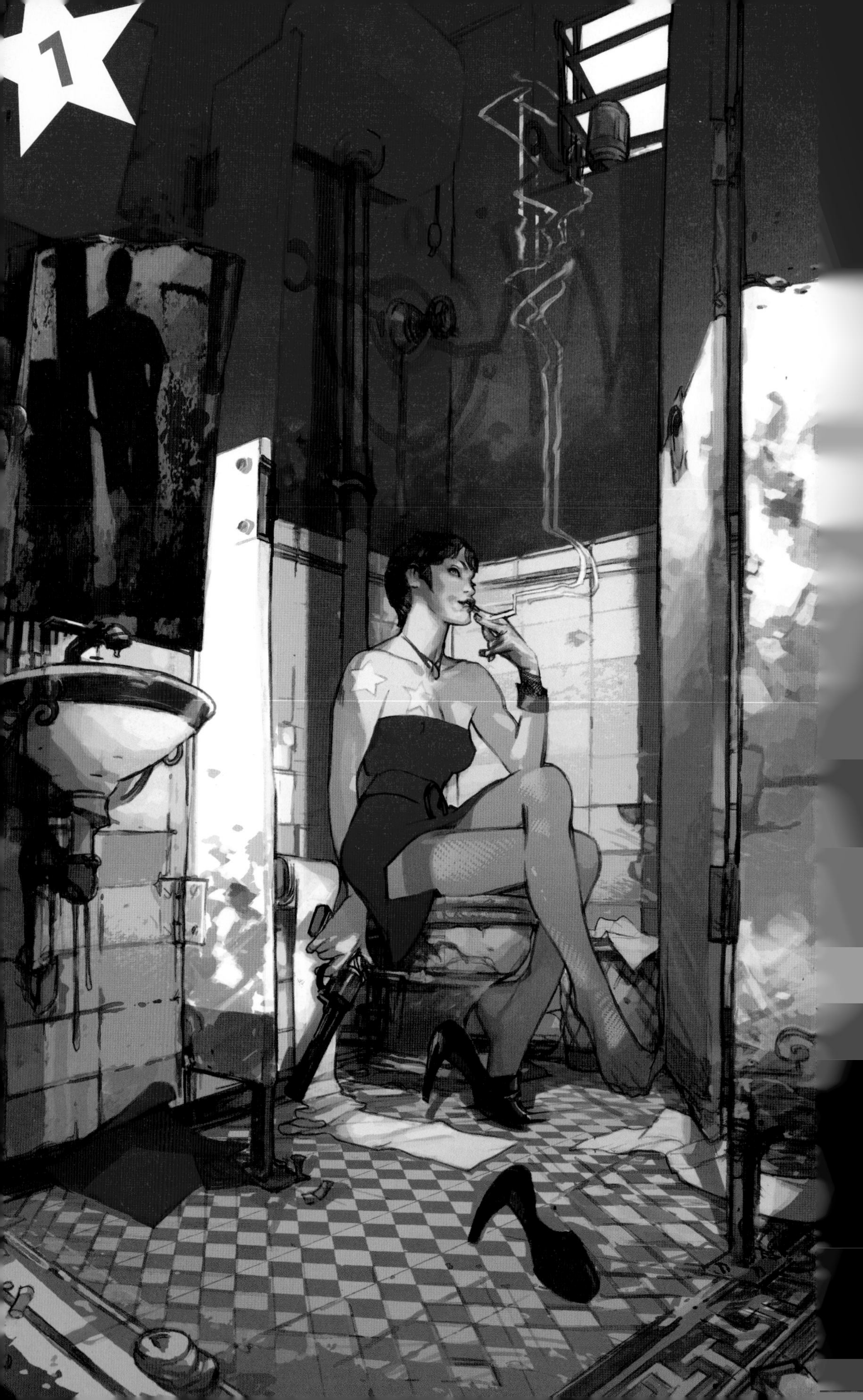
1

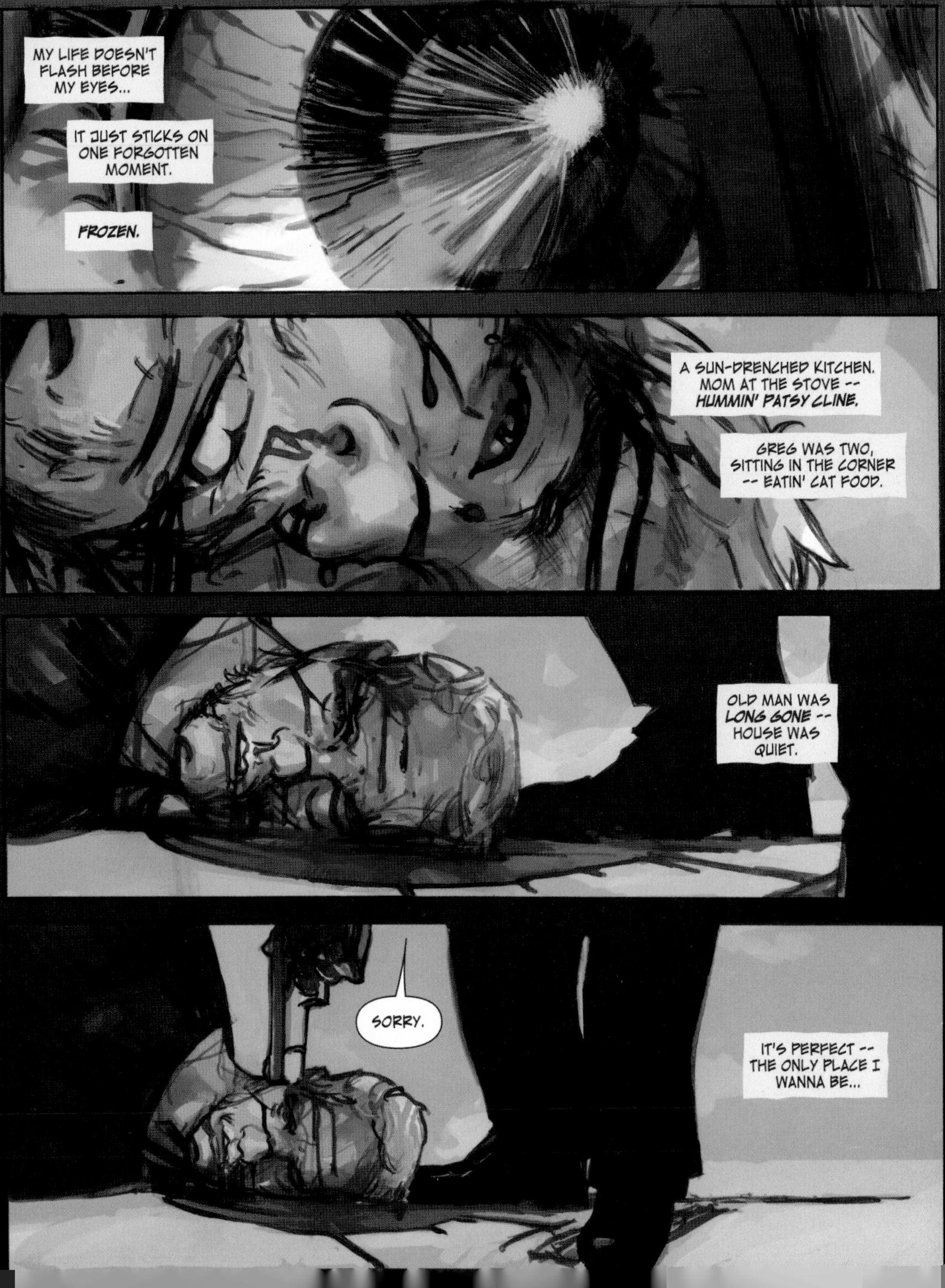
MY LIFE DOESN'T FLASH BEFORE MY EYES...
IT JUST STICKS ON ONE FORGOTTEN MOMENT.
FROZEN.
A SUN-DRENCHED KITCHEN. MOM AT THE STOVE -- HUMMIN' PATSY CLINE.
GREG WAS TWO, SITTING IN THE CORNER -- EATIN' CAT FOOD.
OLD MAN WAS LONG GONE -- HOUSE WAS QUIET.
SORRY.
IT'S PERFECT -- THE ONLY PLACE I WANNA BE...

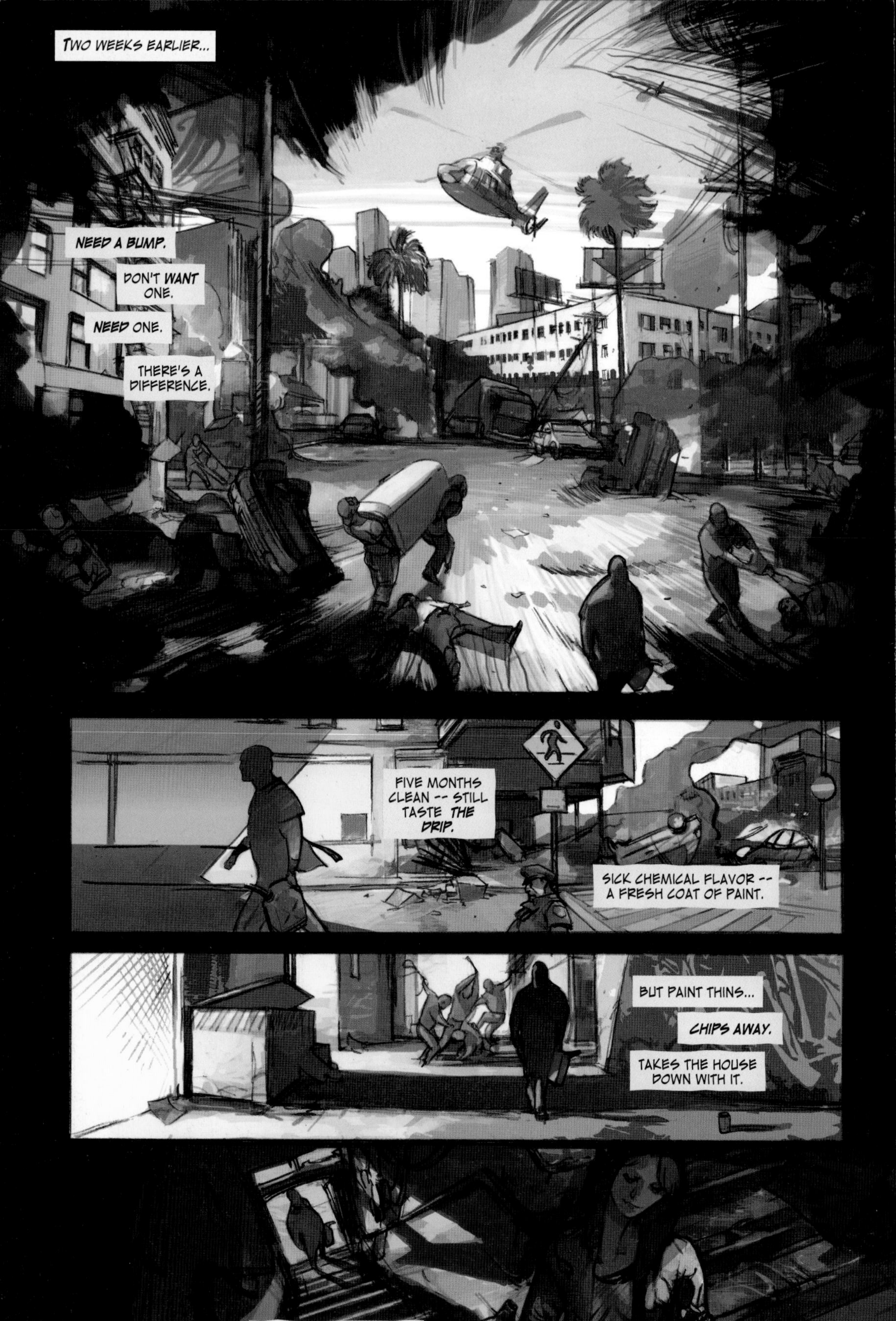
TWO WEEKS EARLIER...
NEED A BUMP.
DON'T WANT ONE.
NEED ONE.
THERE'S A DIFFERENCE.
FIVE MONTHS CLEAN -- STILL TASTE THE DRIP.
SICK CHEMICAL FLAVOR -- A FRESH COAT OF PAINT.
BUT PAINT THINS...
CHIPS AWAY.
TAKES THE HOUSE DOWN WITH IT.

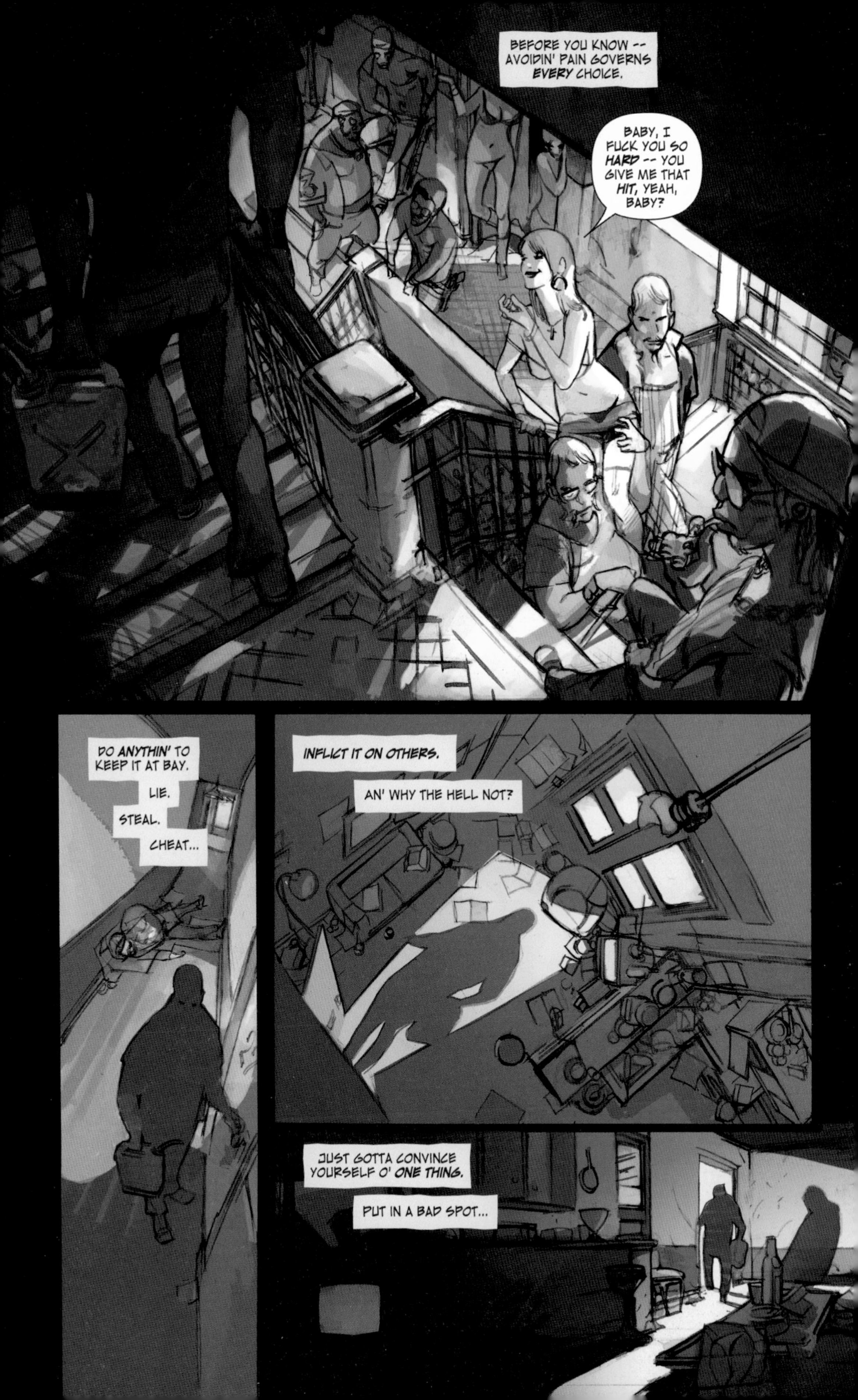
BEFORE YOU KNOW -- AVOIDIN' PAIN GOVERNS EVERY CHOICE.
BABY, I FUCK YOU SO HARD -- YOU GIVE ME THAT HIT, YEAH, BABY?
DO ANYTHIN' TO KEEP IT AT BAY.
LIE.
STEAL.
CHEAT...
INFLICT IT ON OTHERS.
AN' WHY THE HELL NOT?
JUST GOTTA CONVINCE YOURSELF O' ONE THING.
PUT IN A BAD SPOT...

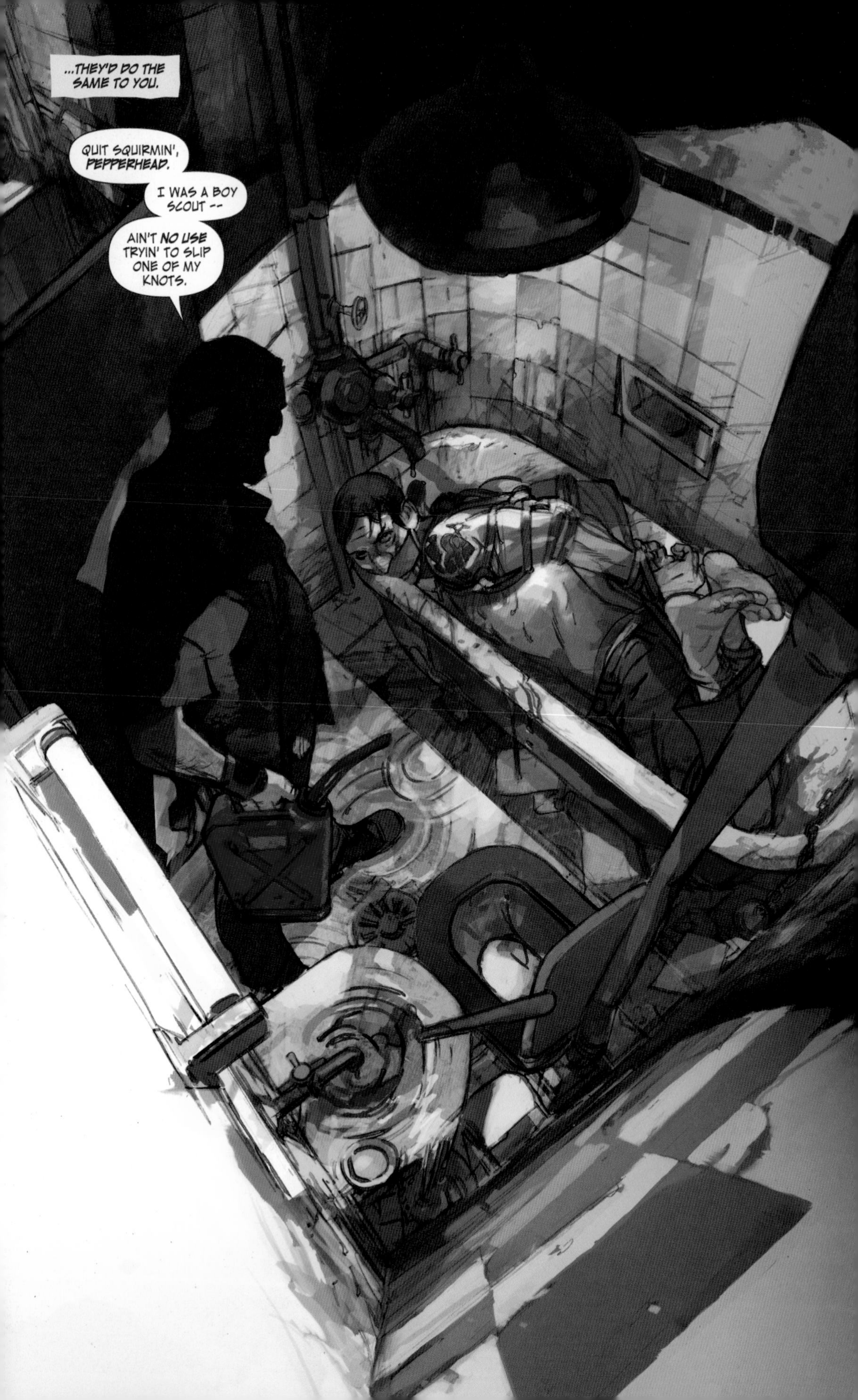
...THEY'D DO THE SAME TO YOU.
QUIT SQUIRMIN', PEPPERHEAD.
I WAS A BOY SCOUT --
AIN'T NO USE TRYIN' TO SLIP ONE OF MY KNOTS.

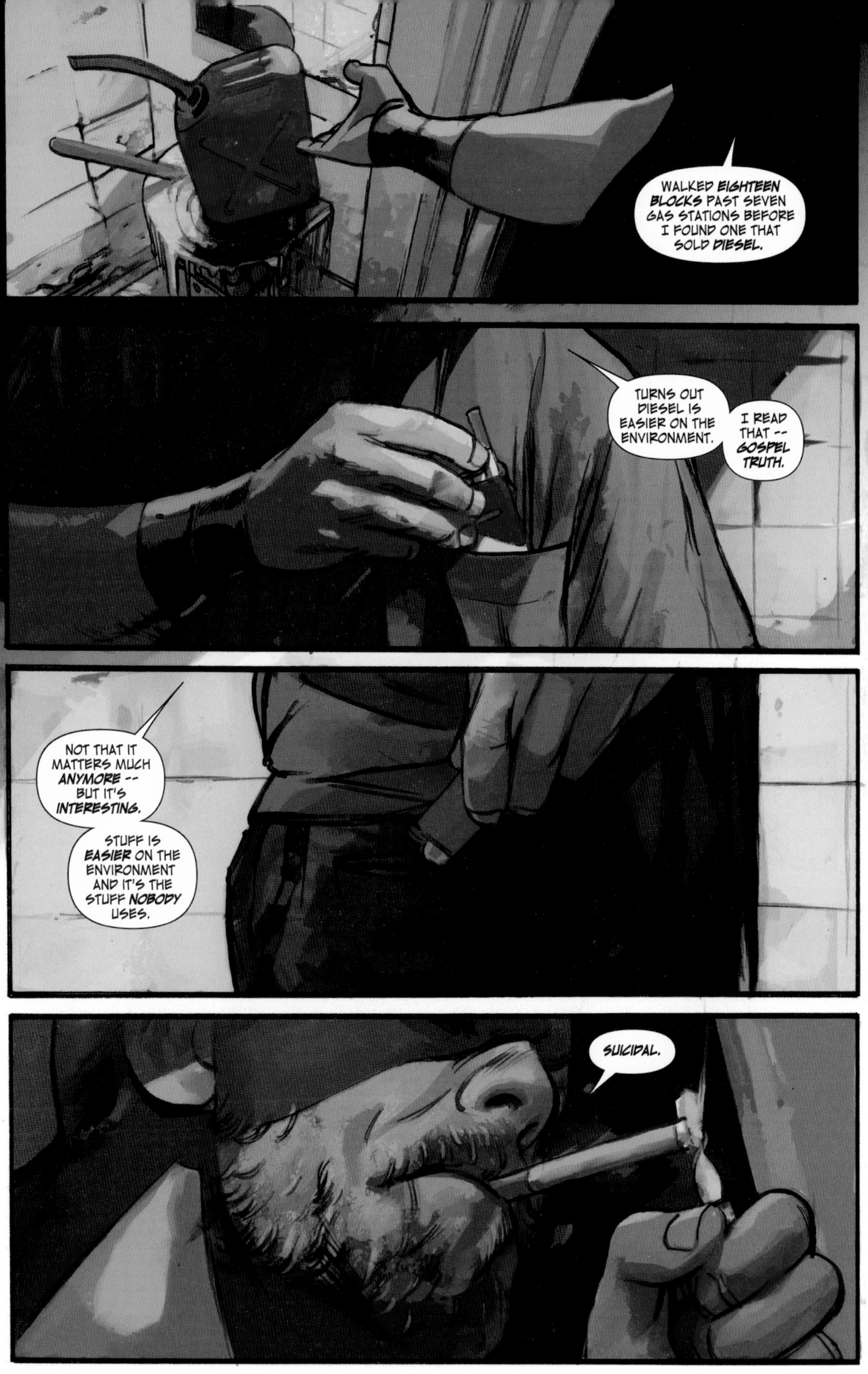
WALKED EIGHTEEN BLOCKS PAST SEVEN GAS STATIONS BEFORE I FOUND ONE THAT SOLD DIESEL.
TURNS OUT DIESEL IS EASIER ON THE ENVIRONMENT.
I READ THAT -- GOSPEL TRUTH.
NOT THAT IT MATTERS MUCH ANYMORE -- BUT IT'S INTERESTING.
STUFF IS EASIER ON THE ENVIRONMENT AND IT'S THE STUFF NOBODY USES.
SUICIDAL.

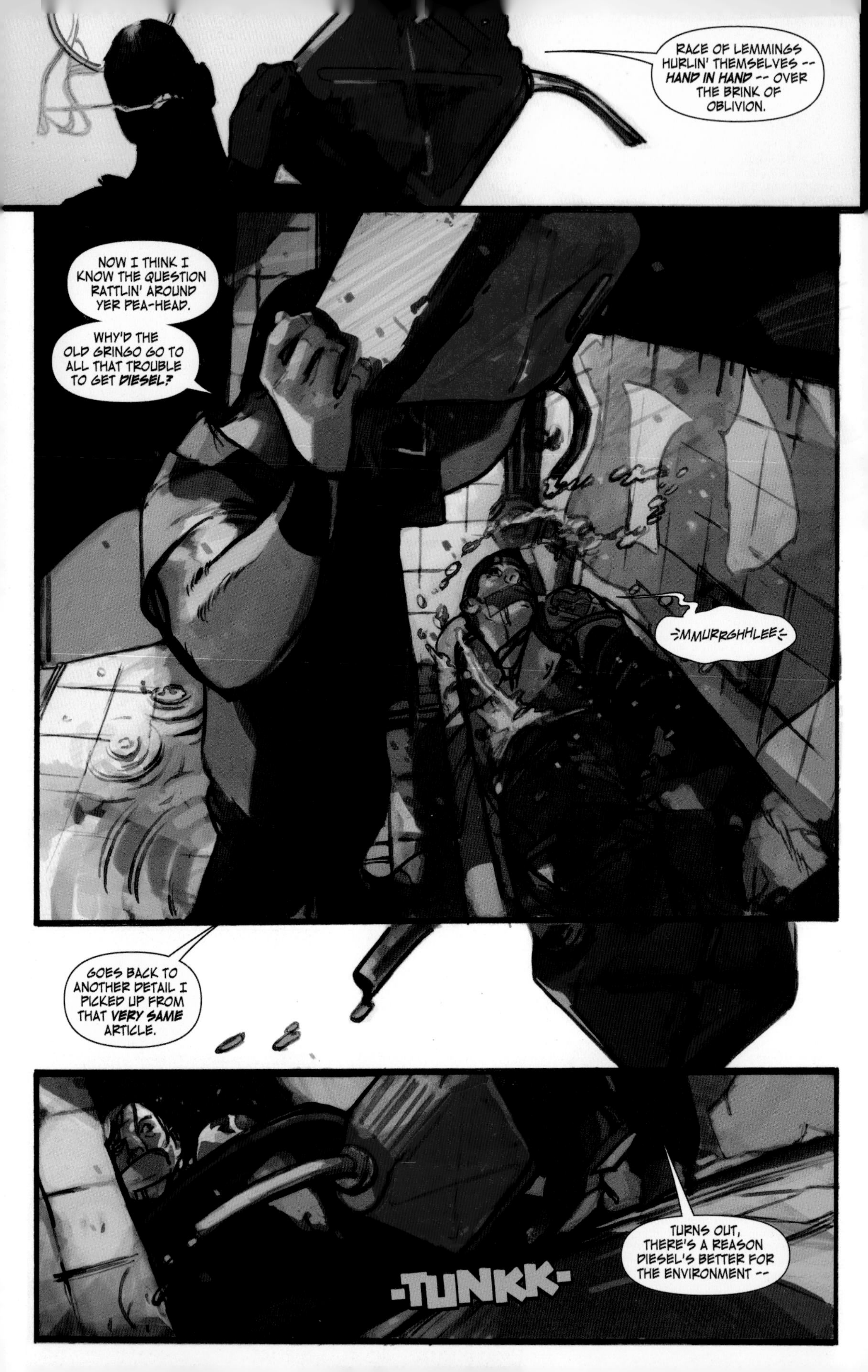
RACE OF LEMMINGS HURLIN' THEMSELVES -- HAND IN HAND -- OVER THE BRINK OF OBLIVION.
NOW I THINK I KNOW THE QUESTION RATTLIN' AROUND YER PEA-HEAD.
WHY'D THE OLD GRINGO GO TO ALL THAT TROUBLE TO GET DIESEL?
-MMURRGHHLEE-
GOES BACK TO ANOTHER DETAIL I PICKED UP FROM THAT VERY SAME ARTICLE.
TURNS OUT, THERE'S A REASON DIESEL'S BETTER FOR THE ENVIRONMENT --
-TUNKK-

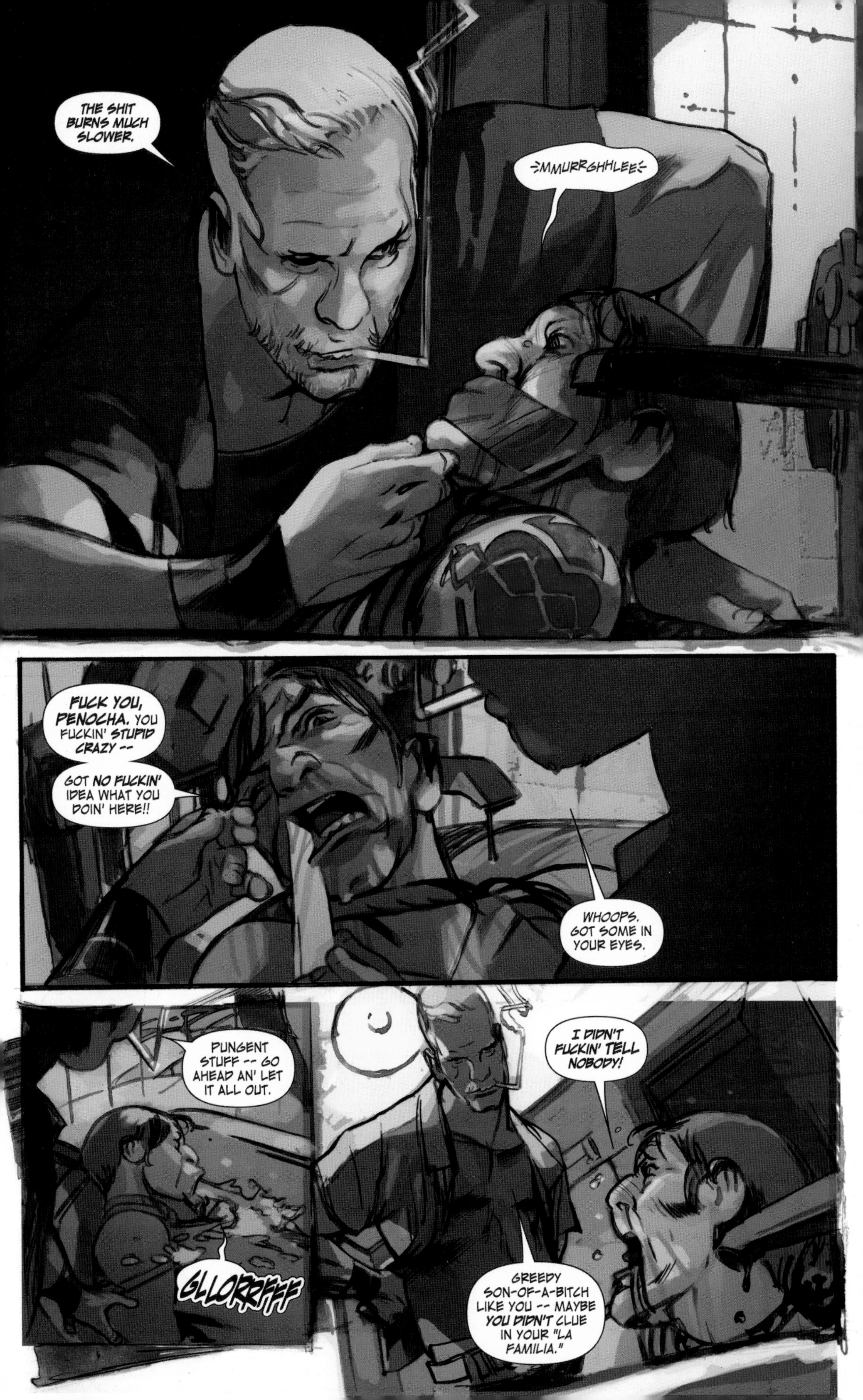
THE SHIT BURNS MUCH SLOWER.
MMURRGHHLEE
FUCK YOU, PENOCHA. YOU FUCKIN' STUPID CRAZY --
GOT NO FUCKIN' IDEA WHAT YOU DOIN' HERE!!
WHOOPS. GOT SOME IN YOUR EYES.
PUNGENT STUFF -- GO AHEAD AN' LET IT ALL OUT.
GLLORRFFF
I DIDN'T FUCKIN' TELL NOBODY!
GREEDY SON-OF-A-BITCH LIKE YOU -- MAYBE YOU DIDN'T CLUE IN YOUR "LA FAMILIA."

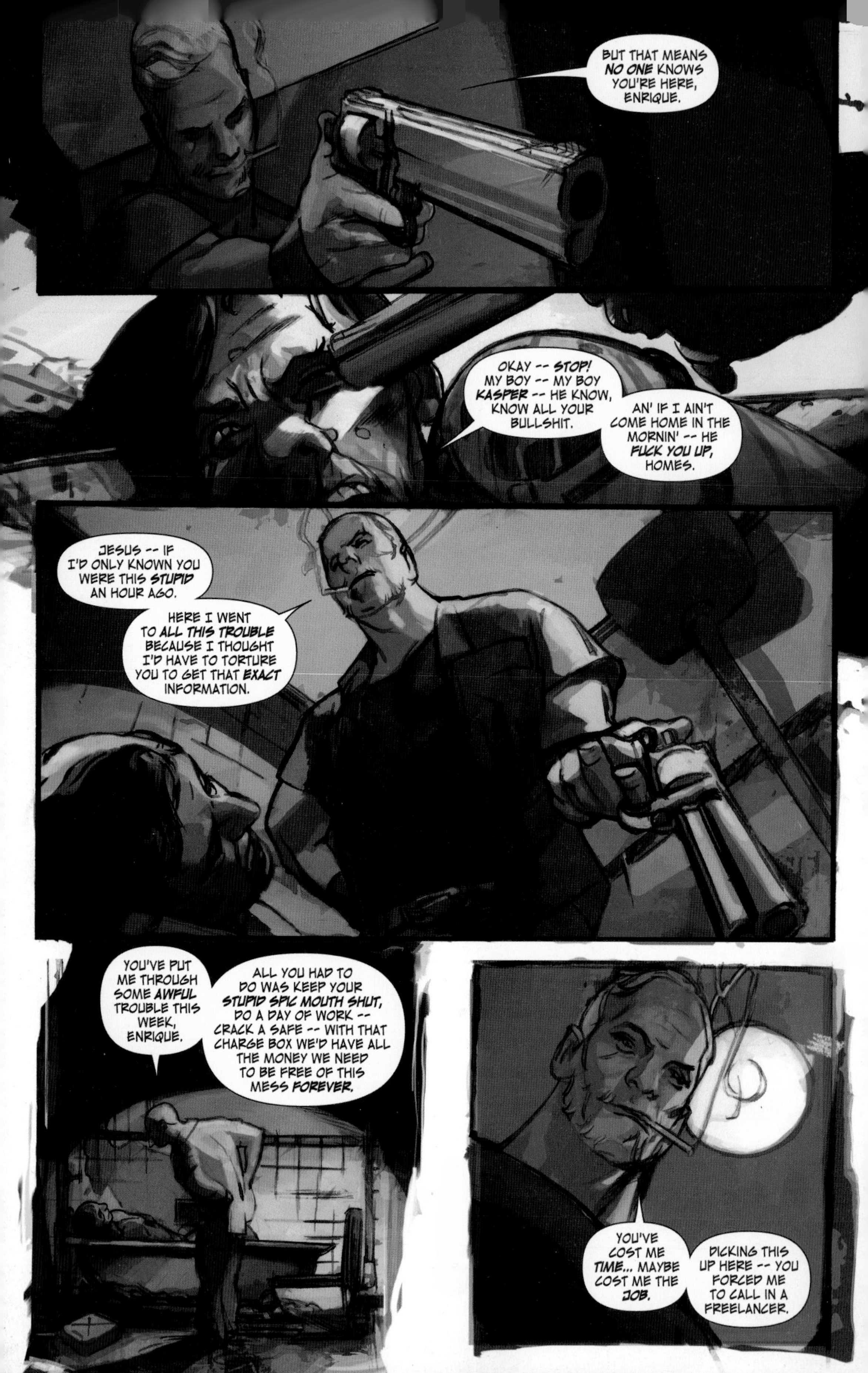
BUT THAT MEANS NO ONE KNOWS YOU'RE HERE, ENRIQUE.
OKAY -- STOP! MY BOY -- MY BOY KASPER -- HE KNOW, KNOW ALL YOUR BULLSHIT.
AN' IF I AIN'T COME HOME IN THE MORNIN' -- HE FUCK YOU UP, HOMES.
JESUS -- IF I'D ONLY KNOWN YOU WERE THIS STUPID AN HOUR AGO.
HERE I WENT TO ALL THIS TROUBLE BECAUSE I THOUGHT I'D HAVE TO TORTURE YOU TO GET THAT EXACT INFORMATION.
YOU'VE PUT ME THROUGH SOME AWFUL TROUBLE THIS WEEK, ENRIQUE.
ALL YOU HAD TO DO WAS KEEP YOUR STUPID SPIC MOUTH SHUT, DO A DAY OF WORK -- CRACK A SAFE -- WITH THAT CHARGE BOX WE'D HAVE ALL THE MONEY WE NEED TO BE FREE OF THIS MESS FOREVER.
YOU'VE COST ME TIME... MAYBE COST ME THE JOB.
DICKING THIS UP HERE -- YOU FORCED ME TO CALL IN A FREELANCER.

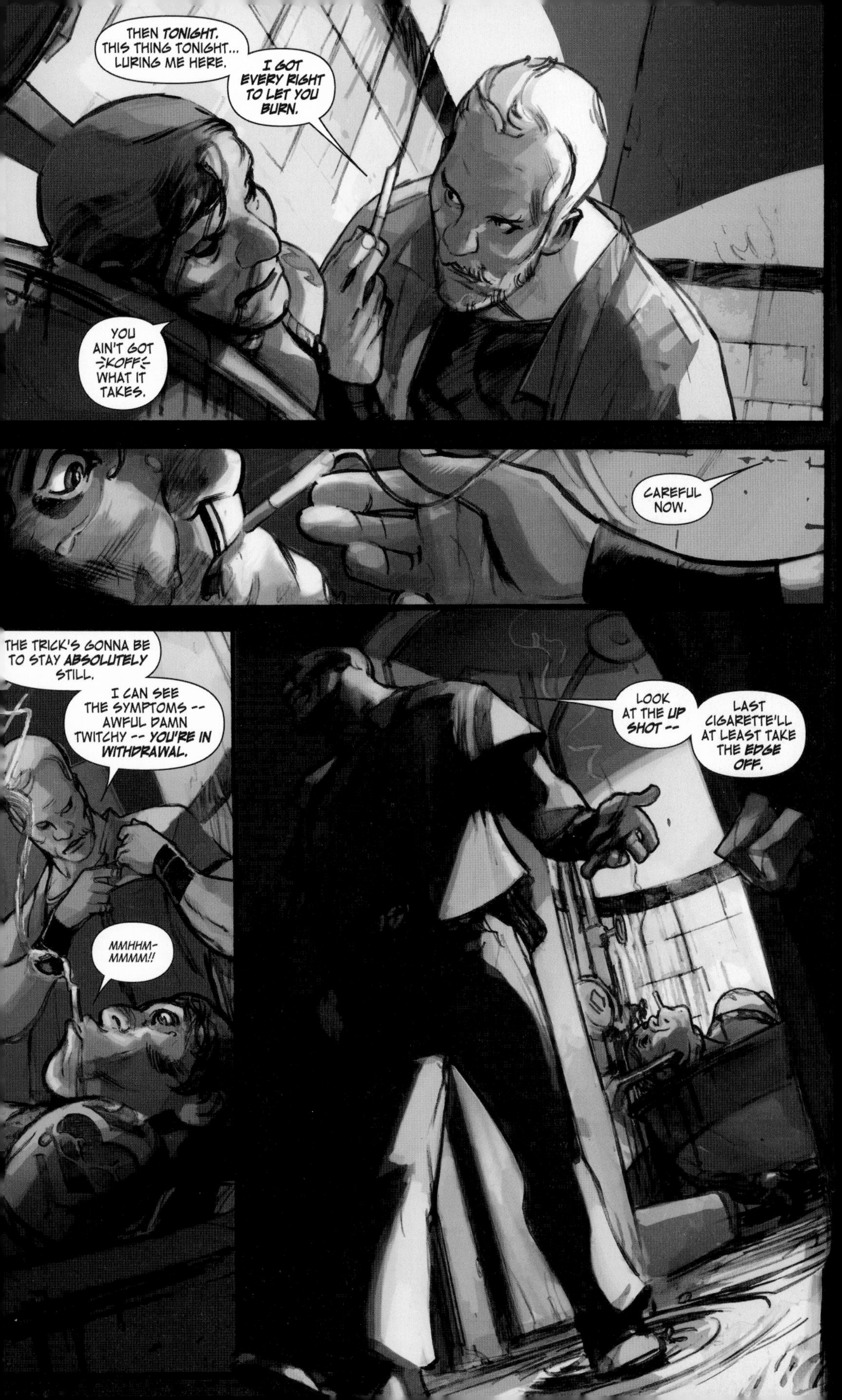

THEN TONIGHT. THIS THING TONIGHT... LURING ME HERE.
I GOT EVERY RIGHT TO LET YOU BURN.
YOU AIN'T GOT =KOFF= WHAT IT TAKES.
CAREFUL NOW.
THE TRICK'S GONNA BE TO STAY ABSOLUTELY STILL.
I CAN SEE THE SYMPTOMS -- AWFUL DAMN TWITCHY -- YOU'RE IN WITHDRAWAL.
MMHHM-MMMM!!
LOOK AT THE UP SHOT --
LAST CIGARETTE'LL AT LEAST TAKE THE EDGE OFF.

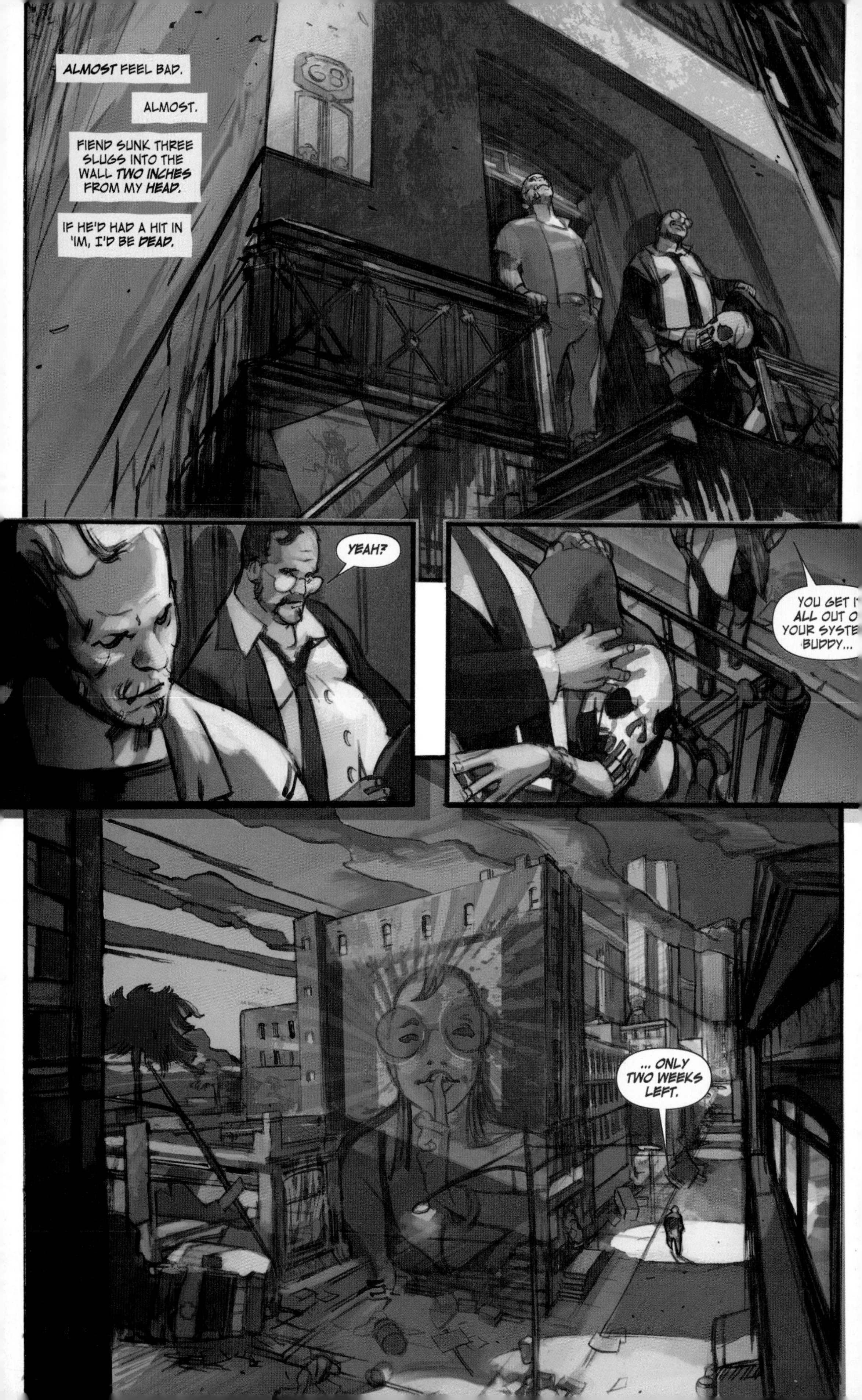
ALMOST FEEL BAD.
ALMOST.
FIEND SUNK THREE SLUGS INTO THE WALL TWO INCHES FROM MY HEAD.
IF HE'D HAD A HIT IN 'IM, I'D BE DEAD.
YEAH?
YOU GET I
ALL OUT O
YOUR SYSTE
BUDDY...
... ONLY TWO WEEKS LEFT.

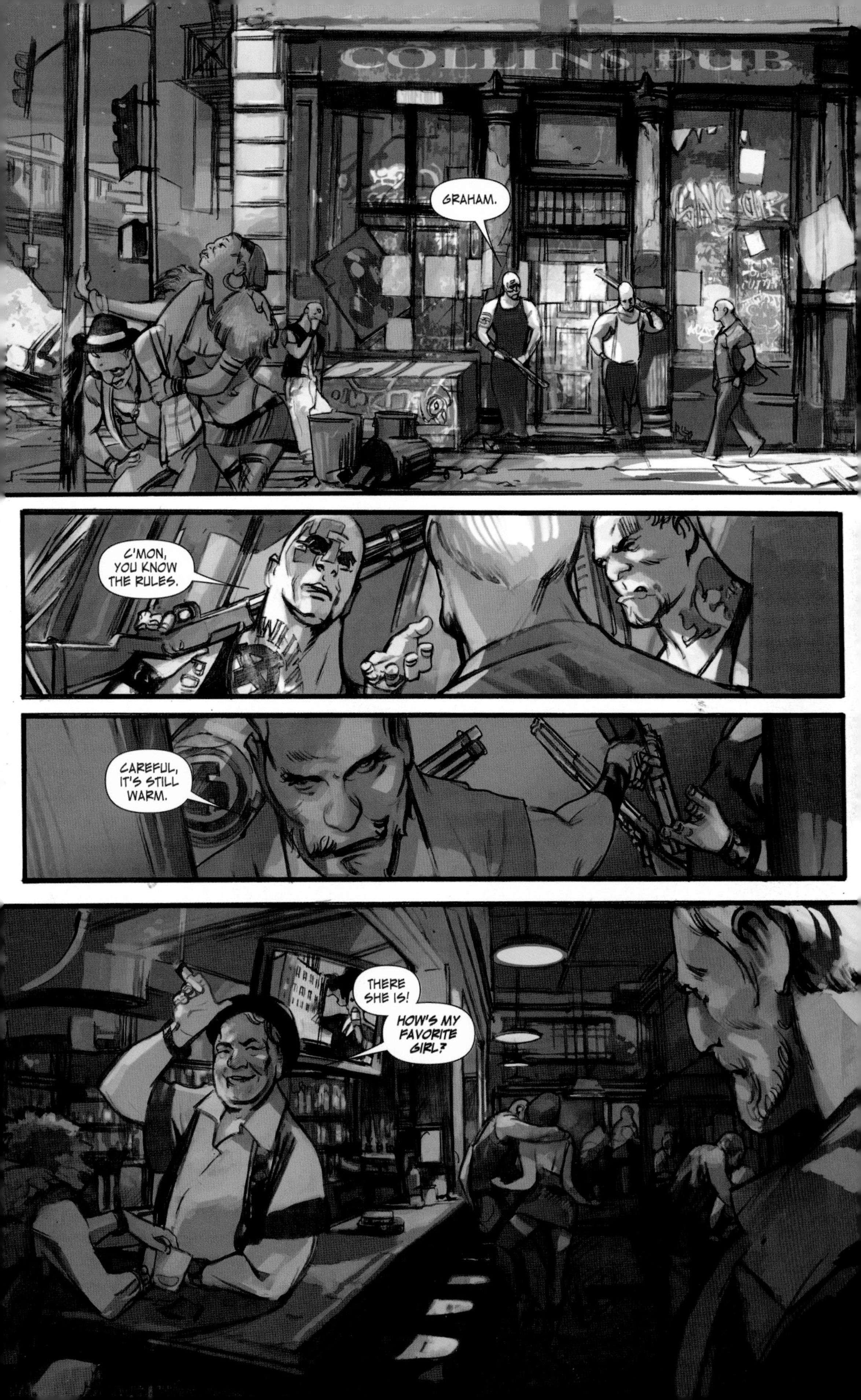
COLLINS PUB
GRAHAM.
C'MON, YOU KNOW THE RULES.
CAREFUL, IT'S STILL WARM.
THERE SHE IS!
HOW'S MY FAVORITE GIRL?

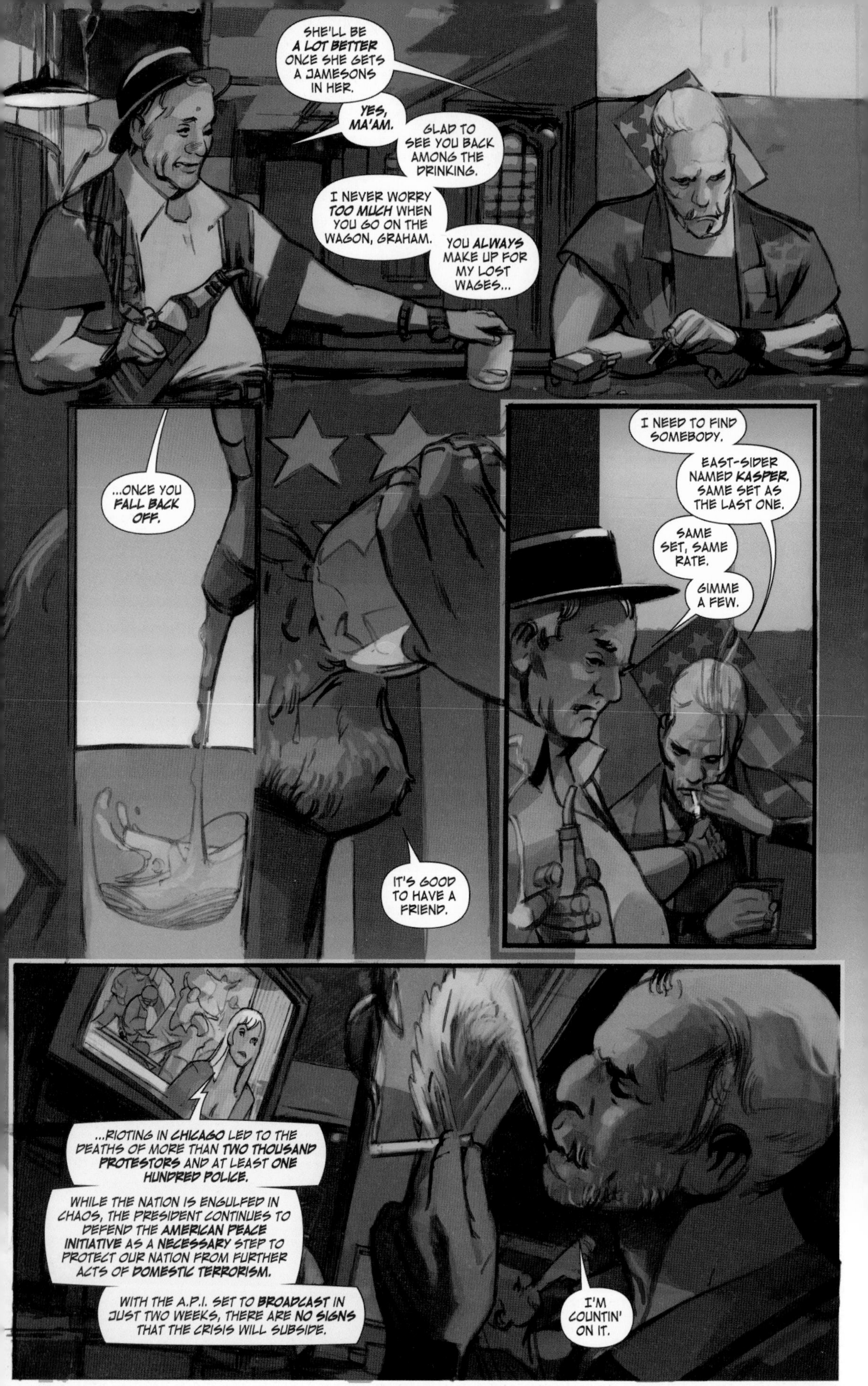
SHE'LL BE A LOT BETTER ONCE SHE GETS A JAMESONS IN HER.
YES, MA'AM.
GLAD TO SEE YOU BACK AMONG THE DRINKING.
I NEVER WORRY TOO MUCH WHEN YOU GO ON THE WAGON, GRAHAM.
YOU ALWAYS MAKE UP FOR MY LOST WAGES...
...ONCE YOU FALL BACK OFF.
IT'S GOOD TO HAVE A FRIEND.
I NEED TO FIND SOMEBODY.
EAST-SIDER NAMED KASPER. SAME SET AS THE LAST ONE.
SAME SET, SAME RATE.
GIMME A FEW.
...RIOTING IN CHICAGO LED TO THE DEATHS OF MORE THAN TWO THOUSAND PROTESTORS AND AT LEAST ONE HUNDRED POLICE.
WHILE THE NATION IS ENGULFED IN CHAOS, THE PRESIDENT CONTINUES TO DEFEND THE AMERICAN PEACE INITIATIVE AS A NECESSARY STEP TO PROTECT OUR NATION FROM FURTHER ACTS OF DOMESTIC TERRORISM.
WITH THE A.P.I. SET TO BROADCAST IN JUST TWO WEEKS, THERE ARE NO SIGNS THAT THE CRISIS WILL SUBSIDE.
I'M COUNTIN' ON IT.

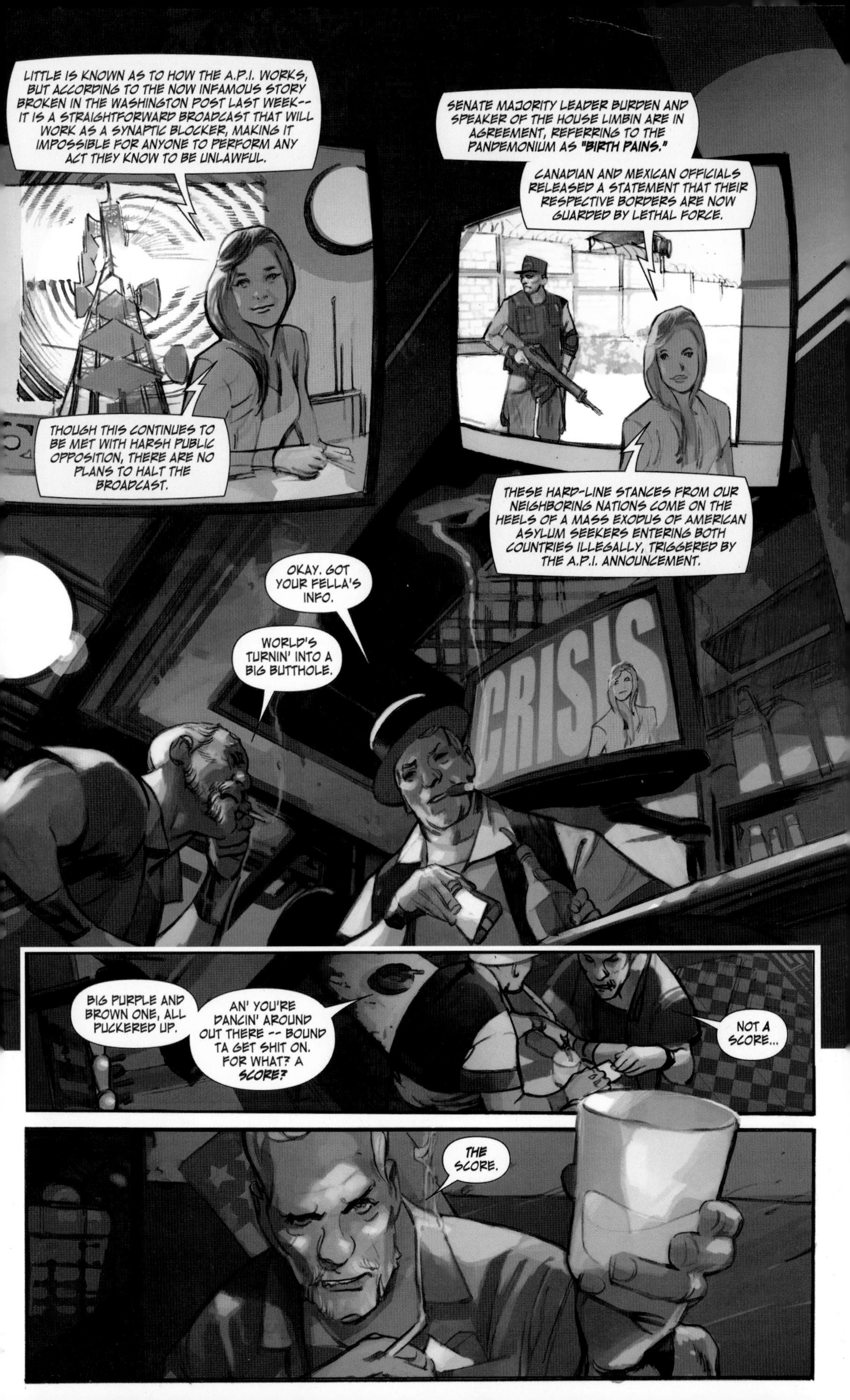
LITTLE IS KNOWN AS TO HOW THE A.P.I. WORKS, BUT ACCORDING TO THE NOW INFAMOUS STORY BROKEN IN THE WASHINGTON POST LAST WEEK-- IT IS A STRAIGHTFORWARD BROADCAST THAT WILL WORK AS A SYNAPTIC BLOCKER, MAKING IT IMPOSSIBLE FOR ANYONE TO PERFORM ANY ACT THEY KNOW TO BE UNLAWFUL.
THOUGH THIS CONTINUES TO BE MET WITH HARSH PUBLIC OPPOSITION, THERE ARE NO PLANS TO HALT THE BROADCAST.
SENATE MAJORITY LEADER BURDEN AND SPEAKER OF THE HOUSE LIMBIN ARE IN AGREEMENT, REFERRING TO THE PANDEMONIUM AS "BIRTH PAINS."
CANADIAN AND MEXICAN OFFICIALS RELEASED A STATEMENT THAT THEIR RESPECTIVE BORDERS ARE NOW GUARDED BY LETHAL FORCE.
THESE HARD-LINE STANCES FROM OUR NEIGHBORING NATIONS COME ON THE HEELS OF A MASS EXODUS OF AMERICAN ASYLUM SEEKERS ENTERING BOTH COUNTRIES ILLEGALLY, TRIGGERED BY THE A.P.I. ANNOUNCEMENT.
OKAY. GOT YOUR FELLA'S INFO.
WORLD'S TURNIN' INTO A BIG BUTTHOLE.
CRISIS
BIG PURPLE AND BROWN ONE, ALL PUCKERED UP.
AN' YOU'RE DANCIN' AROUND OUT THERE -- BOUND TA GET SHIT ON. FOR WHAT? A SCORE?
NOT A SCORE...
THE SCORE.

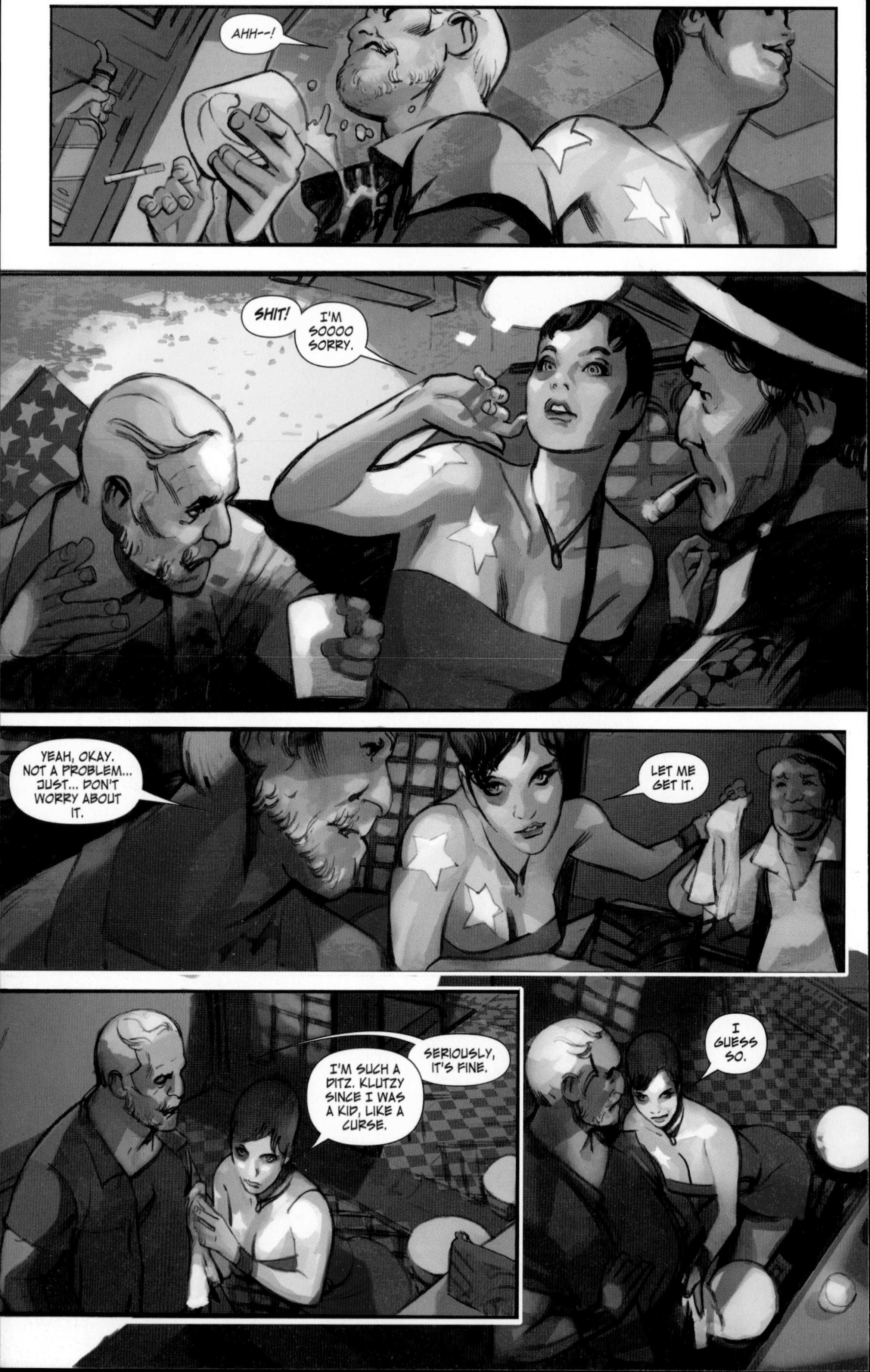
AHH--!
SHIT!
I'M SOOOO SORRY.
YEAH, OKAY. NOT A PROBLEM... JUST... DON'T WORRY ABOUT IT.
LET ME GET IT.
I'M SUCH A DITZ. KLUTZY SINCE I WAS A KID, LIKE A CURSE.
SERIOUSLY, IT'S FINE.
I GUESS SO.

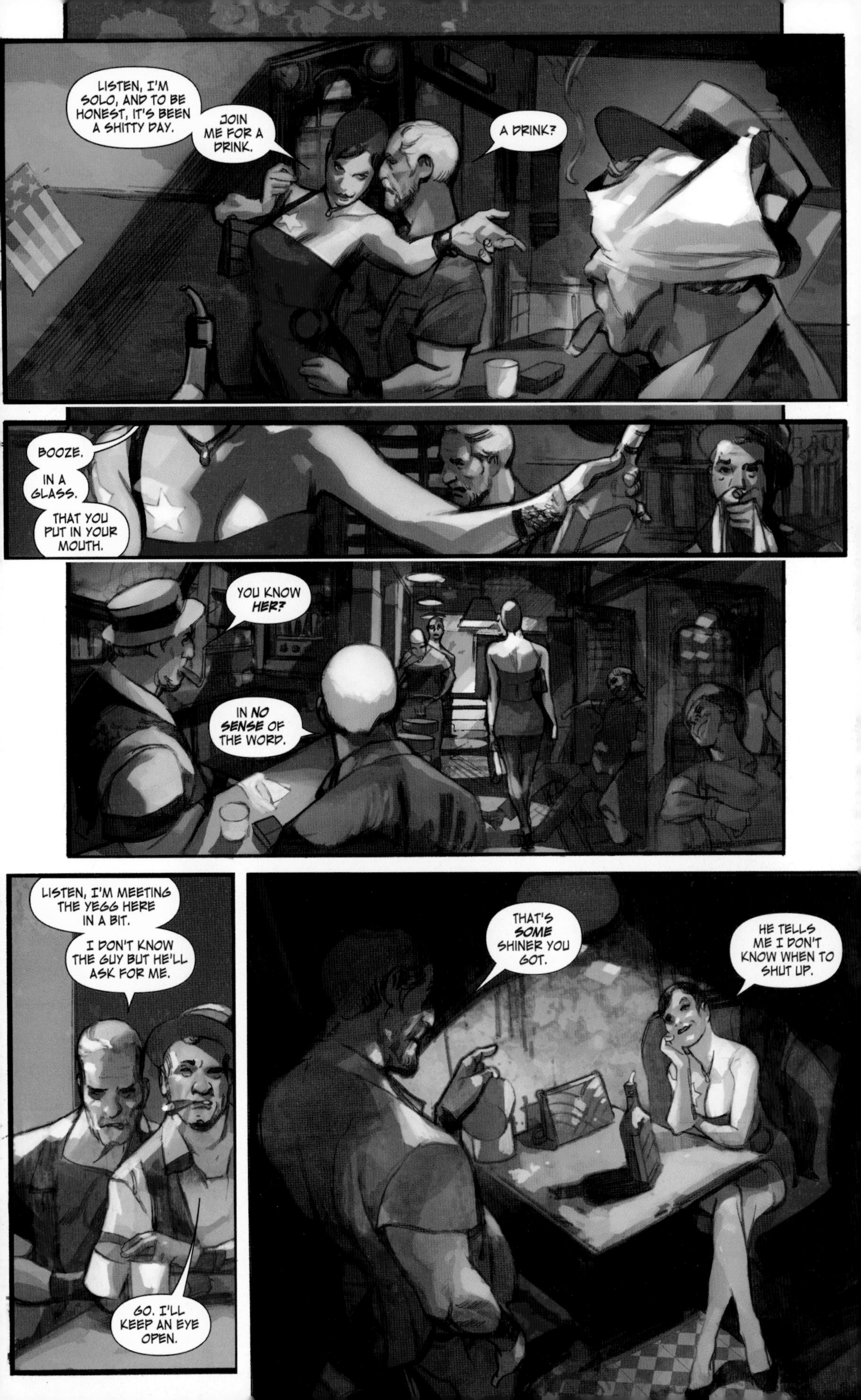
LISTEN, I'M SOLO, AND TO BE HONEST, IT'S BEEN A SHITTY DAY.
JOIN ME FOR A DRINK.
A DRINK?
BOOZE.
IN A GLASS.
THAT YOU PUT IN YOUR MOUTH.
YOU KNOW HER?
IN NO SENSE OF THE WORD.
LISTEN, I'M MEETING THE YEGG HERE IN A BIT.
I DON'T KNOW THE GUY BUT HE'LL ASK FOR ME.
GO. I'LL KEEP AN EYE OPEN.
THAT'S SOME SHINER YOU GOT.
HE TELLS ME I DON'T KNOW WHEN TO SHUT UP.

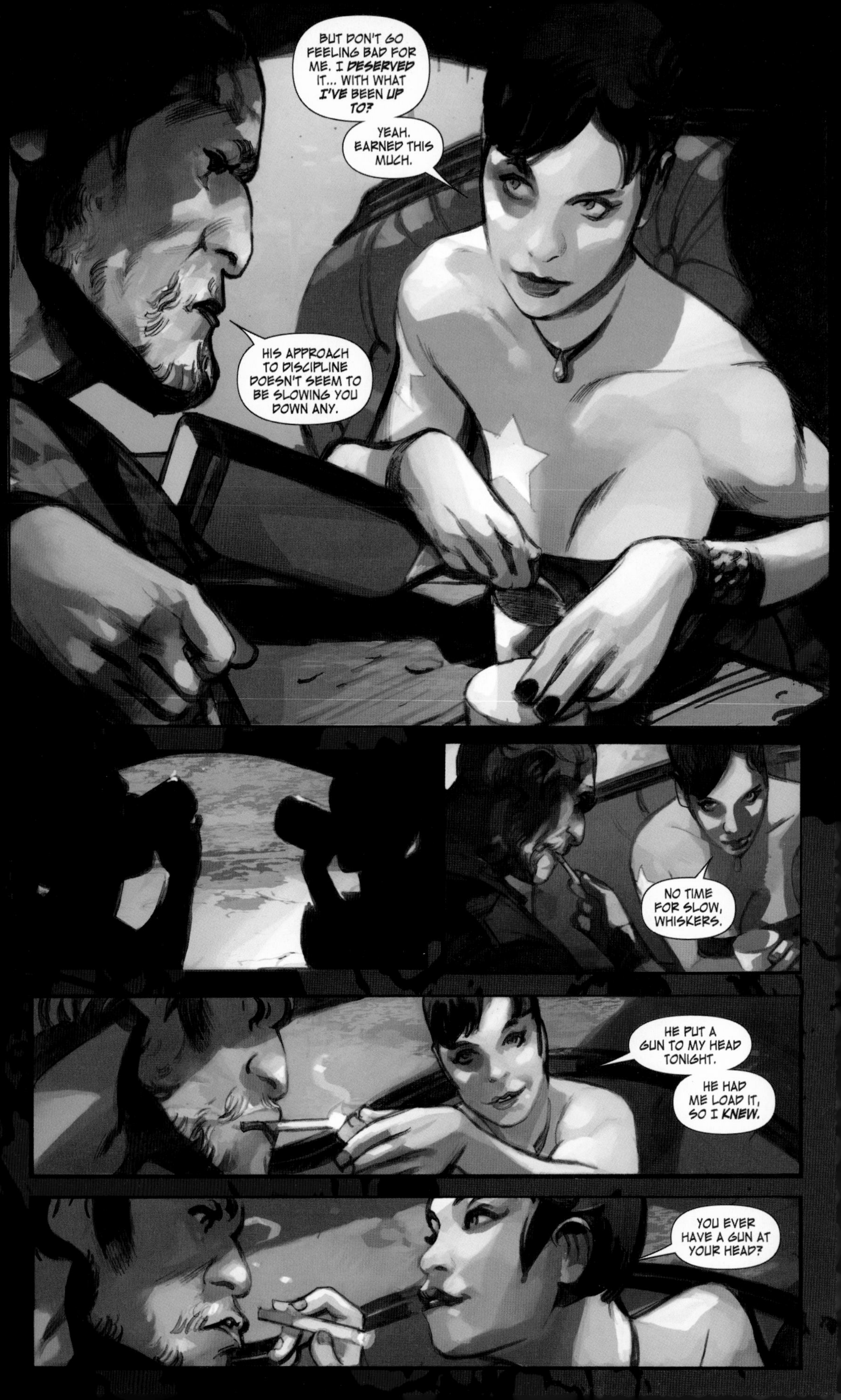
BUT DON'T GO FEELING BAD FOR ME. I DESERVED IT... WITH WHAT I'VE BEEN UP TO?
YEAH. EARNED THIS MUCH.
HIS APPROACH TO DISCIPLINE DOESN'T SEEM TO BE SLOWING YOU DOWN ANY.
NO TIME FOR SLOW, WHISKERS.
HE PUT A GUN TO MY HEAD TONIGHT.
HE HAD ME LOAD IT, SO I KNEW.
YOU EVER HAVE A GUN AT YOUR HEAD?

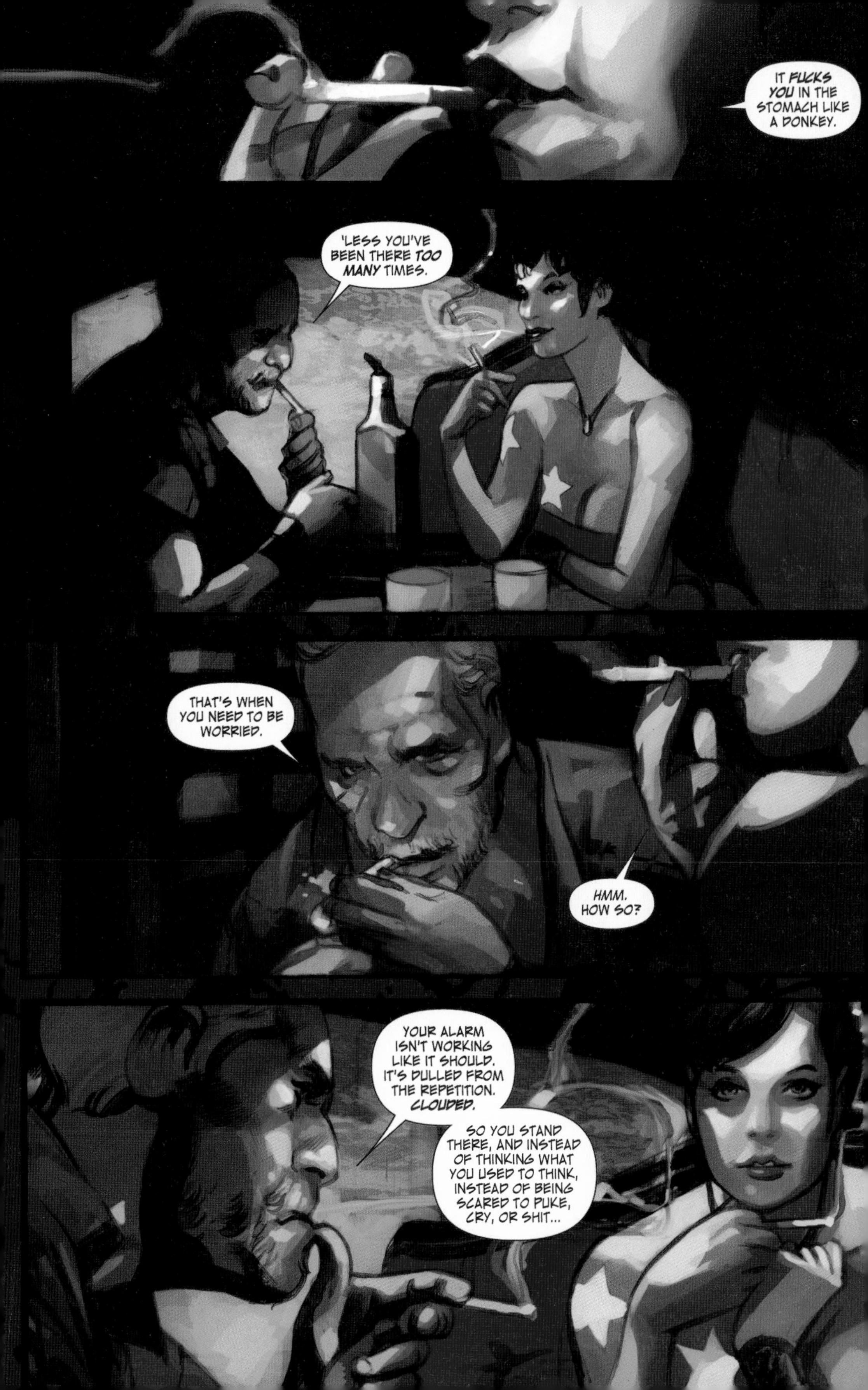
IT FUCKS YOU IN THE STOMACH LIKE A DONKEY.
'LESS YOU'VE BEEN THERE TOO MANY TIMES.
THAT'S WHEN YOU NEED TO BE WORRIED.
HMM. HOW SO?
YOUR ALARM ISN'T WORKING LIKE IT SHOULD. IT'S DULLED FROM THE REPETITION. CLOUDED.
SO YOU STAND THERE, AND INSTEAD OF THINKING WHAT YOU USED TO THINK, INSTEAD OF BEING SCARED TO PUKE, CRY, OR SHIT...

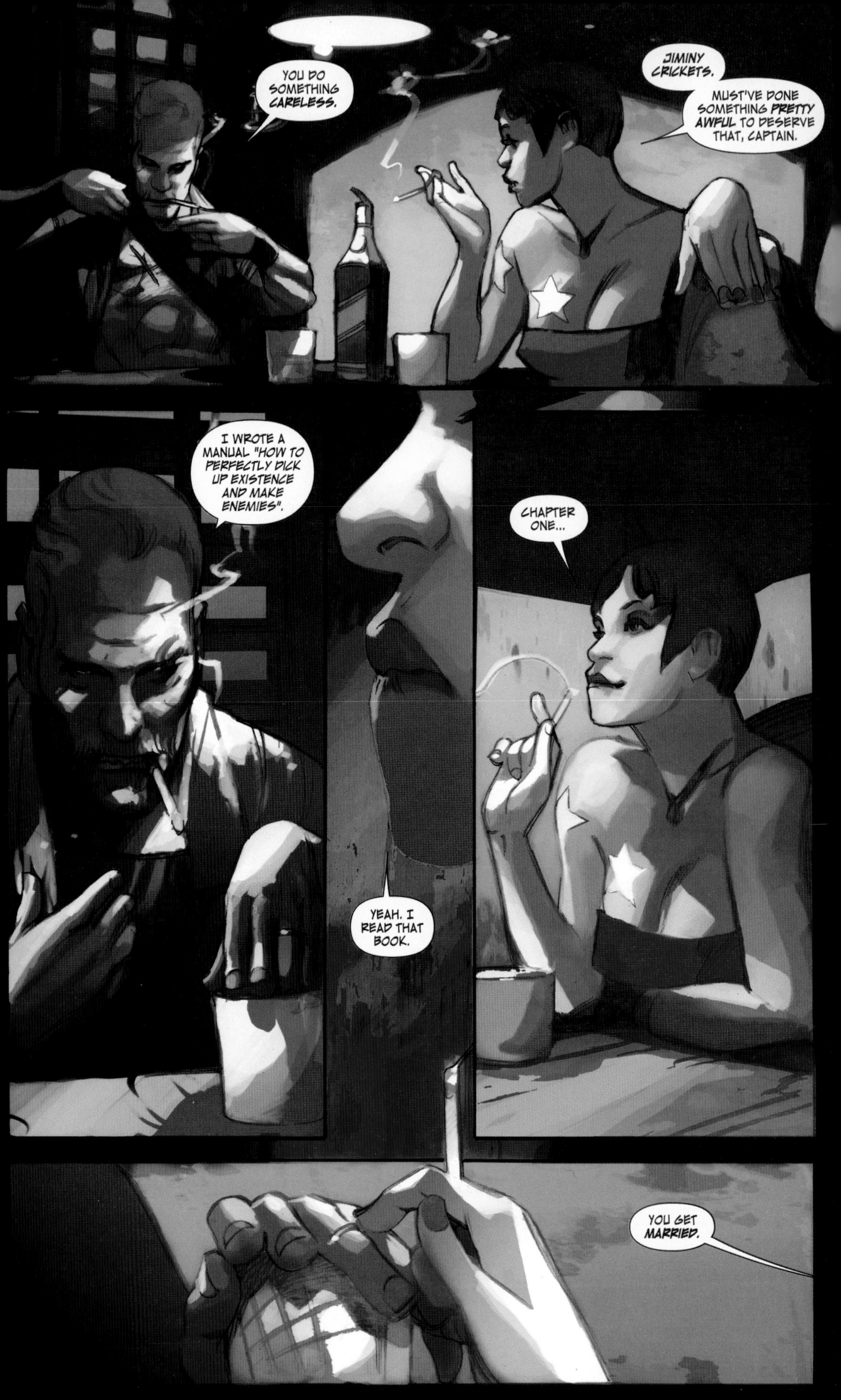
YOU DO SOMETHING CARELESS.
JIMINY CRICKETS.
MUST'VE DONE SOMETHING PRETTY AWFUL TO DESERVE THAT, CAPTAIN.
I WROTE A MANUAL "HOW TO PERFECTLY DICK UP EXISTENCE AND MAKE ENEMIES".
YEAH. I READ THAT BOOK.
CHAPTER ONE...
YOU GET MARRIED.

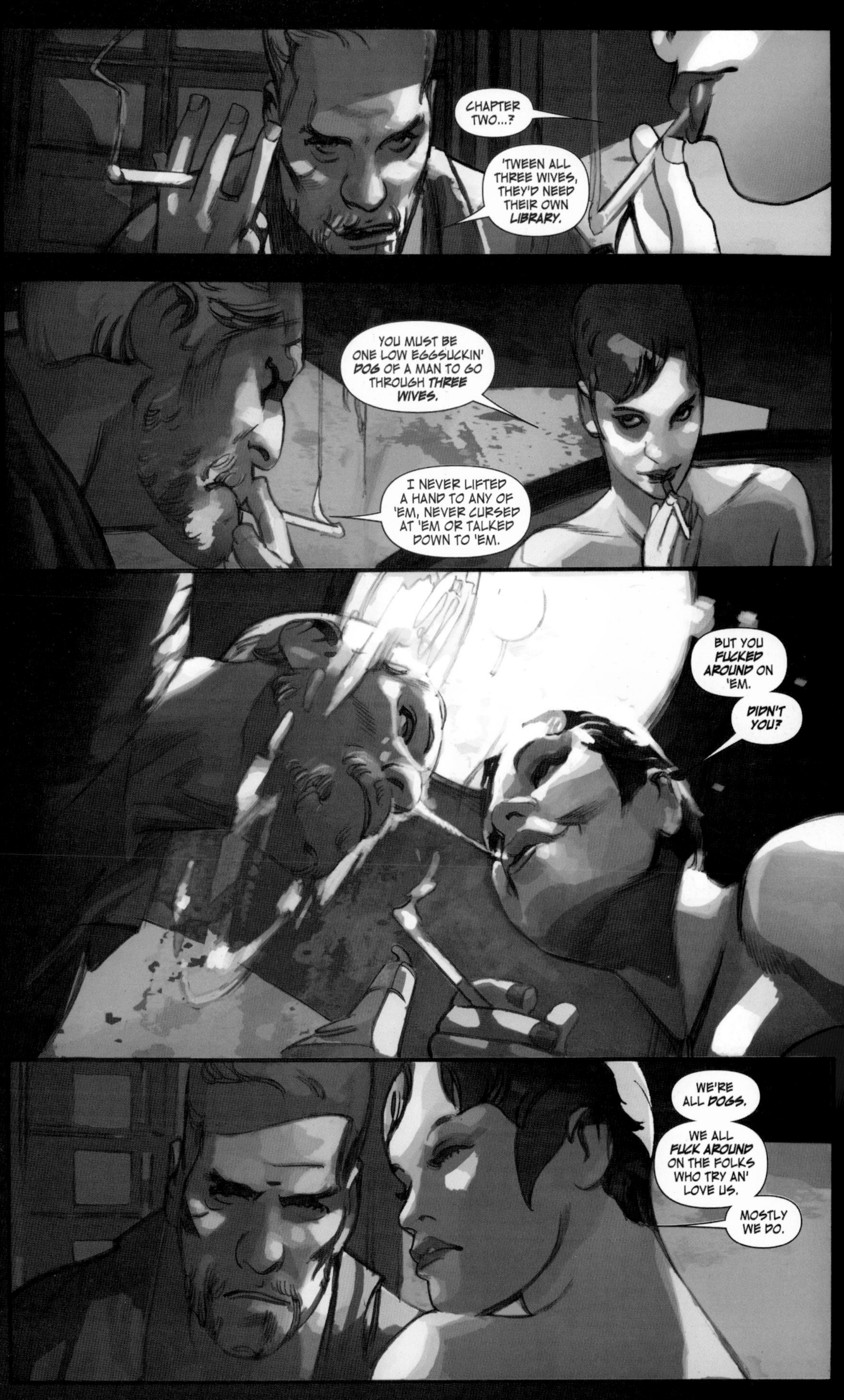
CHAPTER TWO...?
'TWEEN ALL THREE WIVES, THEY'D NEED THEIR OWN LIBRARY.
YOU MUST BE ONE LOW EGGSUCKIN' DOG OF A MAN TO GO THROUGH THREE WIVES.
I NEVER LIFTED A HAND TO ANY OF 'EM, NEVER CURSED AT 'EM OR TALKED DOWN TO 'EM.
BUT YOU FUCKED AROUND ON 'EM.
DIDN'T YOU?
WE'RE ALL DOGS.
WE ALL FUCK AROUND ON THE FOLKS WHO TRY AN' LOVE US.
MOSTLY WE DO.

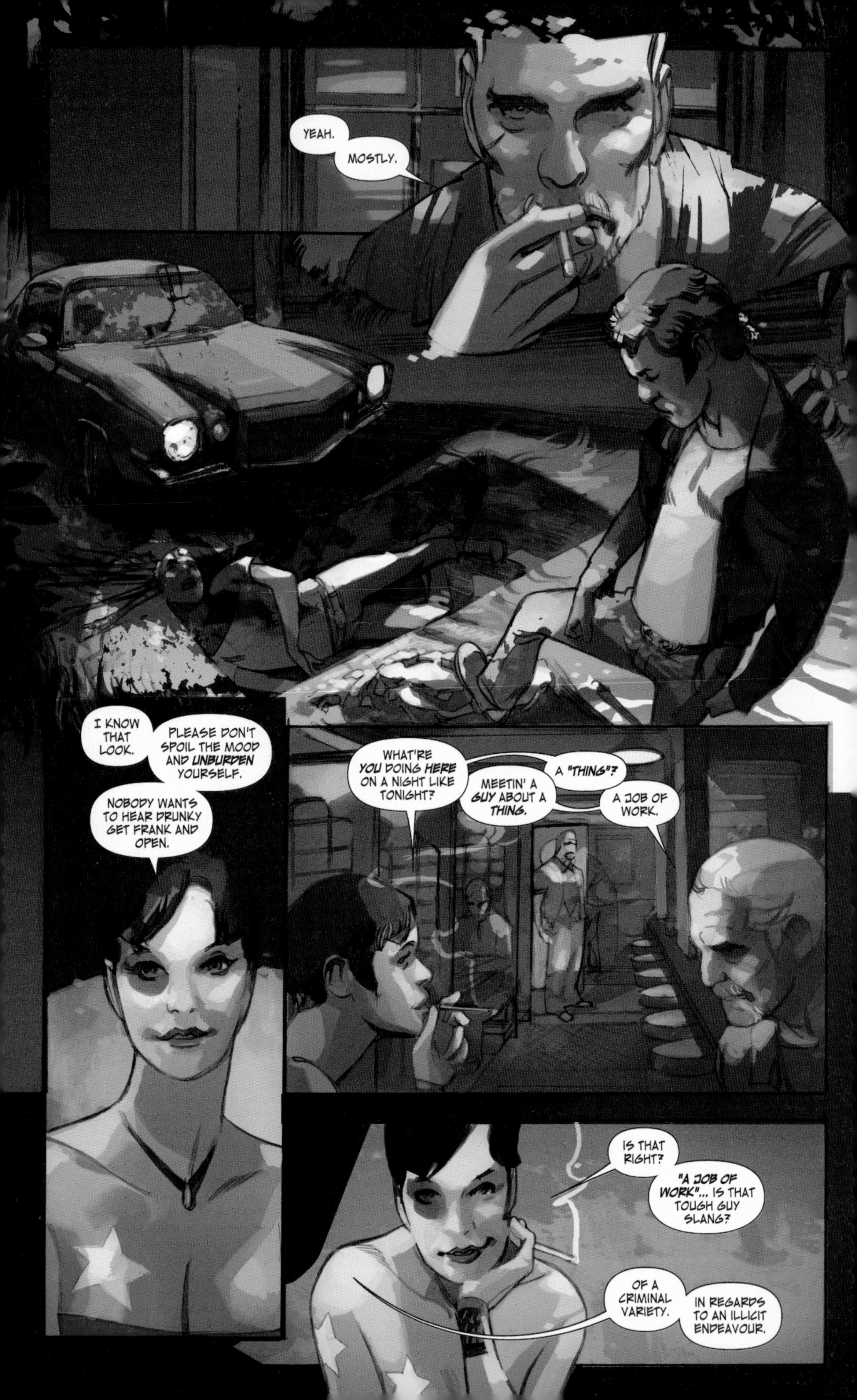

YEAH.
MOSTLY.
I KNOW THAT LOOK.
PLEASE DON'T SPOIL THE MOOD AND UNBURDEN YOURSELF.
NOBODY WANTS TO HEAR DRUNKY GET FRANK AND OPEN.
WHAT'RE YOU DOING HERE ON A NIGHT LIKE TONIGHT?
MEETIN' A GUY ABOUT A THING.
A "THING"?
A JOB OF WORK.
IS THAT RIGHT?
"A JOB OF WORK"... IS THAT TOUGH GUY SLANG?
OF A CRIMINAL VARIETY.
IN REGARDS TO AN ILLICIT ENDEAVOUR.

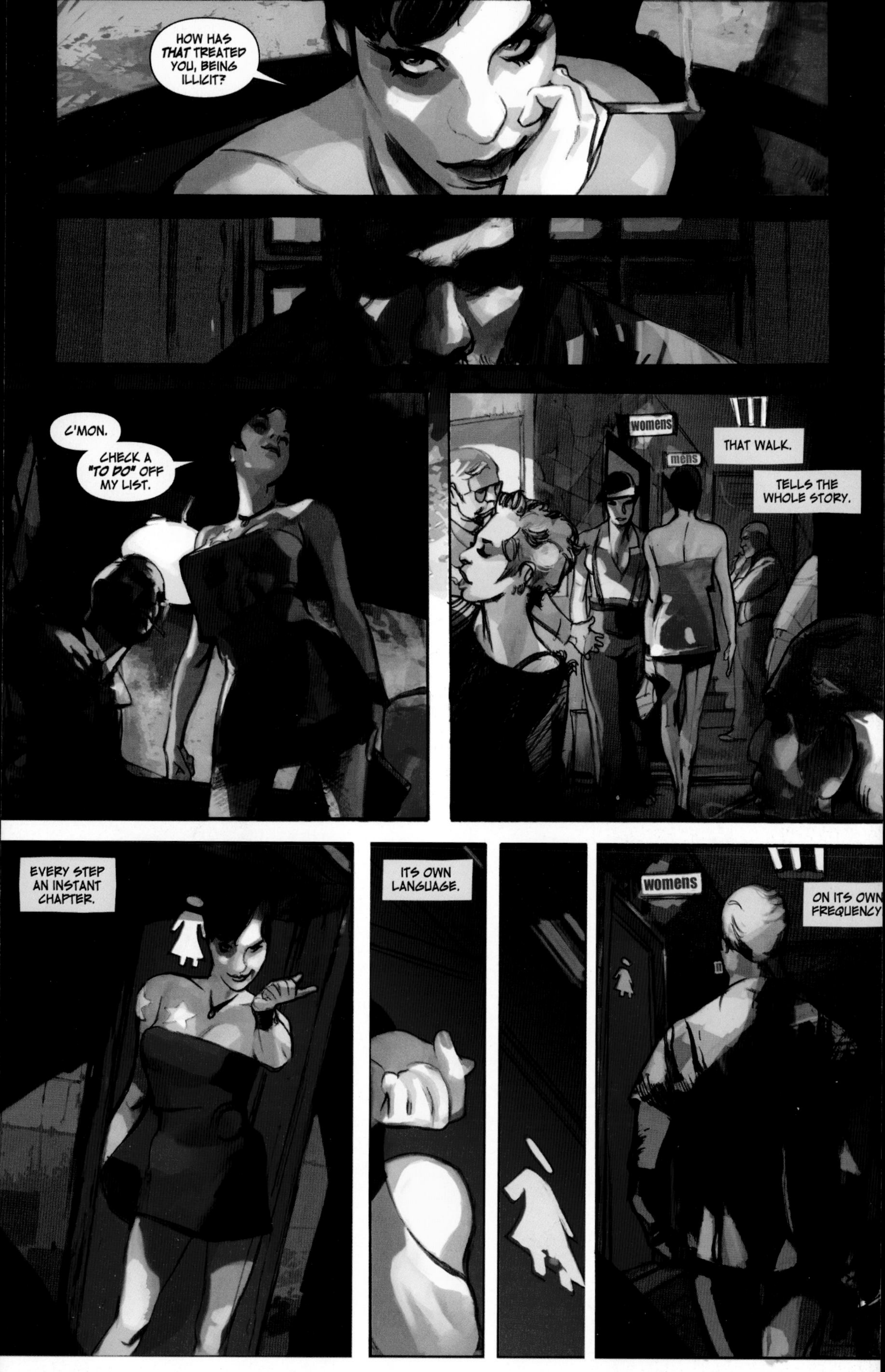
HOW HAS *THAT* TREATED YOU, BEING ILLICIT?
C'MON.
CHECK A *"TO DO"* OFF MY LIST.
womens
mens
THAT WALK.
TELLS THE WHOLE STORY.
EVERY STEP AN INSTANT CHAPTER.
ITS OWN LANGUAGE.
womens
ON ITS OWN FREQUENCY

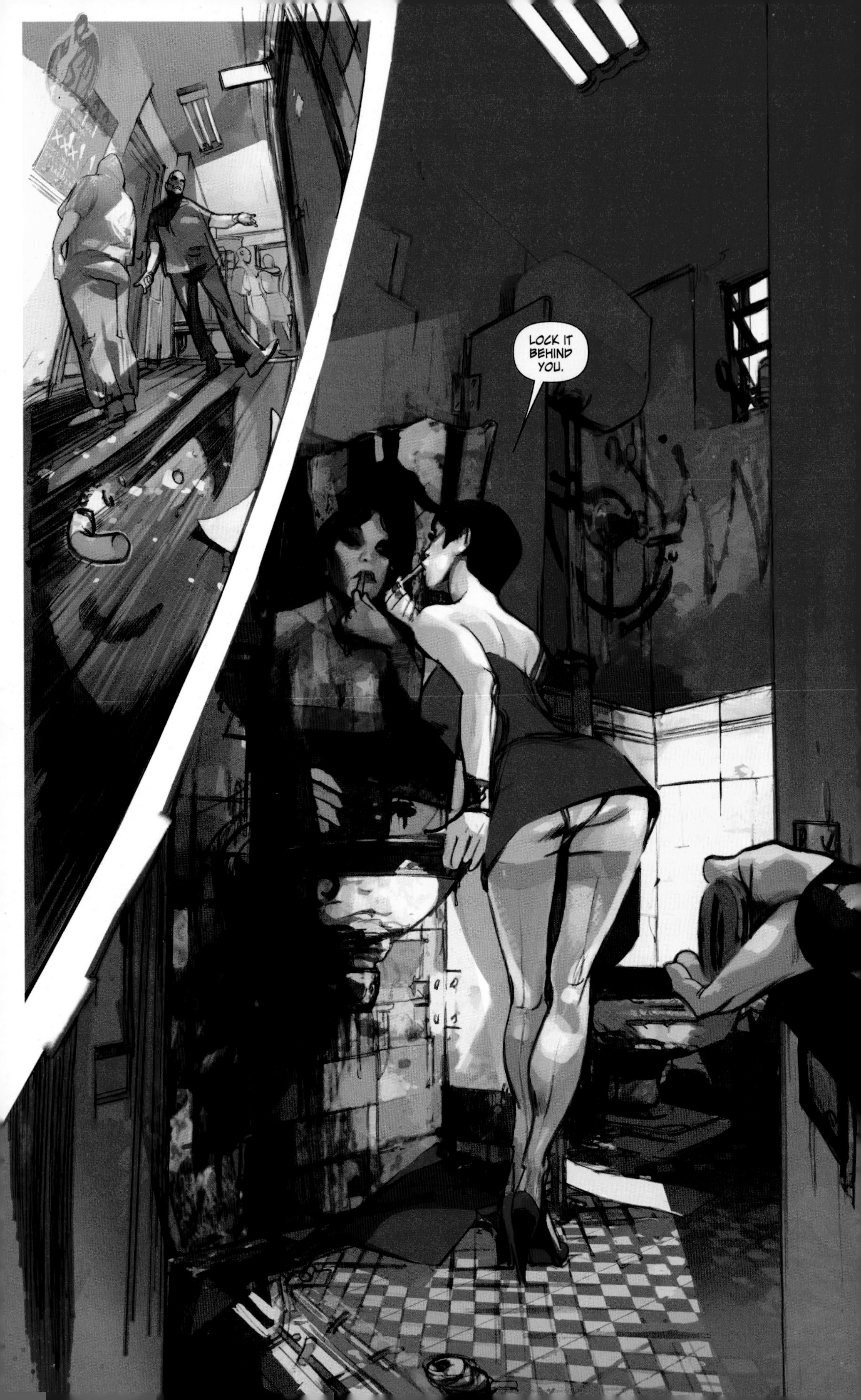
LOCK IT BEHIND YOU.

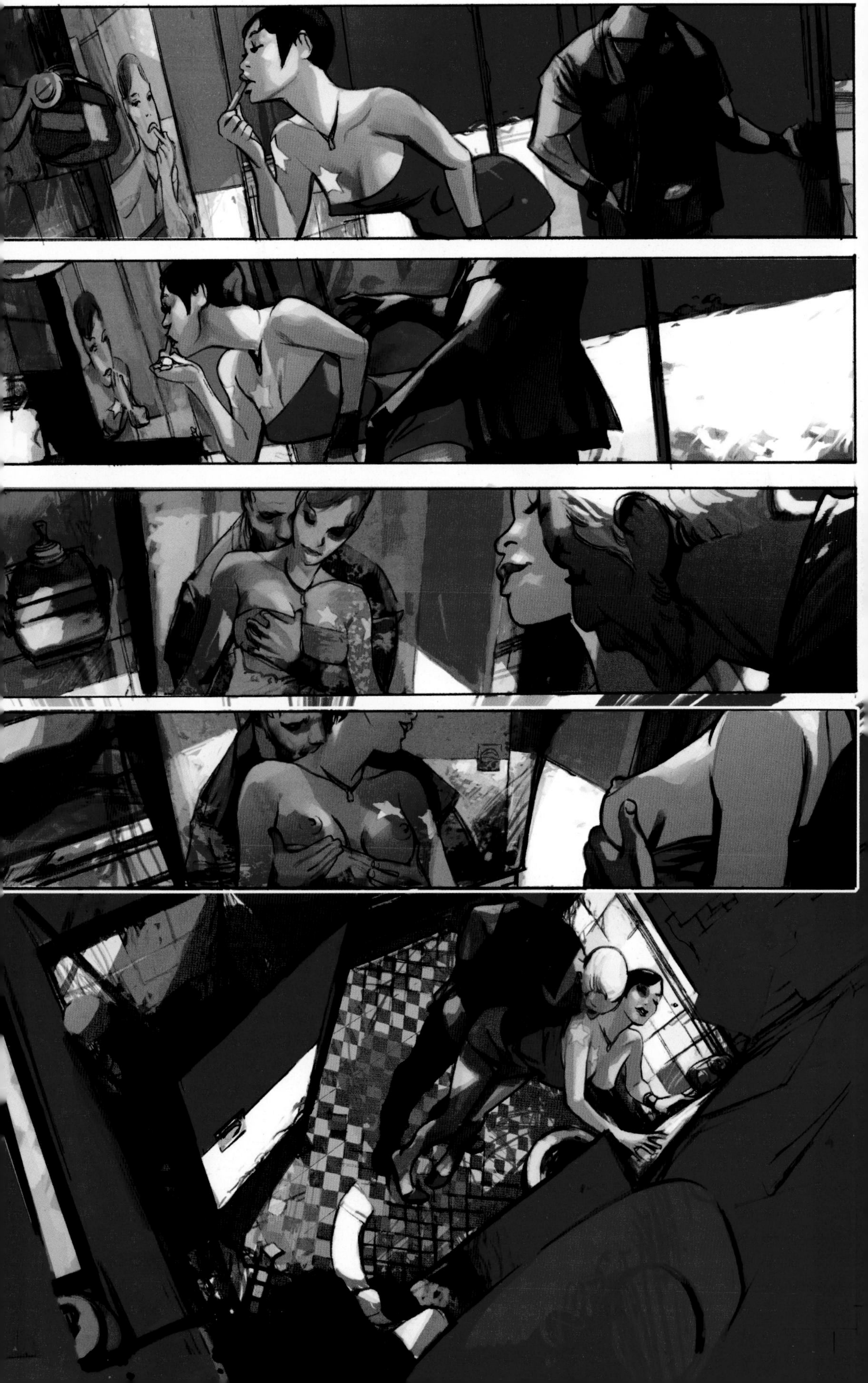

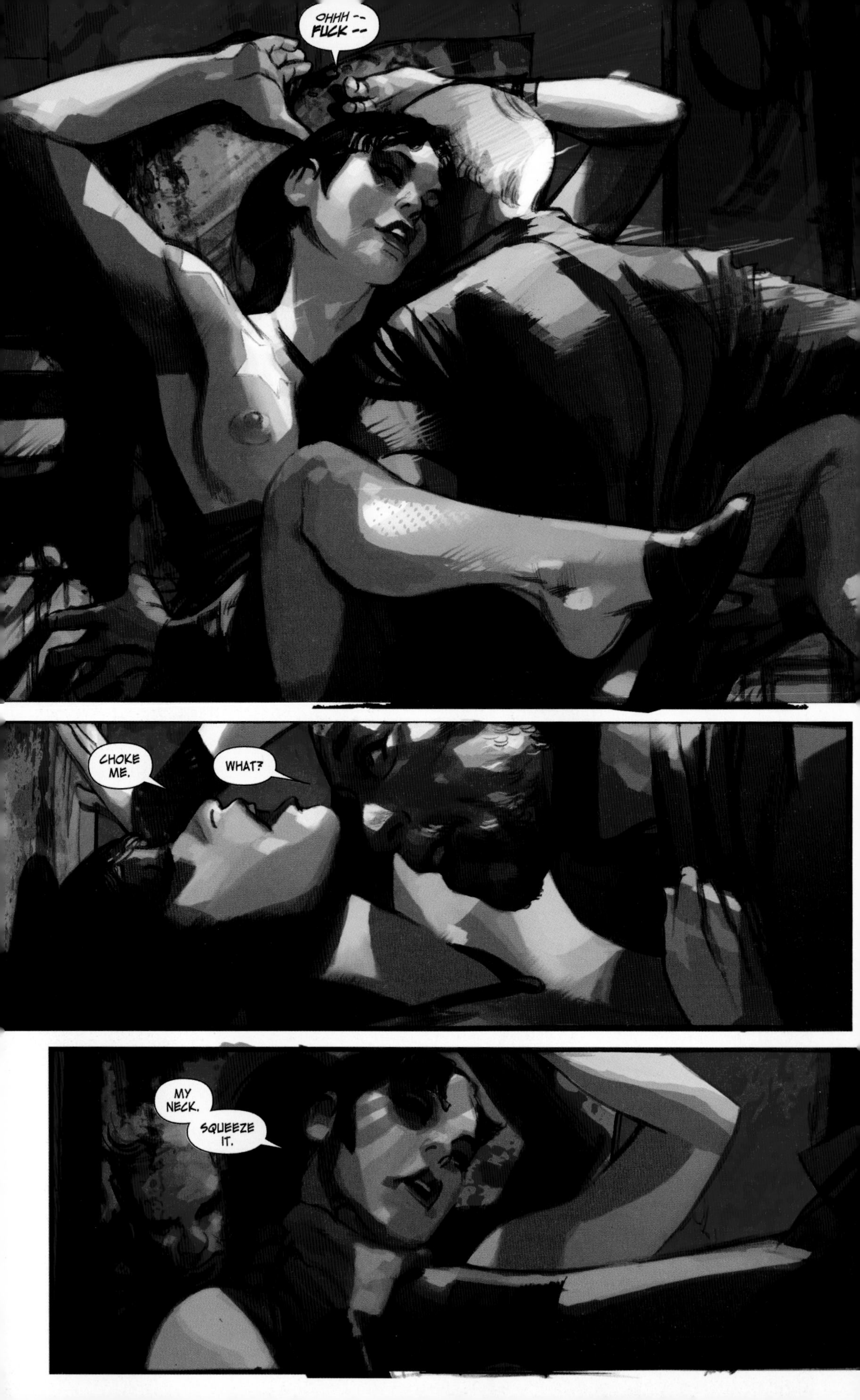
OHHH --
FUCK --
CHOKE ME.
WHAT?
MY NECK.
SQUEEZE IT.

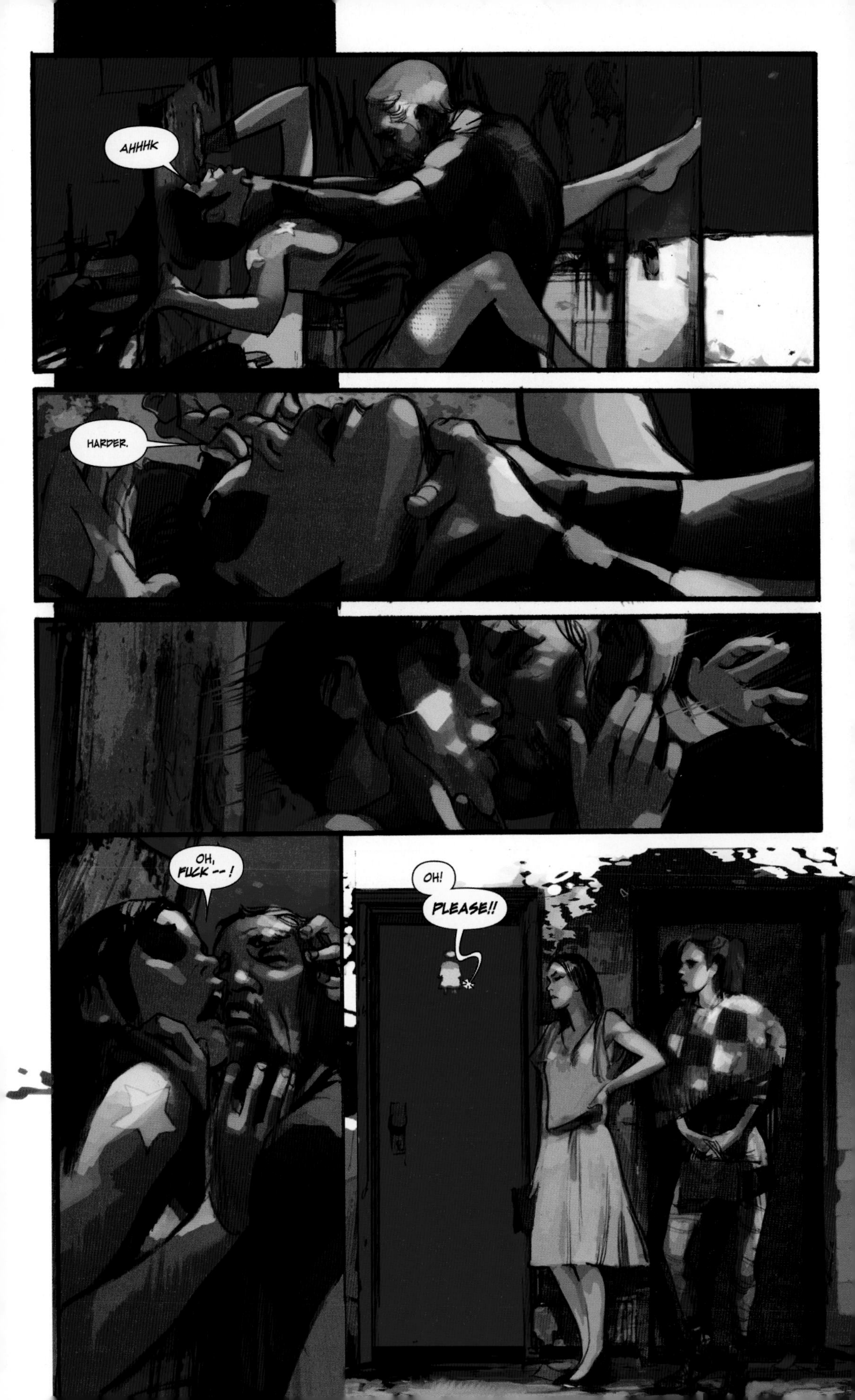
AHHHK
HARDER.
OH, FUCK -- !
OH!
PLEASE!!

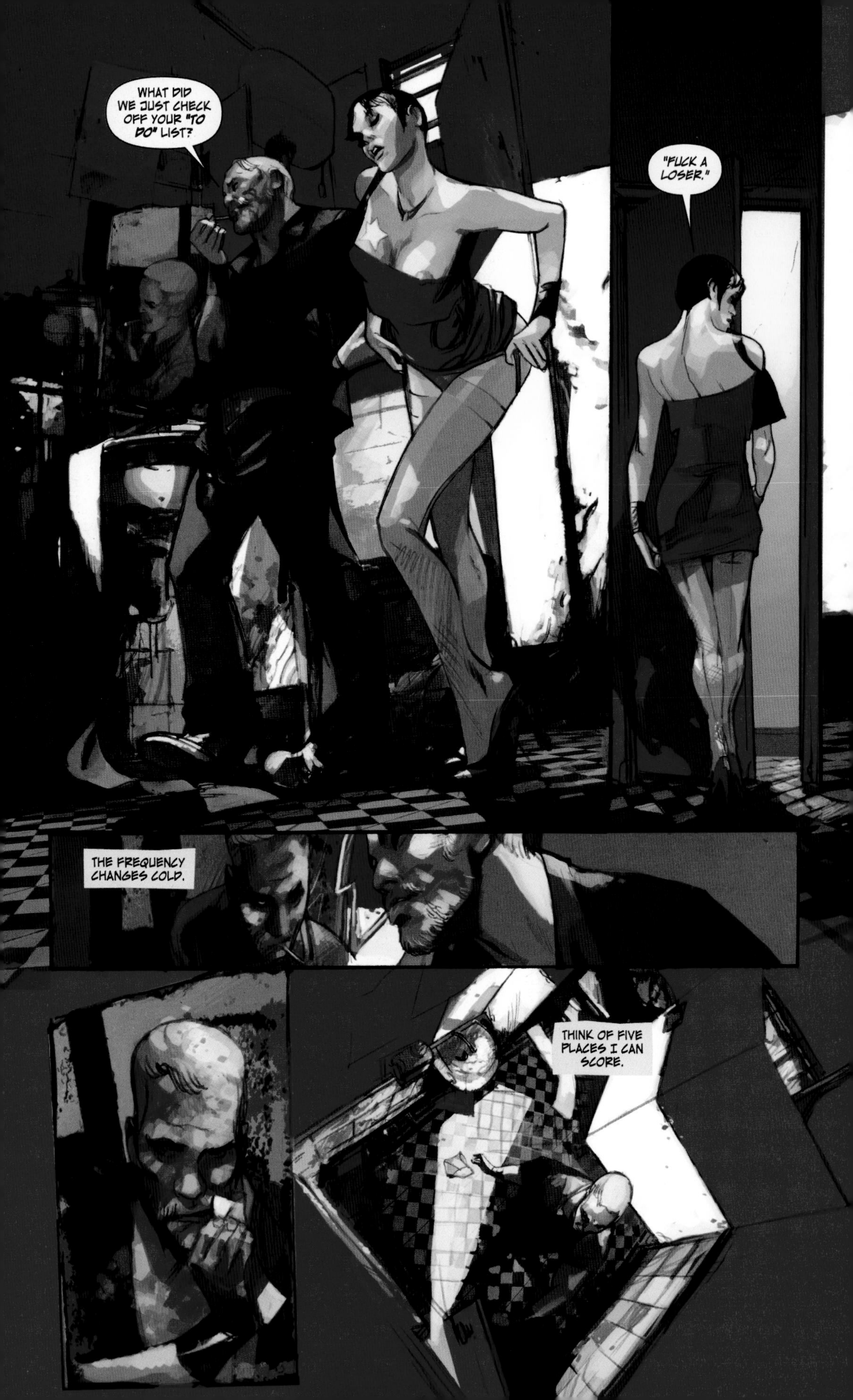
WHAT DID WE JUST CHECK OFF YOUR "TO DO" LIST?
"FUCK A LOSER."
THE FREQUENCY CHANGES COLD.
THINK OF FIVE PLACES I CAN SCORE.

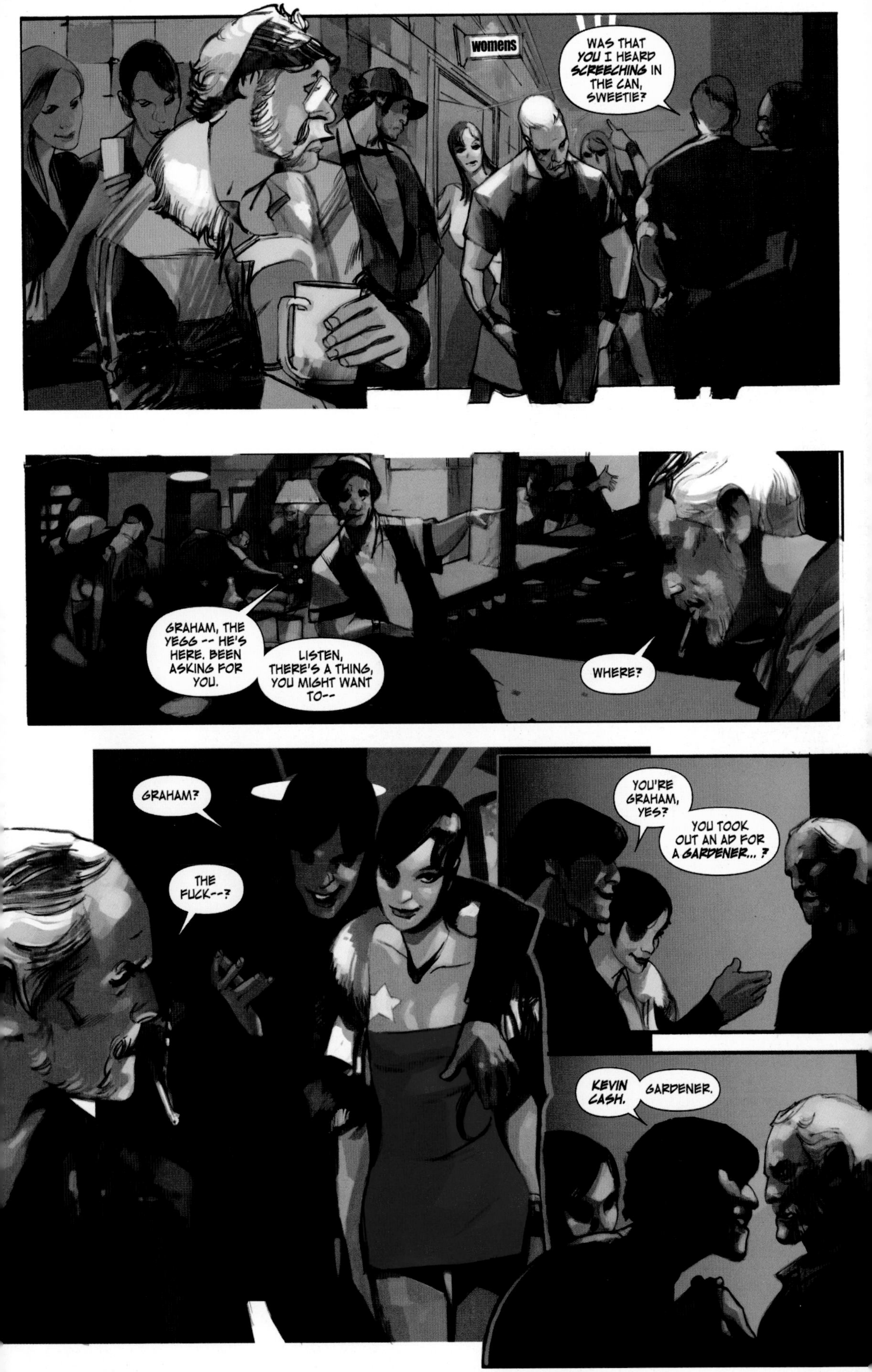
womens
WAS THAT YOU I HEARD SCREECHING IN THE CAN, SWEETIE?
GRAHAM, THE YEGG -- HE'S HERE. BEEN ASKING FOR YOU.
LISTEN, THERE'S A THING, YOU MIGHT WANT TO--
WHERE?
GRAHAM?
THE FUCK--?
YOU'RE GRAHAM, YES?
YOU TOOK OUT AN AD FOR A GARDENER...?
KEVIN CASH.
GARDENER.

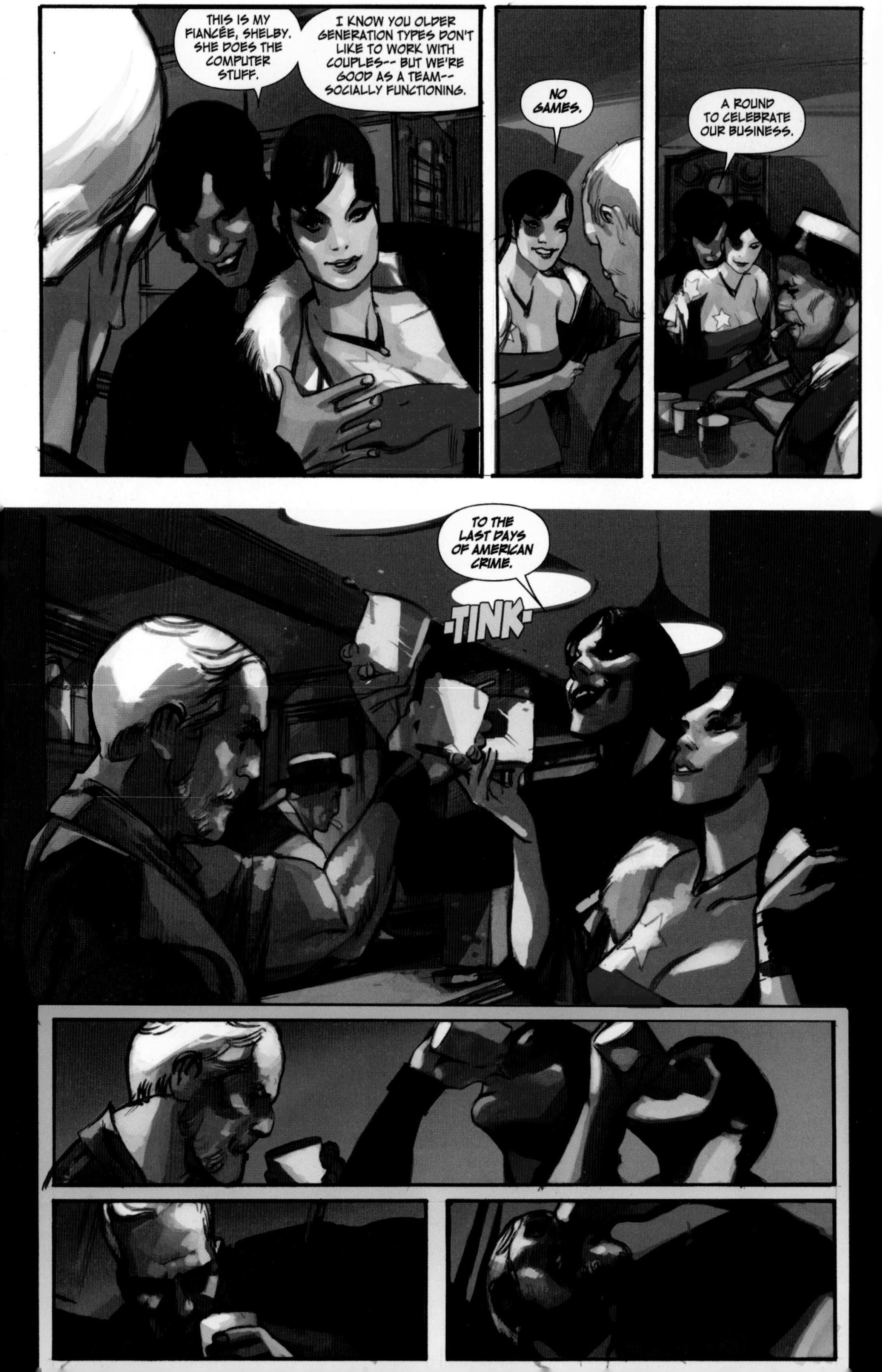
THIS IS MY FIANCÉE, SHELBY. SHE DOES THE COMPUTER STUFF.
I KNOW YOU OLDER GENERATION TYPES DON'T LIKE TO WORK WITH COUPLES-- BUT WE'RE GOOD AS A TEAM-- SOCIALLY FUNCTIONING.
NO GAMES.
A ROUND TO CELEBRATE OUR BUSINESS.
TO THE LAST DAYS OF AMERICAN CRIME.
-TINK-

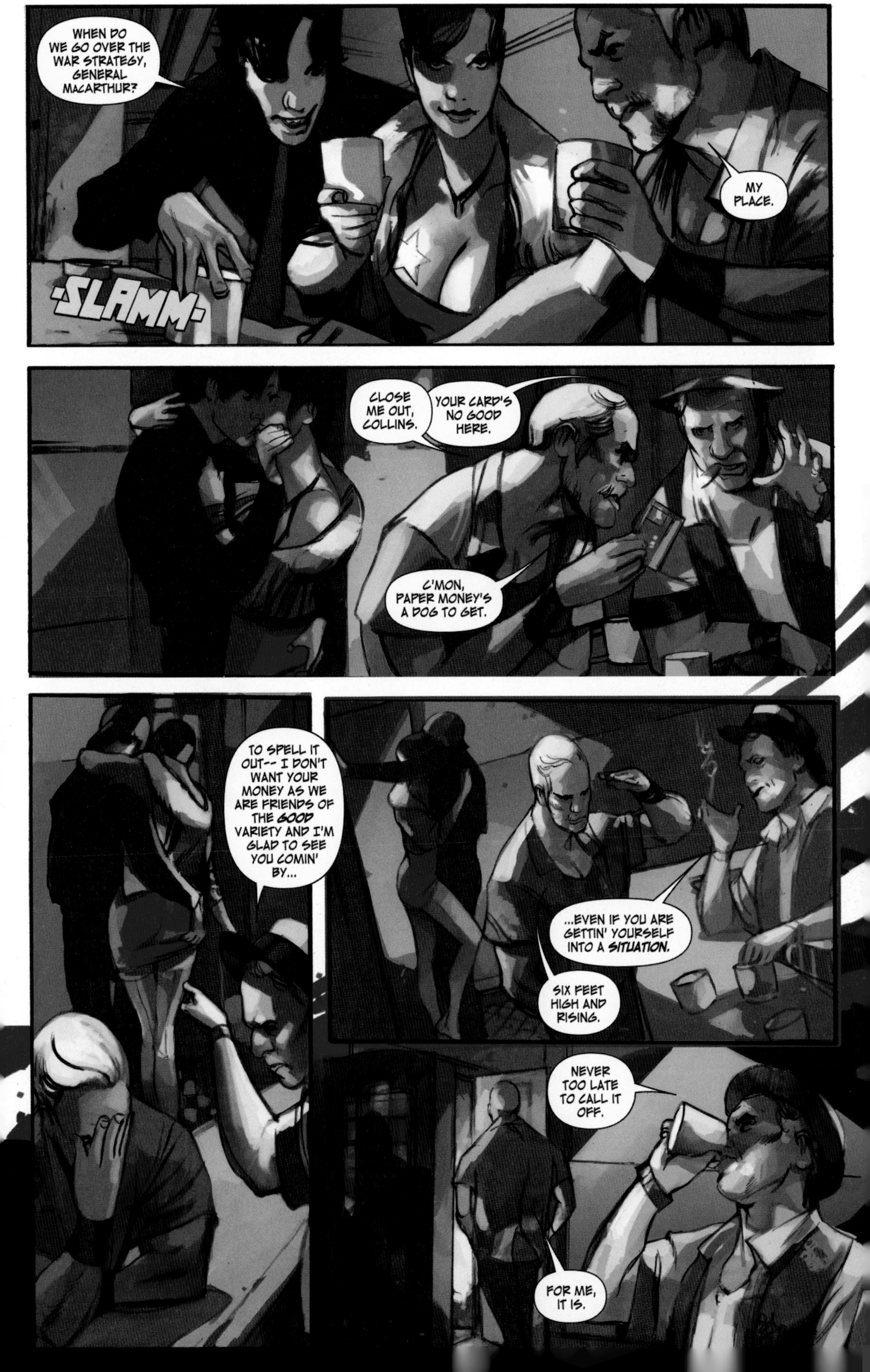
WHEN DO WE GO OVER THE WAR STRATEGY, GENERAL MacARTHUR?
MY PLACE.
-SLAMM-
CLOSE ME OUT, COLLINS.
YOUR CARD'S NO GOOD HERE.
C'MON, PAPER MONEY'S A DOG TO GET.
TO SPELL IT OUT-- I DON'T WANT YOUR MONEY AS WE ARE FRIENDS OF THE GOOD VARIETY AND I'M GLAD TO SEE YOU COMIN' BY...
...EVEN IF YOU ARE GETTIN' YOURSELF INTO A SITUATION.
SIX FEET HIGH AND RISING.
NEVER TOO LATE TO CALL IT OFF.
FOR ME, IT IS.

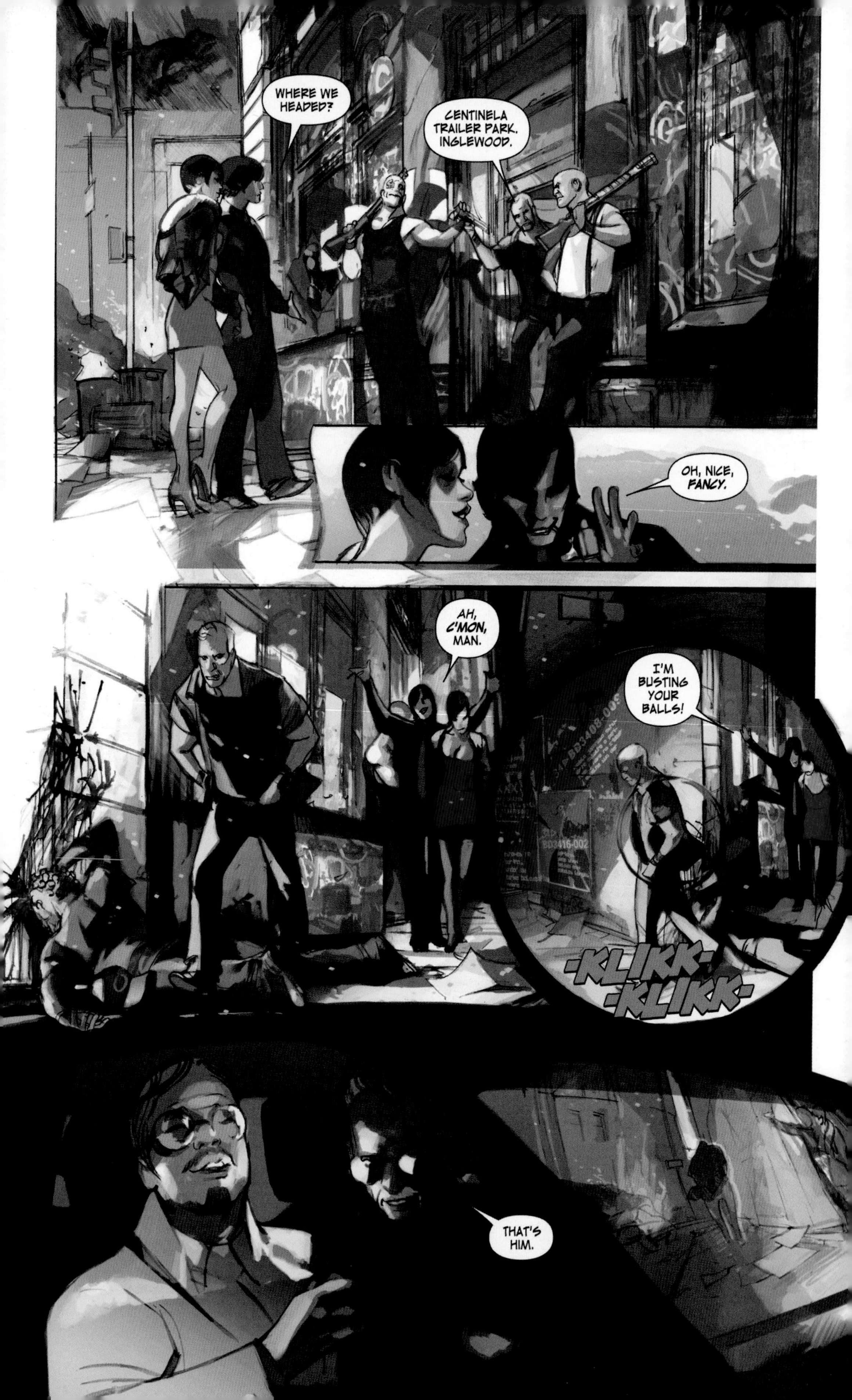
WHERE WE HEADED?
CENTINELA TRAILER PARK. INGLEWOOD.
OH, NICE, FANCY.
AH, C'MON, MAN.
I'M BUSTING YOUR BALLS!
-KLIKK- -KLIKK-
THAT'S HIM.

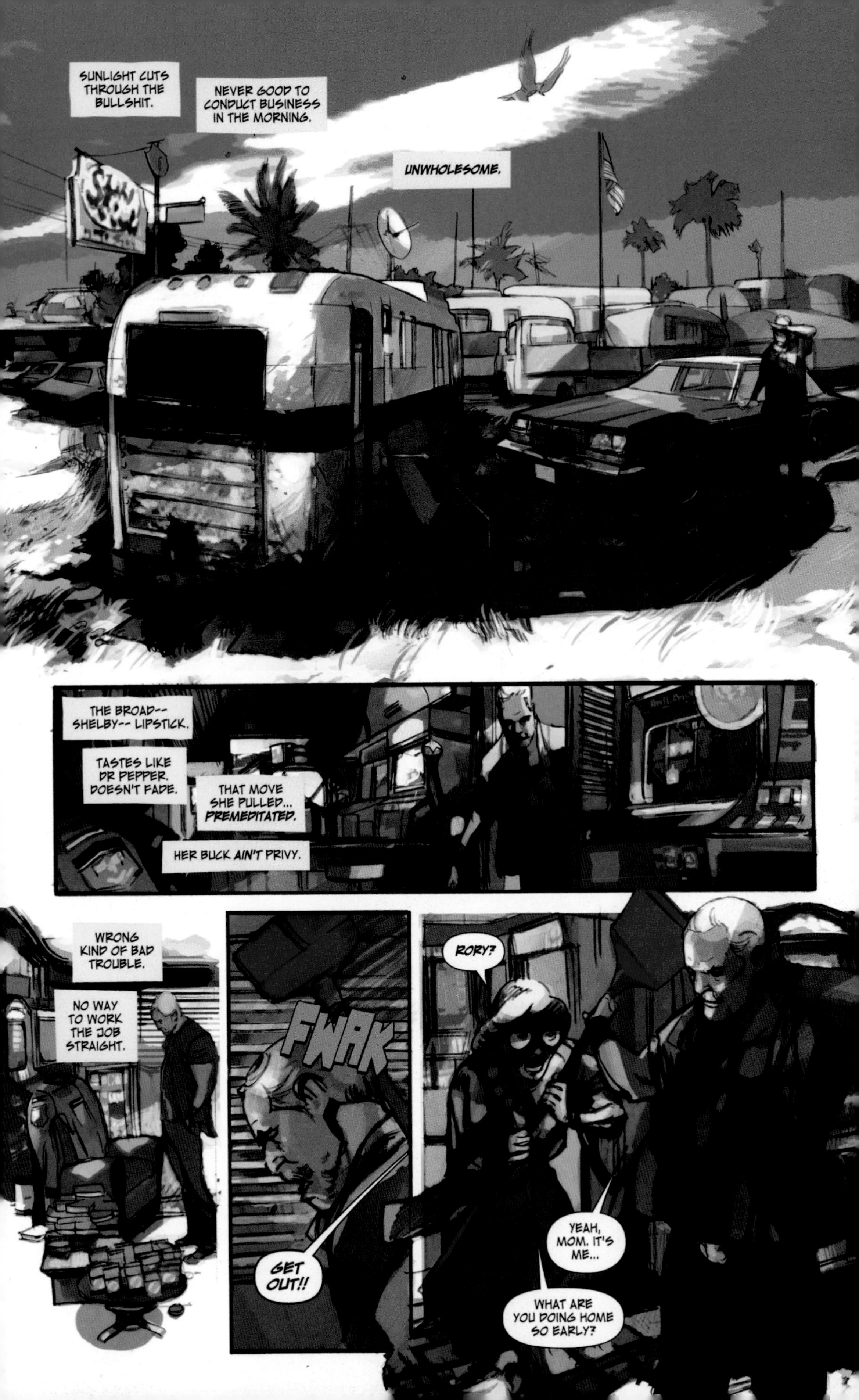
SUNLIGHT CUTS THROUGH THE BULLSHIT.
NEVER GOOD TO CONDUCT BUSINESS IN THE MORNING.
UNWHOLESOME.
THE BROAD-- SHELBY-- LIPSTICK.
TASTES LIKE DR PEPPER. DOESN'T FADE.
THAT MOVE SHE PULLED... PREMEDITATED.
HER BUCK AIN'T PRIVY.
WRONG KIND OF BAD TROUBLE.
NO WAY TO WORK THE JOB STRAIGHT.
FWAK
GET OUT!!
RORY?
YEAH, MOM. IT'S ME...
WHAT ARE YOU DOING HOME SO EARLY?

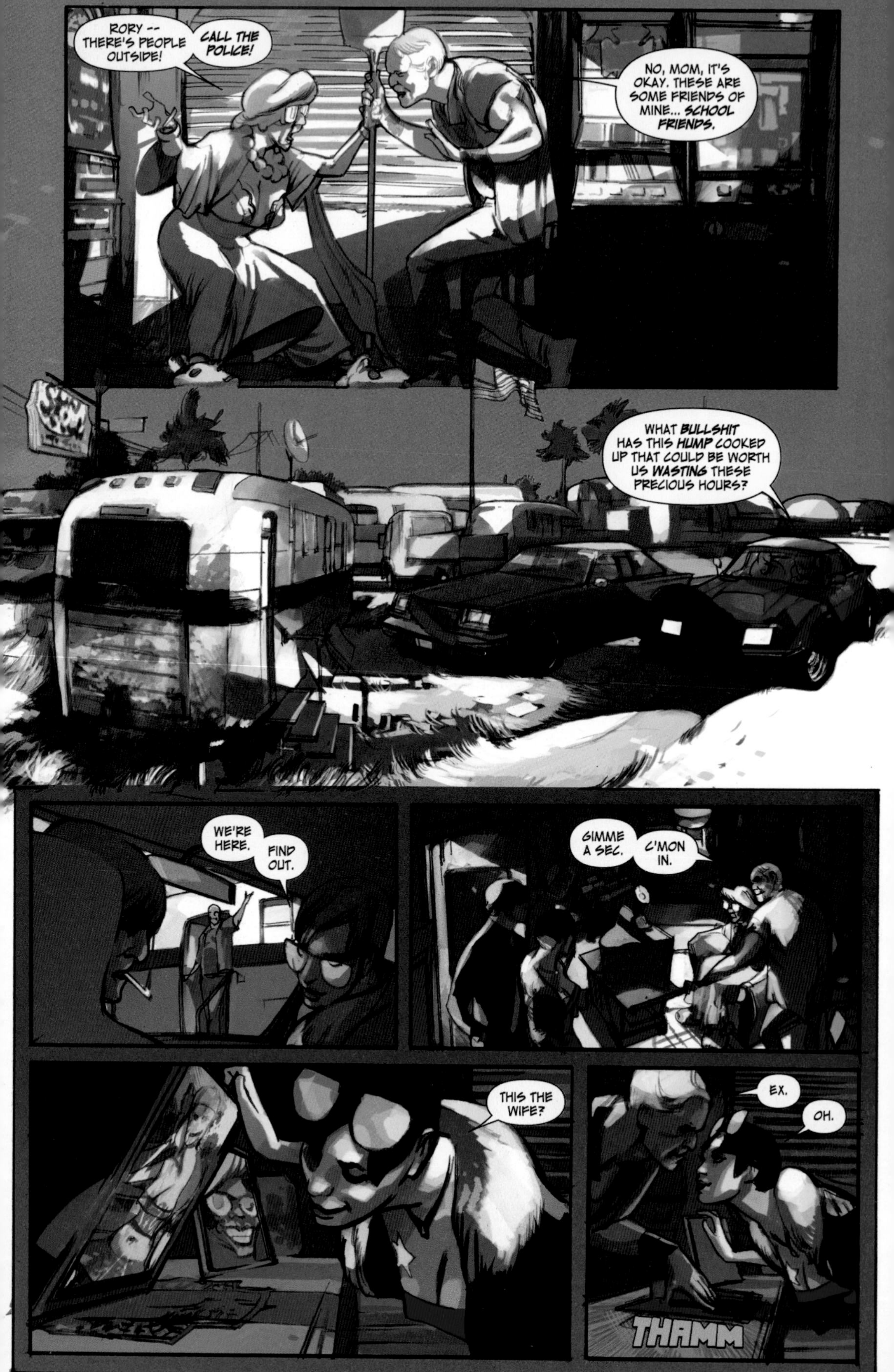
RORY -- THERE'S PEOPLE OUTSIDE!
CALL THE POLICE!
NO, MOM, IT'S OKAY. THESE ARE SOME FRIENDS OF MINE... SCHOOL FRIENDS.
WHAT BULLSHIT HAS THIS HUMP COOKED UP THAT COULD BE WORTH US WASTING THESE PRECIOUS HOURS?
WE'RE HERE.
FIND OUT.
GIMME A SEC.
C'MON IN.
THIS THE WIFE?
EX.
OH.
THAMM

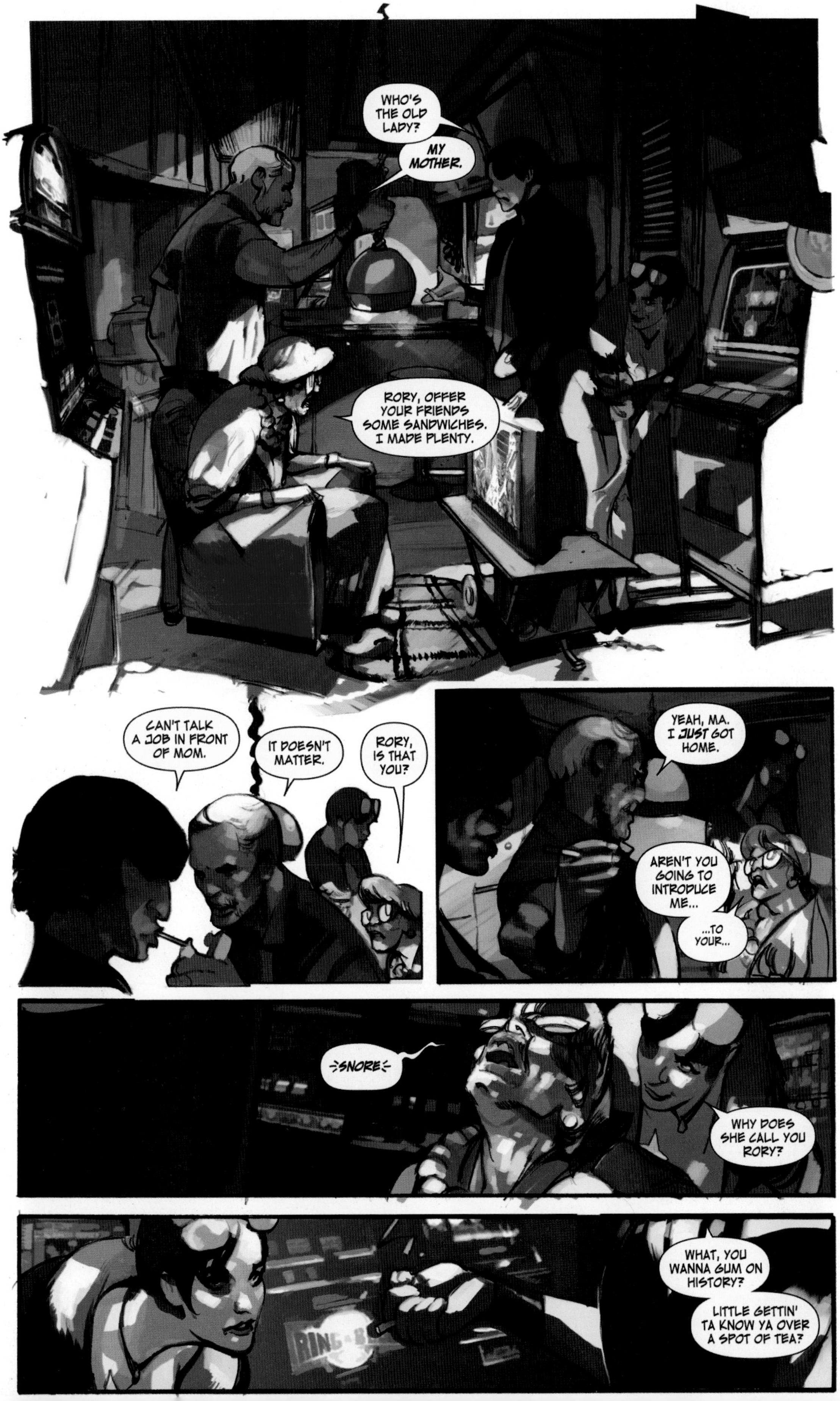
WHO'S THE OLD LADY?
MY MOTHER.
RORY, OFFER YOUR FRIENDS SOME SANDWICHES. I MADE PLENTY.
CAN'T TALK A JOB IN FRONT OF MOM.
IT DOESN'T MATTER.
RORY, IS THAT YOU?
YEAH, MA. I JUST GOT HOME.
AREN'T YOU GOING TO INTRODUCE ME...
...TO YOUR...
=SNORE=
WHY DOES SHE CALL YOU RORY?
WHAT, YOU WANNA GUM ON HISTORY?
LITTLE GETTIN' TA KNOW YA OVER A SPOT OF TEA?

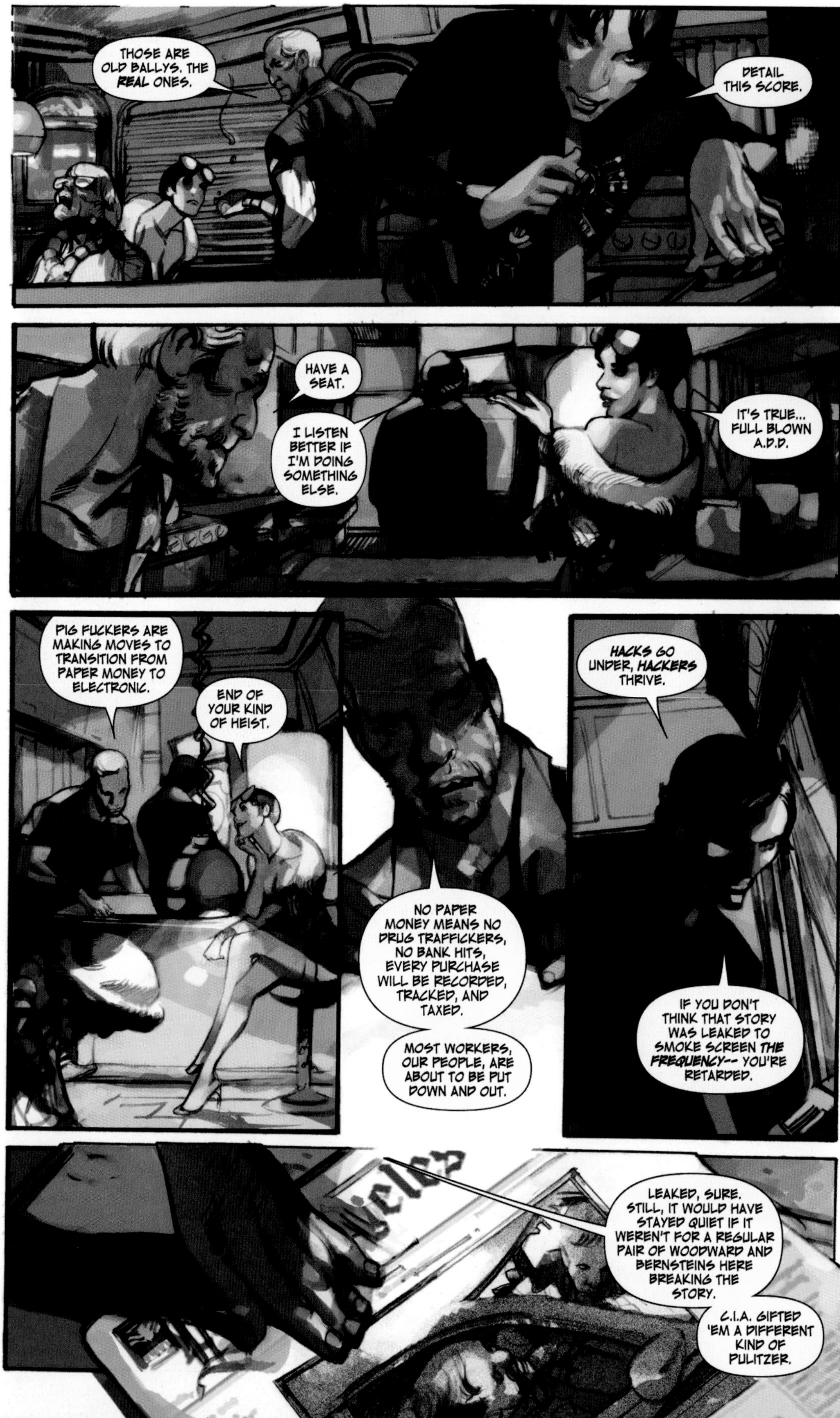
THOSE ARE OLD BALLYS. THE REAL ONES.
DETAIL THIS SCORE.
HAVE A SEAT.
I LISTEN BETTER IF I'M DOING SOMETHING ELSE.
IT'S TRUE... FULL BLOWN A.D.D.
PIG FUCKERS ARE MAKING MOVES TO TRANSITION FROM PAPER MONEY TO ELECTRONIC.
END OF YOUR KIND OF HEIST.
NO PAPER MONEY MEANS NO DRUG TRAFFICKERS, NO BANK HITS, EVERY PURCHASE WILL BE RECORDED, TRACKED, AND TAXED.
MOST WORKERS, OUR PEOPLE, ARE ABOUT TO BE PUT DOWN AND OUT.
HACKS GO UNDER, HACKERS THRIVE.
IF YOU DON'T THINK THAT STORY WAS LEAKED TO SMOKE SCREEN THE FREQUENCY-- YOU'RE RETARDED.
LEAKED, SURE. STILL, IT WOULD HAVE STAYED QUIET IF IT WEREN'T FOR A REGULAR PAIR OF WOODWARD AND BERNSTEINS HERE BREAKING THE STORY.
C.I.A. GIFTED 'EM A DIFFERENT KIND OF PULITZER.

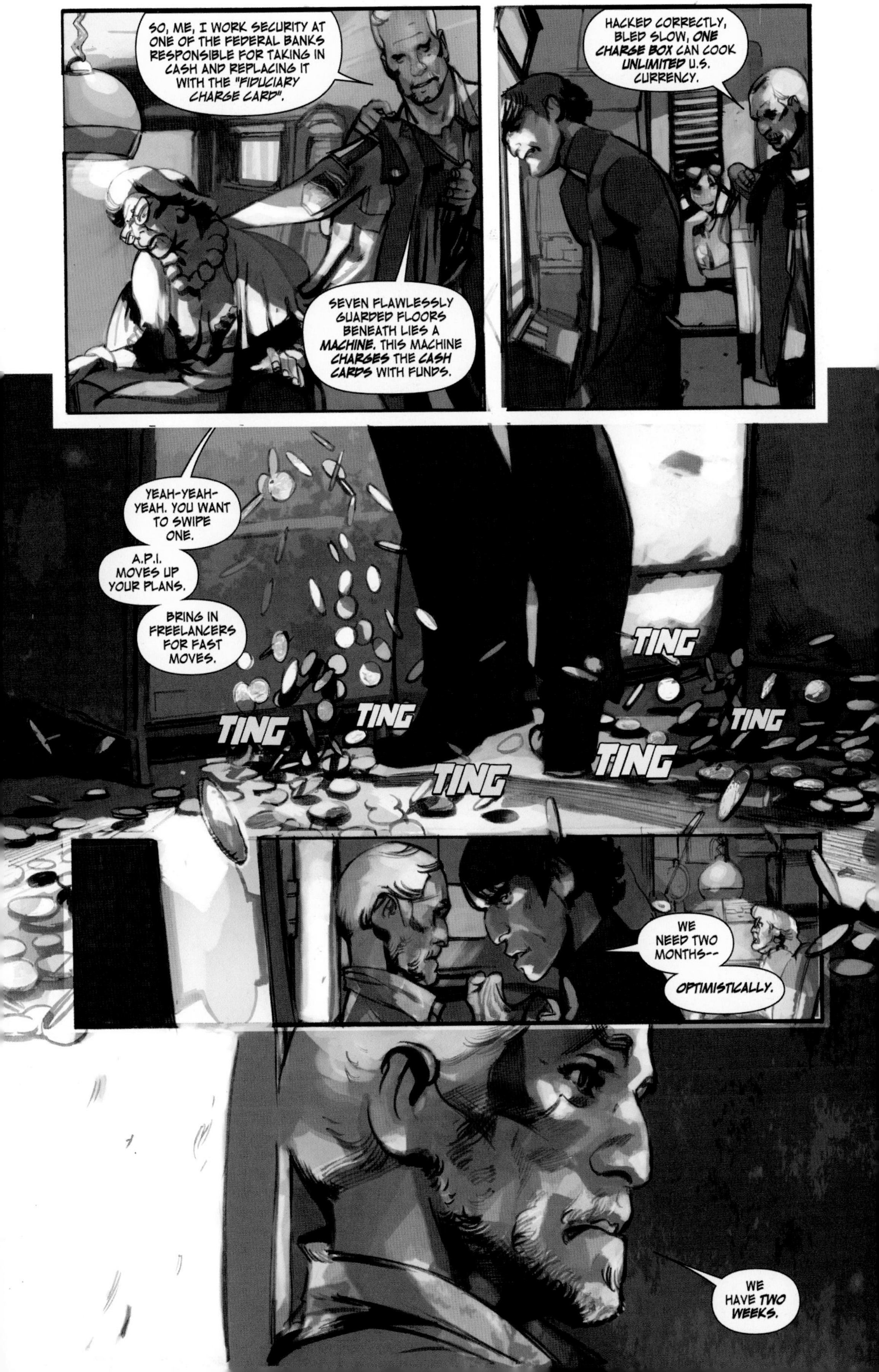
SO, ME, I WORK SECURITY AT ONE OF THE FEDERAL BANKS RESPONSIBLE FOR TAKING IN CASH AND REPLACING IT WITH THE "FIDUCIARY CHARGE CARD".
SEVEN FLAWLESSLY GUARDED FLOORS BENEATH LIES A MACHINE. THIS MACHINE CHARGES THE CASH CARDS WITH FUNDS.
HACKED CORRECTLY, BLED SLOW, ONE CHARGE BOX CAN COOK UNLIMITED U.S. CURRENCY.
YEAH-YEAH-YEAH. YOU WANT TO SWIPE ONE.
A.P.I. MOVES UP YOUR PLANS.
BRING IN FREELANCERS FOR FAST MOVES.
TING
TING
TING
TING
TING
TING
WE NEED TWO MONTHS--
OPTIMISTICALLY.
WE HAVE TWO WEEKS.

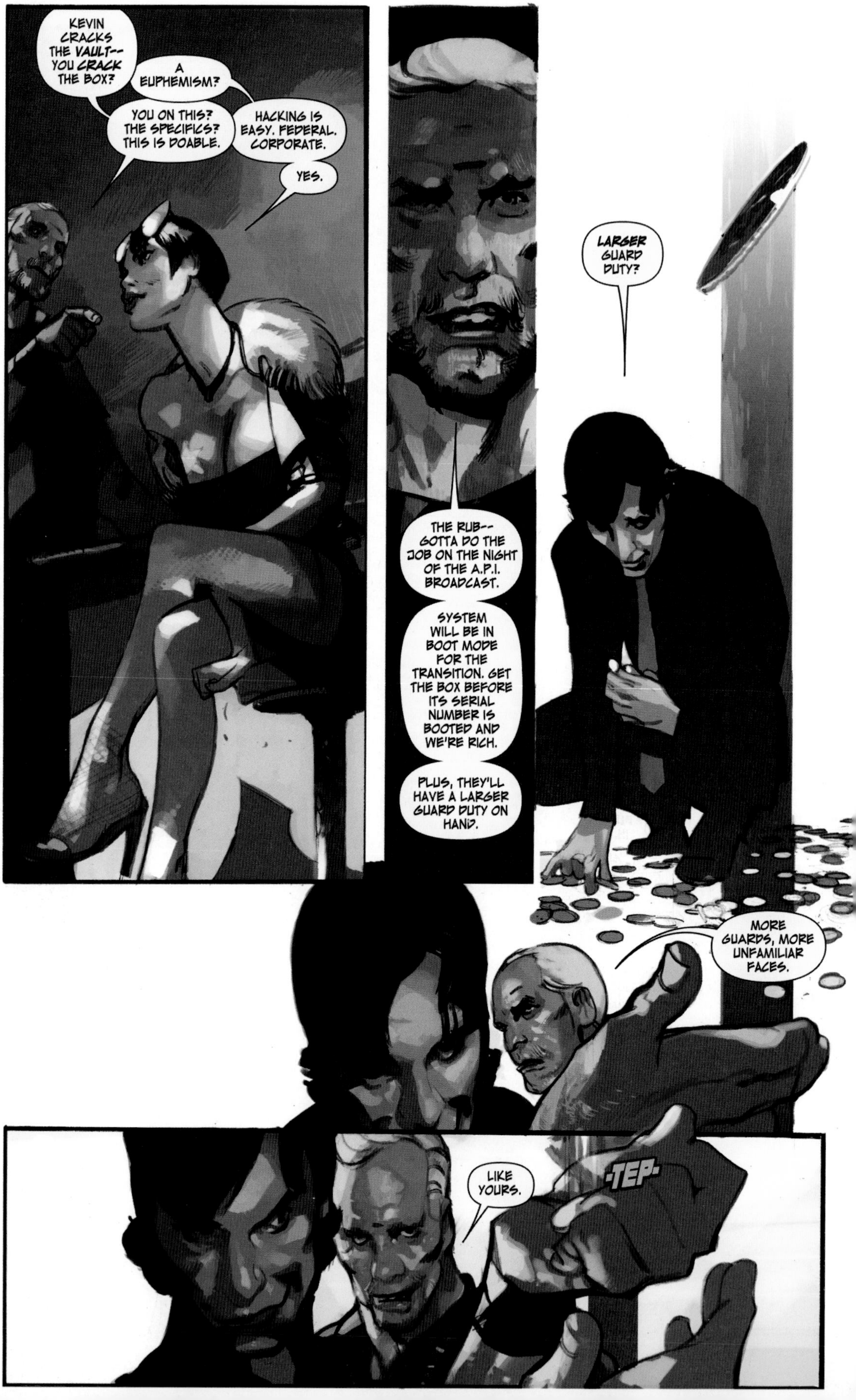
KEVIN CRACKS THE VAULT-- YOU CRACK THE BOX?
A EUPHEMISM?
YOU ON THIS? THE SPECIFICS? THIS IS DOABLE.
HACKING IS EASY. FEDERAL. CORPORATE.
YES.
THE RUB-- GOTTA DO THE JOB ON THE NIGHT OF THE A.P.I. BROADCAST.
SYSTEM WILL BE IN BOOT MODE FOR THE TRANSITION. GET THE BOX BEFORE ITS SERIAL NUMBER IS BOOTED AND WE'RE RICH.
PLUS, THEY'LL HAVE A LARGER GUARD DUTY ON HAND.
LARGER GUARD DUTY?
MORE GUARDS, MORE UNFAMILIAR FACES.
LIKE YOURS.
-TEP-

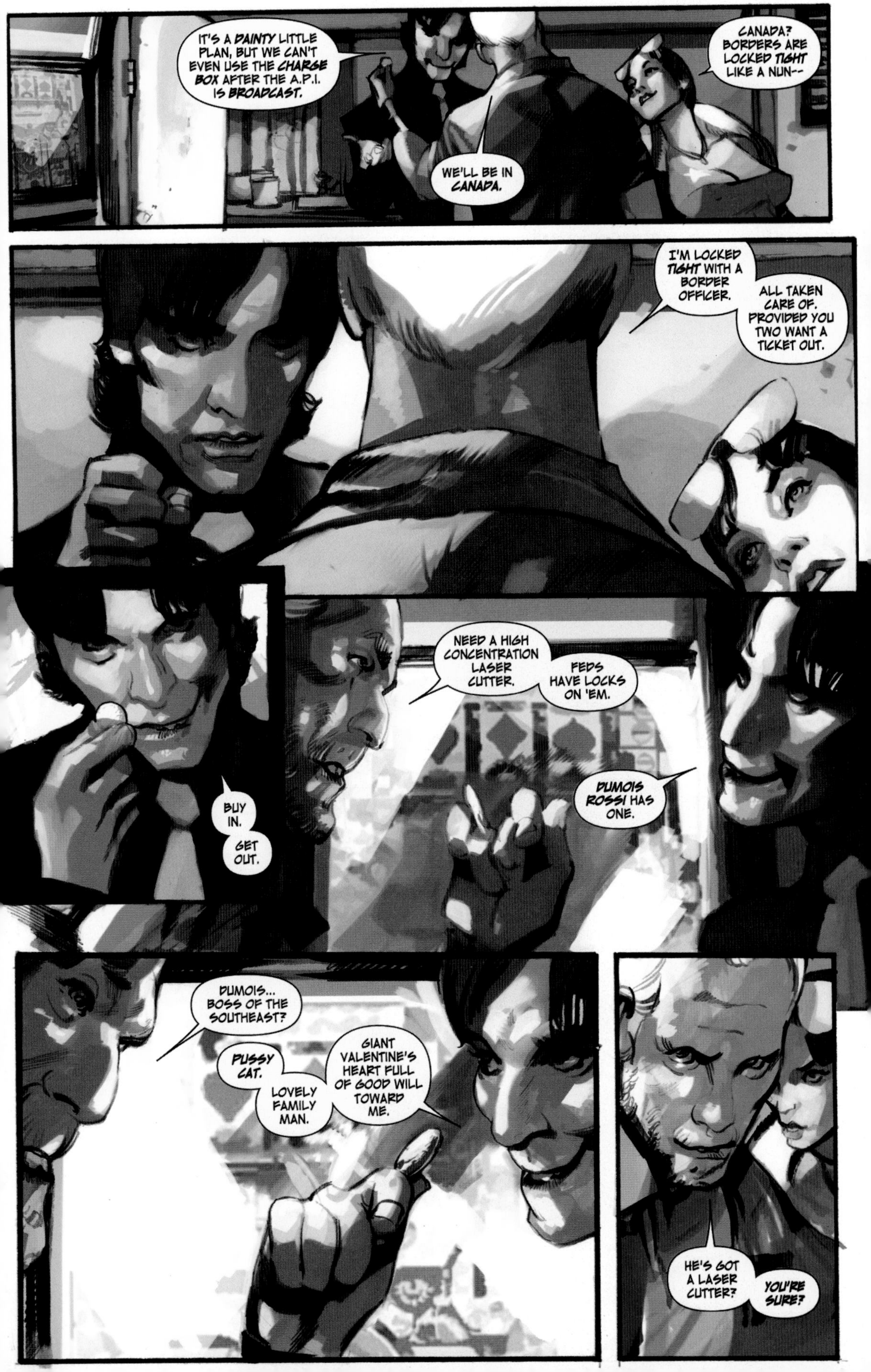

IT'S A DAINTY LITTLE PLAN, BUT WE CAN'T EVEN USE THE CHARGE BOX AFTER THE A.P.I. IS BROADCAST.
WE'LL BE IN CANADA.
CANADA? BORDERS ARE LOCKED TIGHT LIKE A NUN--
I'M LOCKED TIGHT WITH A BORDER OFFICER.
ALL TAKEN CARE OF. PROVIDED YOU TWO WANT A TICKET OUT.
BUY IN.
GET OUT.
NEED A HIGH CONCENTRATION LASER CUTTER.
FEDS HAVE LOCKS ON 'EM.
DUMOIS ROSSI HAS ONE.
DUMOIS... BOSS OF THE SOUTHEAST?
PUSSY CAT.
LOVELY FAMILY MAN.
GIANT VALENTINE'S HEART FULL OF GOOD WILL TOWARD ME.
HE'S GOT A LASER CUTTER?
YOU'RE SURE?

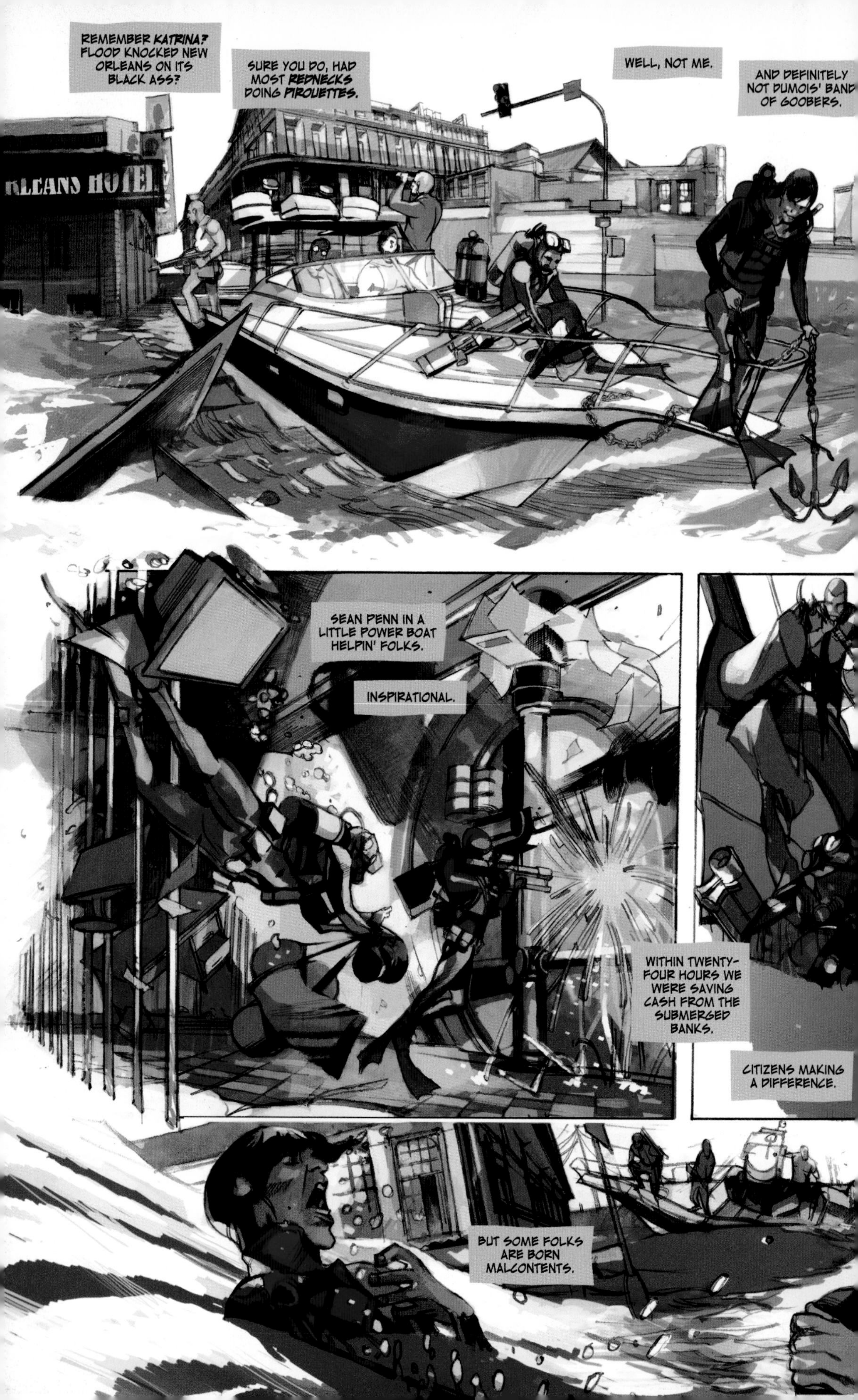
REMEMBER KATRINA? FLOOD KNOCKED NEW ORLEANS ON ITS BLACK ASS?
SURE YOU DO, HAD MOST REDNECKS DOING PIROUETTES.
WELL, NOT ME.
AND DEFINITELY NOT DUMOIS' BAND OF GOOBERS.
RLEANS HOTEL
SEAN PENN IN A LITTLE POWER BOAT HELPIN' FOLKS.
INSPIRATIONAL.
WITHIN TWENTY-FOUR HOURS WE WERE SAVING CASH FROM THE SUBMERGED BANKS.
CITIZENS MAKING A DIFFERENCE.
BUT SOME FOLKS ARE BORN MALCONTENTS.

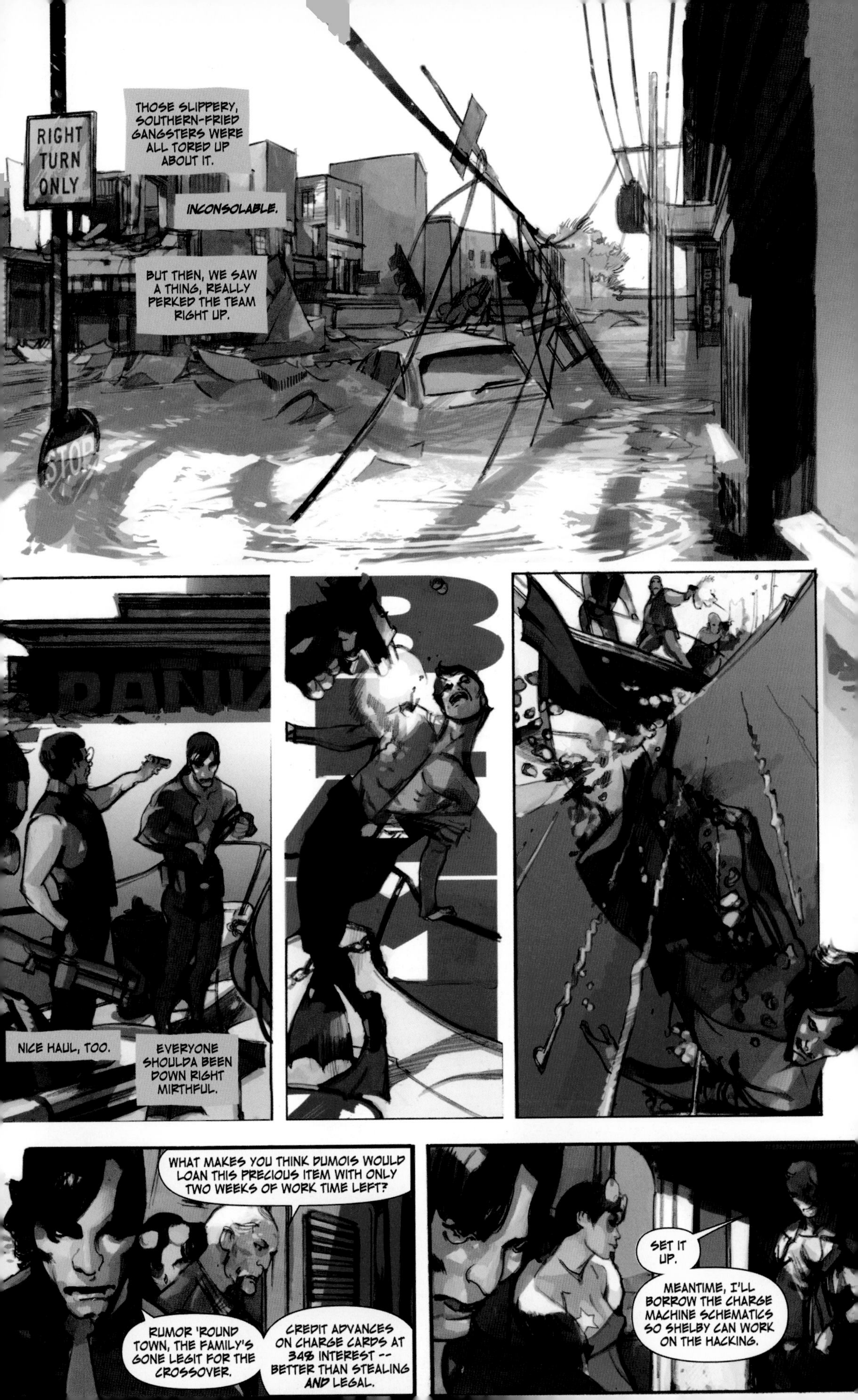
RIGHT TURN ONLY
THOSE SLIPPERY, SOUTHERN-FRIED GANGSTERS WERE ALL TORED UP ABOUT IT.
INCONSOLABLE.
BUT THEN, WE SAW A THING, REALLY PERKED THE TEAM RIGHT UP.
STOP
NICE HAUL, TOO.
EVERYONE SHOULDA BEEN DOWN RIGHT MIRTHFUL.
WHAT MAKES YOU THINK DUMOIS WOULD LOAN THIS PRECIOUS ITEM WITH ONLY TWO WEEKS OF WORK TIME LEFT?
RUMOR 'ROUND TOWN, THE FAMILY'S GONE LEGIT FOR THE CROSSOVER.
CREDIT ADVANCES ON CHARGE CARDS AT 34% INTEREST -- BETTER THAN STEALING *AND* LEGAL.
SET IT UP.
MEANTIME, I'LL BORROW THE CHARGE MACHINE SCHEMATICS SO SHELBY CAN WORK ON THE HACKING.

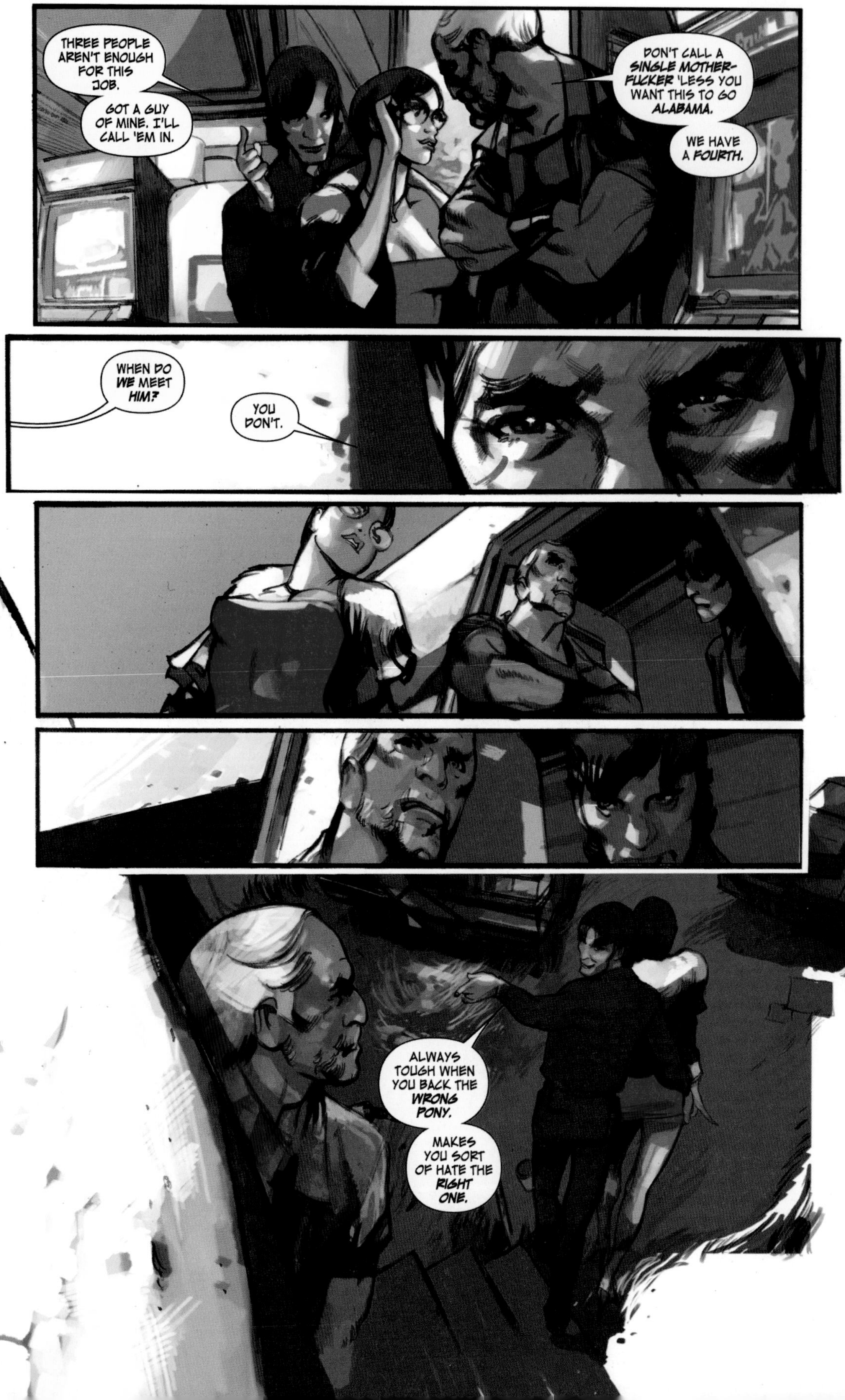
THREE PEOPLE AREN'T ENOUGH FOR THIS JOB.
GOT A GUY OF MINE. I'LL CALL 'EM IN.
DON'T CALL A SINGLE MOTHER-FUCKER 'LESS YOU WANT THIS TO GO ALABAMA.
WE HAVE A FOURTH.
WHEN DO WE MEET HIM?
YOU DON'T.
ALWAYS TOUGH WHEN YOU BACK THE WRONG PONY.
MAKES YOU SORT OF HATE THE RIGHT ONE.

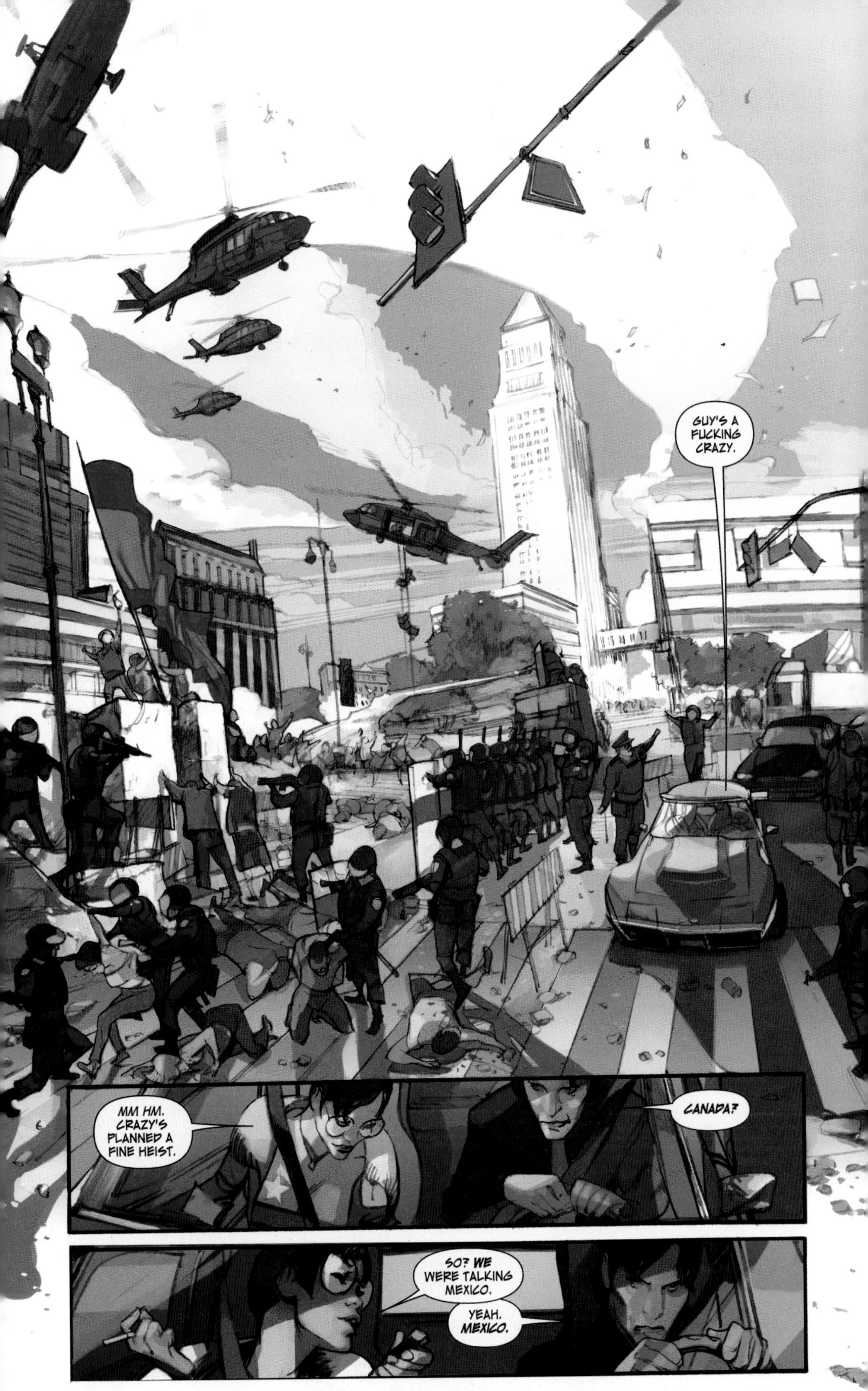
GUY'S A FUCKING CRAZY.
MM HM. CRAZY'S PLANNED A FINE HEIST.
CANADA?
SO? WE WERE TALKING MEXICO.
YEAH. MEXICO.

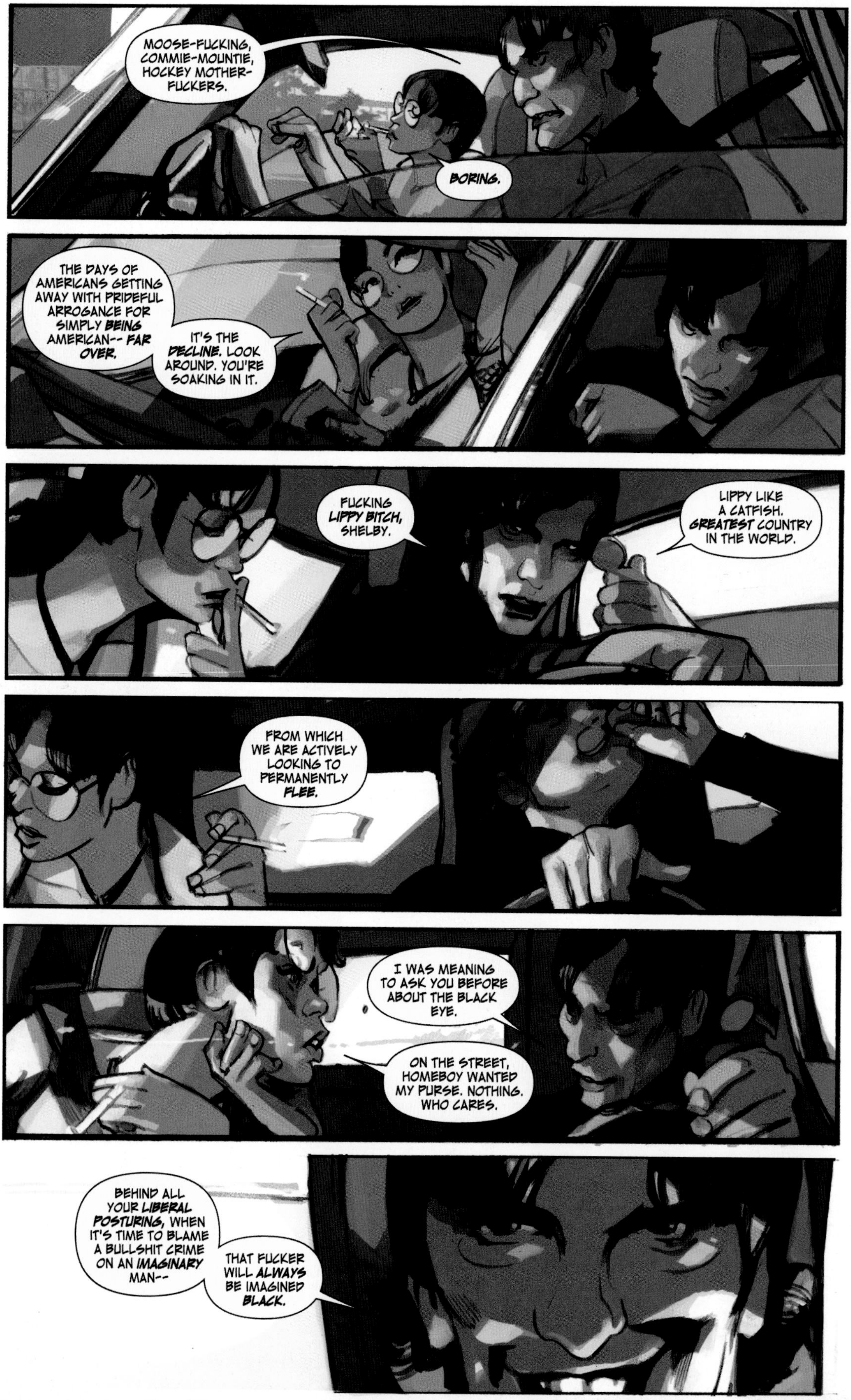
MOOSE-FUCKING, COMMIE-MOUNTIE, HOCKEY MOTHER-FUCKERS.
BORING.
THE DAYS OF AMERICANS GETTING AWAY WITH PRIDEFUL ARROGANCE FOR SIMPLY BEING AMERICAN-- FAR OVER.
IT'S THE DECLINE. LOOK AROUND. YOU'RE SOAKING IN IT.
FUCKING LIPPY BITCH, SHELBY.
LIPPY LIKE A CATFISH. GREATEST COUNTRY IN THE WORLD.
FROM WHICH WE ARE ACTIVELY LOOKING TO PERMANENTLY FLEE.
I WAS MEANING TO ASK YOU BEFORE ABOUT THE BLACK EYE.
ON THE STREET, HOMEBOY WANTED MY PURSE. NOTHING. WHO CARES.
BEHIND ALL YOUR LIBERAL POSTURING, WHEN IT'S TIME TO BLAME A BULLSHIT CRIME ON AN IMAGINARY MAN--
THAT FUCKER WILL ALWAYS BE IMAGINED BLACK.

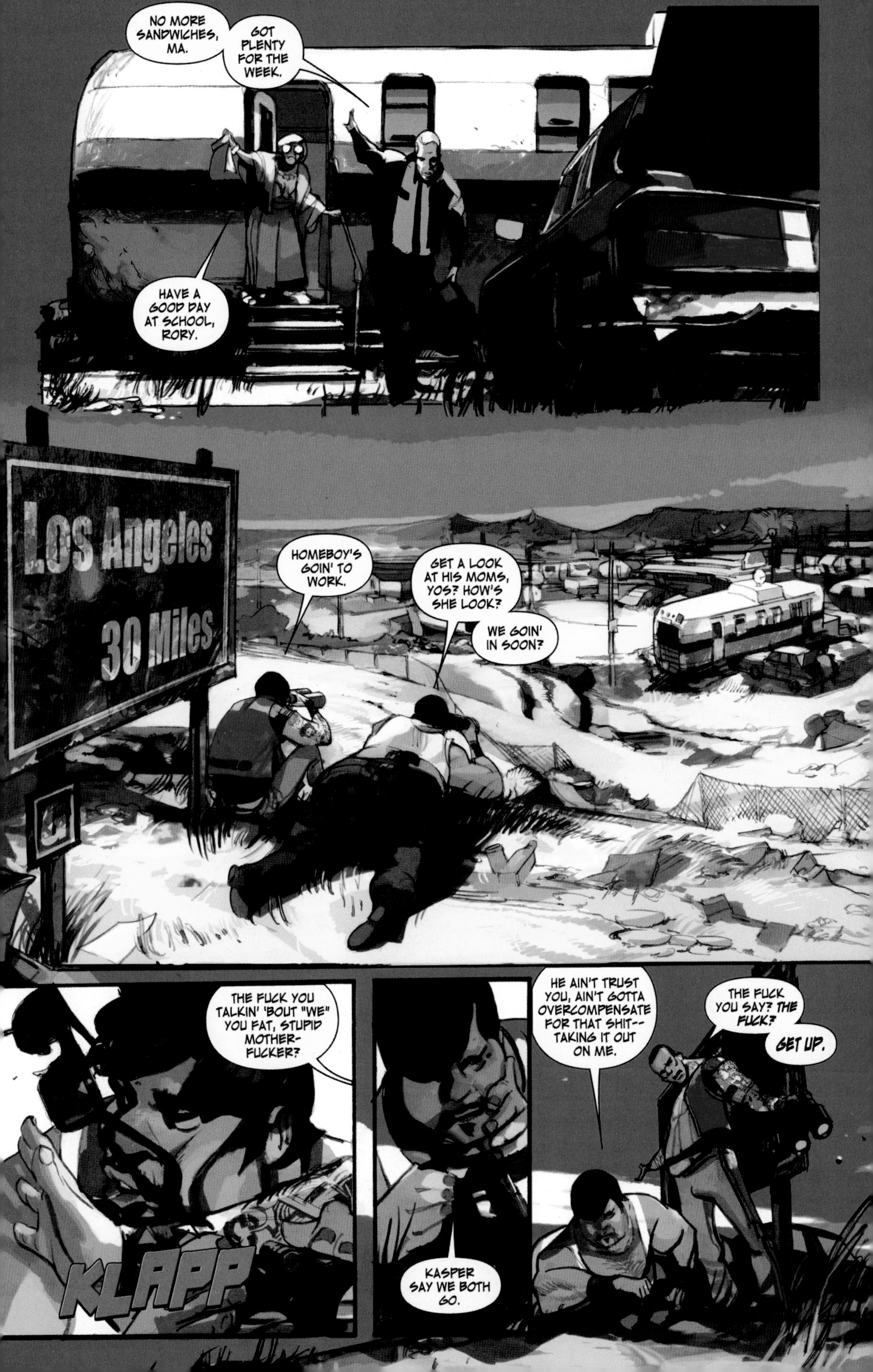
NO MORE SANDWICHES, MA.
GOT PLENTY FOR THE WEEK.
HAVE A GOOD DAY AT SCHOOL, RORY.
Los Angeles
30 Miles
HOMEBOY'S GOIN' TO WORK.
GET A LOOK AT HIS MOMS, YOS? HOW'S SHE LOOK?
WE GOIN' IN SOON?
THE FUCK YOU TALKIN' 'BOUT "WE" YOU FAT, STUPID MOTHER-FUCKER?
KLAPP
KASPER SAY WE BOTH GO.
HE AIN'T TRUST YOU, AIN'T GOTTA OVERCOMPENSATE FOR THAT SHIT-- TAKING IT OUT ON ME.
THE FUCK YOU SAY? THE FUCK?
GET UP.

YO, GO EASY.

I'LL KILL THE MOMS, TOXICO. YOU GRAB THAT OTHER SHIT.

I'LL DO IT. BE COOL.

CHICO, MAN, YOU SICK-ASS PANOCHA.

GUESS IT'S GOOD, KNOW WHERE TA TURN IF I EVER WANT AN OLD WOMAN *MURDERED* AND *MOLESTED*.

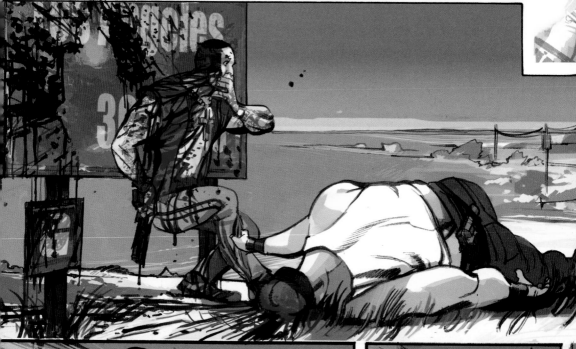

GAA--

BLAMM

THE GHOST OF ENRIQUE HAUNTS.

BLAMM-
BLAMM-

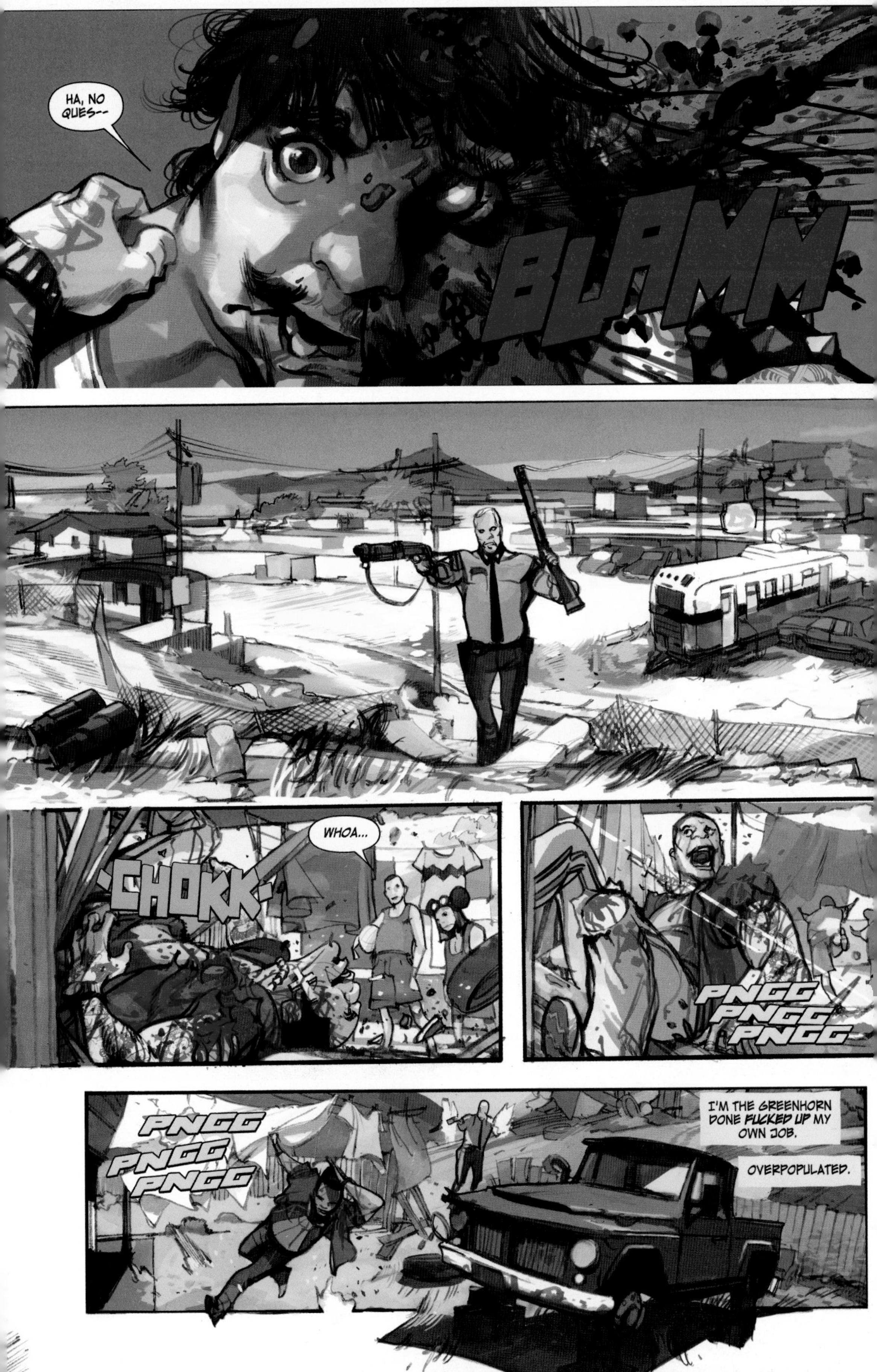
HA, NO QUES--
BLAMM
WHOA...
CHOKK
PNGG PNGG PNGG
PNGG PNGG PNGG
I'M THE GREENHORN DONE FUCKED UP MY OWN JOB.
OVERPOPULATED.

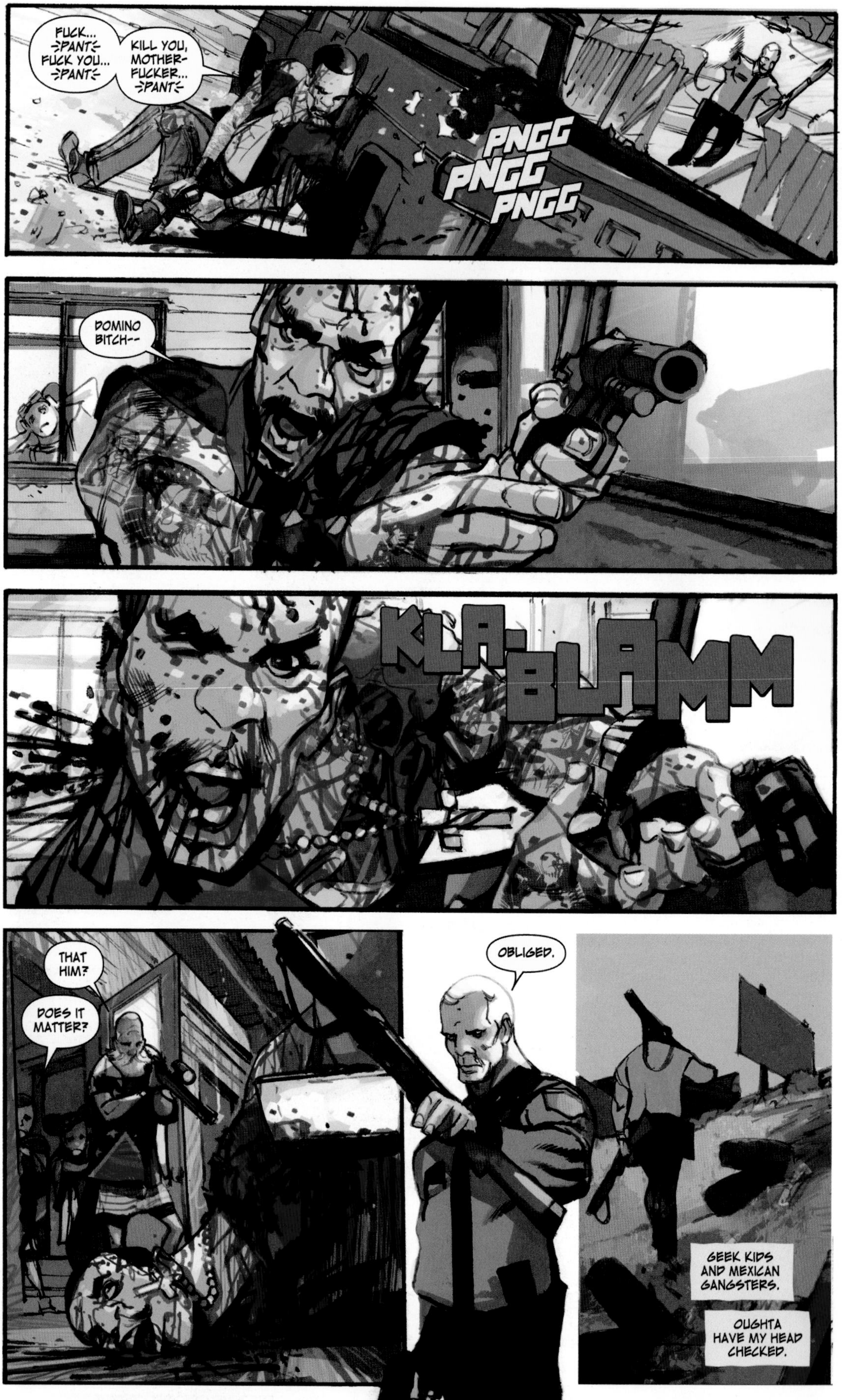
FUCK... -PANT- FUCK YOU... -PANT-
KILL YOU, MOTHER-FUCKER... -PANT-
PNGG PNGG PNGG
DOMINO BITCH--
KLA-BLAMM
THAT HIM?
DOES IT MATTER?
OBLIGED.
GEEK KIDS AND MEXICAN GANGSTERS.
OUGHTA HAVE MY HEAD CHECKED.

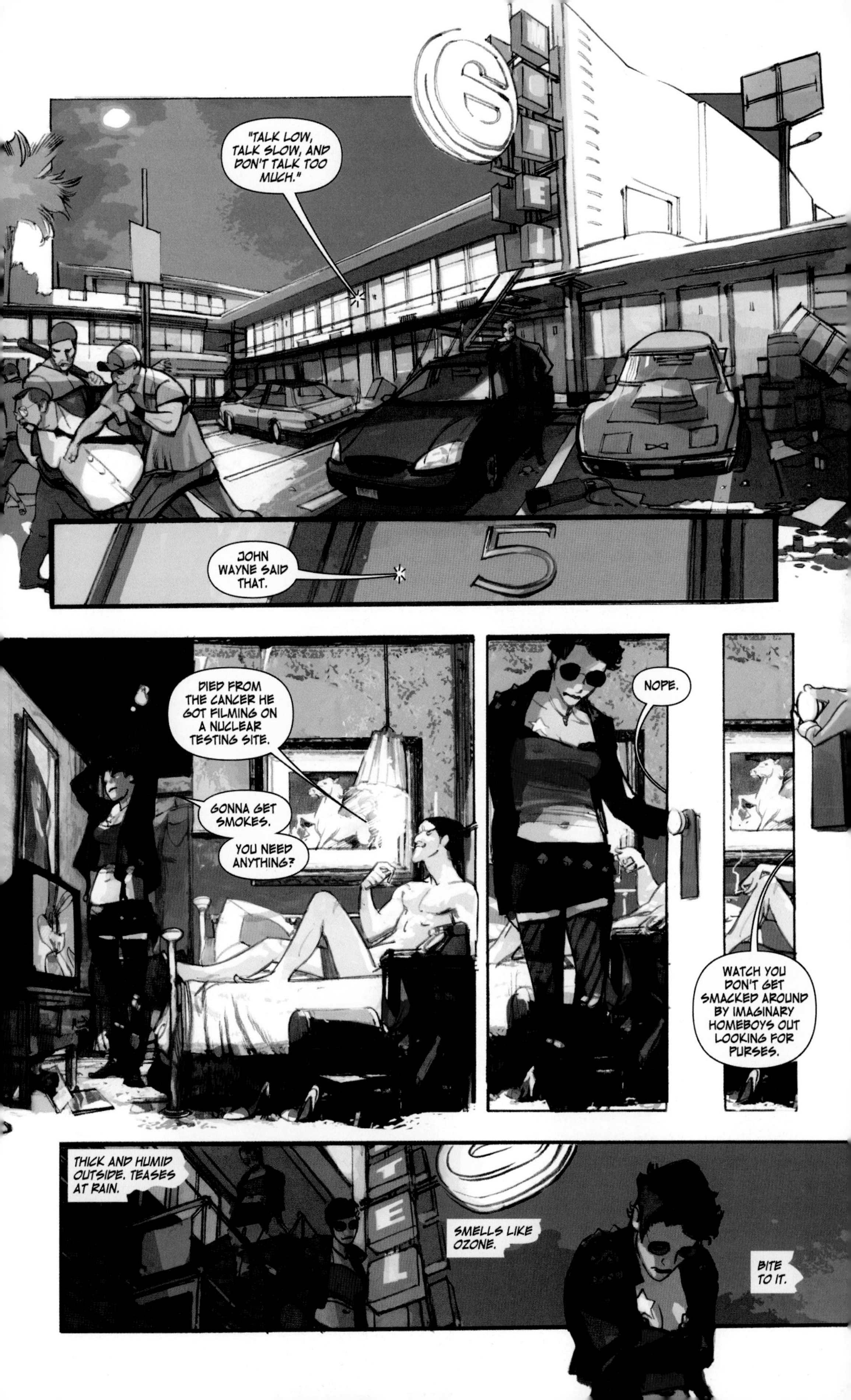
"TALK LOW, TALK SLOW, AND DON'T TALK TOO MUCH."
JOHN WAYNE SAID THAT.
5
DIED FROM THE CANCER HE GOT FILMING ON A NUCLEAR TESTING SITE.
GONNA GET SMOKES.
YOU NEED ANYTHING?
NOPE.
WATCH YOU DON'T GET SMACKED AROUND BY IMAGINARY HOMEBOYS OUT LOOKING FOR PURSES.
THICK AND HUMID OUTSIDE. TEASES AT RAIN.
SMELLS LIKE OZONE.
BITE TO IT.

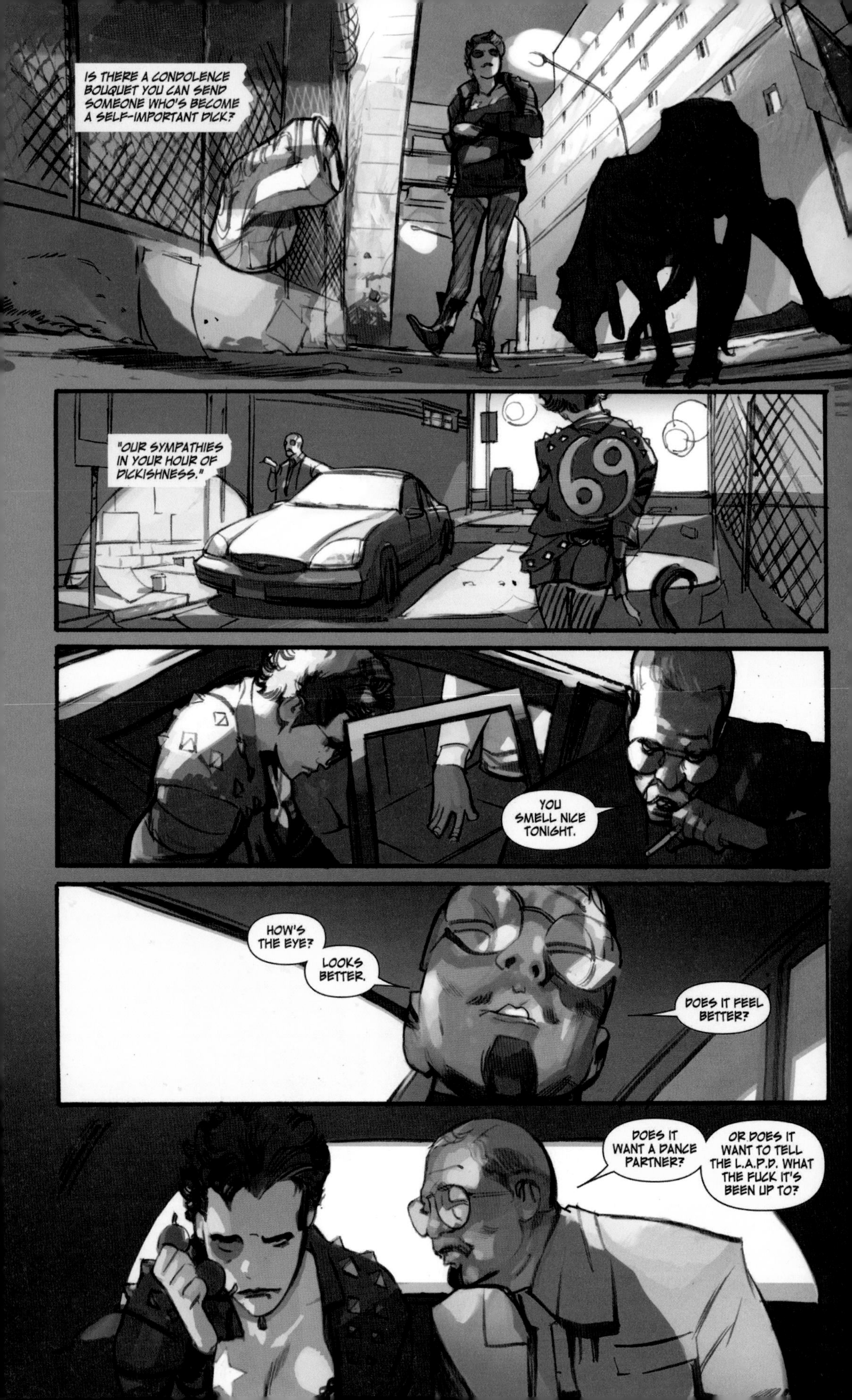

IS THERE A CONDOLENCE BOUQUET YOU CAN SEND SOMEONE WHO'S BECOME A SELF-IMPORTANT DICK?
"OUR SYMPATHIES IN YOUR HOUR OF DICKISHNESS."
YOU SMELL NICE TONIGHT.
HOW'S THE EYE?
LOOKS BETTER.
DOES IT FEEL BETTER?
DOES IT WANT A DANCE PARTNER?
OR DOES IT WANT TO TELL THE L.A.P.D. WHAT THE FUCK IT'S BEEN UP TO?

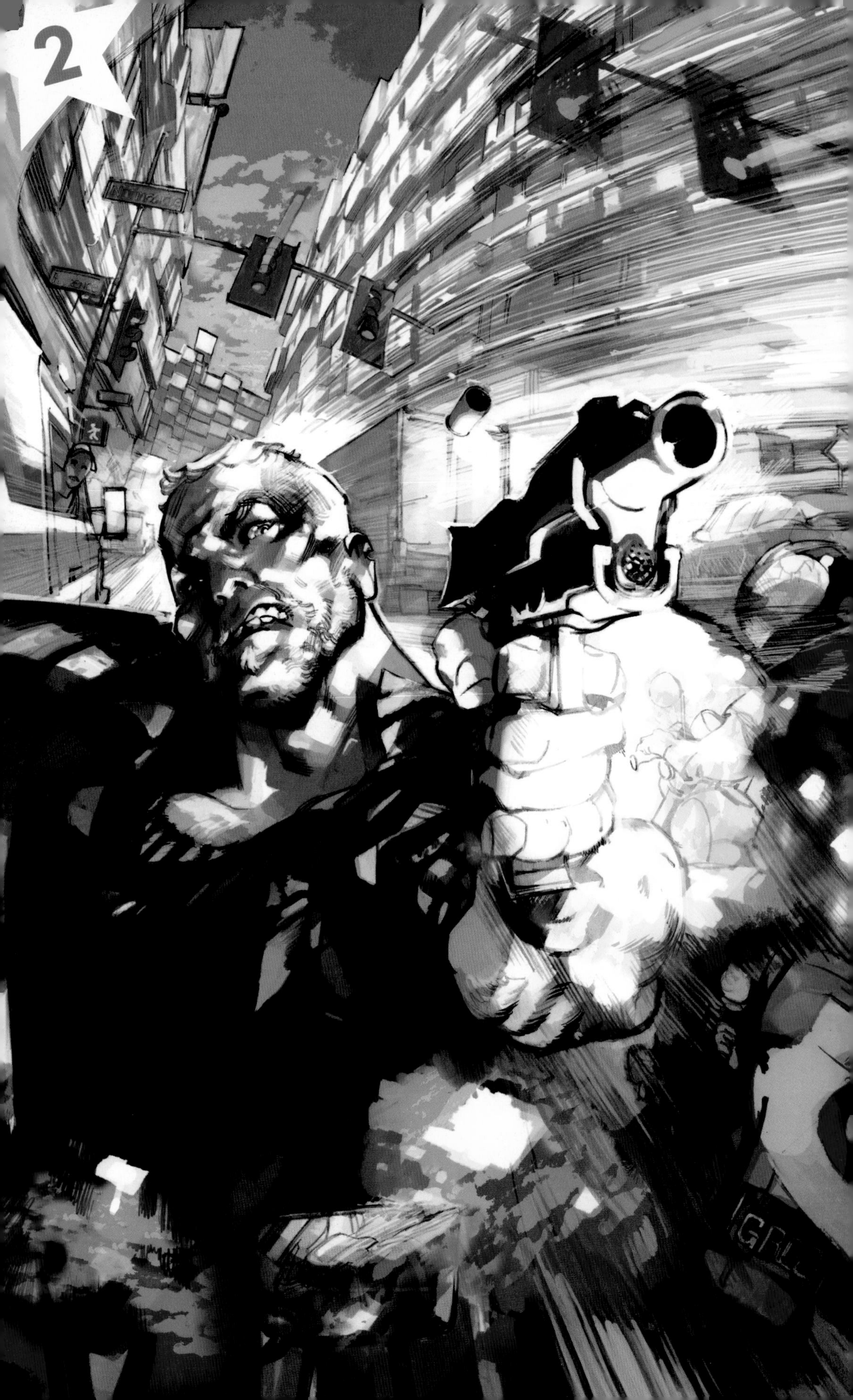
2

SEVEN DAYS UNTIL BROADCAST

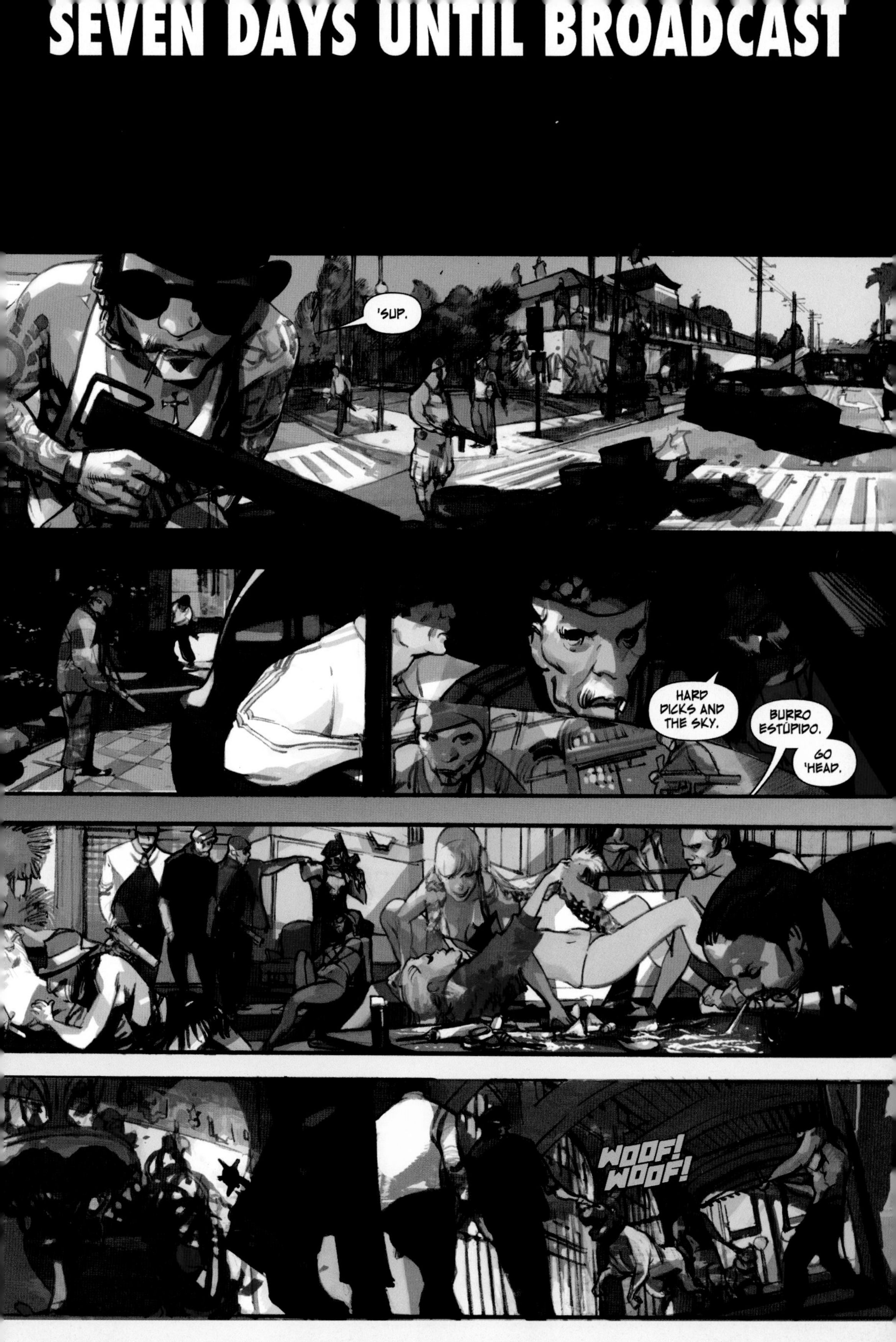

'SUP.
HARD DICKS AND THE SKY.
BURRO ESTÚPIDO.
GO 'HEAD.
WOOF! WOOF!

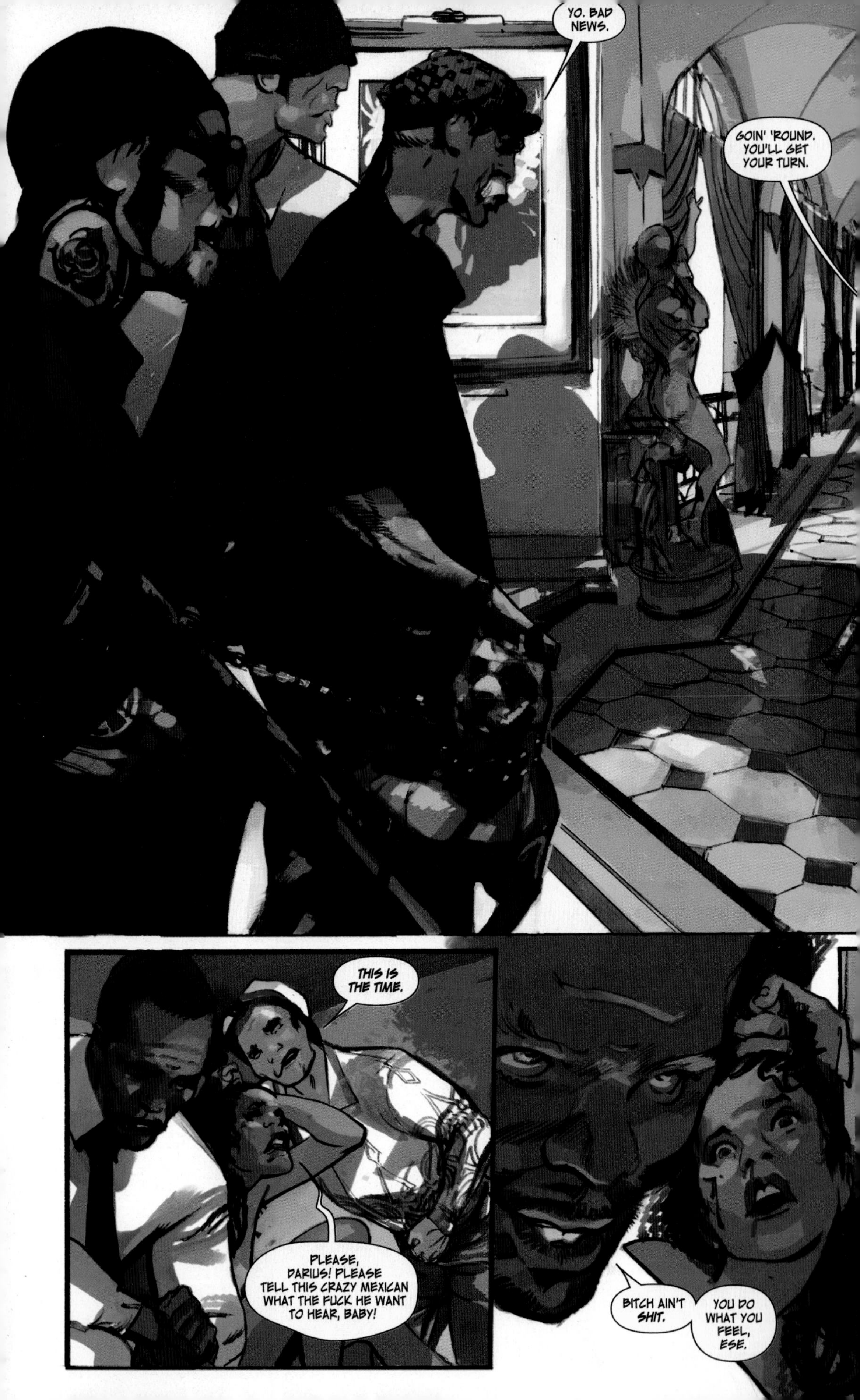
YO. BAD NEWS.
GOIN' 'ROUND. YOU'LL GET YOUR TURN.
THIS IS THE TIME.
PLEASE, DARIUS! PLEASE TELL THIS CRAZY MEXICAN WHAT THE FUCK HE WANT TO HEAR, BABY!
BITCH AIN'T SHIT.
YOU DO WHAT YOU FEEL, ESE.

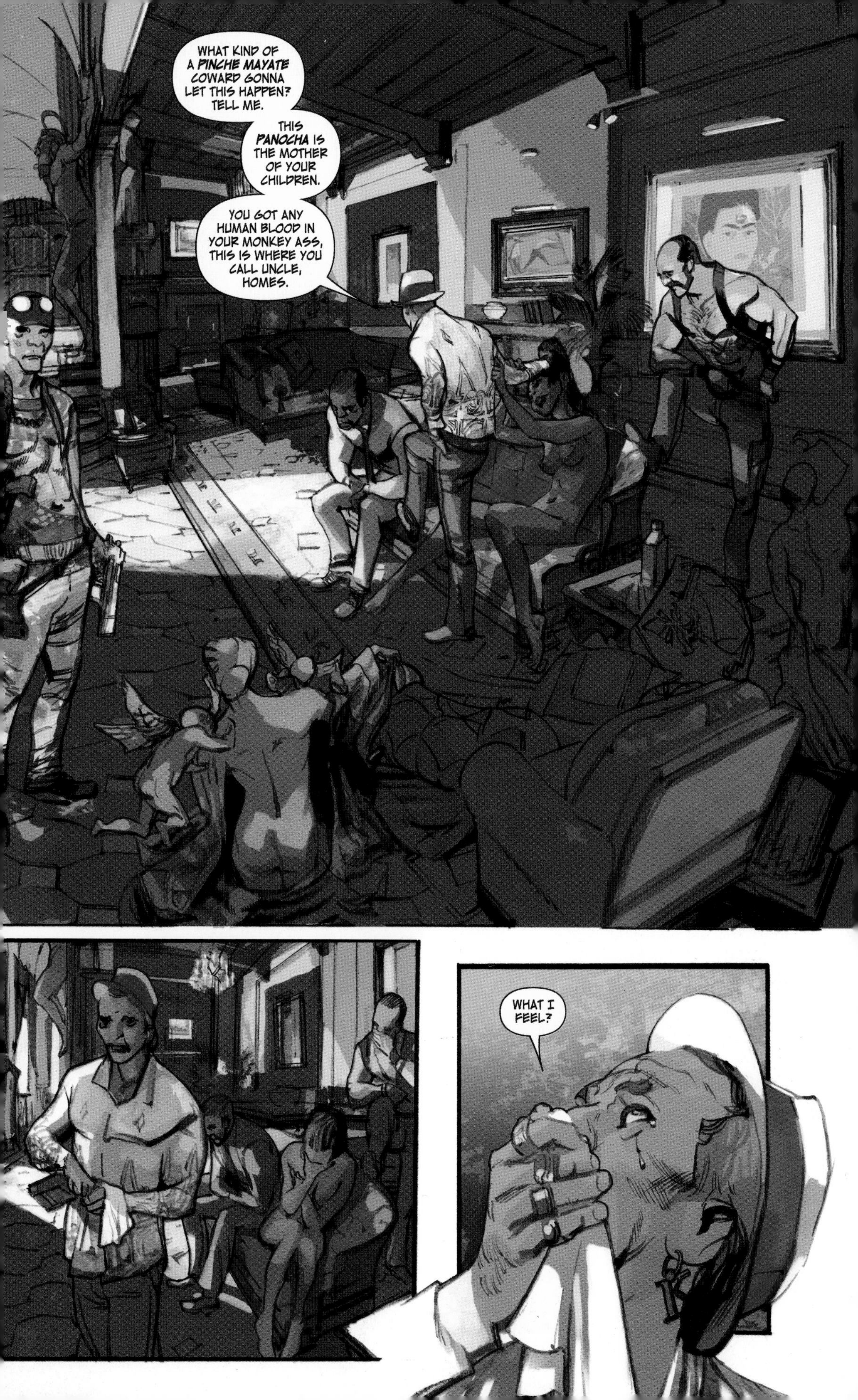
WHAT KIND OF A PINCHE MAYATE COWARD GONNA LET THIS HAPPEN? TELL ME.
THIS PANOCHA IS THE MOTHER OF YOUR CHILDREN.
YOU GOT ANY HUMAN BLOOD IN YOUR MONKEY ASS, THIS IS WHERE YOU CALL UNCLE, HOMES.
WHAT I FEEL?

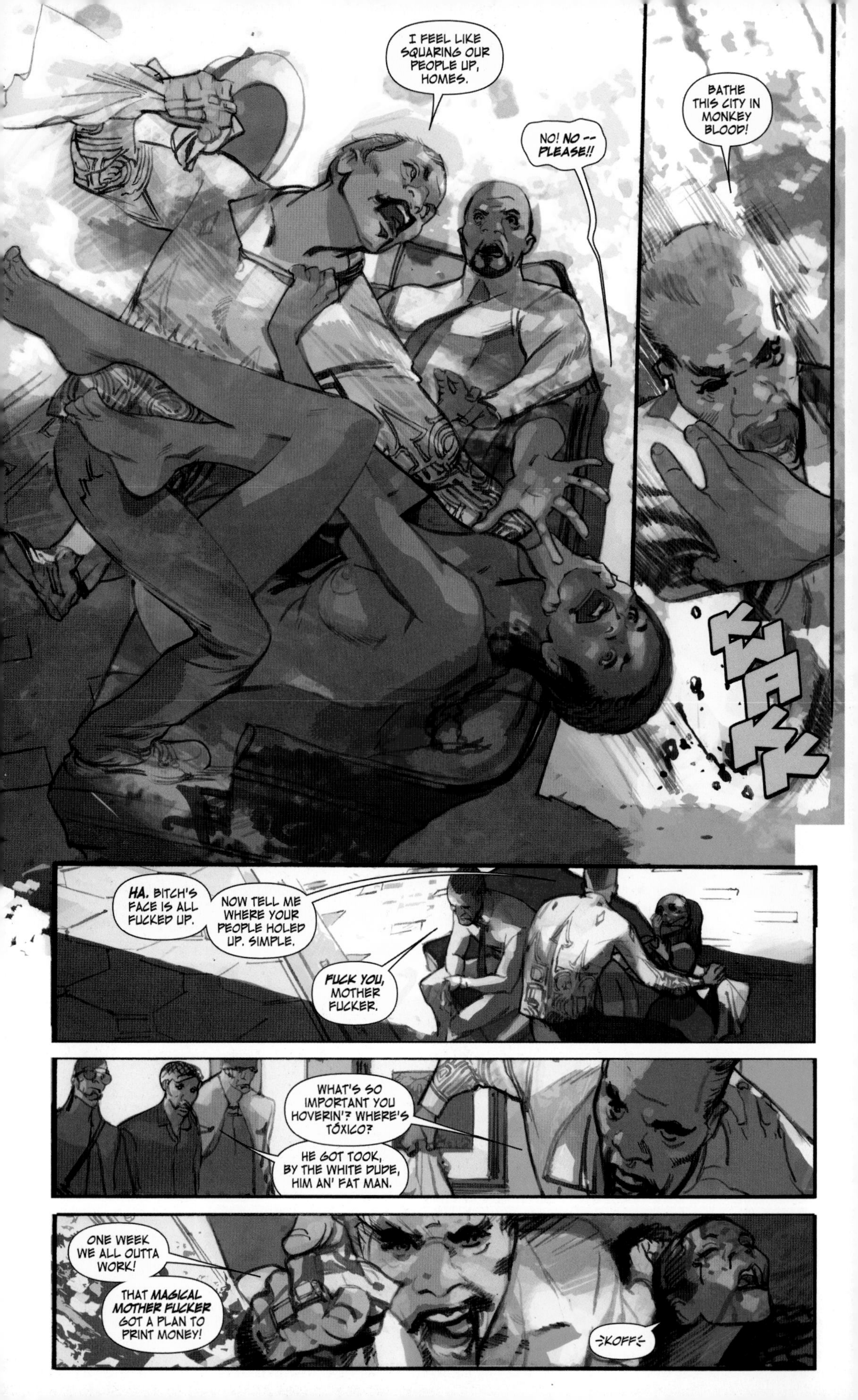
I FEEL LIKE SQUARING OUR PEOPLE UP, HOMES.
NO! NO -- PLEASE!!
BATHE THIS CITY IN MONKEY BLOOD!
KWAKK
HA. BITCH'S FACE IS ALL FUCKED UP.
NOW TELL ME WHERE YOUR PEOPLE HOLED UP. SIMPLE.
FUCK YOU, MOTHER FUCKER.
WHAT'S SO IMPORTANT YOU HOVERIN'? WHERE'S TÓXICO?
HE GOT TOOK, BY THE WHITE DUDE, HIM AN' FAT MAN.
ONE WEEK WE ALL OUTTA WORK!
THAT MAGICAL MOTHER FUCKER GOT A PLAN TO PRINT MONEY!
KOFF

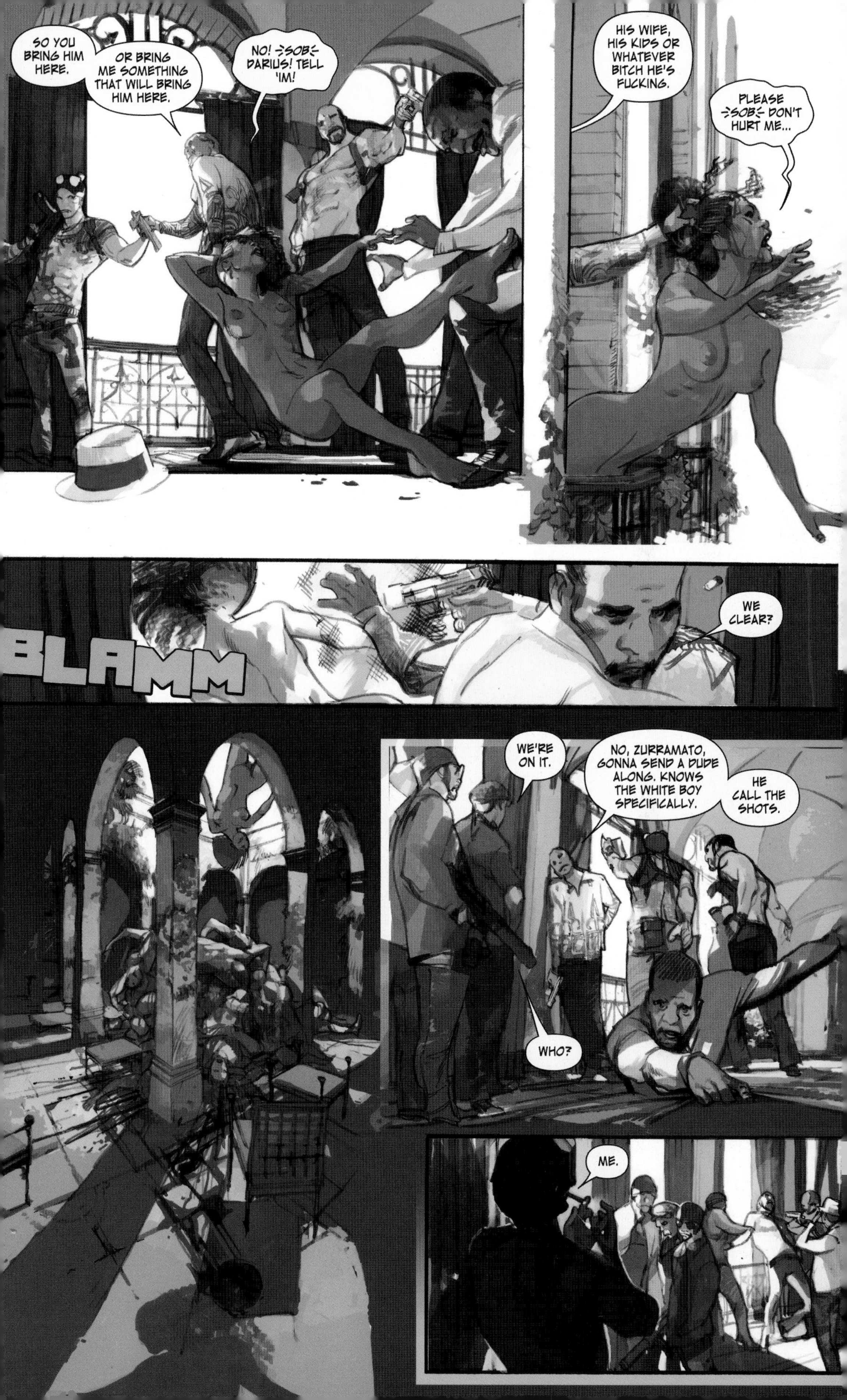
SO YOU BRING HIM HERE.
OR BRING ME SOMETHING THAT WILL BRING HIM HERE.
NO! -SOB- DARIUS! TELL 'IM!
HIS WIFE, HIS KIDS OR WHATEVER BITCH HE'S FUCKING.
PLEASE -SOB- DON'T HURT ME...
BLAMM
WE CLEAR?
WE'RE ON IT.
NO, ZURRAMATO, GONNA SEND A DUDE ALONG. KNOWS THE WHITE BOY SPECIFICALLY.
HE CALL THE SHOTS.
WHO?
ME.

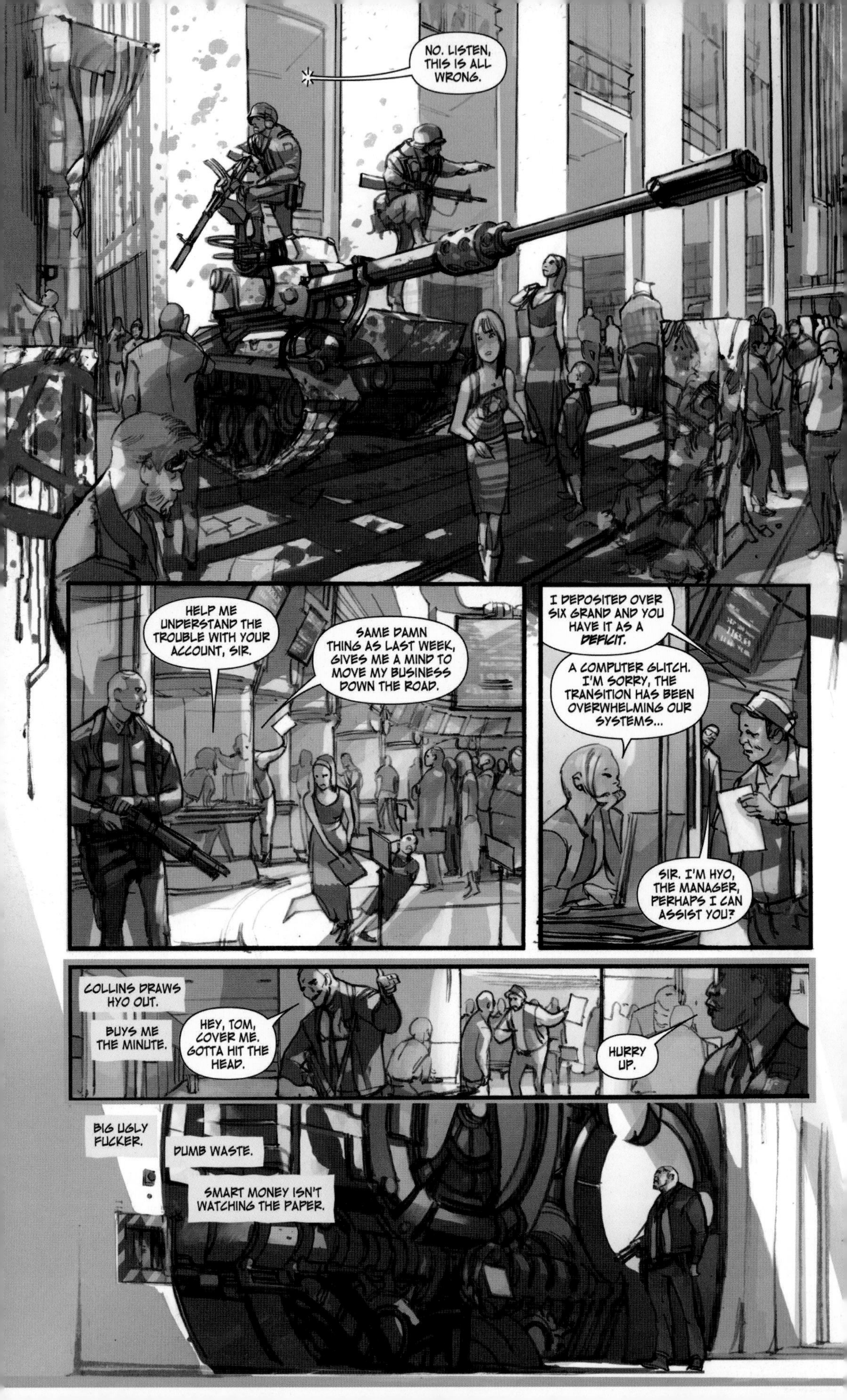
NO. LISTEN, THIS IS ALL WRONG.
HELP ME UNDERSTAND THE TROUBLE WITH YOUR ACCOUNT, SIR.
SAME DAMN THING AS LAST WEEK, GIVES ME A MIND TO MOVE MY BUSINESS DOWN THE ROAD.
I DEPOSITED OVER SIX GRAND AND YOU HAVE IT AS A DEFICIT.
A COMPUTER GLITCH. I'M SORRY, THE TRANSITION HAS BEEN OVERWHELMING OUR SYSTEMS...
SIR. I'M HYO, THE MANAGER, PERHAPS I CAN ASSIST YOU?
COLLINS DRAWS HYO OUT.
BUYS ME THE MINUTE.
HEY, TOM, COVER ME. GOTTA HIT THE HEAD.
HURRY UP.
BIG UGLY FUCKER.
DUMB WASTE.
SMART MONEY ISN'T WATCHING THE PAPER.

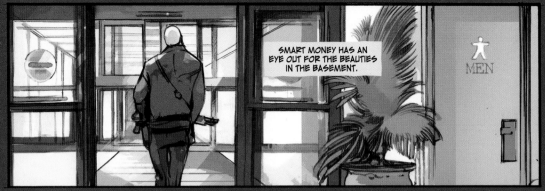
SMART MONEY HAS AN EYE OUT FOR THE BEAUTIES IN THE BASEMENT.

SMART MONEY NEEDS TO GET HIS HACKER GAL THE SYSTEM SCHEMATICS.

SMART MONEY'S BEEN MAKING SOME BAD DECISIONS.

HACKER GAL BAD DECISIONS.

-KLIKK

Copying 1
Copying
from Hyo
Discovered
More in

C'MON, YOU PILE OF DICK.

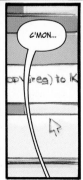
C'MON...

py..rea) to K..GSTONE
Can

MR. BRICKE.

WHAT ARE YOU DOING IN MY OFFICE?

MR. HYO... I'M...

LISTEN...

HYO MANAGER

OH, I AM LISTENING VERY CLOSELY TO THIS.

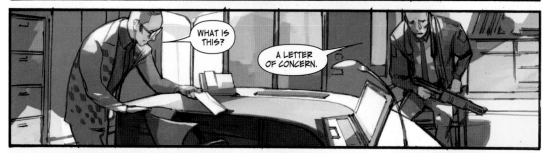

WHAT IS THIS?

A LETTER OF CONCERN.

YOU HAVE TO UNDERSTAND WHY I WANTED TO DROP IT ANONYMOUSLY.

SHH.

YOU ARE TELLING ME THAT MY HEAD OF SECURITY, THE MAN WHO HIRED YOU...

YEAH. ME AND A FEW OF THE GUARDS, WE THOUGHT YOU SHOULD KNOW.

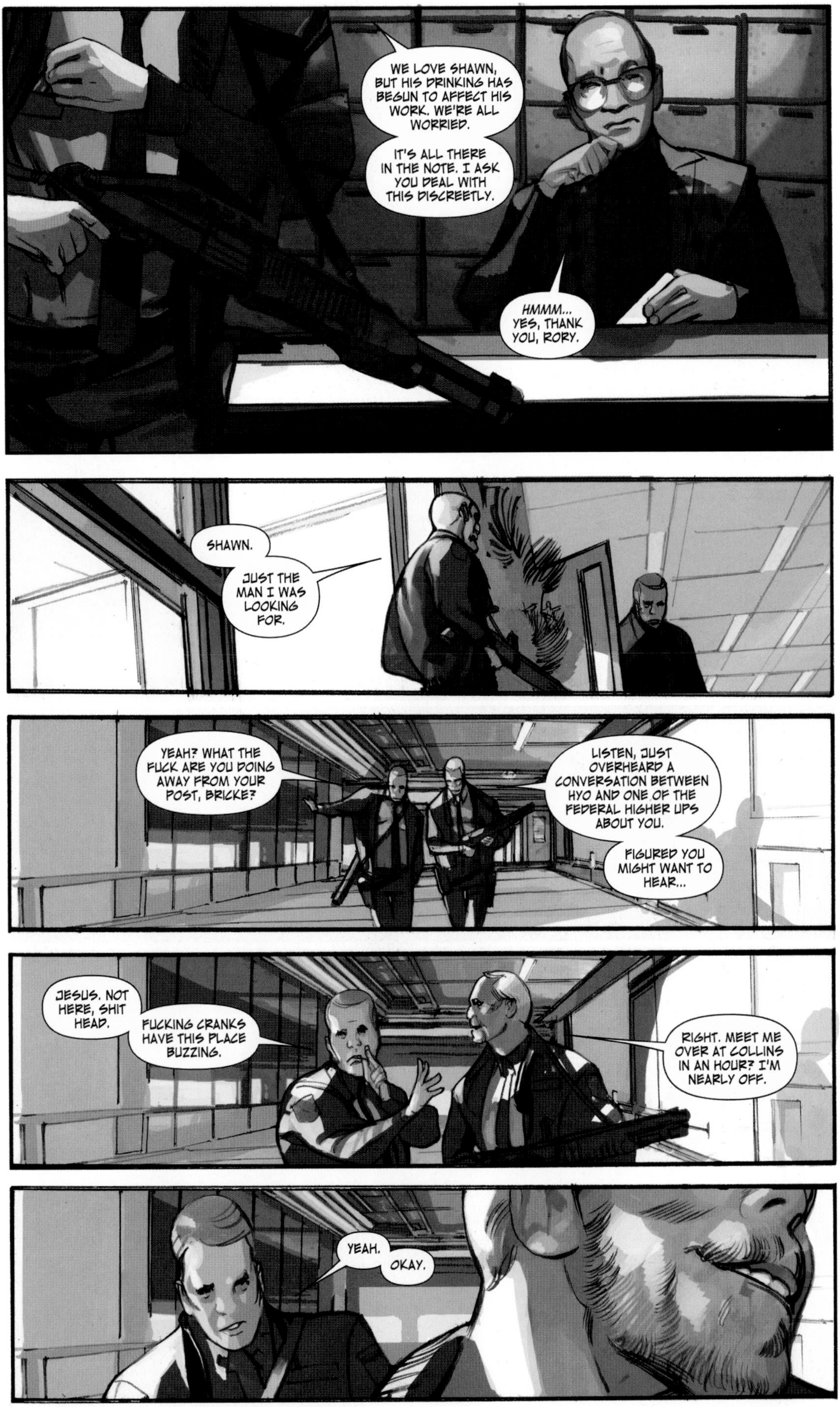
WE LOVE SHAWN, BUT HIS DRINKING HAS BEGUN TO AFFECT HIS WORK. WE'RE ALL WORRIED.
IT'S ALL THERE IN THE NOTE. I ASK YOU DEAL WITH THIS DISCREETLY.
HMMM... YES, THANK YOU, RORY.
SHAWN.
JUST THE MAN I WAS LOOKING FOR.
YEAH? WHAT THE FUCK ARE YOU DOING AWAY FROM YOUR POST, BRICKE?
LISTEN, JUST OVERHEARD A CONVERSATION BETWEEN HYO AND ONE OF THE FEDERAL HIGHER UPS ABOUT YOU.
FIGURED YOU MIGHT WANT TO HEAR...
JESUS. NOT HERE, SHIT HEAD.
FUCKING CRANKS HAVE THIS PLACE BUZZING.
RIGHT. MEET ME OVER AT COLLINS IN AN HOUR? I'M NEARLY OFF.
YEAH.
OKAY.

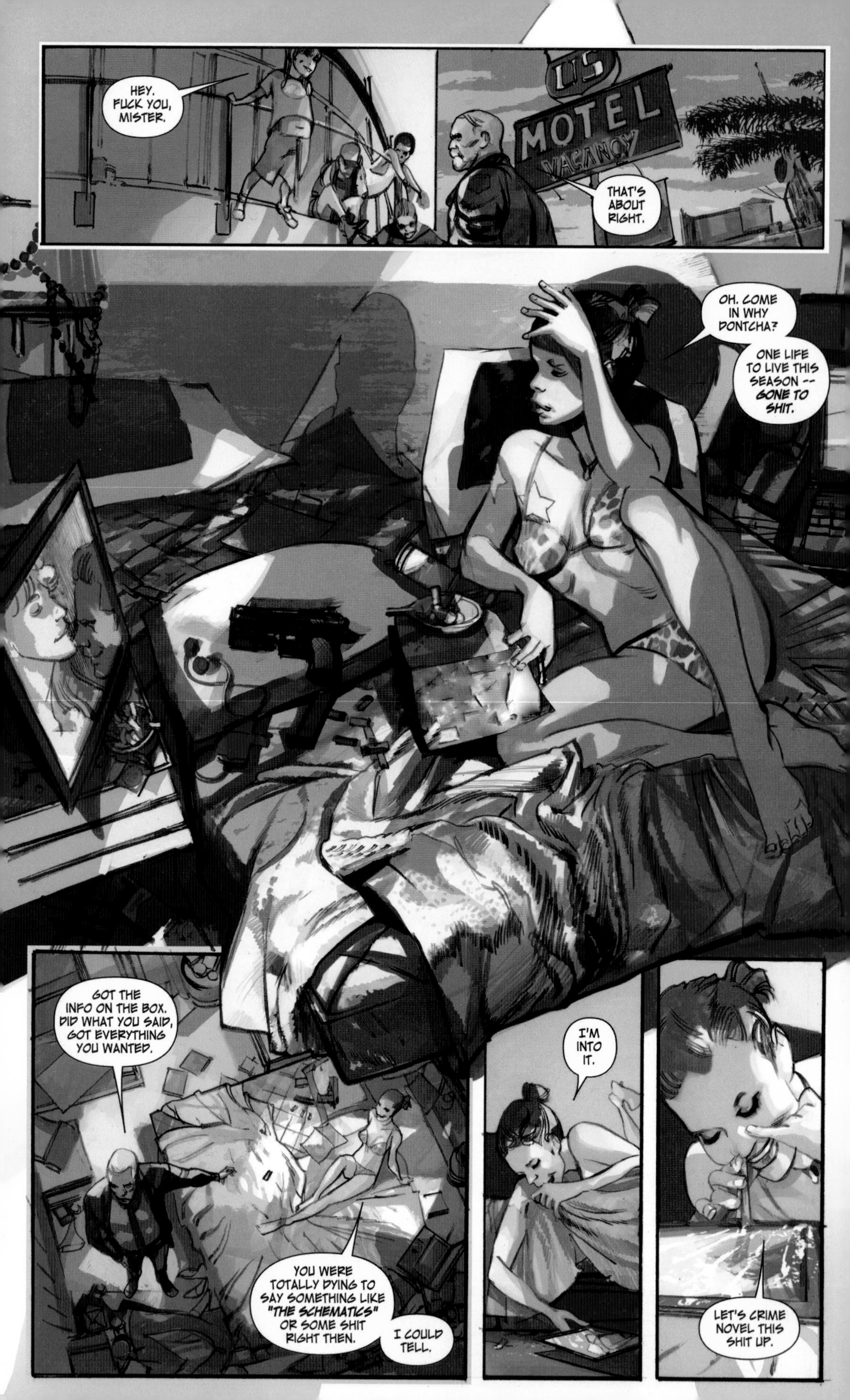
HEY. FUCK YOU, MISTER.
US MOTEL VACANCY
THAT'S ABOUT RIGHT.
OH. COME IN WHY DONTCHA?
ONE LIFE TO LIVE THIS SEASON -- GONE TO SHIT.
GOT THE INFO ON THE BOX. DID WHAT YOU SAID, GOT EVERYTHING YOU WANTED.
YOU WERE TOTALLY DYING TO SAY SOMETHING LIKE "THE SCHEMATICS" OR SOME SHIT RIGHT THEN.
I COULD TELL.
I'M INTO IT.
LET'S CRIME NOVEL THIS SHIT UP.

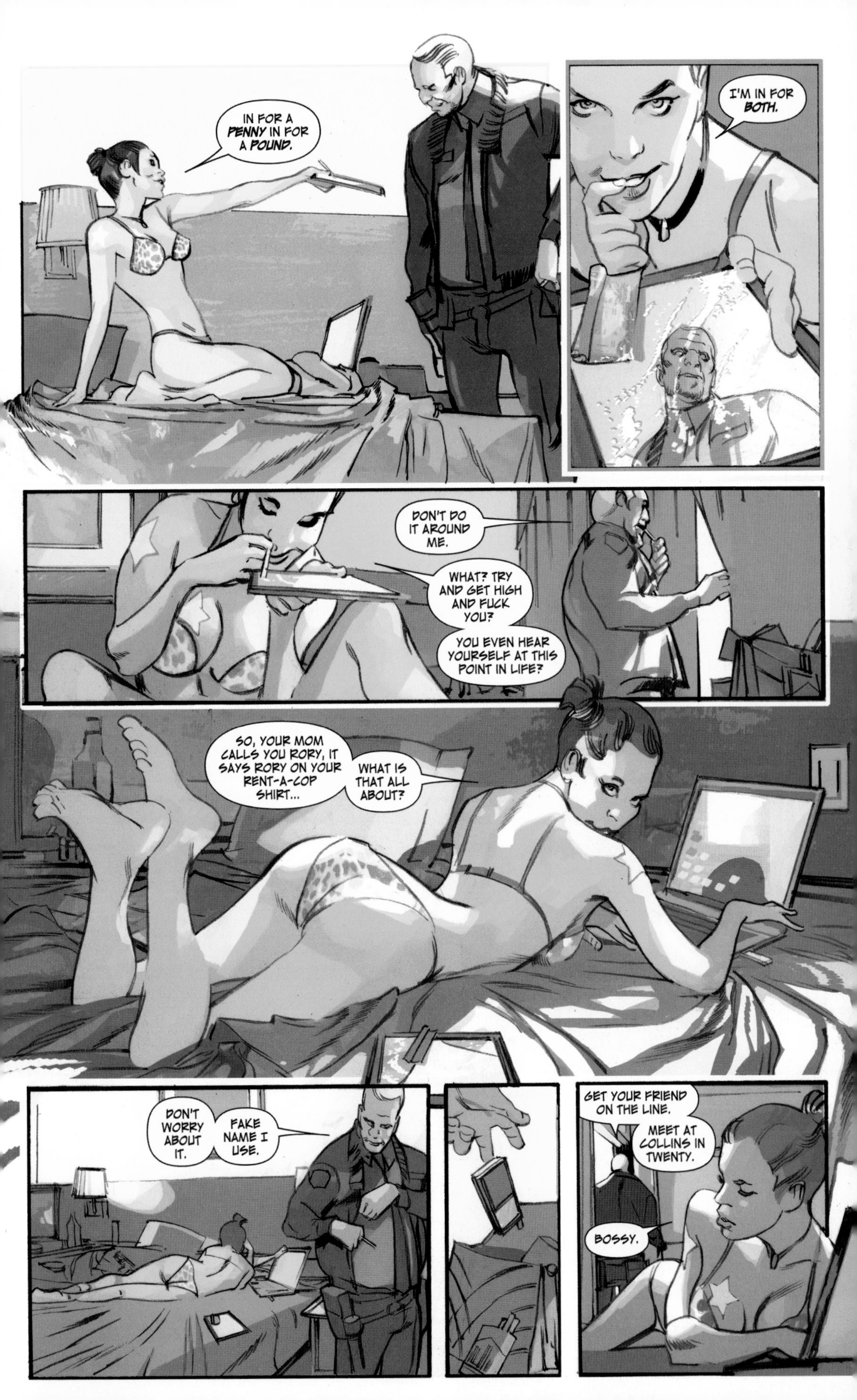
IN FOR A PENNY IN FOR A POUND.
I'M IN FOR BOTH.
DON'T DO IT AROUND ME.
WHAT? TRY AND GET HIGH AND FUCK YOU?
YOU EVEN HEAR YOURSELF AT THIS POINT IN LIFE?
SO, YOUR MOM CALLS YOU RORY, IT SAYS RORY ON YOUR RENT-A-COP SHIRT...
WHAT IS THAT ALL ABOUT?
DON'T WORRY ABOUT IT.
FAKE NAME I USE.
GET YOUR FRIEND ON THE LINE.
MEET AT COLLINS IN TWENTY.
BOSSY.

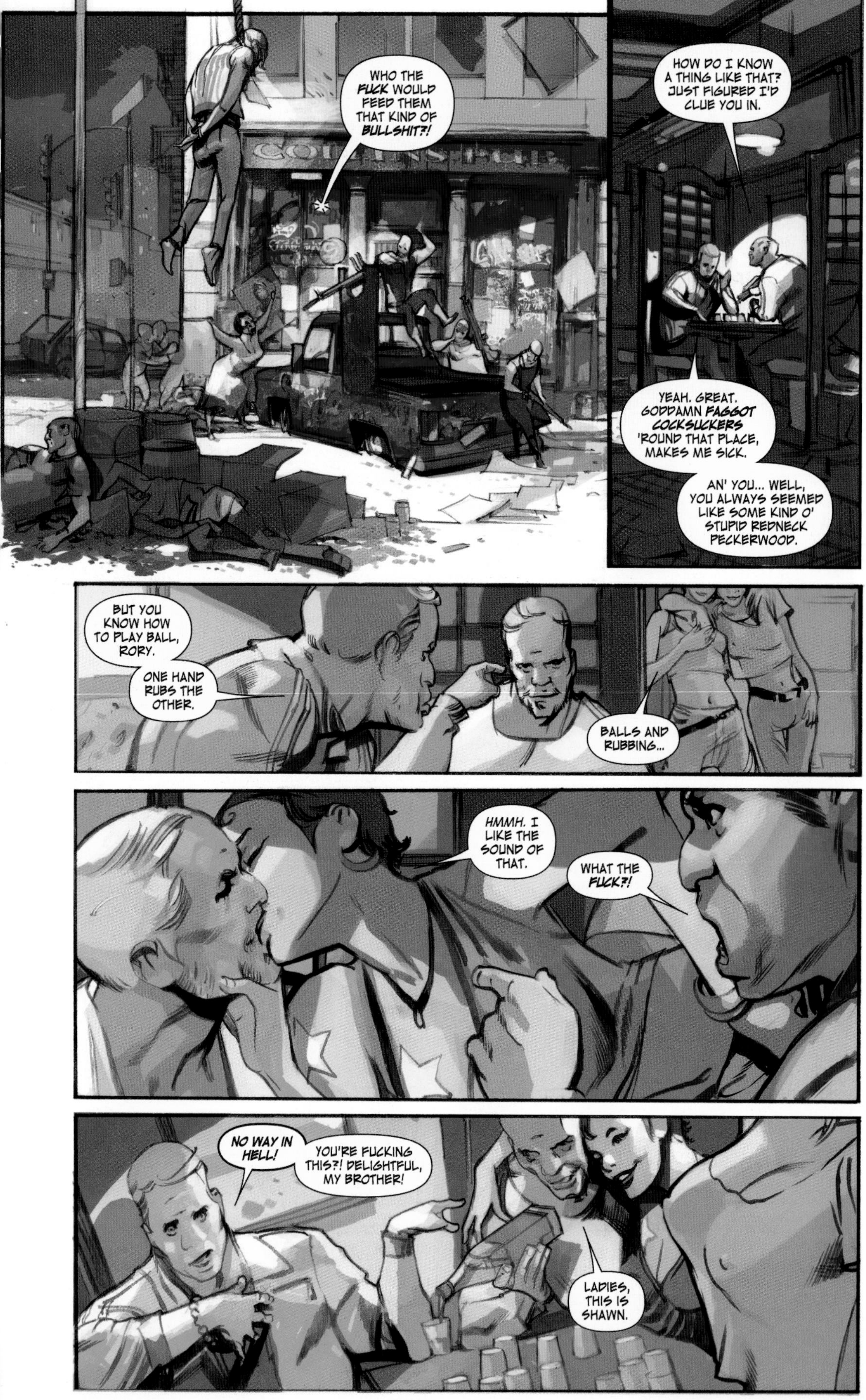
WHO THE FUCK WOULD FEED THEM THAT KIND OF BULLSHIT?!
HOW DO I KNOW A THING LIKE THAT? JUST FIGURED I'D CLUE YOU IN.
YEAH. GREAT. GODDAMN FAGGOT COCKSUCKERS 'ROUND THAT PLACE, MAKES ME SICK.
AN' YOU... WELL, YOU ALWAYS SEEMED LIKE SOME KIND O' STUPID REDNECK PECKERWOOD.
BUT YOU KNOW HOW TO PLAY BALL, RORY.
ONE HAND RUBS THE OTHER.
BALLS AND RUBBING...
HMMH. I LIKE THE SOUND OF THAT.
WHAT THE FUCK?!
NO WAY IN HELL!
YOU'RE FUCKING THIS?! DELIGHTFUL, MY BROTHER!
LADIES, THIS IS SHAWN.

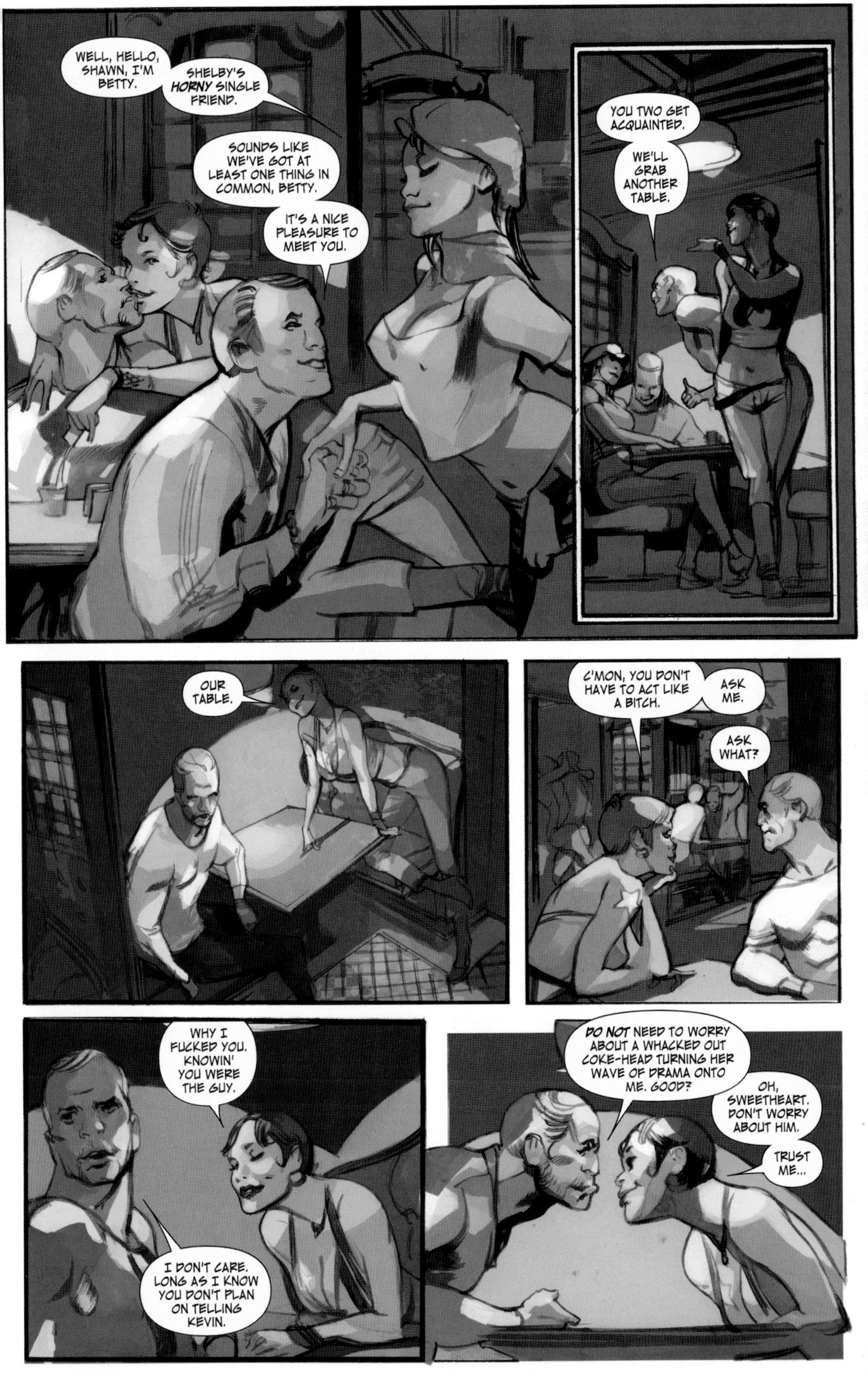
WELL, HELLO, SHAWN, I'M BETTY.
SHELBY'S *HORNY* SINGLE FRIEND.
SOUNDS LIKE WE'VE GOT AT LEAST ONE THING IN COMMON, BETTY.
IT'S A NICE PLEASURE TO MEET YOU.
YOU TWO GET ACQUAINTED.
WE'LL GRAB ANOTHER TABLE.
OUR TABLE.
C'MON, YOU DON'T HAVE TO ACT LIKE A BITCH.
ASK ME.
ASK WHAT?
WHY I FUCKED YOU. KNOWIN' YOU WERE THE GUY.
I DON'T CARE. LONG AS I KNOW YOU DON'T PLAN ON TELLING KEVIN.
DO NOT NEED TO WORRY ABOUT A WHACKED OUT COKE-HEAD TURNING HER WAVE OF DRAMA ONTO ME. GOOD?
OH, SWEETHEART. DON'T WORRY ABOUT HIM.
TRUST ME...

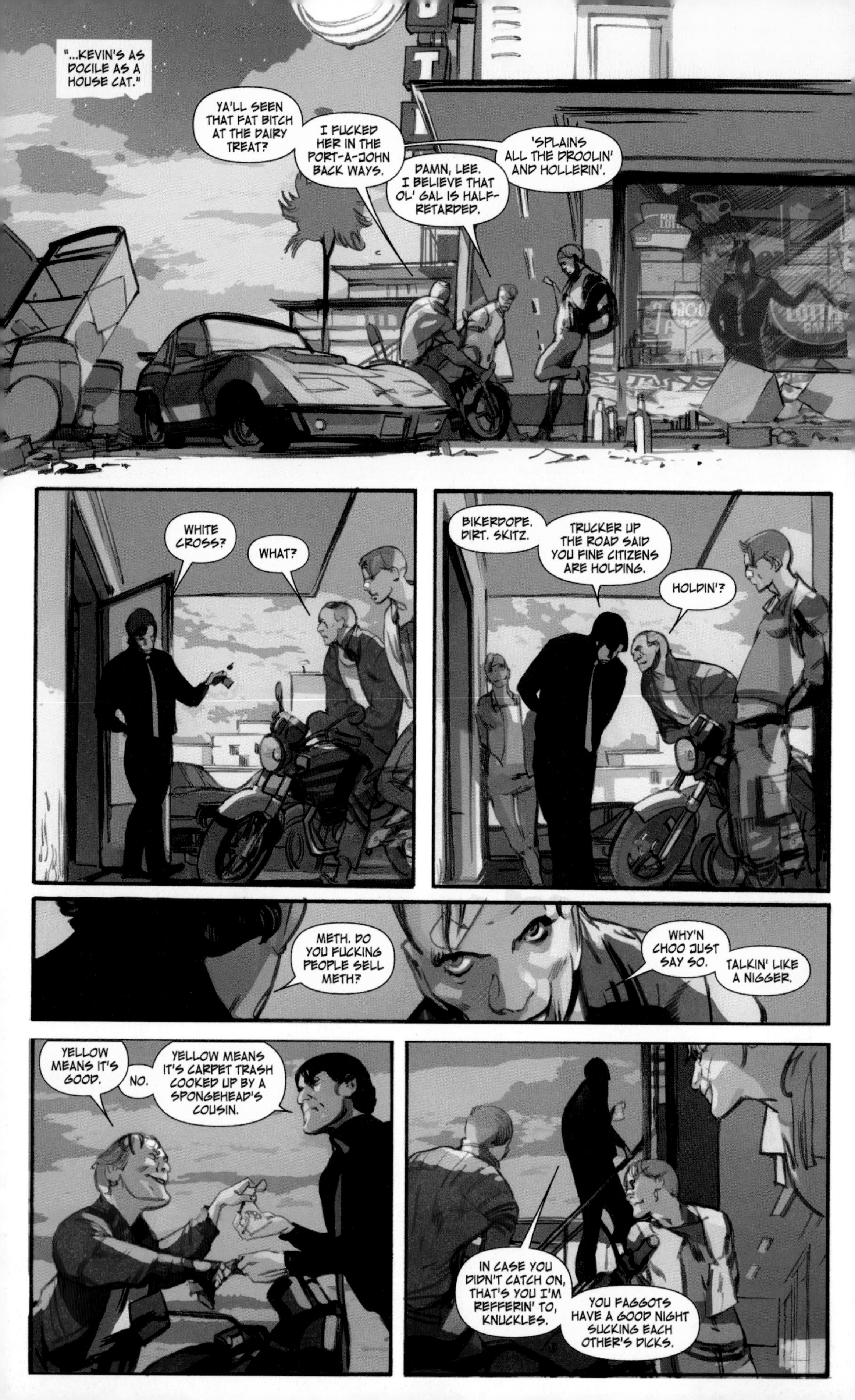
"...KEVIN'S AS DOCILE AS A HOUSE CAT."
YA'LL SEEN THAT FAT BITCH AT THE DAIRY TREAT?
I FUCKED HER IN THE PORT-A-JOHN BACK WAYS.
DAMN, LEE. I BELIEVE THAT OL' GAL IS HALF-RETARDED.
'SPLAINS ALL THE DROOLIN' AND HOLLERIN'.
WHITE CROSS?
WHAT?
BIKERDOPE. DIRT. SKITZ.
TRUCKER UP THE ROAD SAID YOU FINE CITIZENS ARE HOLDING.
HOLDIN'?
METH. DO YOU FUCKING PEOPLE SELL METH?
WHY'N CHOO JUST SAY SO.
TALKIN' LIKE A NIGGER.
YELLOW MEANS IT'S GOOD.
NO.
YELLOW MEANS IT'S CARPET TRASH COOKED UP BY A SPONGEHEAD'S COUSIN.
IN CASE YOU DIDN'T CATCH ON, THAT'S YOU I'M REFFERIN' TO, KNUCKLES.
YOU FAGGOTS HAVE A GOOD NIGHT SUCKING EACH OTHER'S DICKS.

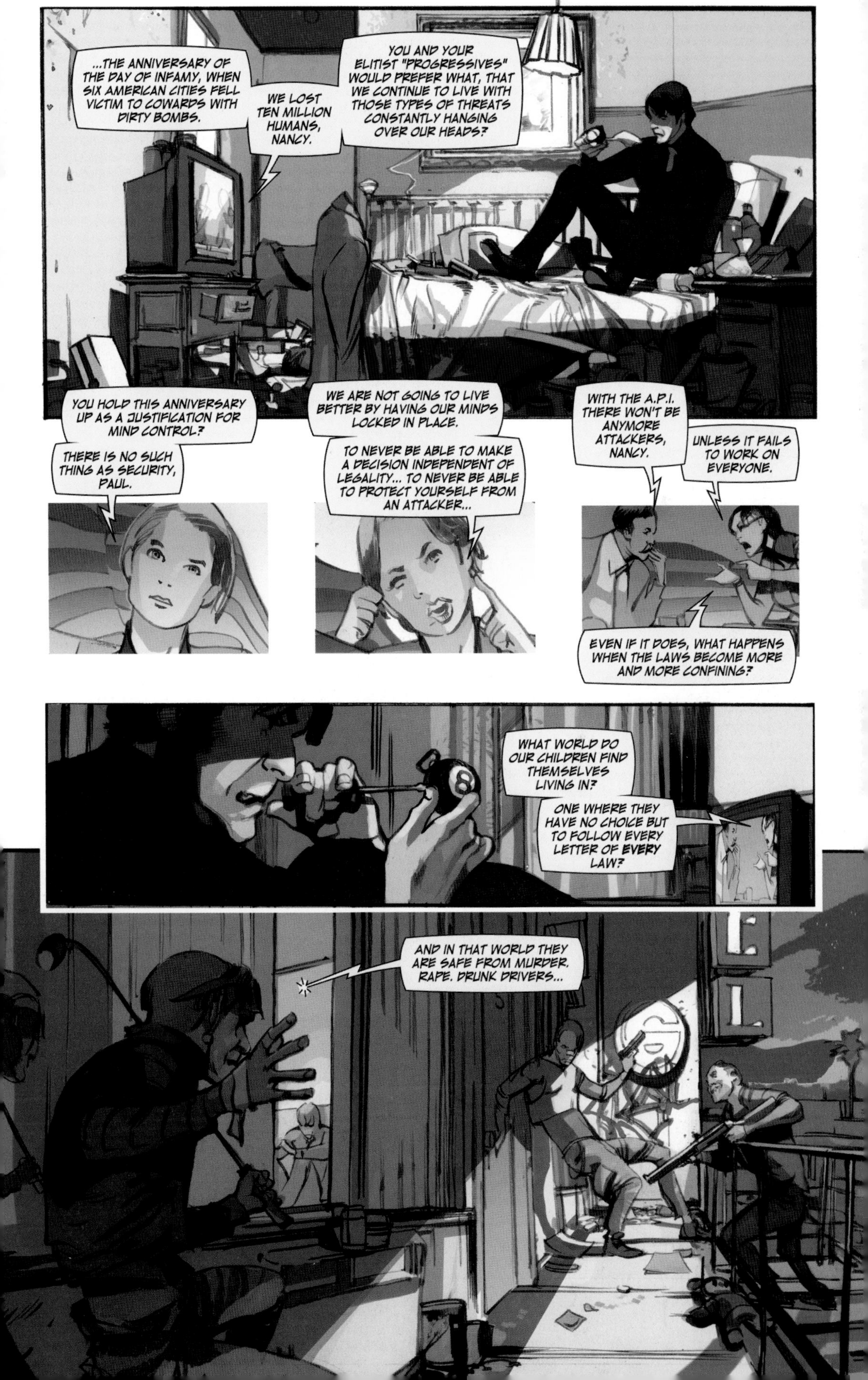
...THE ANNIVERSARY OF THE DAY OF INFAMY, WHEN SIX AMERICAN CITIES FELL VICTIM TO COWARDS WITH DIRTY BOMBS.
WE LOST TEN MILLION HUMANS, NANCY.
YOU AND YOUR ELITIST "PROGRESSIVES" WOULD PREFER WHAT, THAT WE CONTINUE TO LIVE WITH THOSE TYPES OF THREATS CONSTANTLY HANGING OVER OUR HEADS?
YOU HOLD THIS ANNIVERSARY UP AS A JUSTIFICATION FOR MIND CONTROL?
THERE IS NO SUCH THING AS SECURITY, PAUL.
WE ARE NOT GOING TO LIVE BETTER BY HAVING OUR MINDS LOCKED IN PLACE.
TO NEVER BE ABLE TO MAKE A DECISION INDEPENDENT OF LEGALITY... TO NEVER BE ABLE TO PROTECT YOURSELF FROM AN ATTACKER...
WITH THE A.P.I. THERE WON'T BE ANYMORE ATTACKERS, NANCY.
UNLESS IT FAILS TO WORK ON EVERYONE.
EVEN IF IT DOES, WHAT HAPPENS WHEN THE LAWS BECOME MORE AND MORE CONFINING?
WHAT WORLD DO OUR CHILDREN FIND THEMSELVES LIVING IN?
ONE WHERE THEY HAVE NO CHOICE BUT TO FOLLOW EVERY LETTER OF EVERY LAW?
AND IN THAT WORLD THEY ARE SAFE FROM MURDER. RAPE. DRUNK DRIVERS...

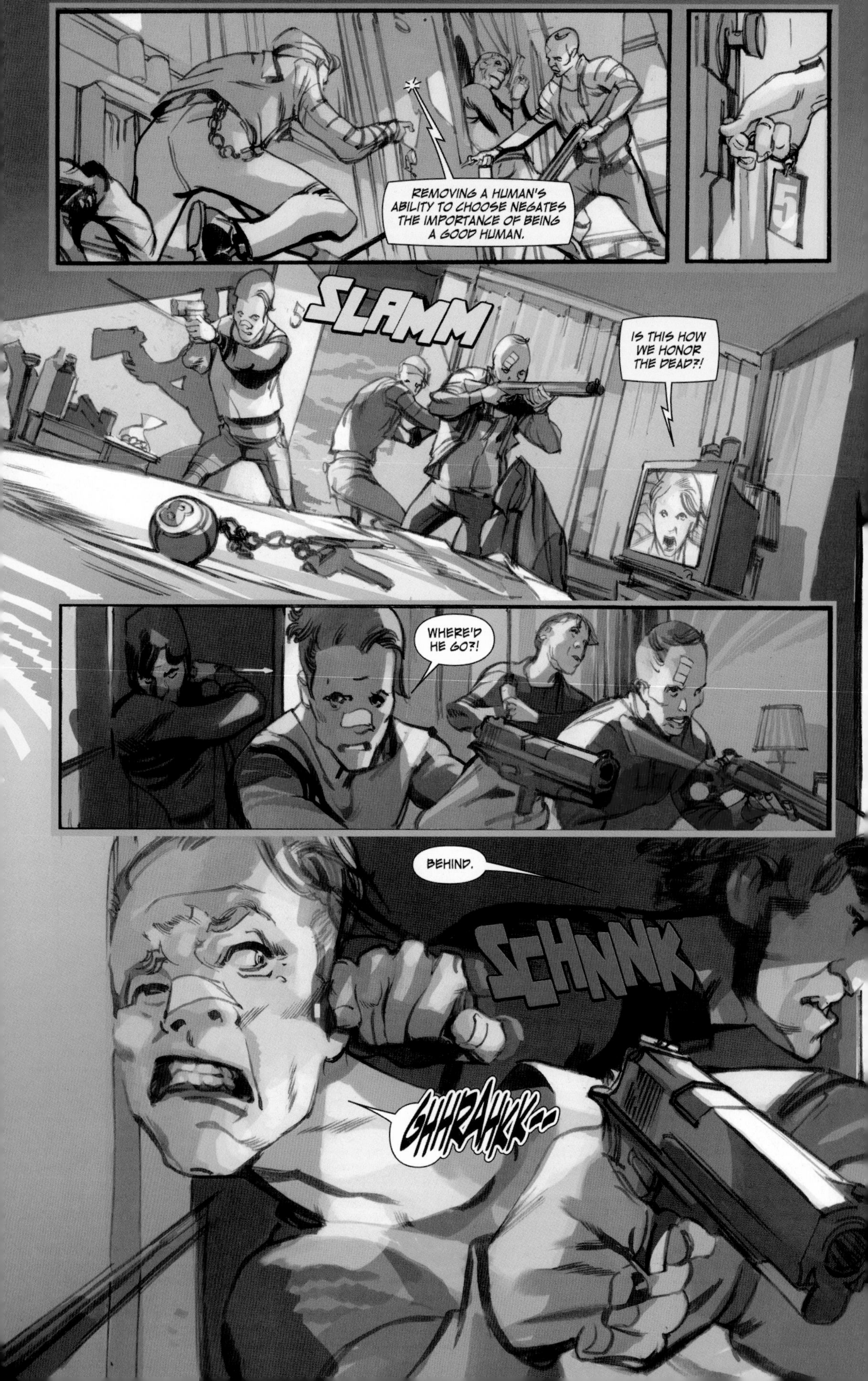
REMOVING A HUMAN'S ABILITY TO CHOOSE NEGATES THE IMPORTANCE OF BEING A GOOD HUMAN.
SLAMM
IS THIS HOW WE HONOR THE DEAD?!
WHERE'D HE GO?!
BEHIND.
SCHNNK

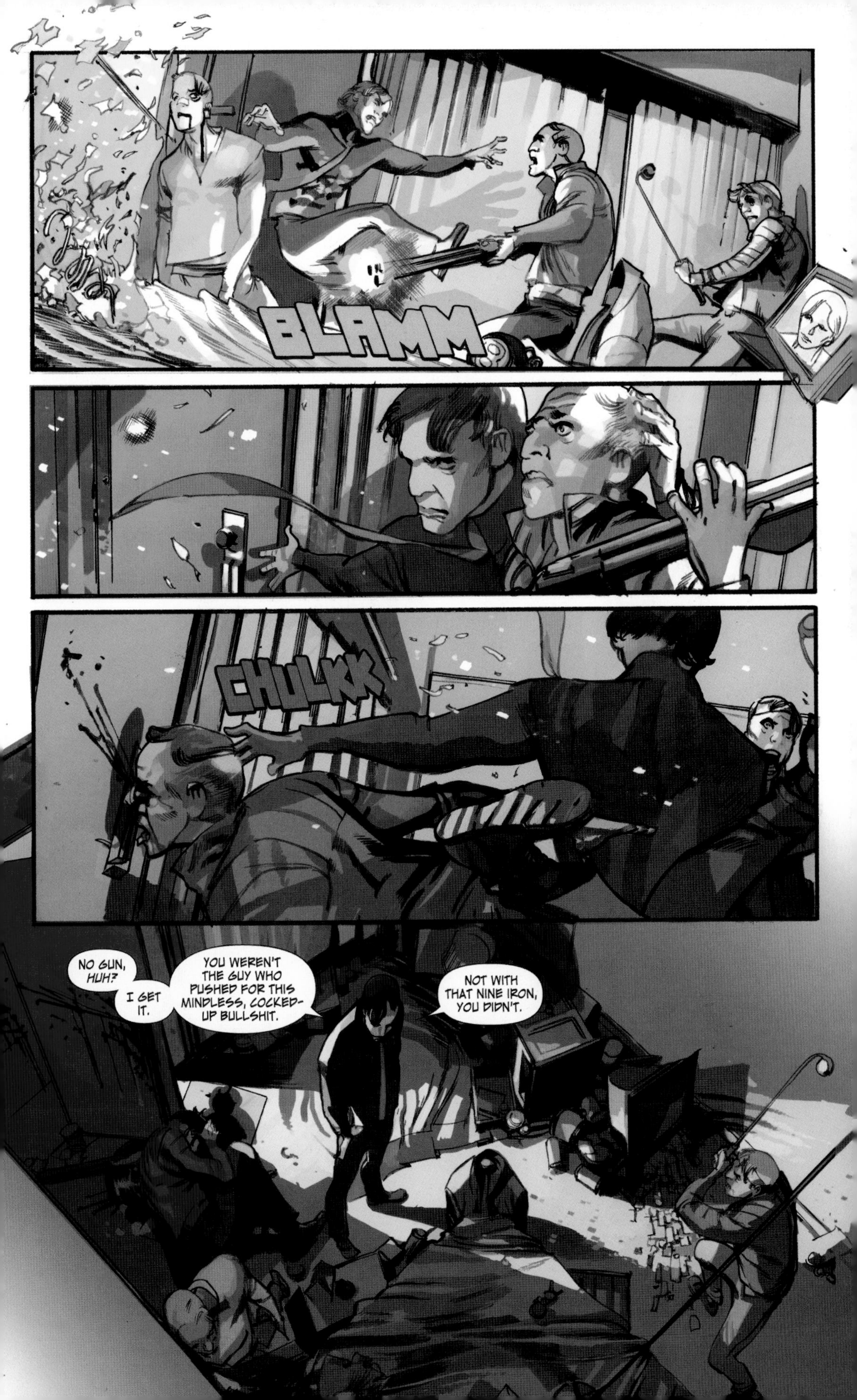
BLAMM
CHULKK
NO GUN, HUH?
I GET IT.
YOU WEREN'T THE GUY WHO PUSHED FOR THIS MINDLESS, COCKED-UP BULLSHIT.
NOT WITH THAT NINE IRON, YOU DIDN'T.

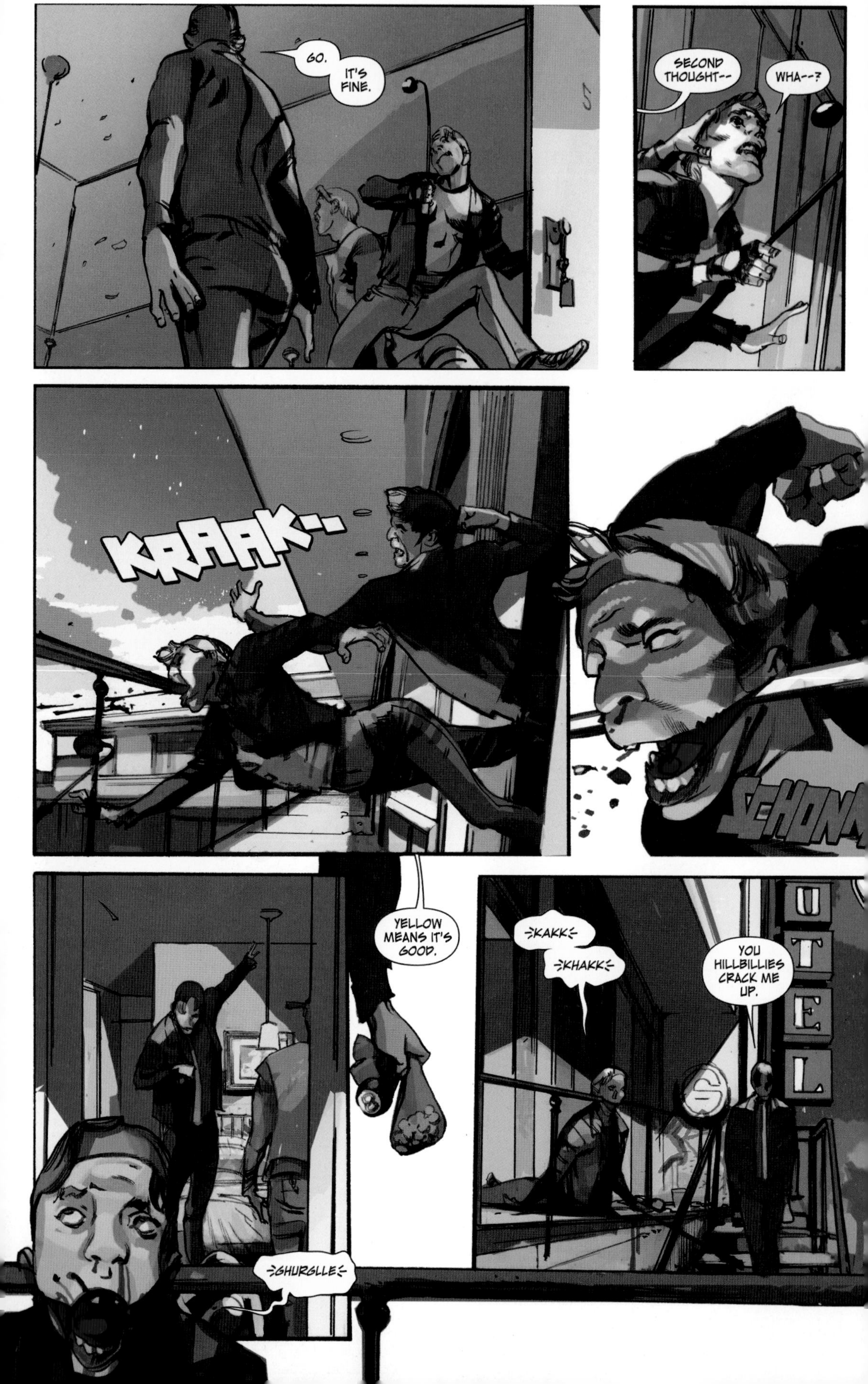
GO.
IT'S FINE.
SECOND THOUGHT--
WHA--?
KRAAK--
SCHON
YELLOW MEANS IT'S GOOD.
GHURGLLE
KAKK
KHAKK
YOU HILLBILLIES CRACK ME UP.
UTEL

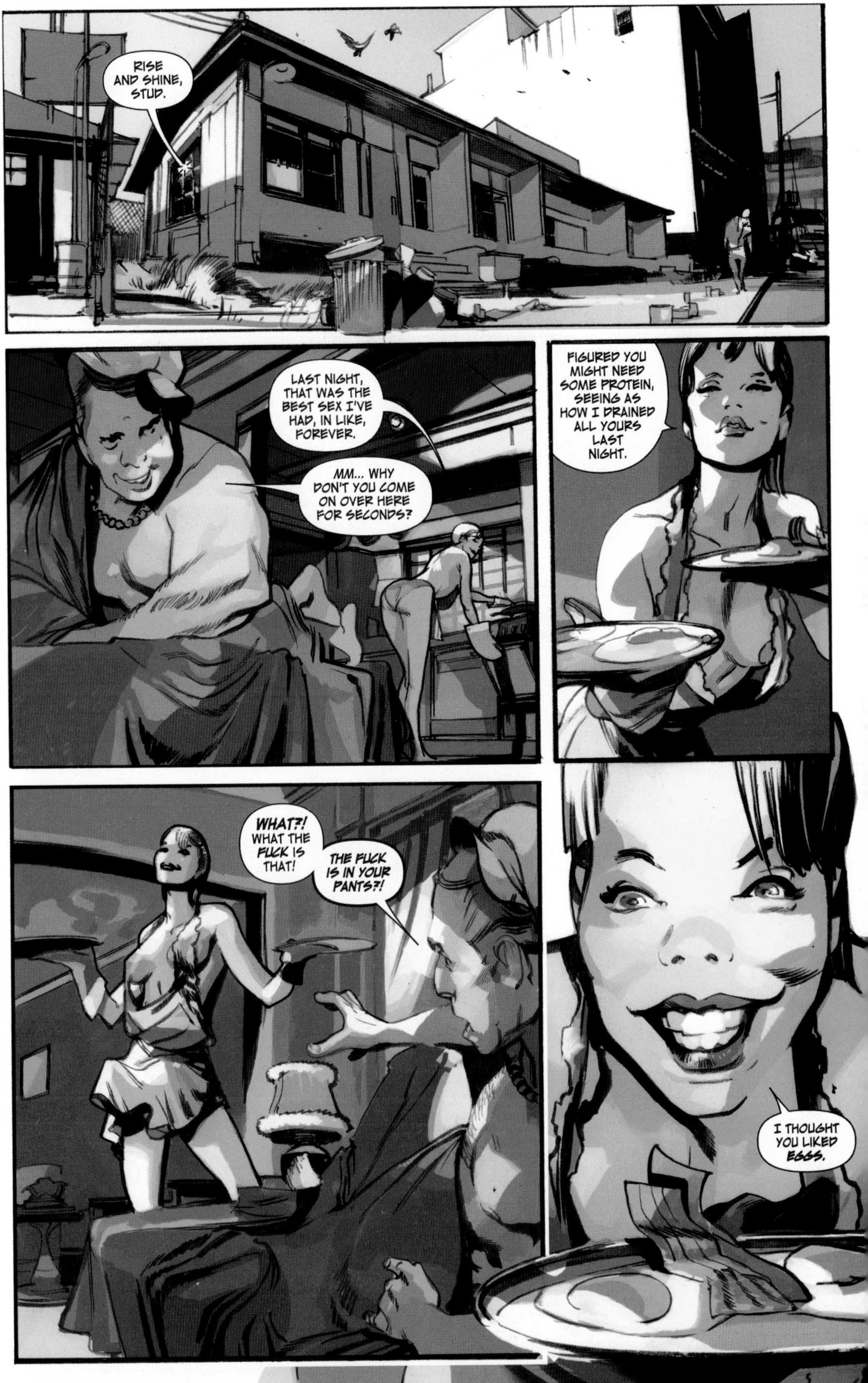
RISE AND SHINE, STUD.
LAST NIGHT, THAT WAS THE BEST SEX I'VE HAD, IN LIKE, FOREVER.
MM... WHY DON'T YOU COME ON OVER HERE FOR SECONDS?
FIGURED YOU MIGHT NEED SOME PROTEIN, SEEING AS HOW I DRAINED ALL YOURS LAST NIGHT.
WHAT?! WHAT THE FUCK IS THAT!
THE FUCK IS IN YOUR PANTS?!
I THOUGHT YOU LIKED EGGS.

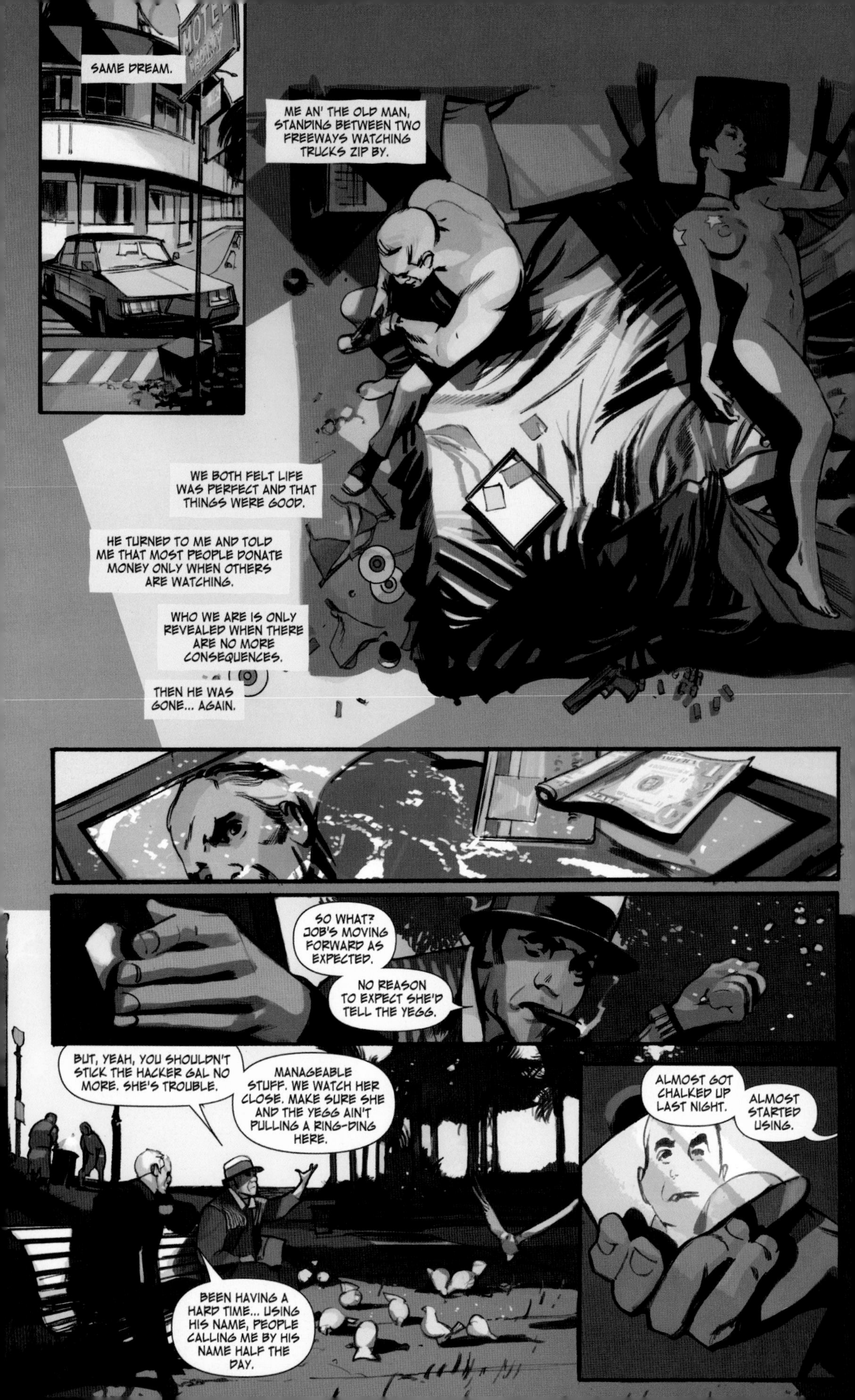
SAME DREAM.
ME AN' THE OLD MAN, STANDING BETWEEN TWO FREEWAYS WATCHING TRUCKS ZIP BY.
WE BOTH FELT LIFE WAS PERFECT AND THAT THINGS WERE GOOD.
HE TURNED TO ME AND TOLD ME THAT MOST PEOPLE DONATE MONEY ONLY WHEN OTHERS ARE WATCHING.
WHO WE ARE IS ONLY REVEALED WHEN THERE ARE NO MORE CONSEQUENCES.
THEN HE WAS GONE... AGAIN.
SO WHAT? JOB'S MOVING FORWARD AS EXPECTED.
NO REASON TO EXPECT SHE'D TELL THE YEGG.
BUT, YEAH, YOU SHOULDN'T STICK THE HACKER GAL NO MORE. SHE'S TROUBLE.
MANAGEABLE STUFF. WE WATCH HER CLOSE. MAKE SURE SHE AND THE YEGG AIN'T PULLING A RING-DING HERE.
BEEN HAVING A HARD TIME... USING HIS NAME, PEOPLE CALLING ME BY HIS NAME HALF THE DAY.
ALMOST GOT CHALKED UP LAST NIGHT.
ALMOST STARTED USING.

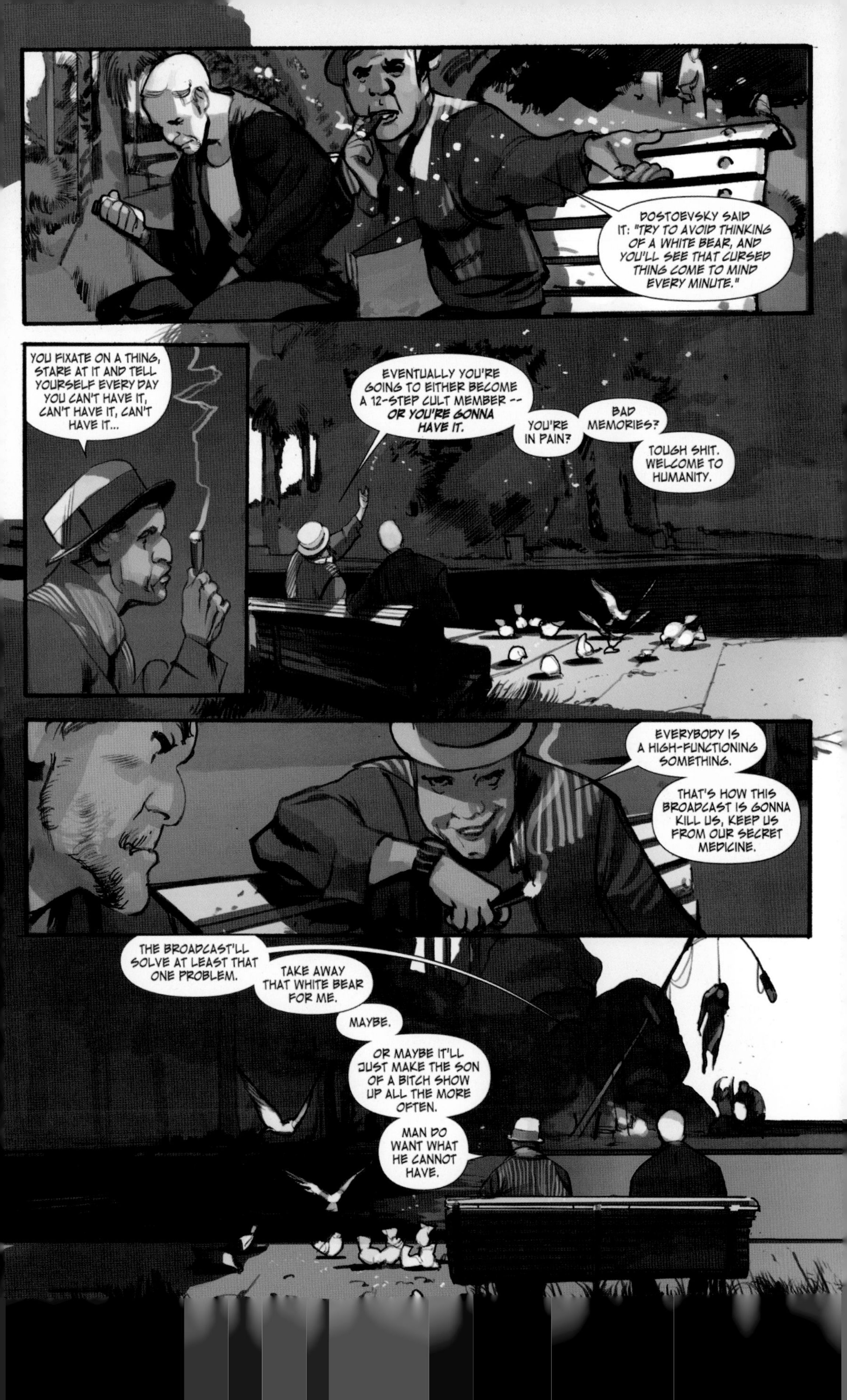
DOSTOEVSKY SAID IT: "TRY TO AVOID THINKING OF A WHITE BEAR, AND YOU'LL SEE THAT CURSED THING COME TO MIND EVERY MINUTE."
YOU FIXATE ON A THING, STARE AT IT AND TELL YOURSELF EVERY DAY YOU CAN'T HAVE IT, CAN'T HAVE IT, CAN'T HAVE IT...
EVENTUALLY YOU'RE GOING TO EITHER BECOME A 12-STEP CULT MEMBER -- OR YOU'RE GONNA HAVE IT.
YOU'RE IN PAIN?
BAD MEMORIES?
TOUGH SHIT. WELCOME TO HUMANITY.
EVERYBODY IS A HIGH-FUNCTIONING SOMETHING.
THAT'S HOW THIS BROADCAST IS GONNA KILL US, KEEP US FROM OUR SECRET MEDICINE.
THE BROADCAST'LL SOLVE AT LEAST THAT ONE PROBLEM.
TAKE AWAY THAT WHITE BEAR FOR ME.
MAYBE.
OR MAYBE IT'LL JUST MAKE THE SON OF A BITCH SHOW UP ALL THE MORE OFTEN.
MAN DO WANT WHAT HE CANNOT HAVE.

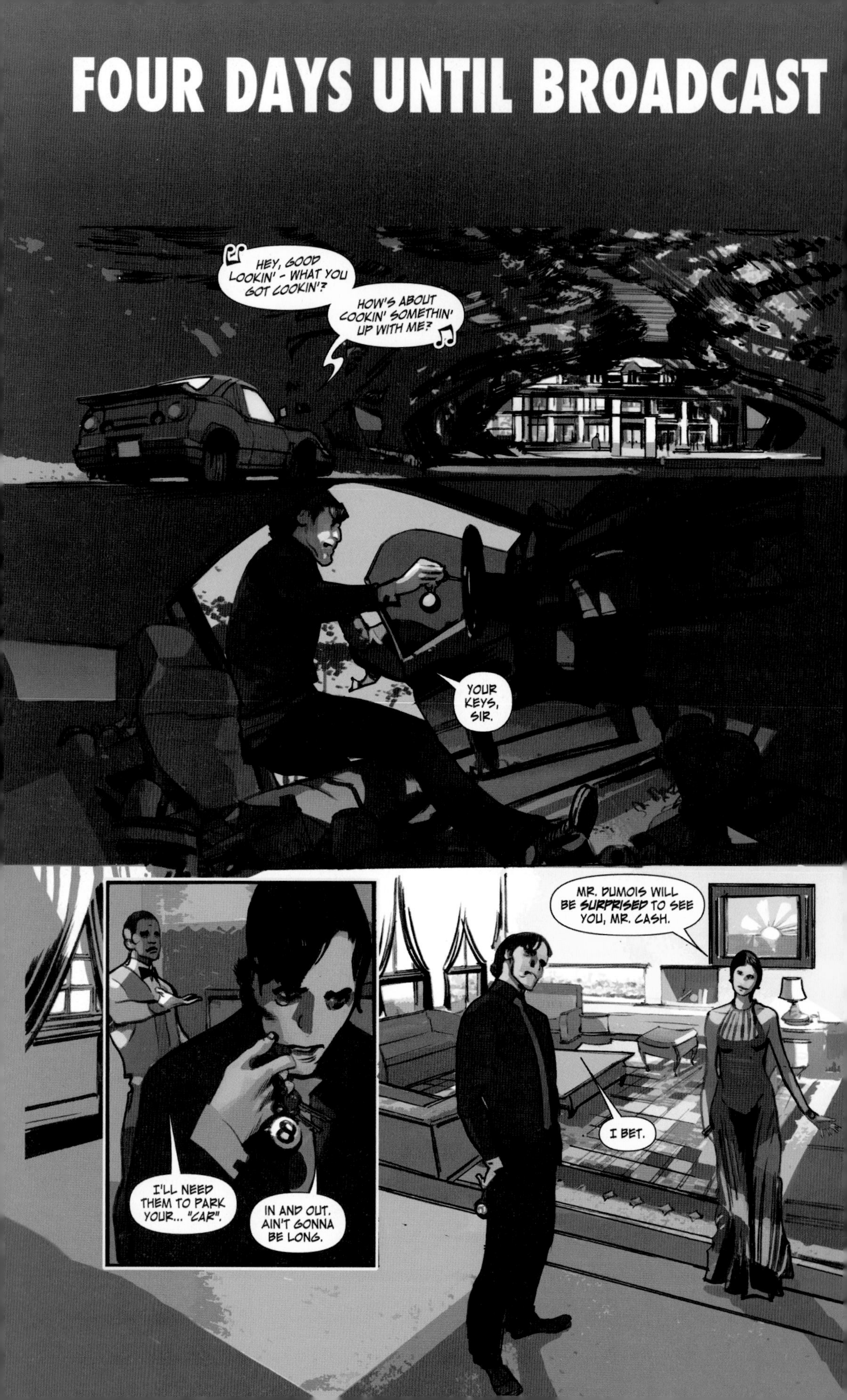
FOUR DAYS UNTIL BROADCAST
HEY, GOOD LOOKIN' - WHAT YOU GOT COOKIN'?
HOW'S ABOUT COOKIN' SOMETHIN' UP WITH ME?
YOUR KEYS, SIR.
I'LL NEED THEM TO PARK YOUR... "CAR".
IN AND OUT. AIN'T GONNA BE LONG.
MR. DUMOIS WILL BE SURPRISED TO SEE YOU, MR. CASH.
I BET.

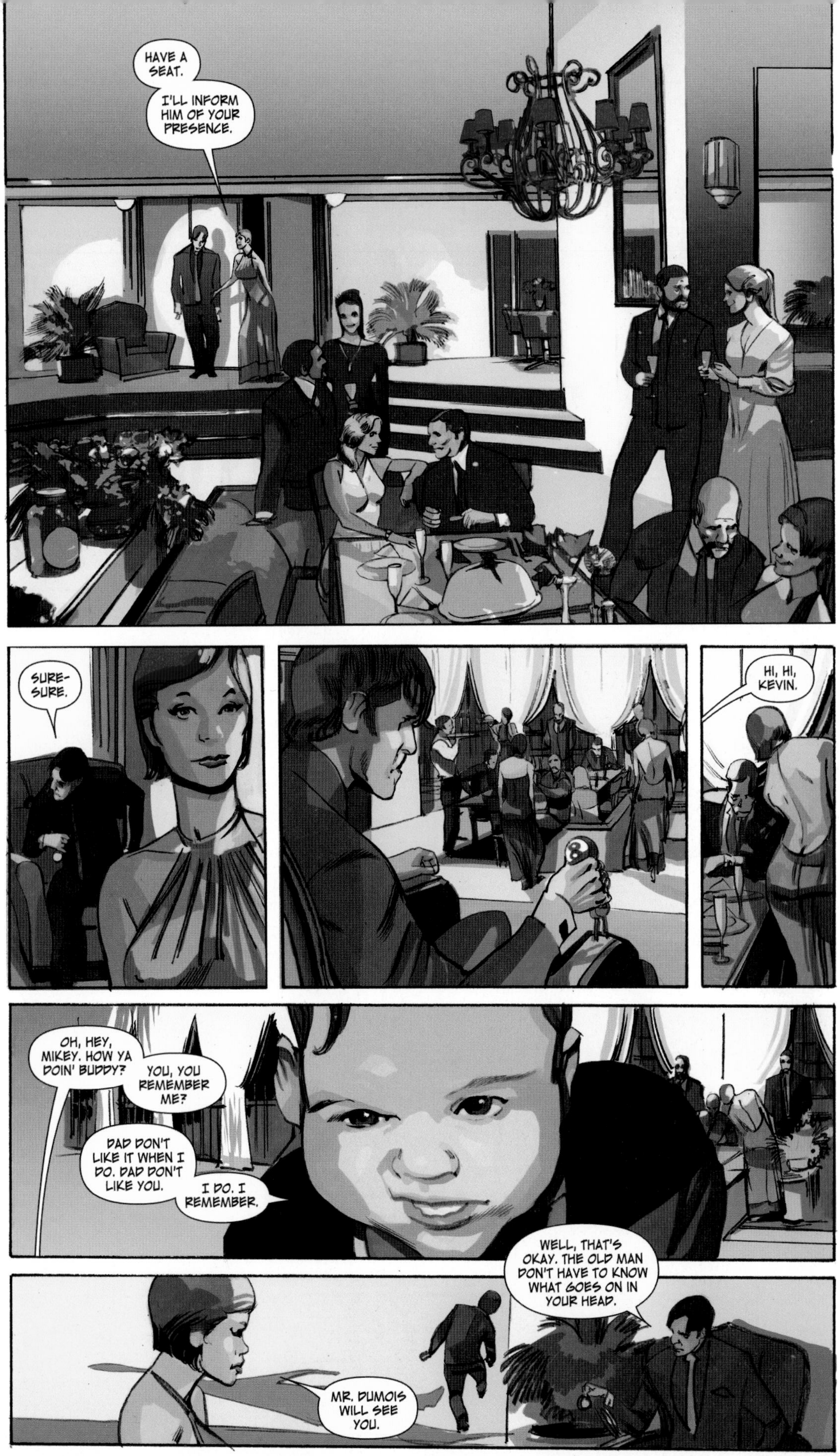
HAVE A SEAT.
I'LL INFORM HIM OF YOUR PRESENCE.
SURE-SURE.
HI, HI, KEVIN.
OH, HEY, MIKEY. HOW YA DOIN' BUDDY?
YOU, YOU REMEMBER ME?
DAD DON'T LIKE IT WHEN I DO. DAD DON'T LIKE YOU.
I DO. I REMEMBER.
WELL, THAT'S OKAY. THE OLD MAN DON'T HAVE TO KNOW WHAT GOES ON IN YOUR HEAD.
MR. DUMOIS WILL SEE YOU.

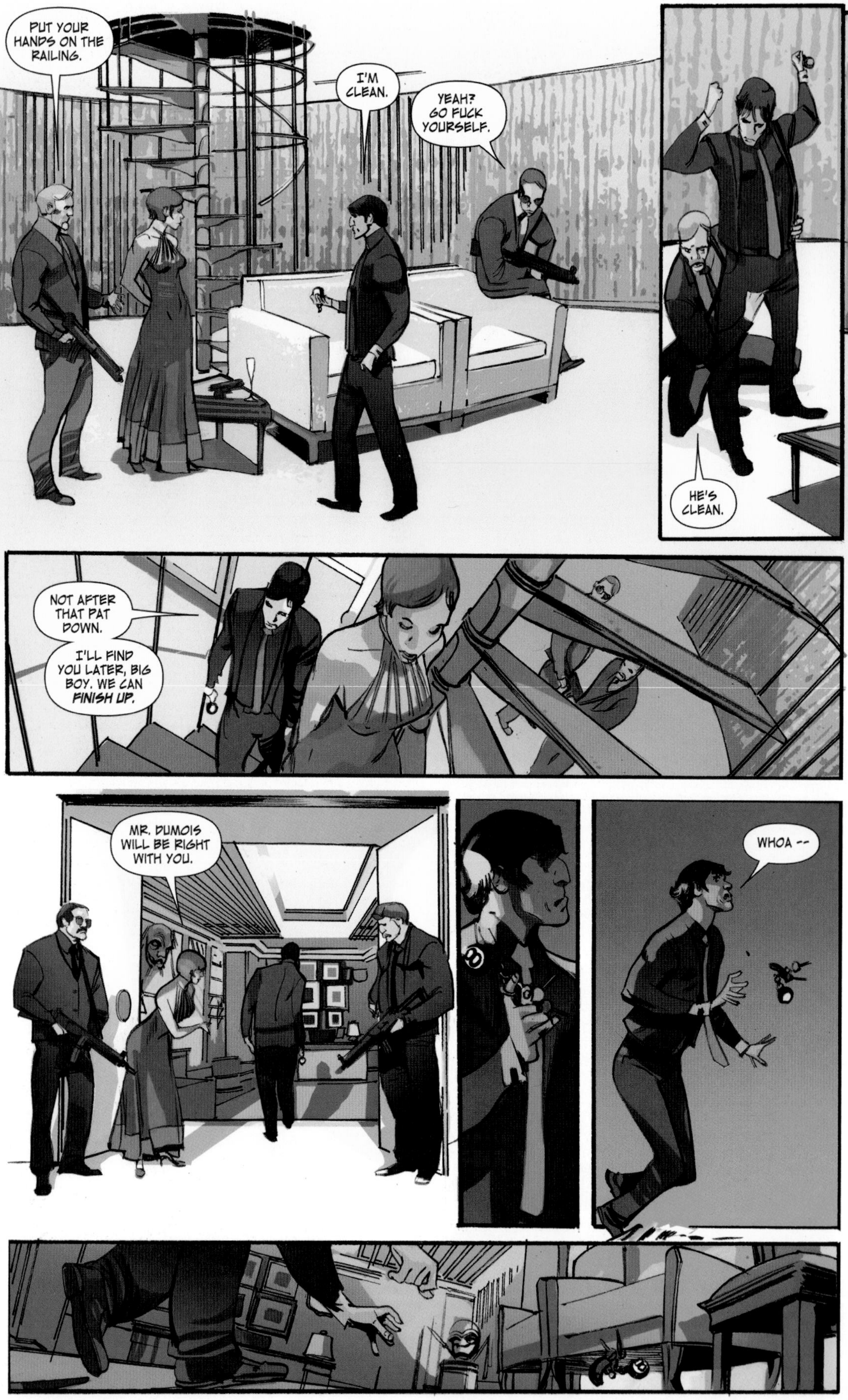
PUT YOUR HANDS ON THE RAILING.
I'M CLEAN.
YEAH? GO FUCK YOURSELF.
HE'S CLEAN.
NOT AFTER THAT PAT DOWN.
I'LL FIND YOU LATER, BIG BOY. WE CAN *FINISH UP.*
MR. DUMOIS WILL BE RIGHT WITH YOU.
WHOA --

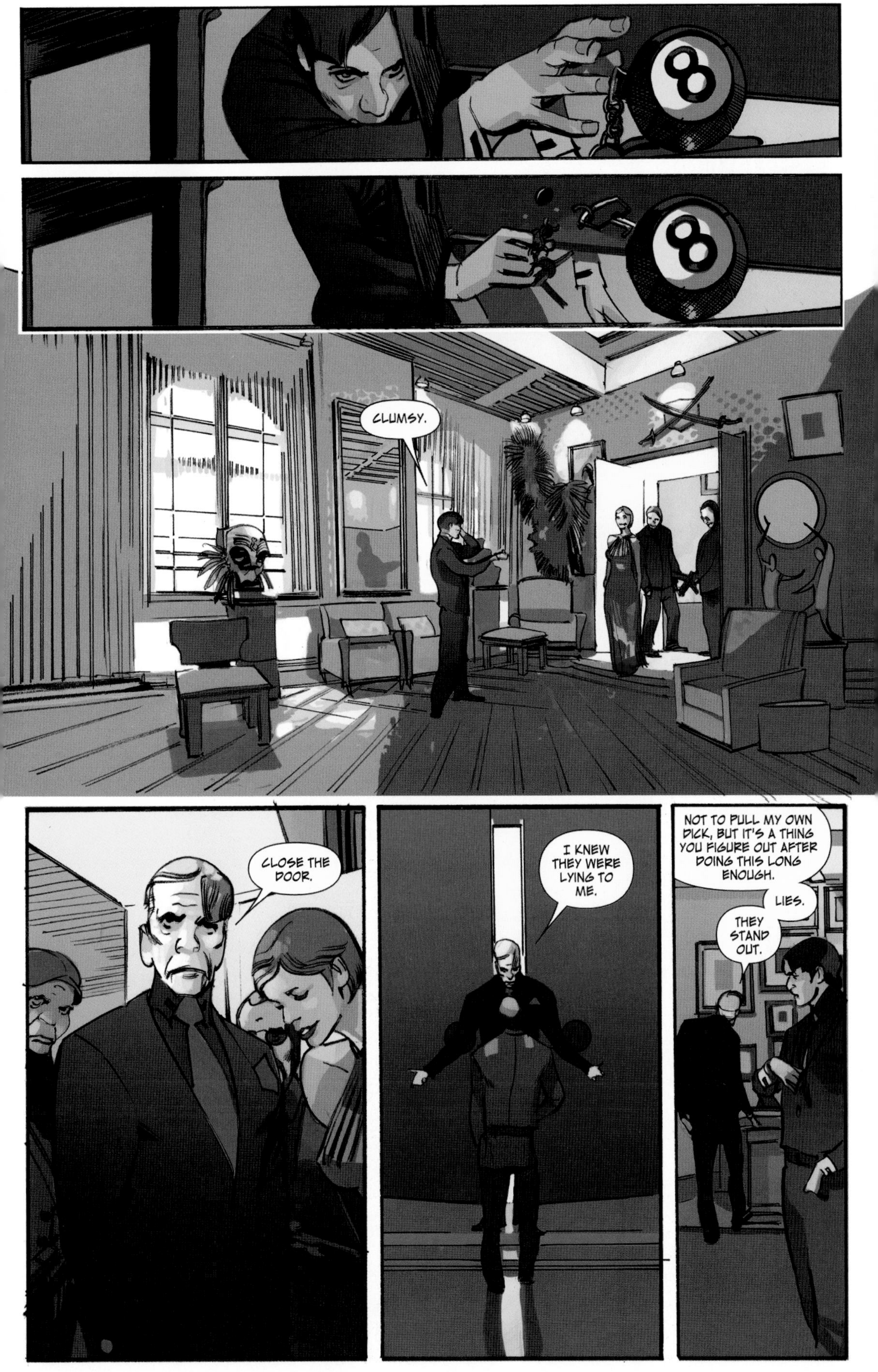
CLUMSY.
CLOSE THE DOOR.
I KNEW THEY WERE LYING TO ME.
NOT TO PULL MY OWN DICK, BUT IT'S A THING YOU FIGURE OUT AFTER DOING THIS LONG ENOUGH.
LIES.
THEY STAND OUT.

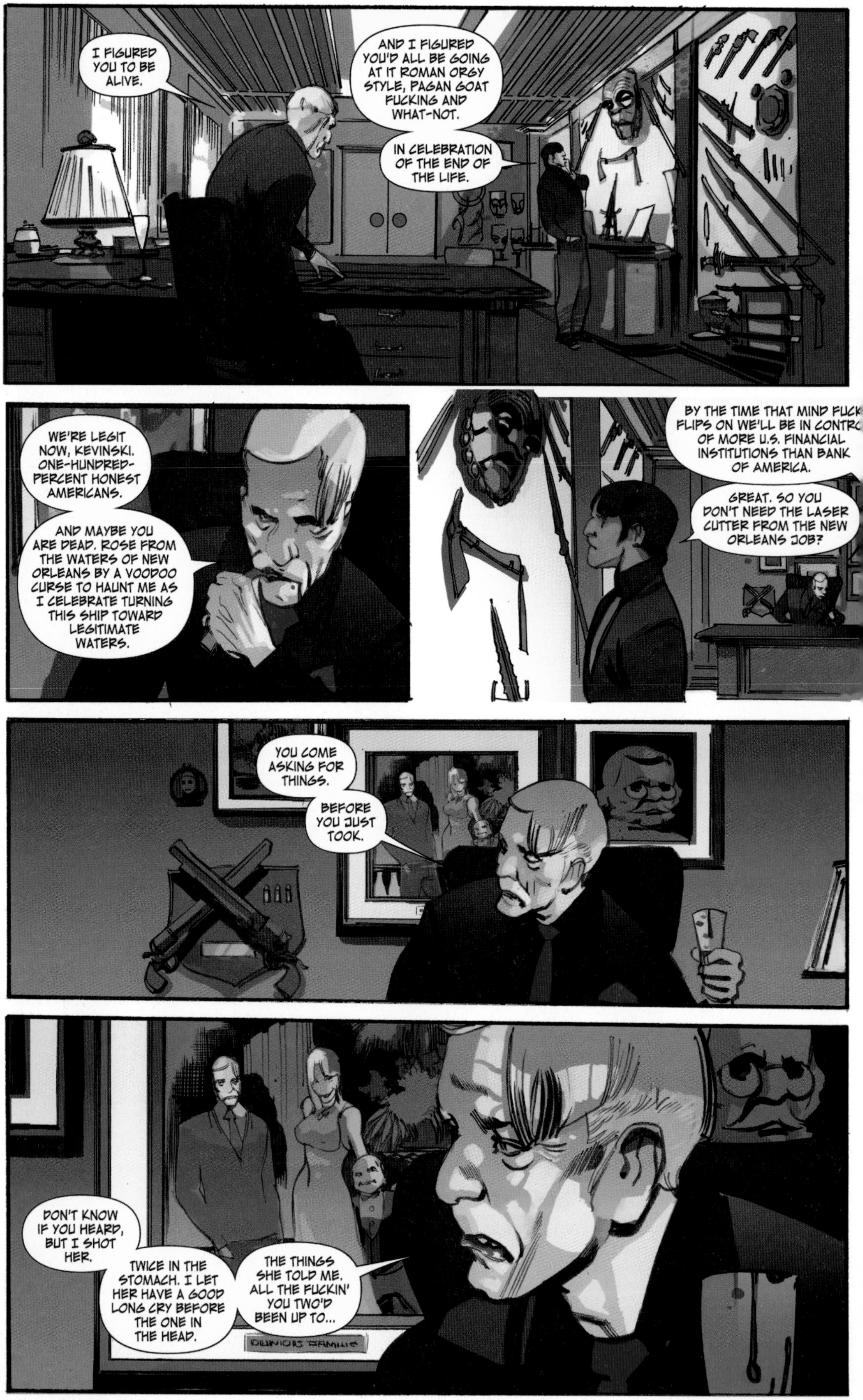
I FIGURED YOU TO BE ALIVE.
AND I FIGURED YOU'D ALL BE GOING AT IT ROMAN ORGY STYLE, PAGAN GOAT FUCKING AND WHAT-NOT.
IN CELEBRATION OF THE END OF THE LIFE.
WE'RE LEGIT NOW, KEVINSKI. ONE-HUNDRED-PERCENT HONEST AMERICANS.
AND MAYBE YOU ARE DEAD. ROSE FROM THE WATERS OF NEW ORLEANS BY A VOODOO CURSE TO HAUNT ME AS I CELEBRATE TURNING THIS SHIP TOWARD LEGITIMATE WATERS.
BY THE TIME THAT MIND FUCK FLIPS ON WE'LL BE IN CONTRO OF MORE U.S. FINANCIAL INSTITUTIONS THAN BANK OF AMERICA.
GREAT. SO YOU DON'T NEED THE LASER CUTTER FROM THE NEW ORLEANS JOB?
YOU COME ASKING FOR THINGS.
BEFORE YOU JUST TOOK.
DON'T KNOW IF YOU HEARD, BUT I SHOT HER.
TWICE IN THE STOMACH. I LET HER HAVE A GOOD LONG CRY BEFORE THE ONE IN THE HEAD.
THE THINGS SHE TOLD ME. ALL THE FUCKIN' YOU TWO'D BEEN UP TO...

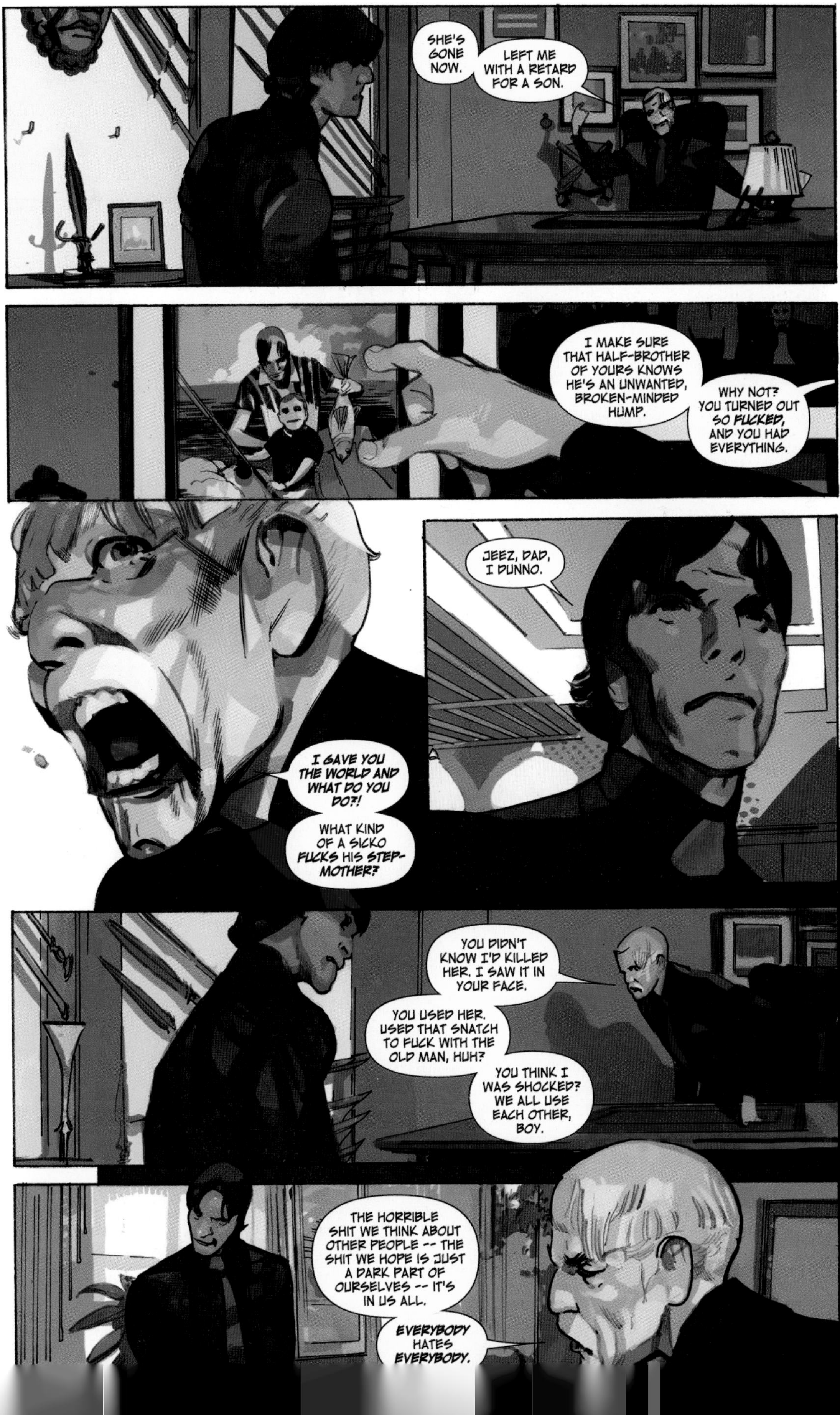
SHE'S GONE NOW.
LEFT ME WITH A RETARD FOR A SON.
I MAKE SURE THAT HALF-BROTHER OF YOURS KNOWS HE'S AN UNWANTED, BROKEN-MINDED HUMP.
WHY NOT? YOU TURNED OUT SO FUCKED, AND YOU HAD EVERYTHING.
I GAVE YOU THE WORLD AND WHAT DO YOU DO?!
WHAT KIND OF A SICKO FUCKS HIS STEP-MOTHER?
JEEZ, DAD, I DUNNO.
YOU DIDN'T KNOW I'D KILLED HER. I SAW IT IN YOUR FACE.
YOU USED HER. USED THAT SNATCH TO FUCK WITH THE OLD MAN, HUH?
YOU THINK I WAS SHOCKED? WE ALL USE EACH OTHER, BOY.
THE HORRIBLE SHIT WE THINK ABOUT OTHER PEOPLE -- THE SHIT WE HOPE IS JUST A DARK PART OF OURSELVES -- IT'S IN US ALL.
EVERYBODY HATES EVERYBODY.

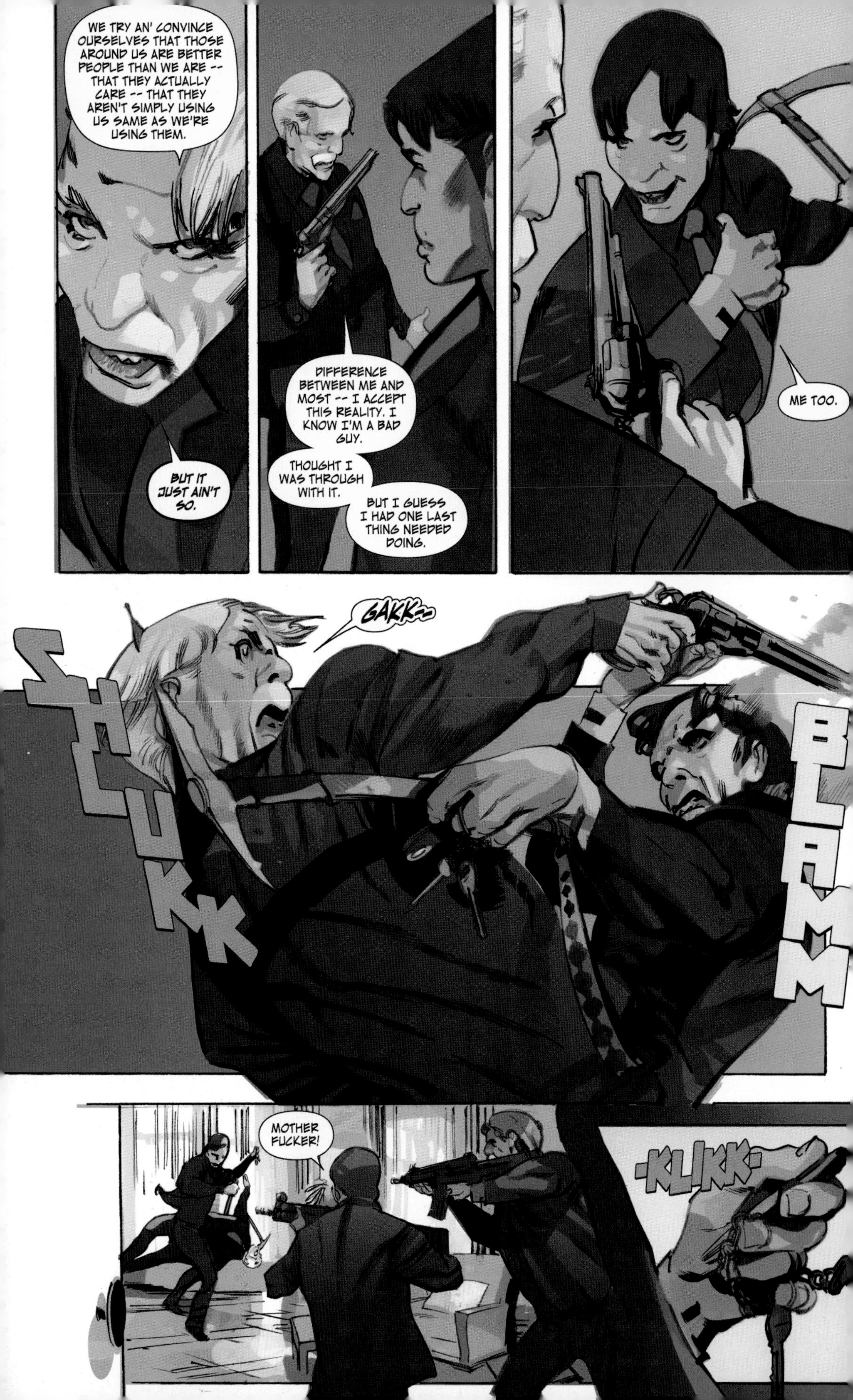
WE TRY AN' CONVINCE OURSELVES THAT THOSE AROUND US ARE BETTER PEOPLE THAN WE ARE -- THAT THEY ACTUALLY CARE -- THAT THEY AREN'T SIMPLY USING US SAME AS WE'RE USING THEM.
BUT IT JUST AIN'T SO.
DIFFERENCE BETWEEN ME AND MOST -- I ACCEPT THIS REALITY. I KNOW I'M A BAD GUY.
THOUGHT I WAS THROUGH WITH IT.
BUT I GUESS I HAD ONE LAST THING NEEDED DOING.
ME TOO.
GAKK--
SHLUKK
BLAMM
MOTHER FUCKER!
-KLIKK-

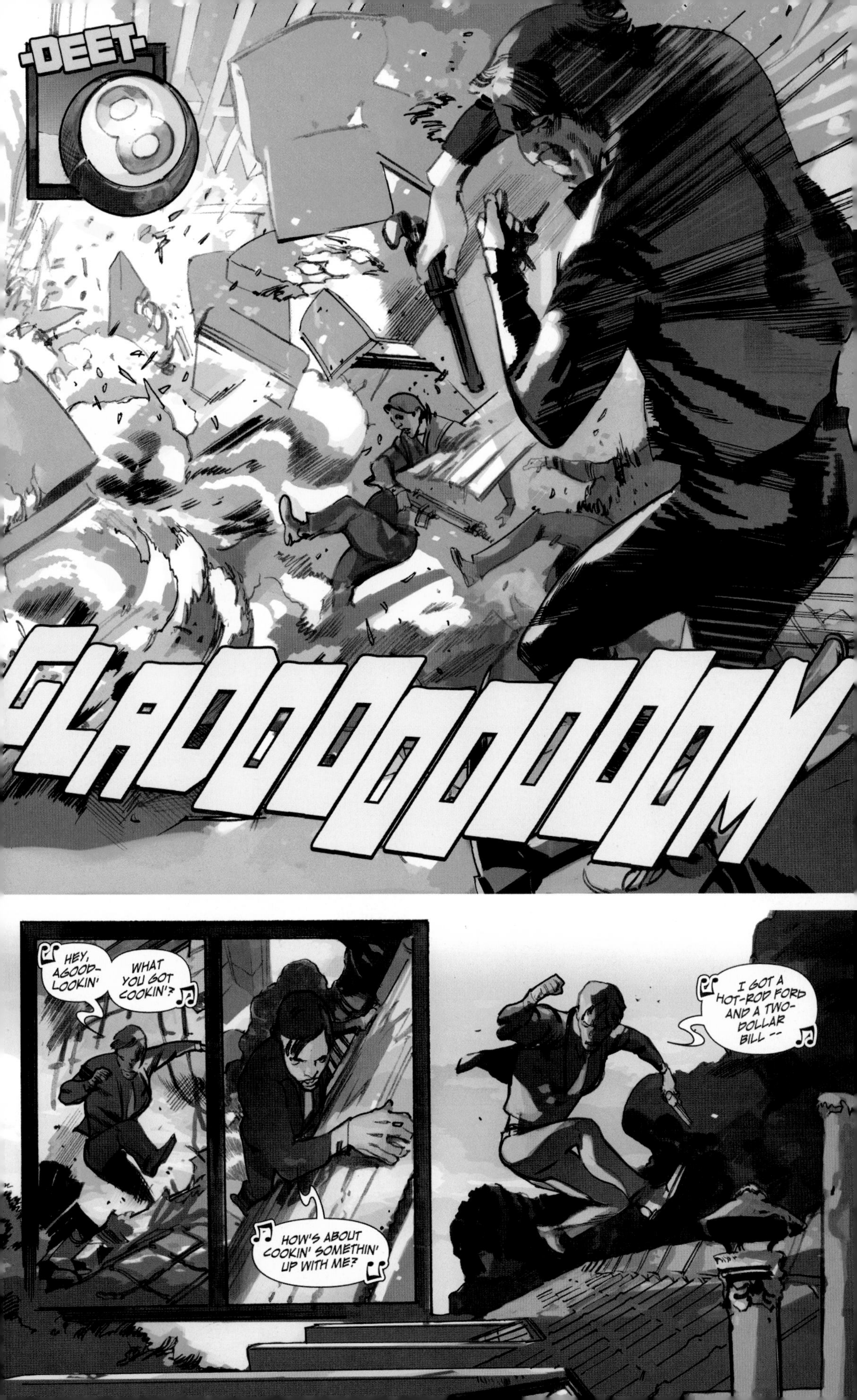
-DEET-
8
CLAOOOOOOOOOM
HEY, AGOOD-LOOKIN'
WHAT YOU GOT COOKIN'?
HOW'S ABOUT COOKIN' SOMETHIN' UP WITH ME?
I GOT A HOT-ROD FORD AND A TWO-DOLLAR BILL --

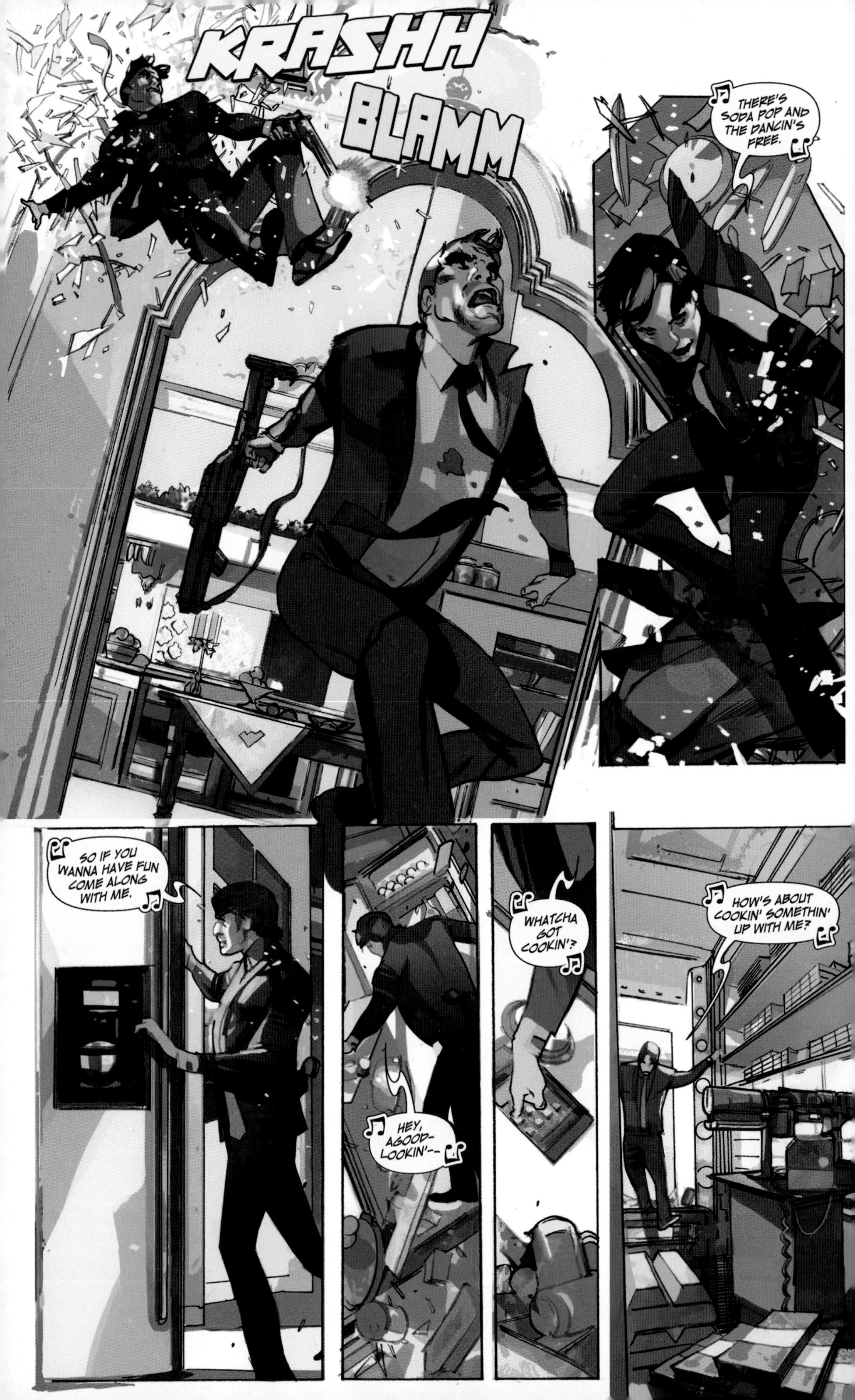
KRASHH
BLAMM
THERE'S SODA POP AND THE DANCIN'S FREE.
SO IF YOU WANNA HAVE FUN COME ALONG WITH ME.
HEY, AGOOD-LOOKIN'--
WHATCHA GOT COOKIN'?
HOW'S ABOUT COOKIN' SOMETHIN' UP WITH ME?

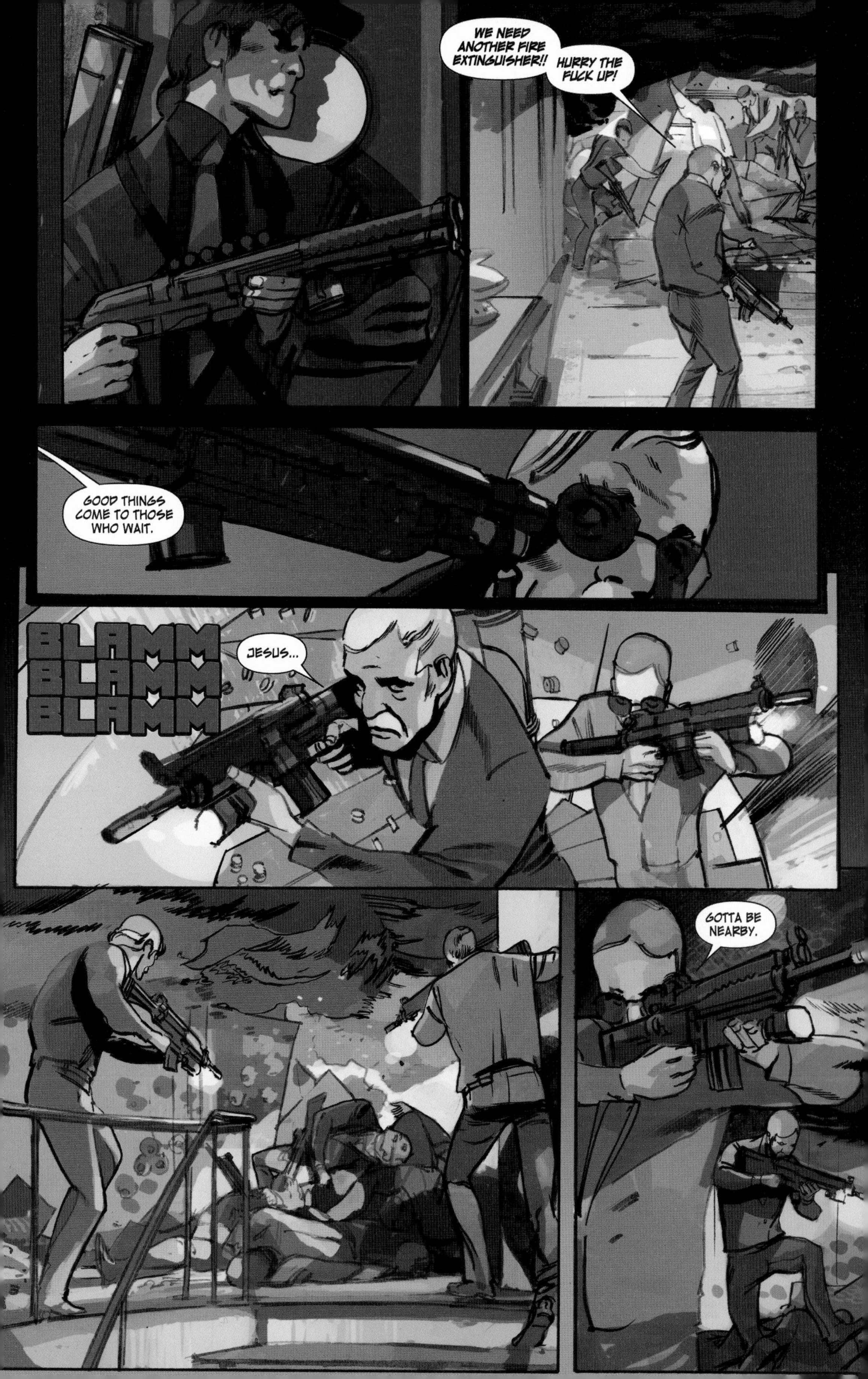
WE NEED ANOTHER FIRE EXTINGUISHER!!
HURRY THE FUCK UP!
GOOD THINGS COME TO THOSE WHO WAIT.
BLAMM BLAMM BLAMM
JESUS...
GOTTA BE NEARBY.

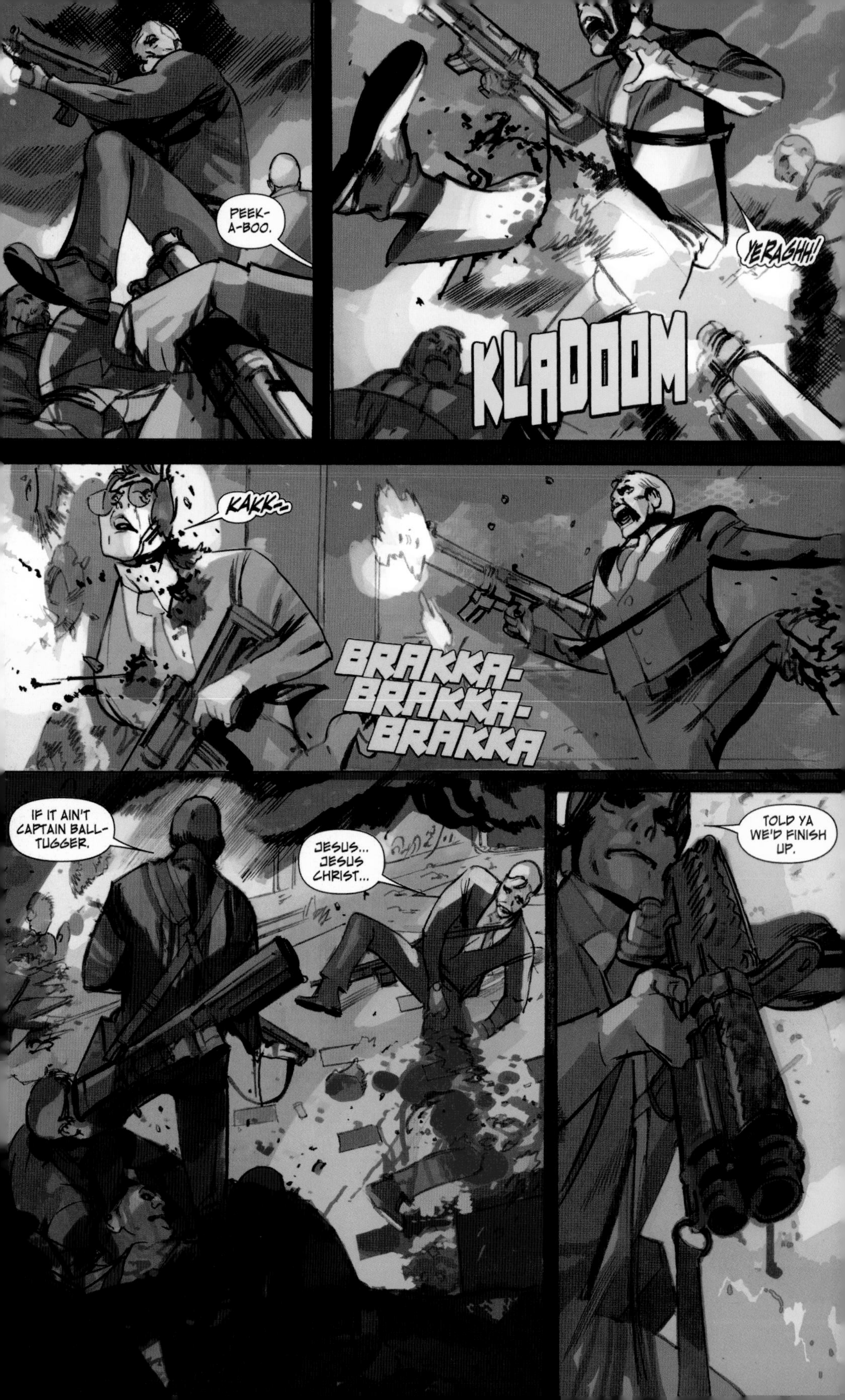
PEEK-A-BOO.
YERAGHH!
KLADOOM
KAKK--
BRAKKA-BRAKKA-BRAKKA
IF IT AIN'T CAPTAIN BALL-TUGGER.
JESUS... JESUS CHRIST...
TOLD YA WE'D FINISH UP.

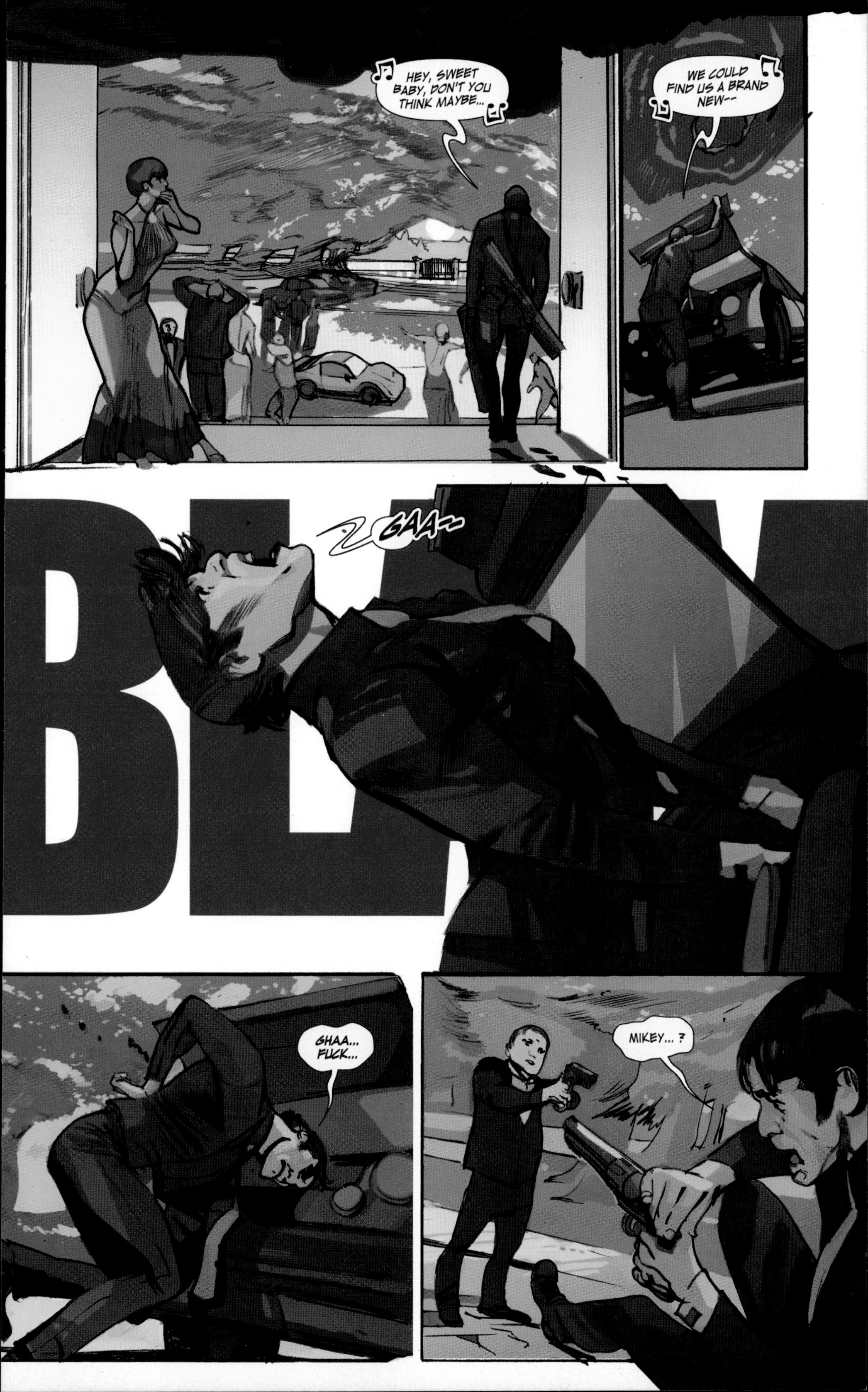
HEY, SWEET BABY, DON'T YOU THINK MAYBE...
WE COULD FIND US A BRAND NEW--
ZGAA--
GHAA... FUCK...
MIKEY... ?

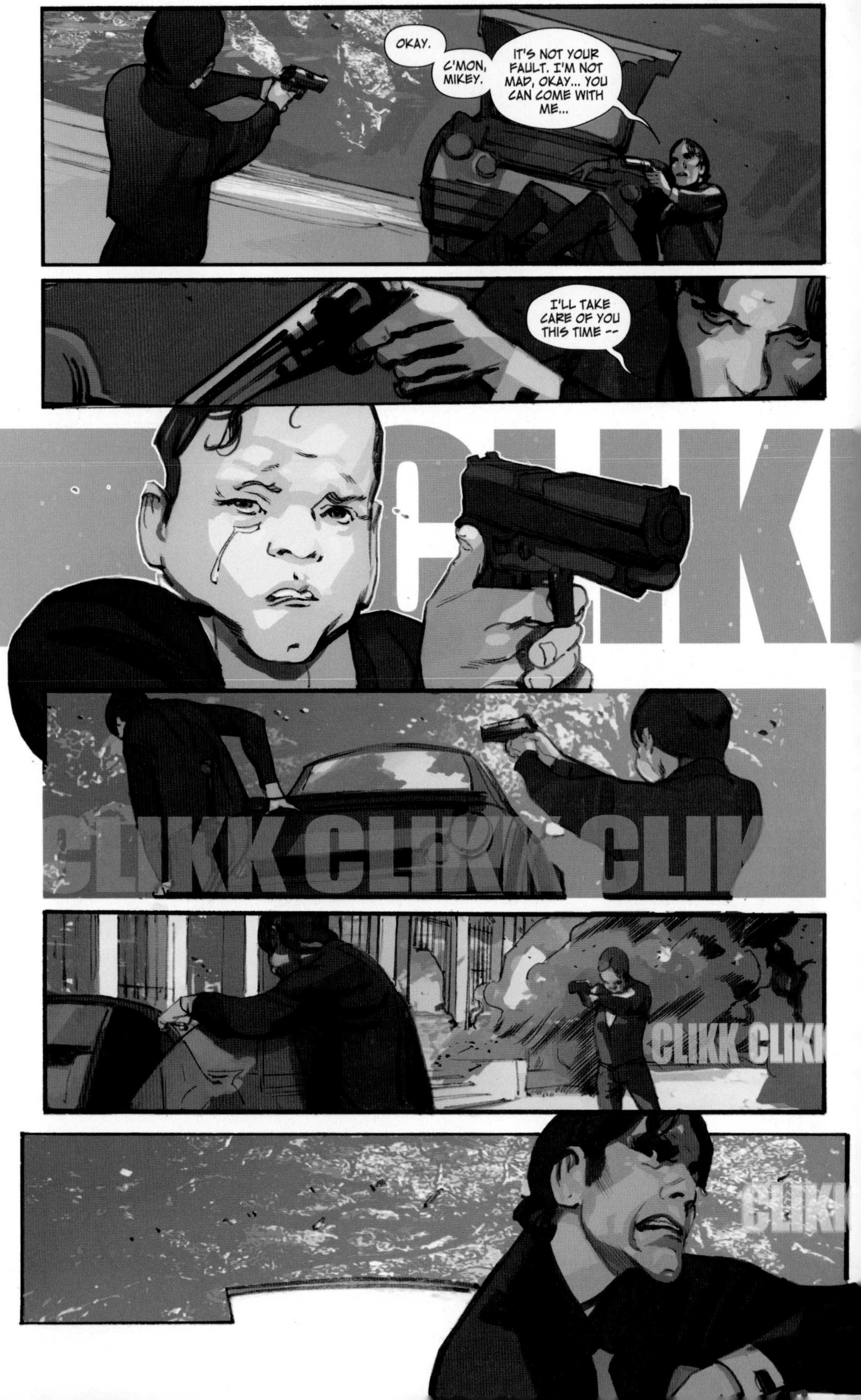

OKAY.
C'MON, MIKEY.
IT'S NOT YOUR FAULT. I'M NOT MAD, OKAY... YOU CAN COME WITH ME...
I'LL TAKE CARE OF YOU THIS TIME --
CLIKK CLIKK
CLIKK CLIKK
CLIKK

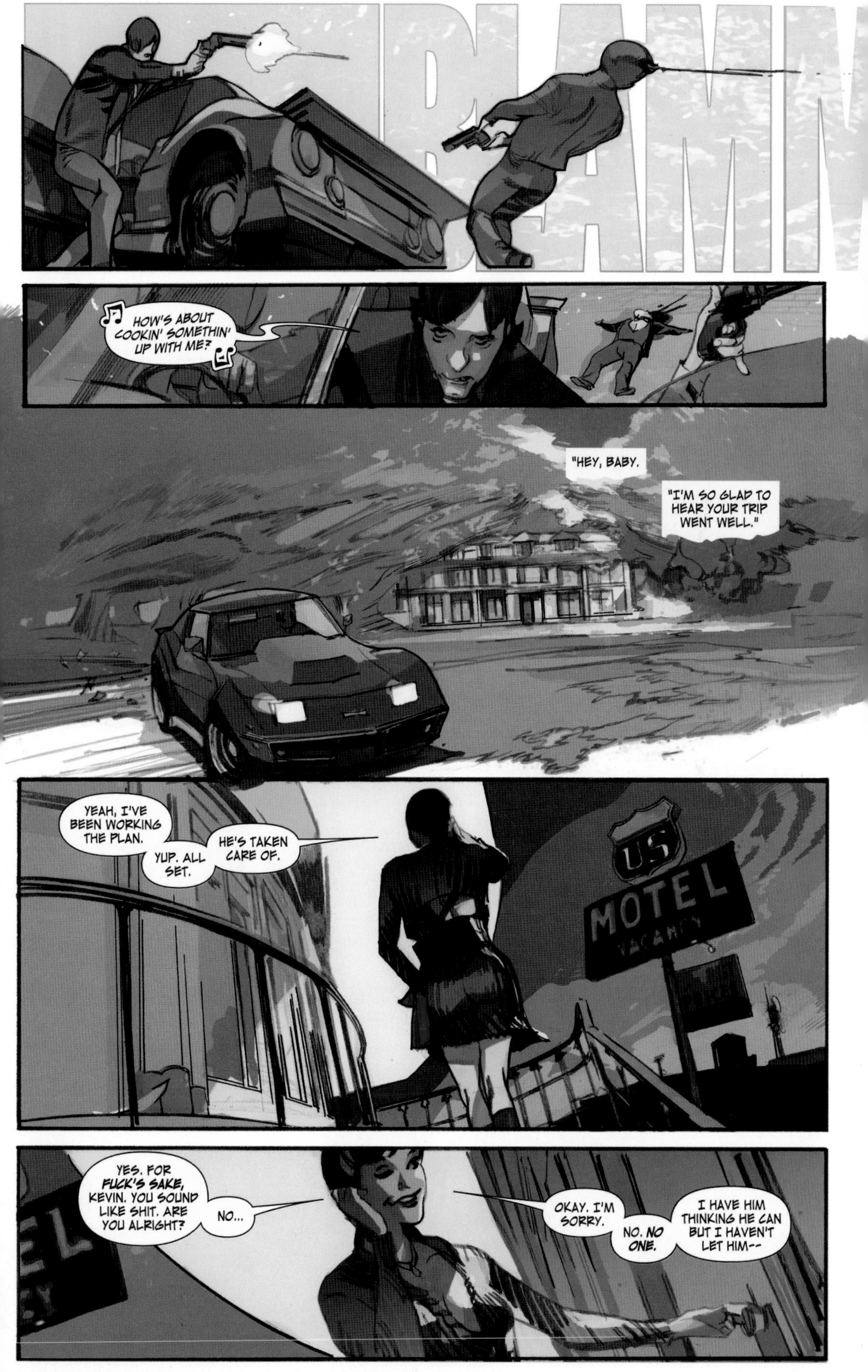
BLAM
HOW'S ABOUT COOKIN' SOMETHIN' UP WITH ME?
"HEY, BABY.
"I'M SO GLAD TO HEAR YOUR TRIP WENT WELL."
YEAH, I'VE BEEN WORKING THE PLAN.
YUP. ALL SET.
HE'S TAKEN CARE OF.
US
MOTEL
YES. FOR FUCK'S SAKE, KEVIN. YOU SOUND LIKE SHIT. ARE YOU ALRIGHT?
NO...
OKAY. I'M SORRY.
NO. NO ONE.
I HAVE HIM THINKING HE CAN BUT I HAVEN'T LET HIM--

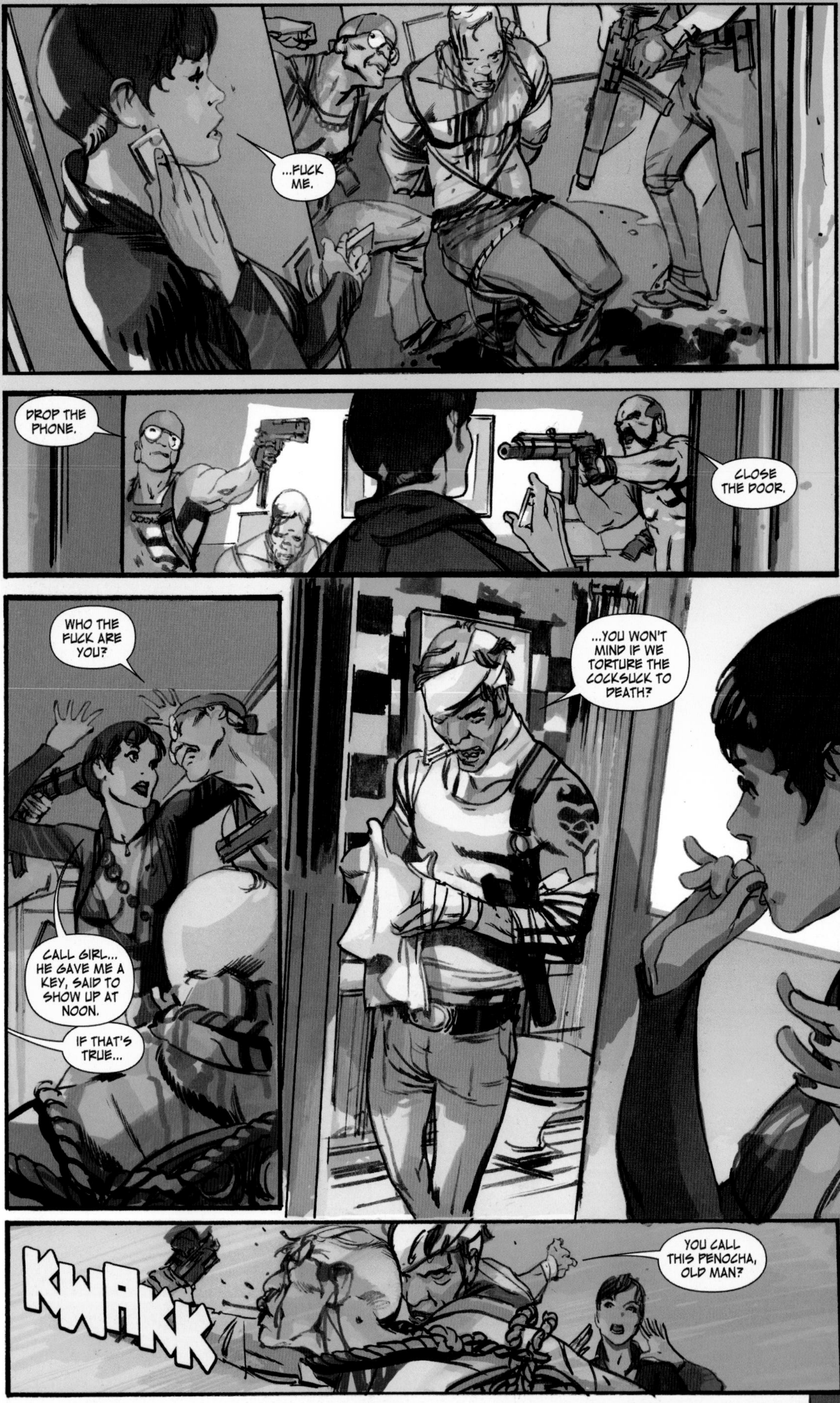
...FUCK ME.
DROP THE PHONE.
CLOSE THE DOOR.
WHO THE FUCK ARE YOU?
CALL GIRL... HE GAVE ME A KEY, SAID TO SHOW UP AT NOON.
IF THAT'S TRUE...
...YOU WON'T MIND IF WE TORTURE THE COCKSUCK TO DEATH?
KWAKK
YOU CALL THIS PENOCHA, OLD MAN?

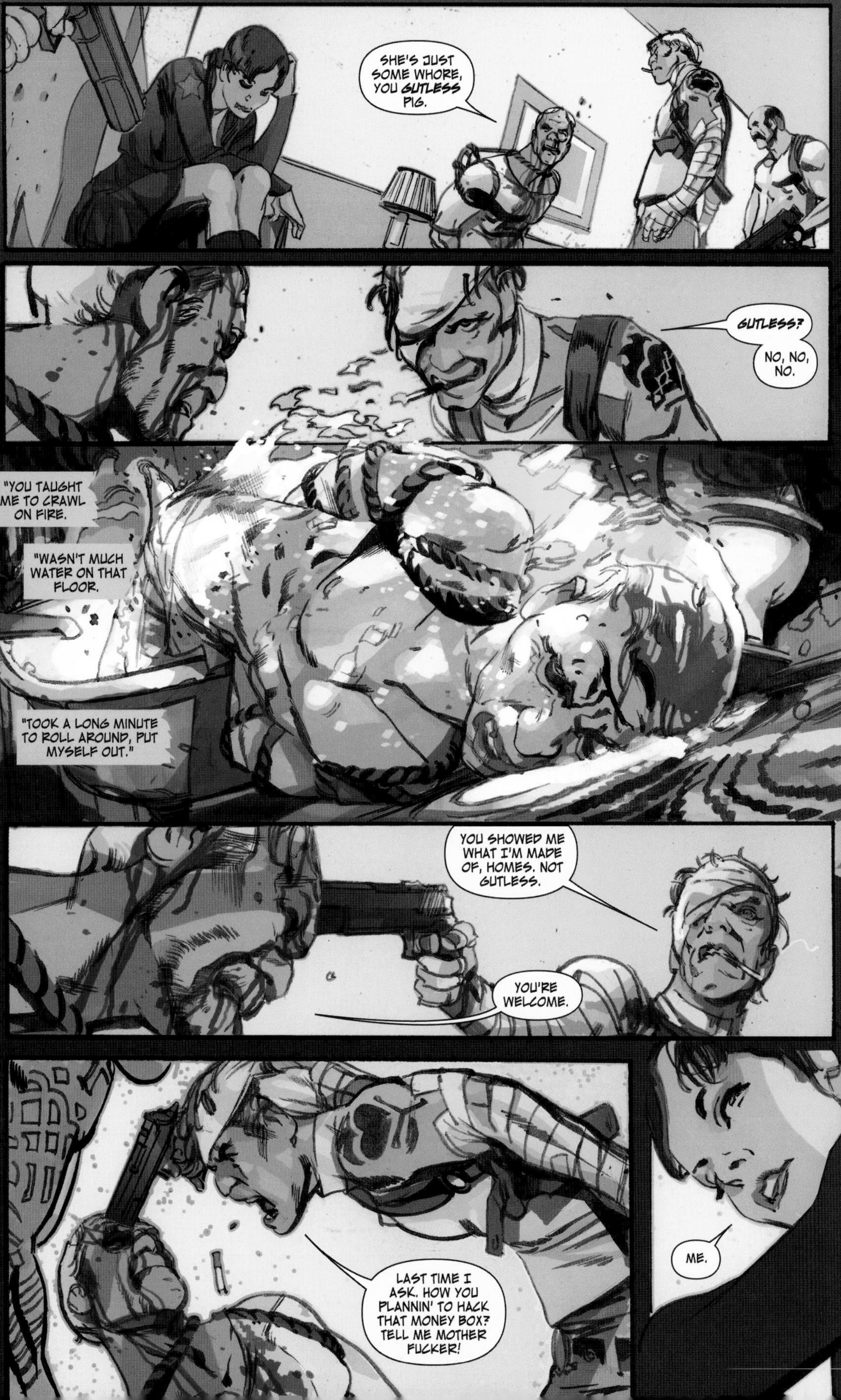
SHE'S JUST SOME WHORE, YOU GUTLESS PIG.
GUTLESS?
NO, NO, NO.
"YOU TAUGHT ME TO CRAWL ON FIRE.
"WASN'T MUCH WATER ON THAT FLOOR.
"TOOK A LONG MINUTE TO ROLL AROUND, PUT MYSELF OUT."
YOU SHOWED ME WHAT I'M MADE OF, HOMES. NOT GUTLESS.
YOU'RE WELCOME.
LAST TIME I ASK. HOW YOU PLANNIN' TO HACK THAT MONEY BOX? TELL ME MOTHER FUCKER!
ME.

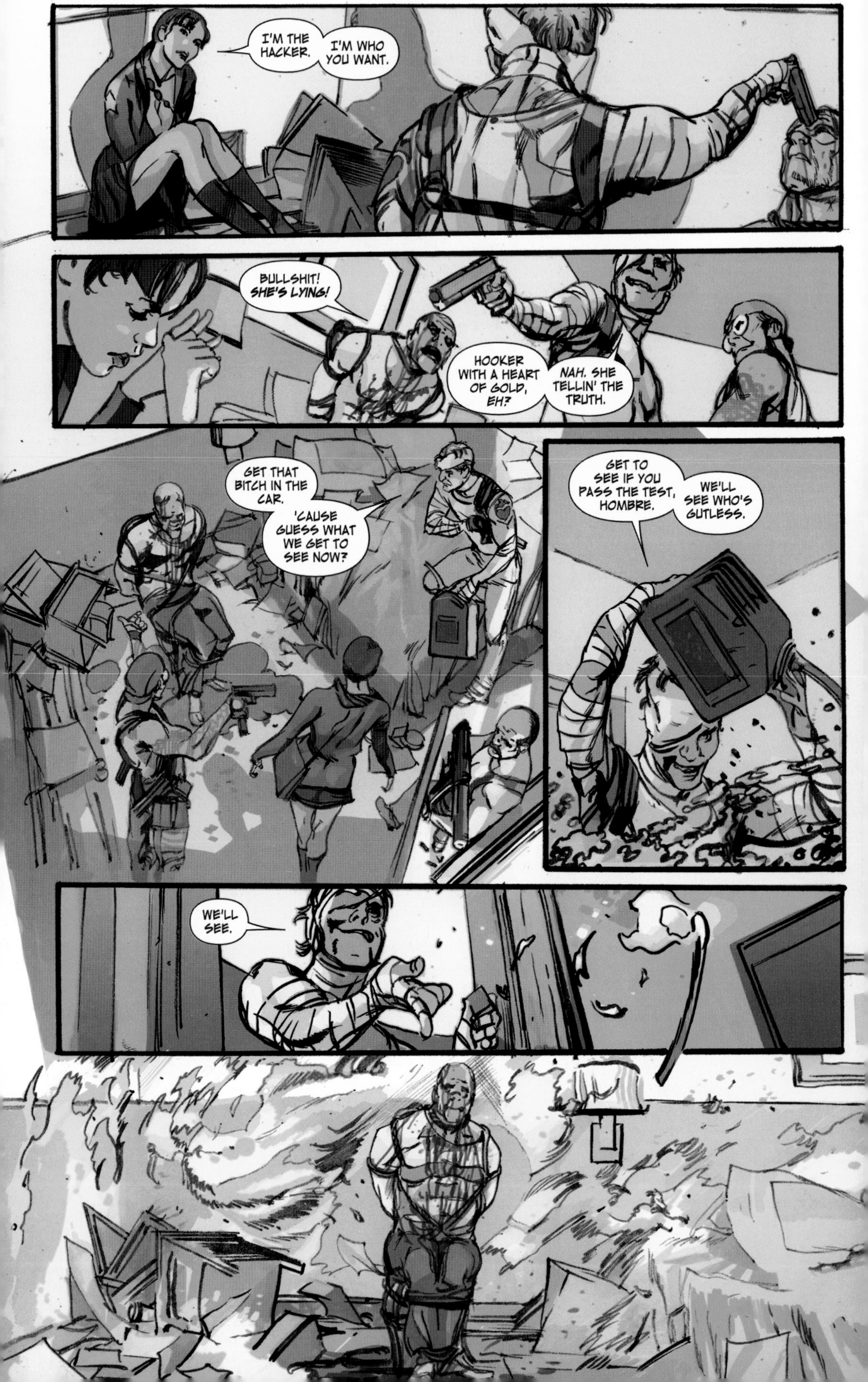
I'M THE HACKER.
I'M WHO YOU WANT.
BULLSHIT! SHE'S LYING!
HOOKER WITH A HEART OF GOLD, EH?
NAH. SHE TELLIN' THE TRUTH.
GET THAT BITCH IN THE CAR.
'CAUSE GUESS WHAT WE GET TO SEE NOW?
GET TO SEE IF YOU PASS THE TEST, HOMBRE.
WE'LL SEE WHO'S GUTLESS.
WE'LL SEE.

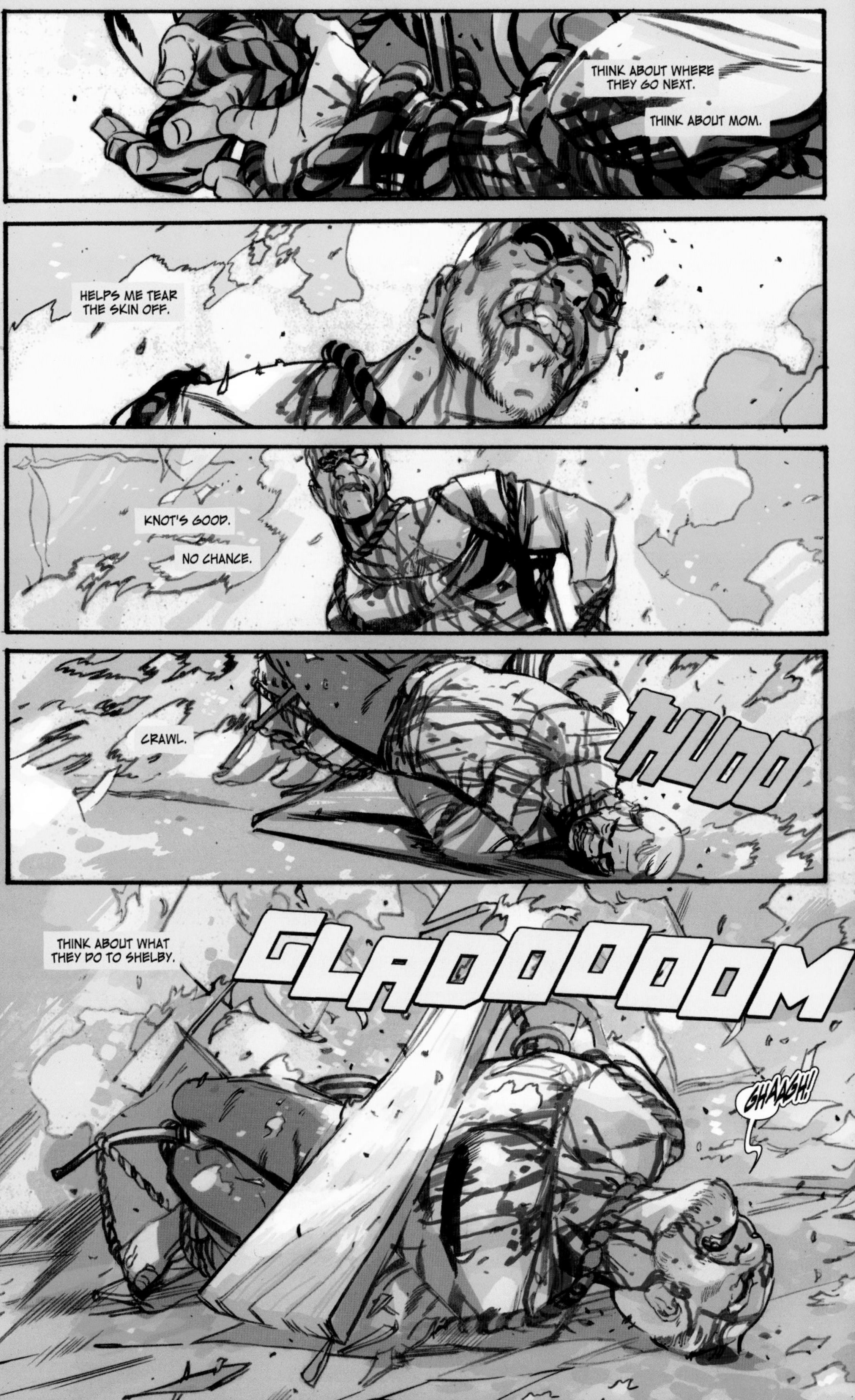
THINK ABOUT WHERE THEY GO NEXT.
THINK ABOUT MOM.
HELPS ME TEAR THE SKIN OFF.
KNOT'S GOOD.
NO CHANCE.
CRAWL.
THUDD
THINK ABOUT WHAT THEY DO TO SHELBY.
GLADOOOOM
GHAASH!

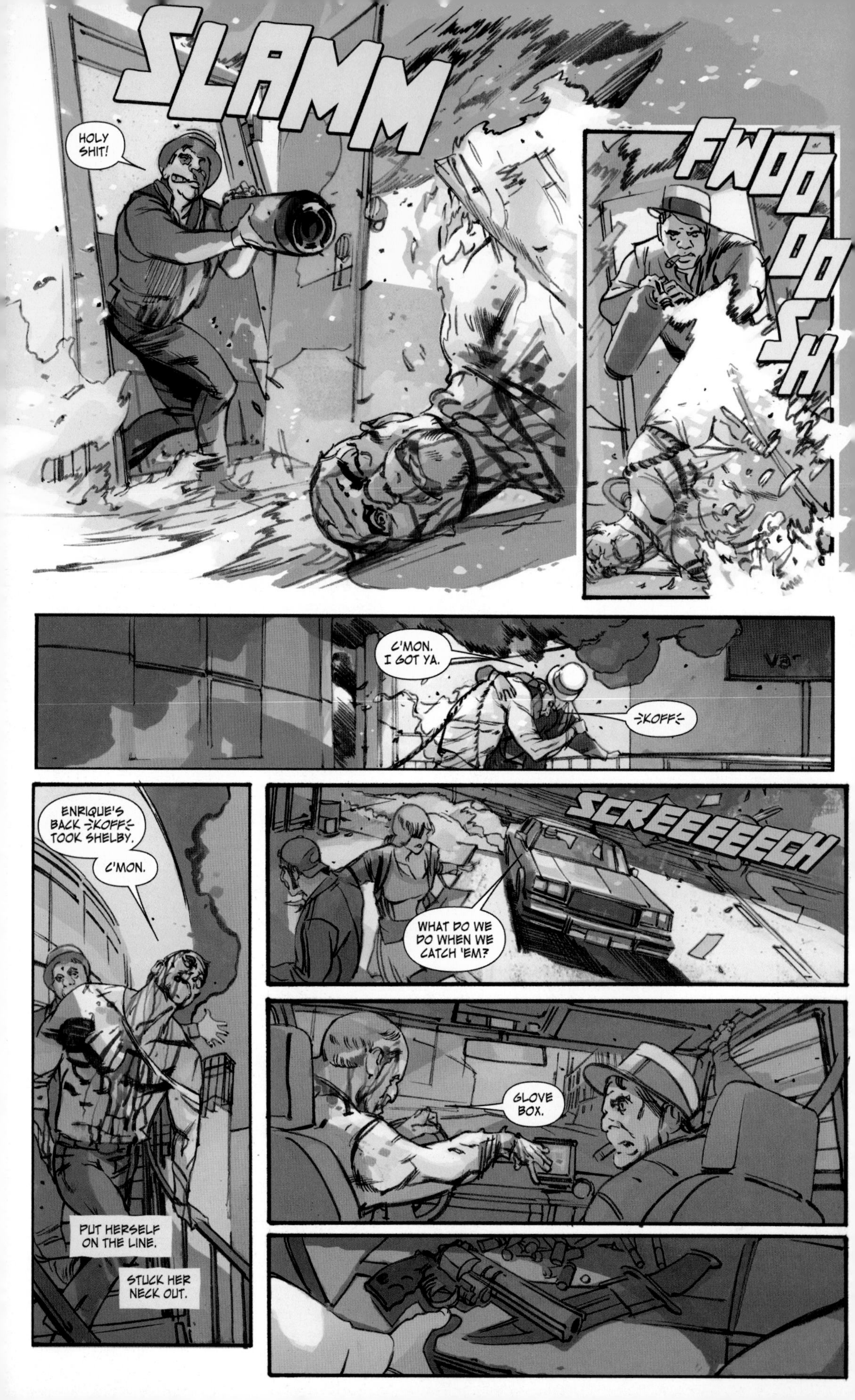
SLAMM
HOLY SHIT!
FWOOOOSH
C'MON. I GOT YA.
-KOFF-
ENRIQUE'S BACK -KOFF- TOOK SHELBY.
C'MON.
PUT HERSELF ON THE LINE.
STUCK HER NECK OUT.
SCREEEEEECH
WHAT DO WE DO WHEN WE CATCH 'EM?
GLOVE BOX.

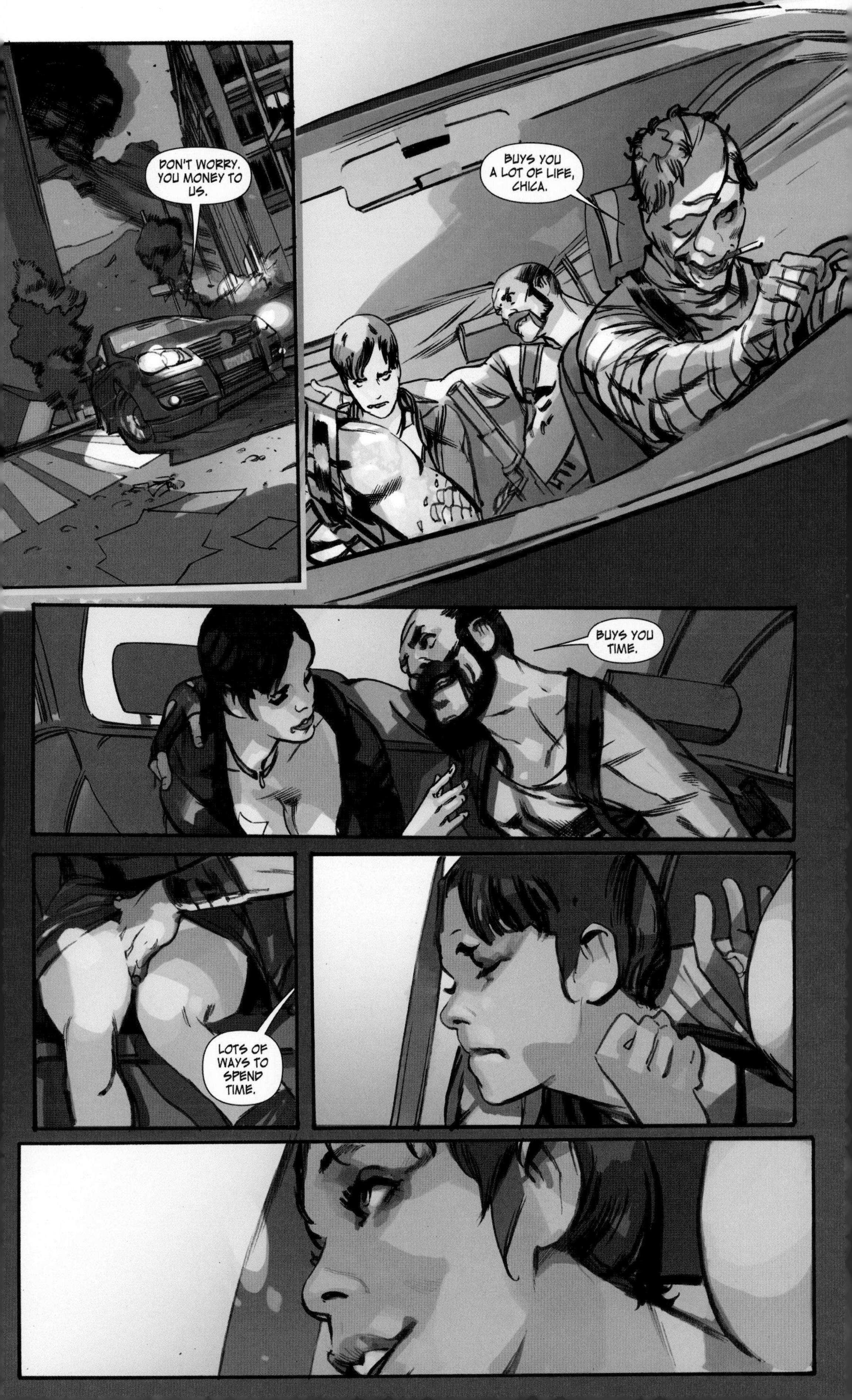
DON'T WORRY. YOU MONEY TO US.
BUYS YOU A LOT OF LIFE, CHICA.
BUYS YOU TIME.
LOTS OF WAYS TO SPEND TIME.

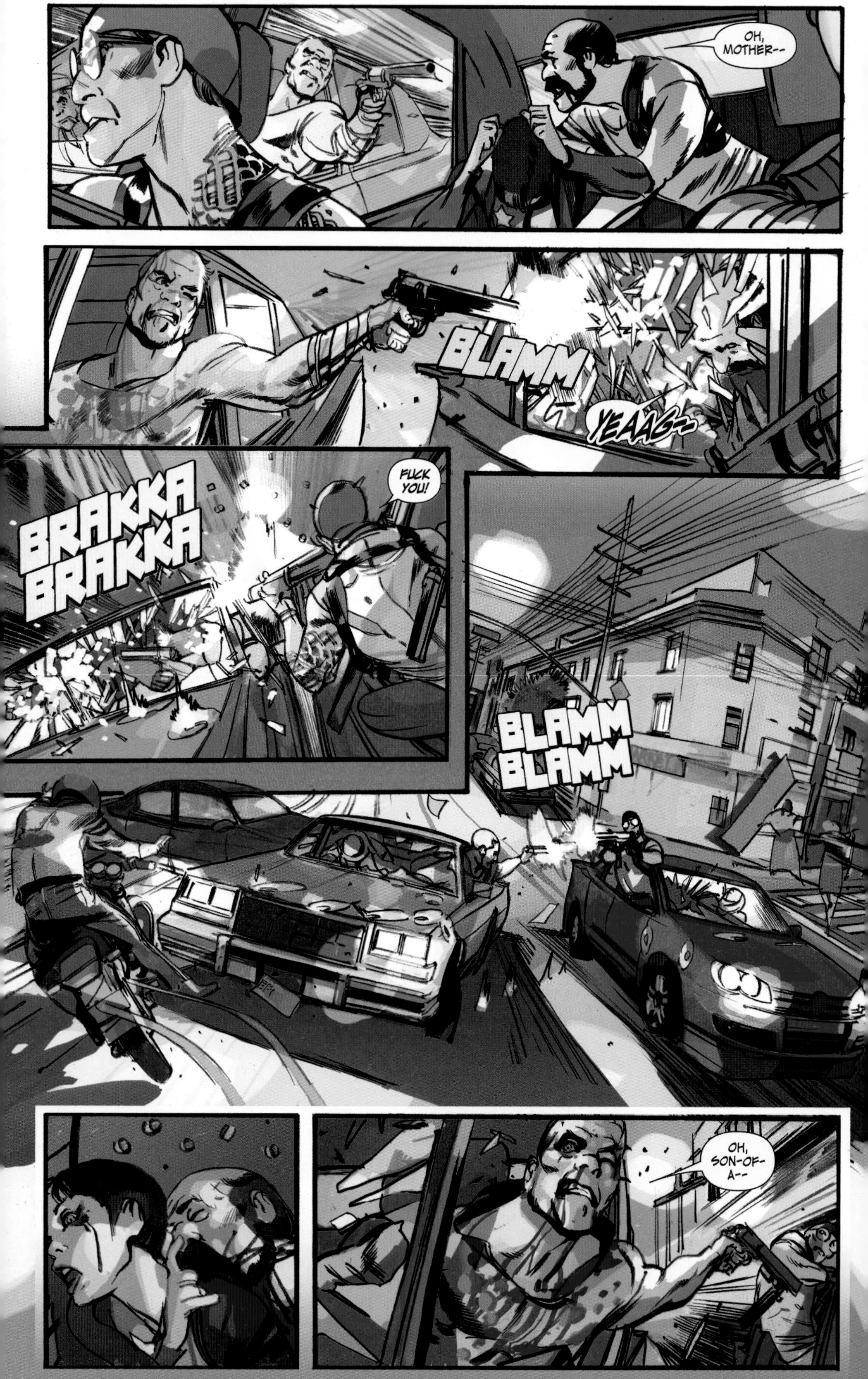
OH, MOTHER--
BLAMM
YEAAG--
BRAKKA BRAKKA
FUCK YOU!
BLAMM BLAMM
OH, SON-OF-A--

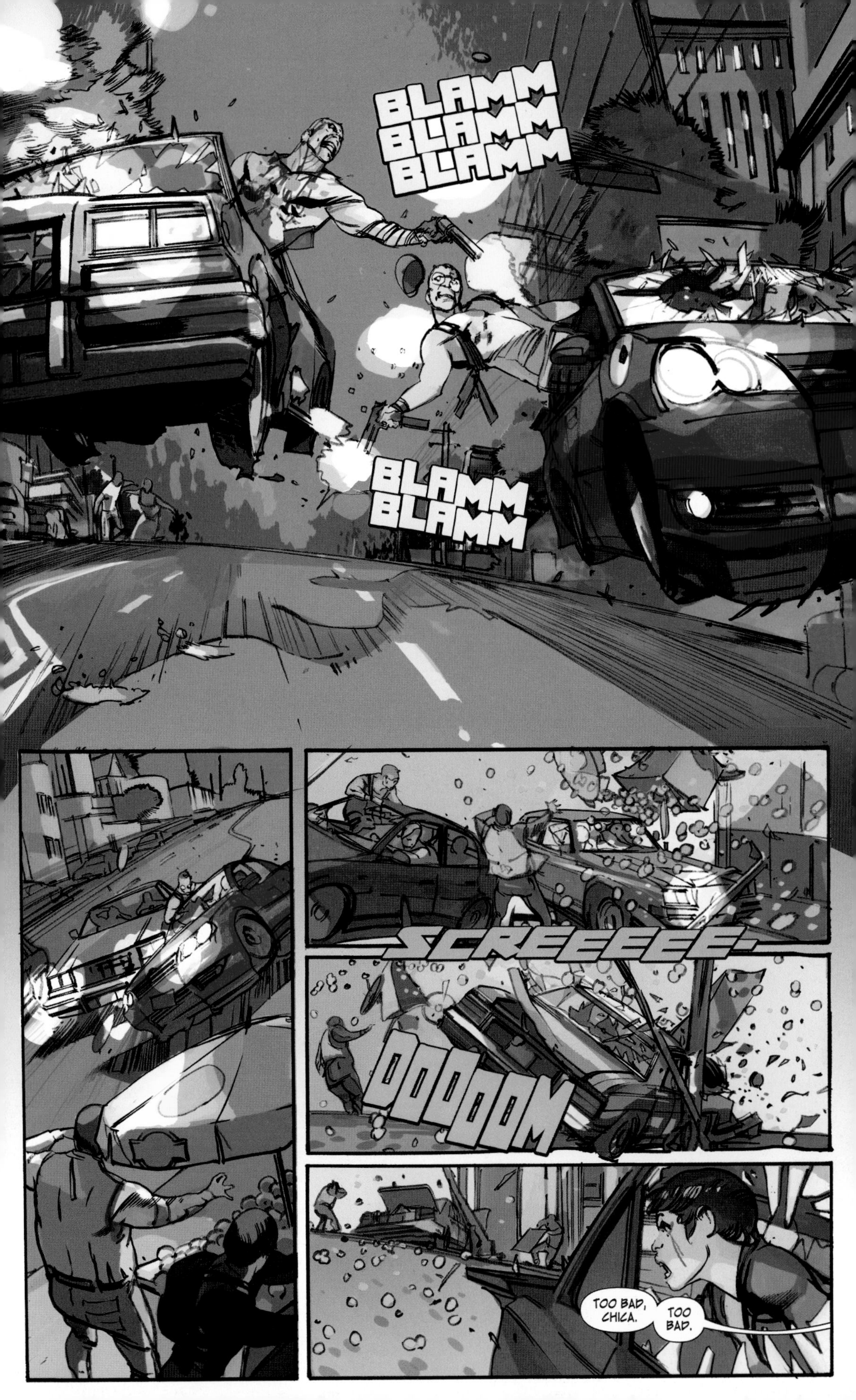
BLAMM
BLAMM
BLAMM
BLAMM
BLAMM
SCREEEEEE
DOOOOOM
TOO BAD, CHICA.
TOO BAD.

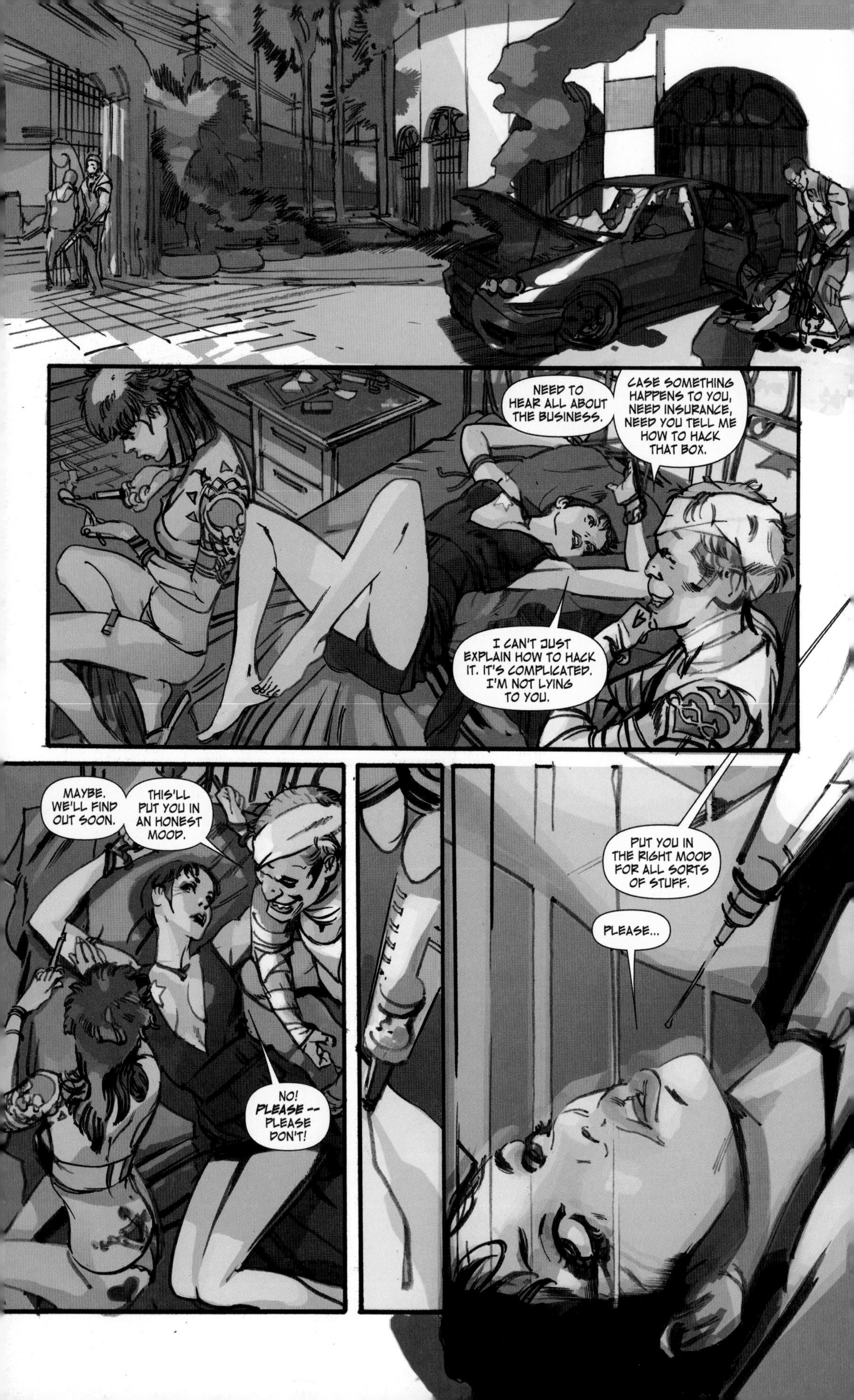
NEED TO HEAR ALL ABOUT THE BUSINESS.
CASE SOMETHING HAPPENS TO YOU, NEED INSURANCE, NEED YOU TELL ME HOW TO HACK THAT BOX.
I CAN'T JUST EXPLAIN HOW TO HACK IT. IT'S COMPLICATED. I'M NOT LYING TO YOU.
MAYBE. WE'LL FIND OUT SOON.
THIS'LL PUT YOU IN AN HONEST MOOD.
NO! *PLEASE* -- PLEASE DON'T!
PUT YOU IN THE RIGHT MOOD FOR ALL SORTS OF STUFF.
PLEASE...

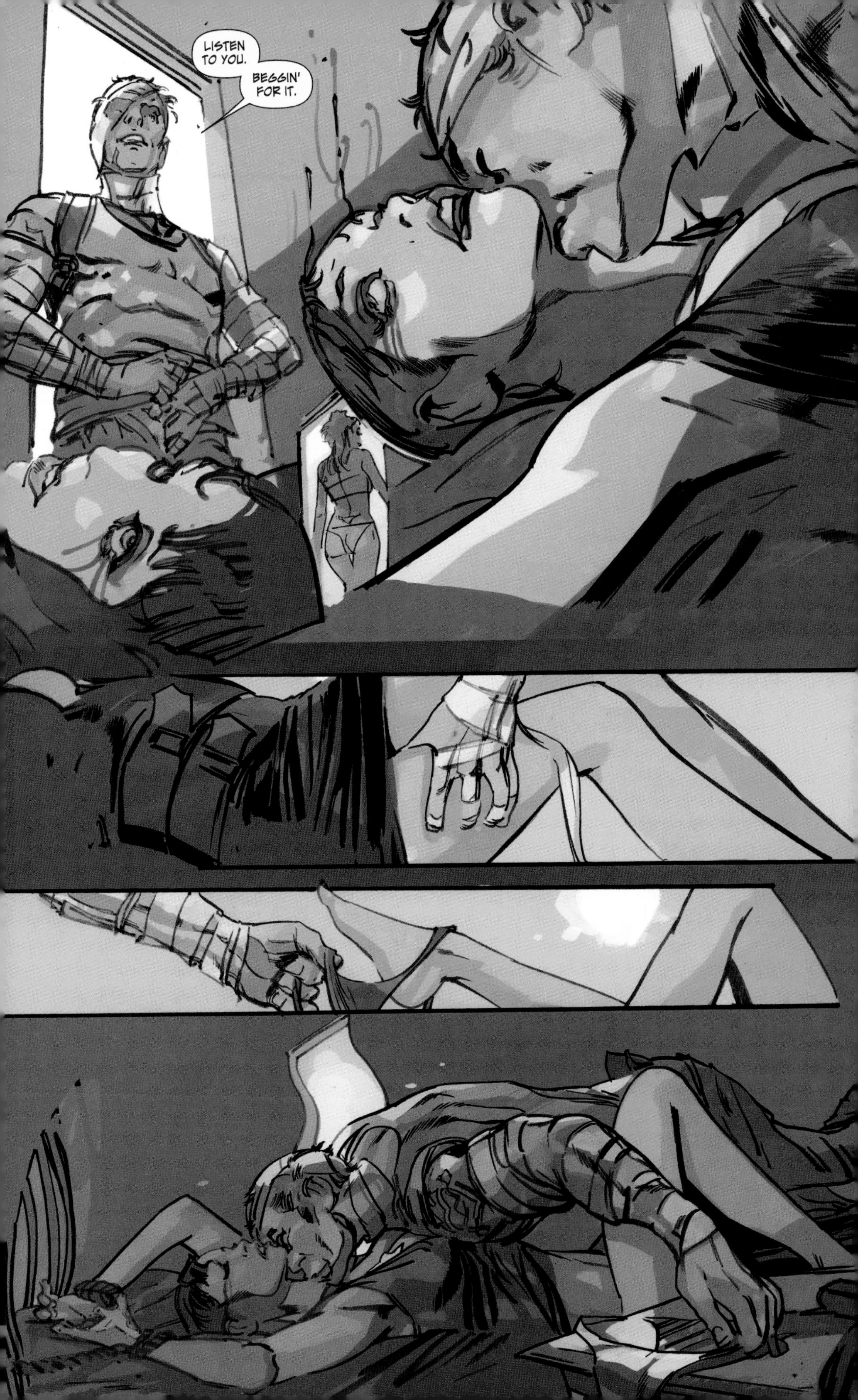
LISTEN TO YOU.
BEGGIN' FOR IT.

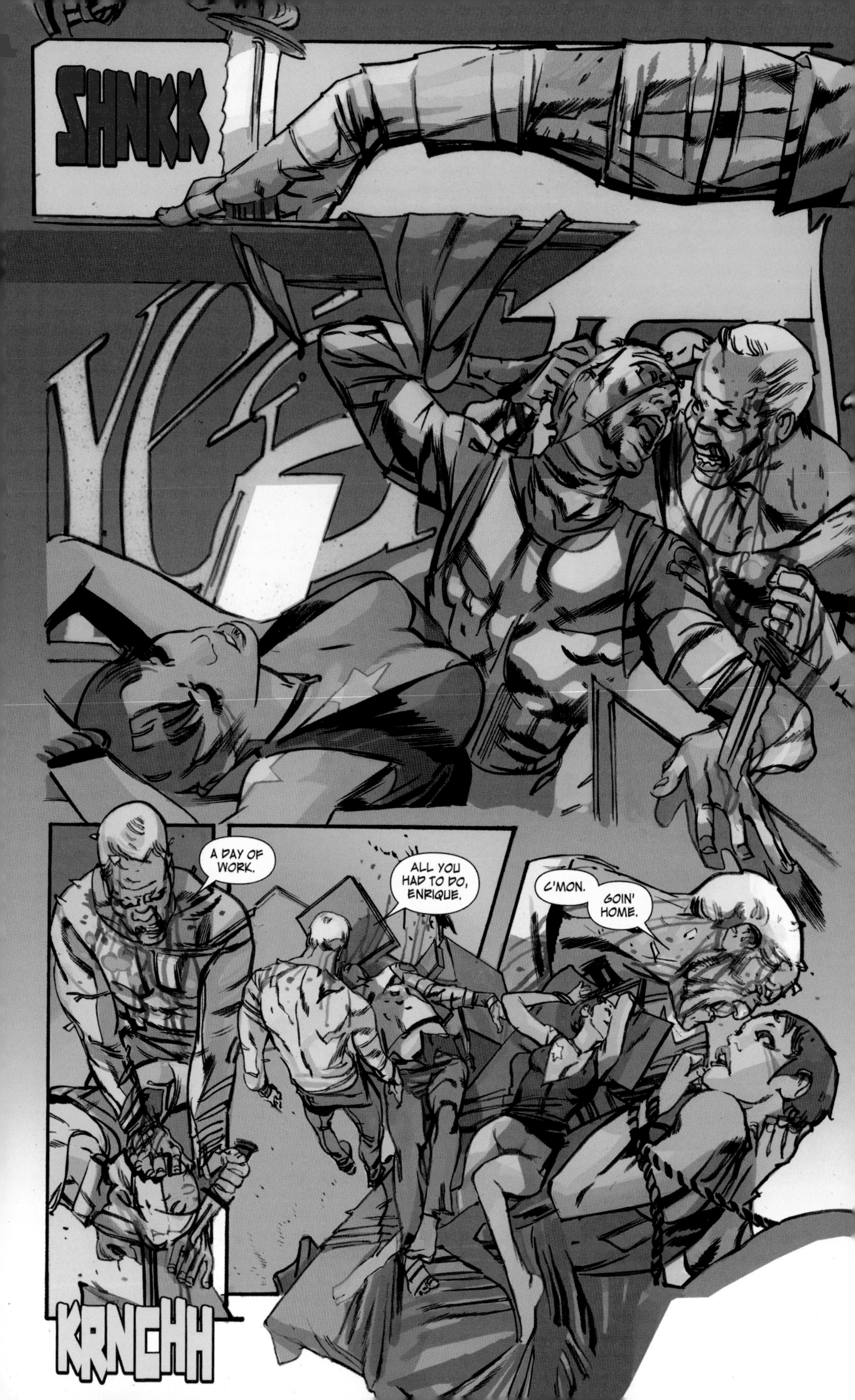
SHNKK
A DAY OF WORK.
ALL YOU HAD TO DO, ENRIQUE.
C'MON.
GOIN' HOME.
KRNCHH

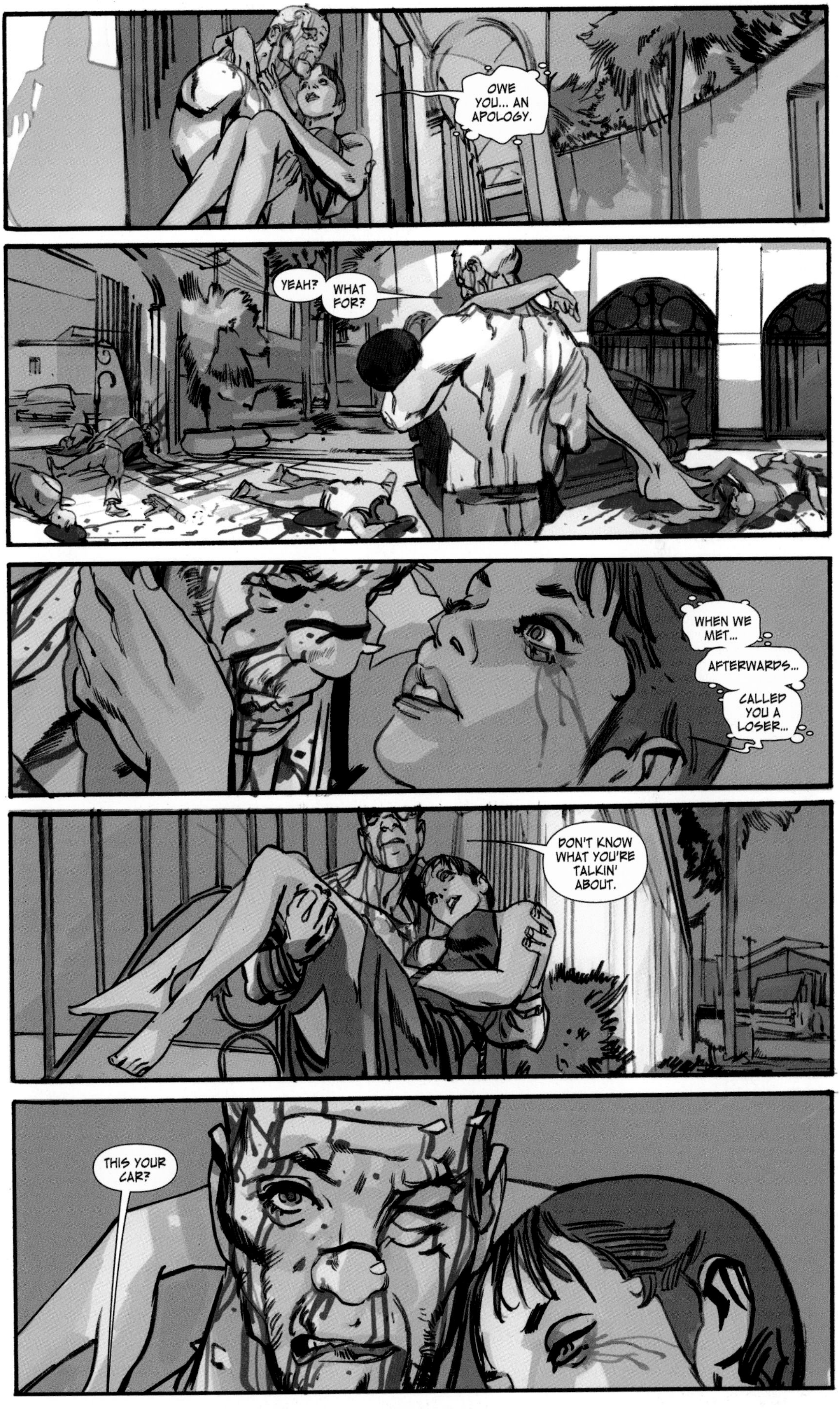
OWE YOU... AN APOLOGY.
YEAH?
WHAT FOR?
WHEN WE MET...
AFTERWARDS...
CALLED YOU A LOSER...
DON'T KNOW WHAT YOU'RE TALKIN' ABOUT.
THIS YOUR CAR?

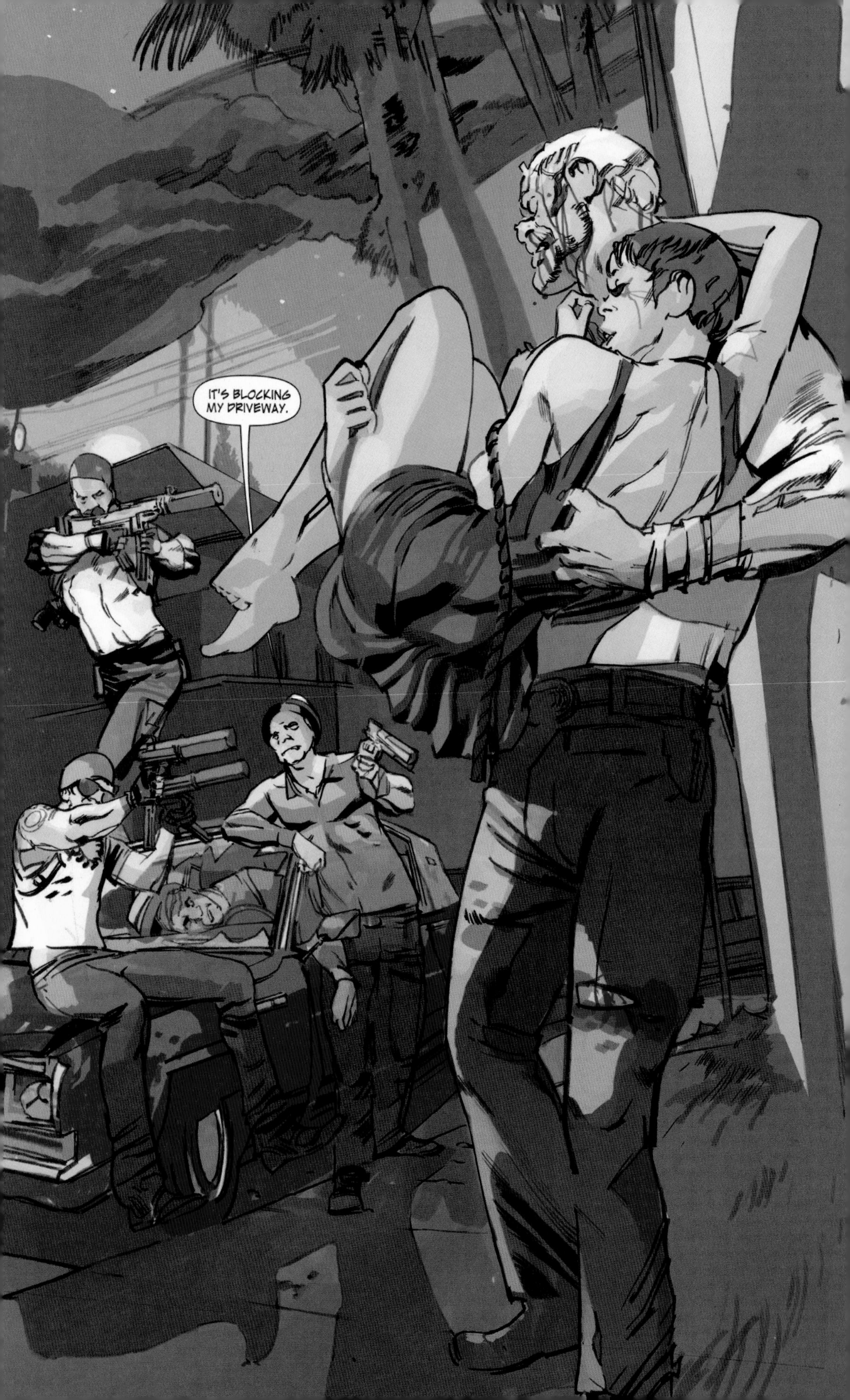
IT'S BLOCKING MY DRIVEWAY.

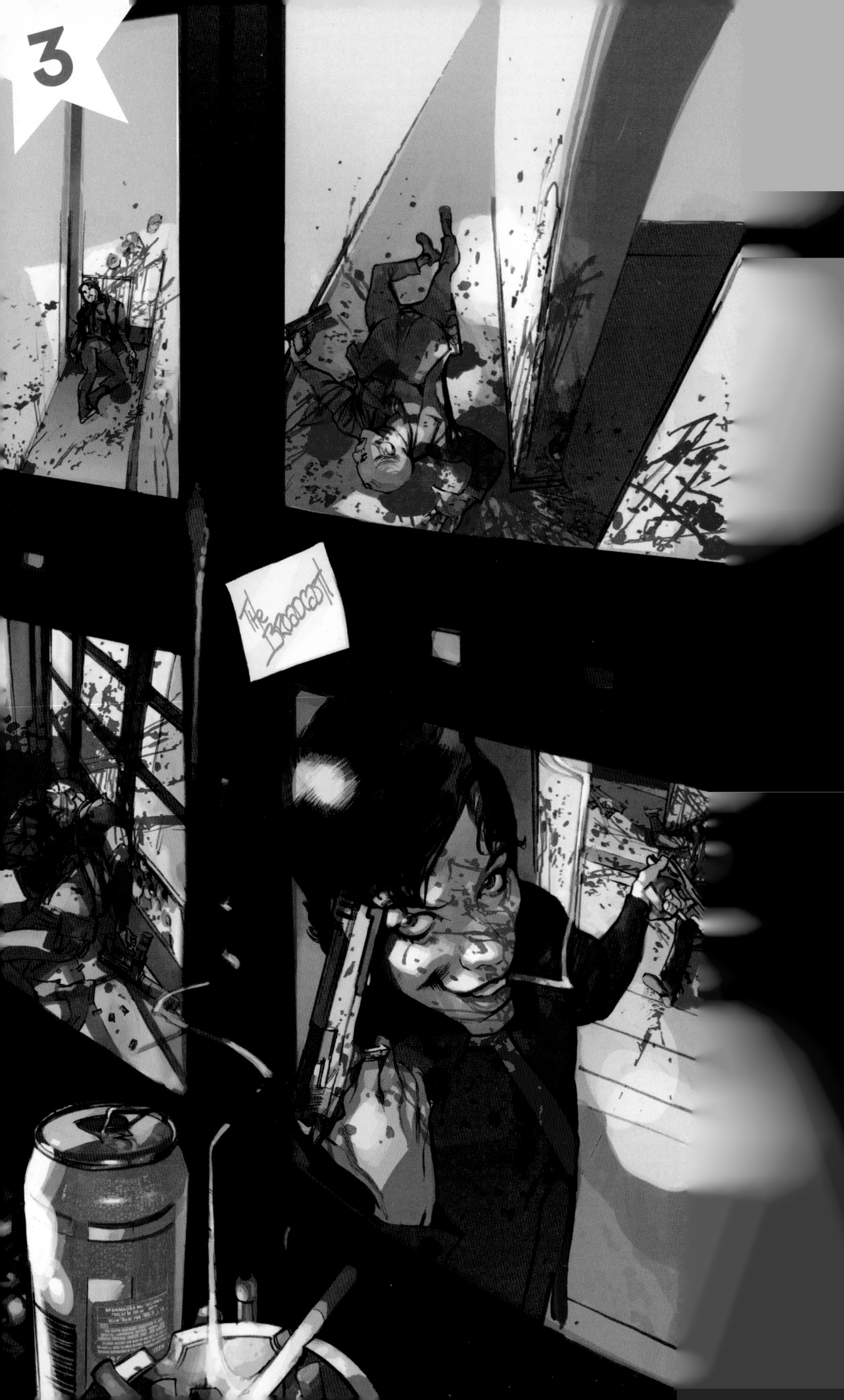
3
The BROADCAST

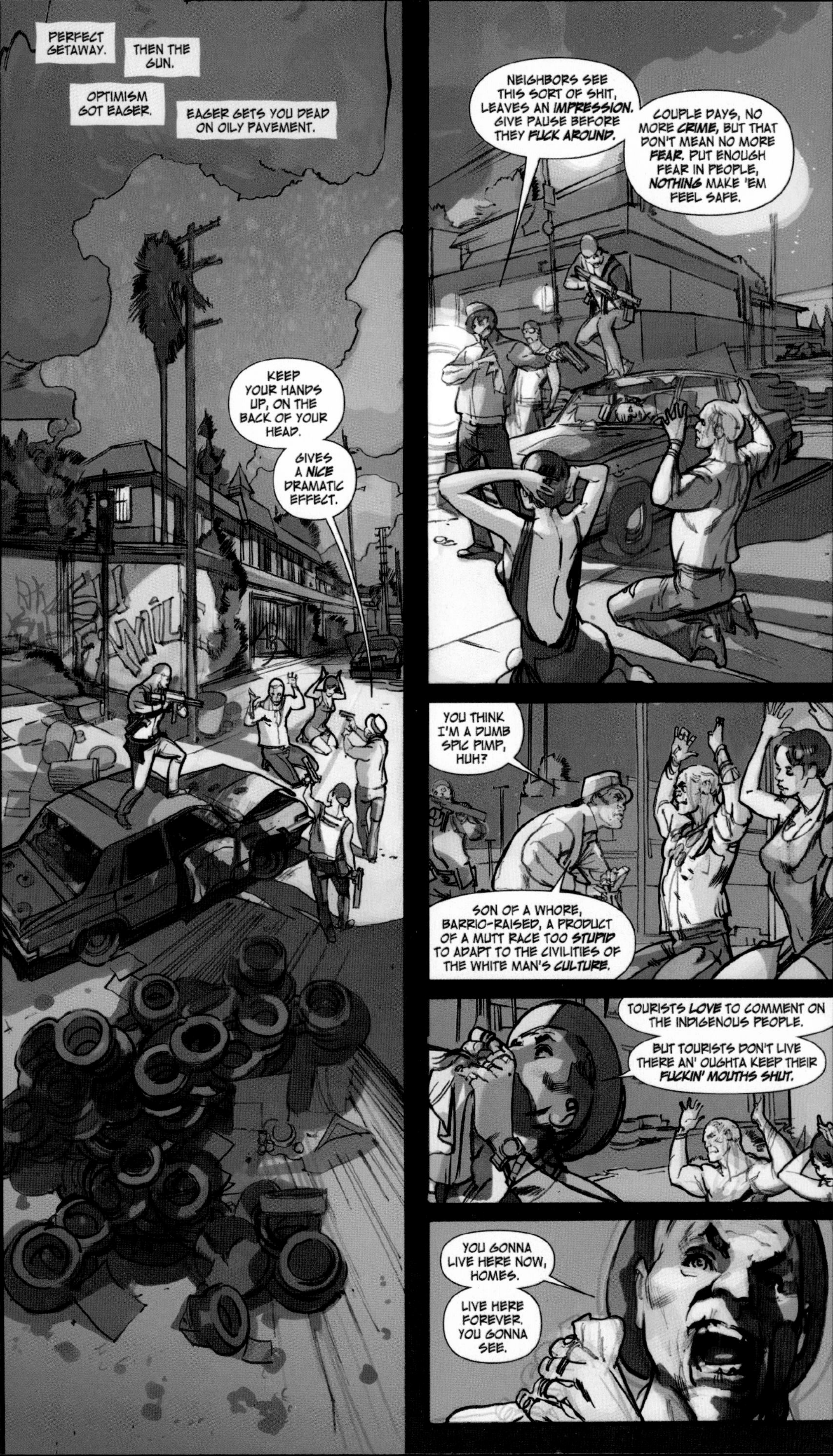
PERFECT GETAWAY.
THEN THE GUN.
OPTIMISM GOT EAGER.
EAGER GETS YOU DEAD ON OILY PAVEMENT.
KEEP YOUR HANDS UP, ON THE BACK OF YOUR HEAD.
GIVES A NICE DRAMATIC EFFECT.
NEIGHBORS SEE THIS SORT OF SHIT, LEAVES AN IMPRESSION. GIVE PAUSE BEFORE THEY FUCK AROUND.
COUPLE DAYS, NO MORE CRIME, BUT THAT DON'T MEAN NO MORE FEAR. PUT ENOUGH FEAR IN PEOPLE, NOTHING MAKE 'EM FEEL SAFE.
YOU THINK I'M A DUMB SPIC PIMP, HUH?
SON OF A WHORE, BARRIO-RAISED, A PRODUCT OF A MUTT RACE TOO STUPID TO ADAPT TO THE CIVILITIES OF THE WHITE MAN'S CULTURE.
TOURISTS LOVE TO COMMENT ON THE INDIGENOUS PEOPLE.
BUT TOURISTS DON'T LIVE THERE AN' OUGHTA KEEP THEIR FUCKIN' MOUTHS SHUT.
YOU GONNA LIVE HERE NOW, HOMES.
LIVE HERE FOREVER. YOU GONNA SEE.

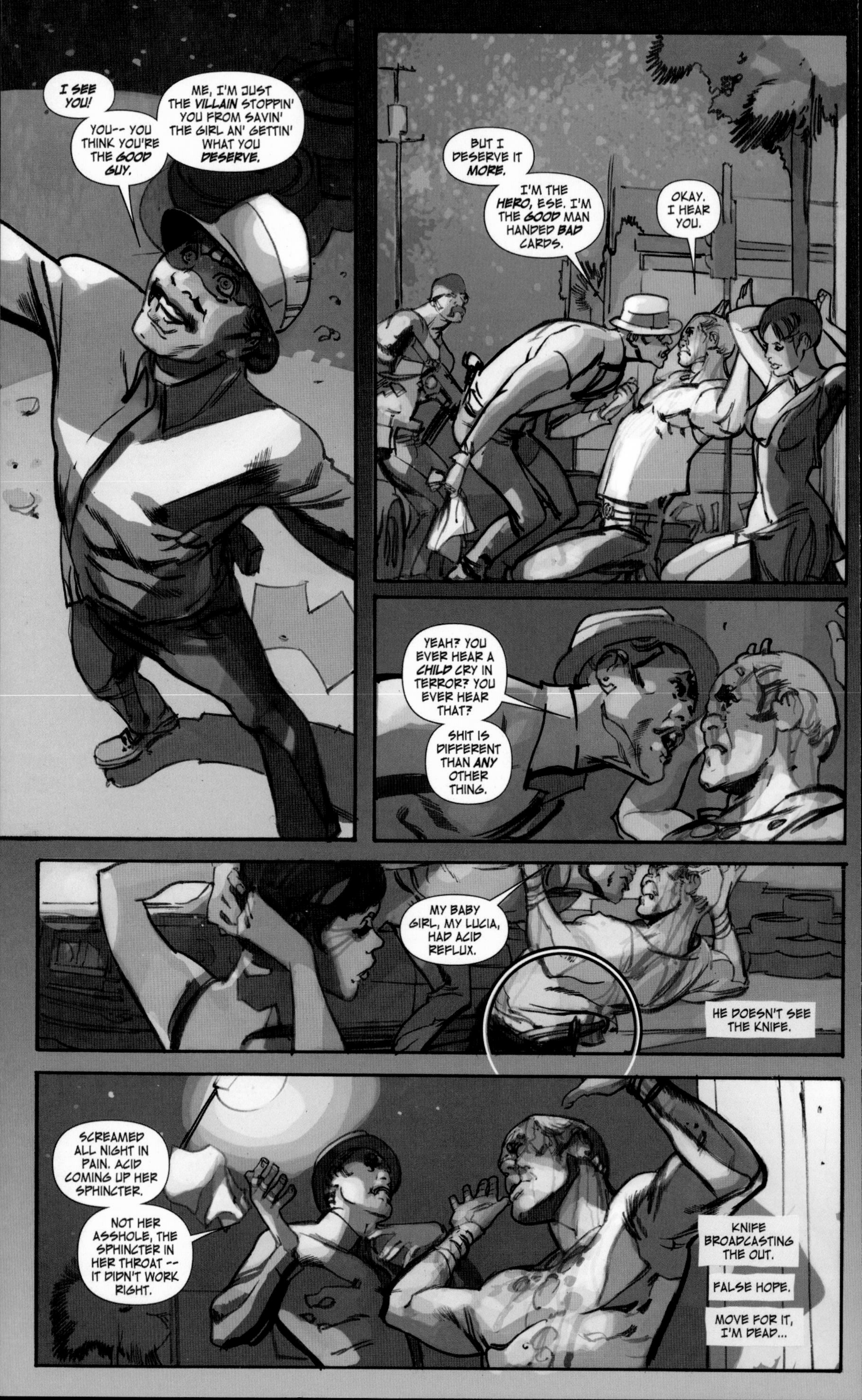
I SEE YOU!
YOU-- YOU THINK YOU'RE THE GOOD GUY.
ME, I'M JUST THE VILLAIN STOPPIN' YOU FROM SAVIN' THE GIRL AN' GETTIN' WHAT YOU DESERVE.
BUT I DESERVE IT MORE.
I'M THE HERO, ESE. I'M THE GOOD MAN HANDED BAD CARDS.
OKAY. I HEAR YOU.
YEAH? YOU EVER HEAR A CHILD CRY IN TERROR? YOU EVER HEAR THAT?
SHIT IS DIFFERENT THAN ANY OTHER THING.
MY BABY GIRL, MY LUCIA, HAD ACID REFLUX.
HE DOESN'T SEE THE KNIFE.
SCREAMED ALL NIGHT IN PAIN. ACID COMING UP HER SPHINCTER.
NOT HER ASSHOLE, THE SPHINCTER IN HER THROAT -- IT DIDN'T WORK RIGHT.
KNIFE BROADCASTING THE OUT.
FALSE HOPE.
MOVE FOR IT, I'M DEAD...

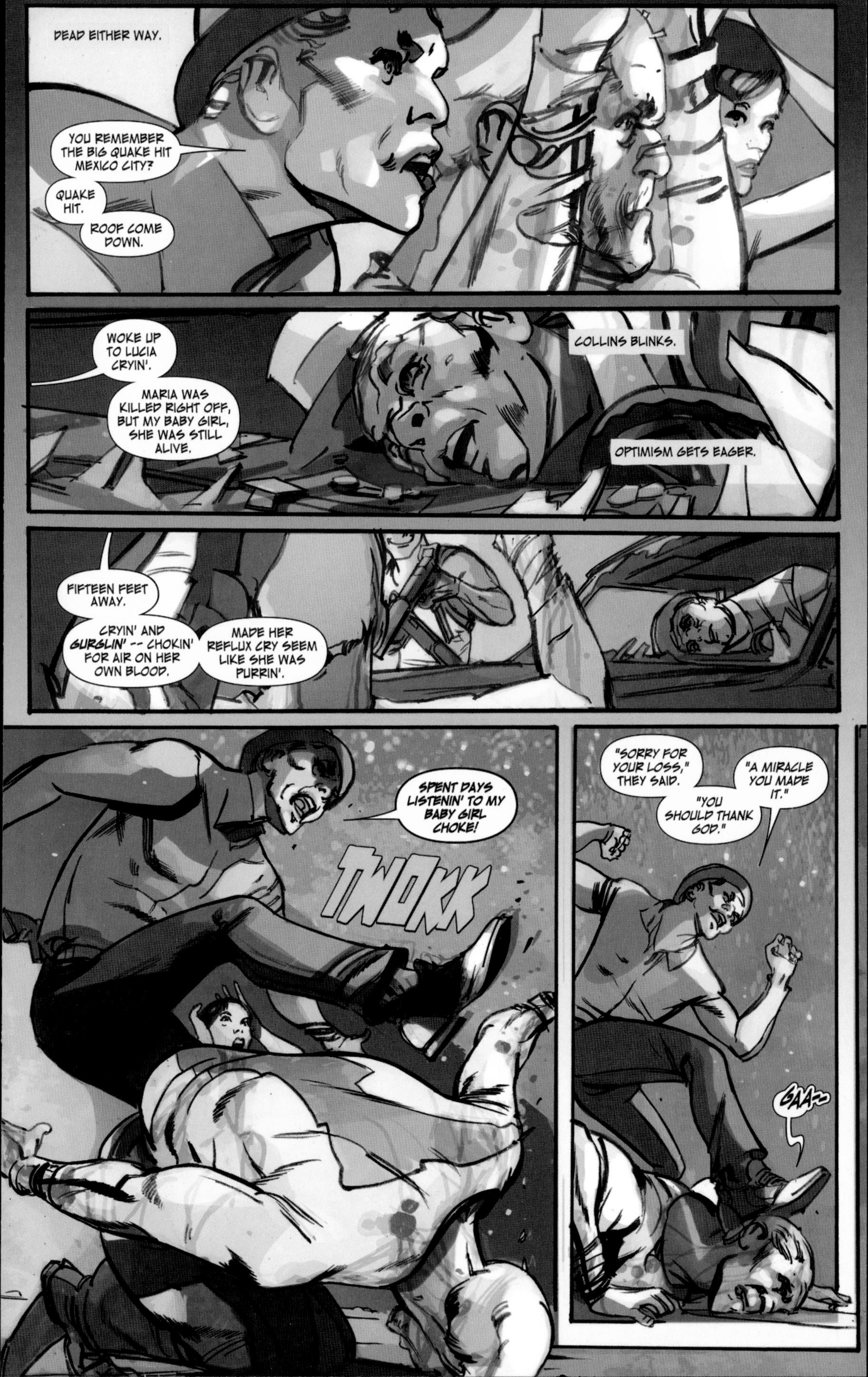
DEAD EITHER WAY.
YOU REMEMBER THE BIG QUAKE HIT MEXICO CITY?
QUAKE HIT.
ROOF COME DOWN.
WOKE UP TO LUCIA CRYIN'.
MARIA WAS KILLED RIGHT OFF, BUT MY BABY GIRL, SHE WAS STILL ALIVE.
COLLINS BLINKS.
OPTIMISM GETS EAGER.
FIFTEEN FEET AWAY.
CRYIN' AND GURGLIN' -- CHOKIN' FOR AIR ON HER OWN BLOOD.
MADE HER REFLUX CRY SEEM LIKE SHE WAS PURRIN'.
SPENT DAYS LISTENIN' TO MY BABY GIRL CHOKE!
TWOKK
"SORRY FOR YOUR LOSS," THEY SAID.
"A MIRACLE YOU MADE IT."
"YOU SHOULD THANK GOD."
GAA--

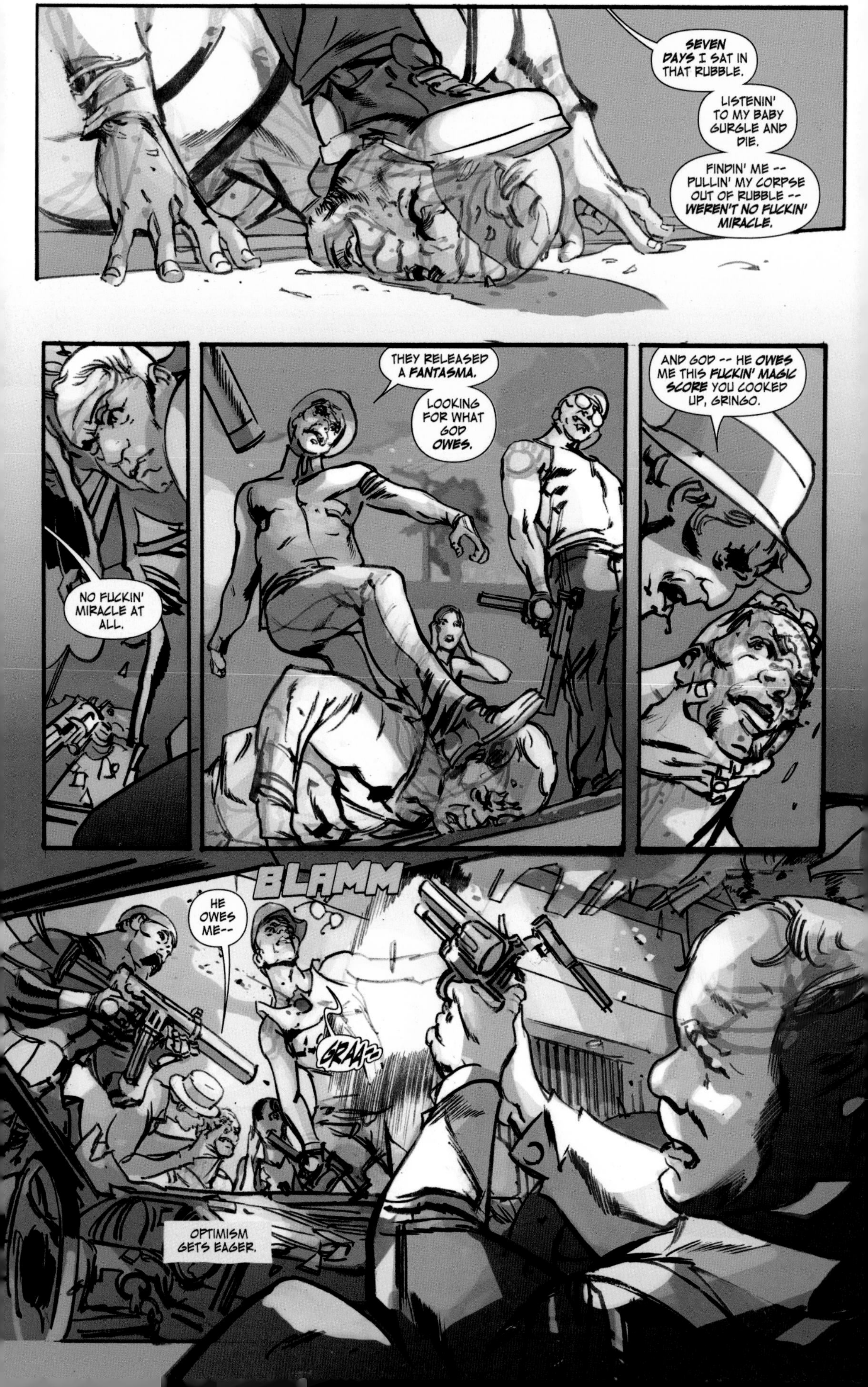
SEVEN DAYS I SAT IN THAT RUBBLE.
LISTENIN' TO MY BABY GURGLE AND DIE.
FINDIN' ME -- PULLIN' MY CORPSE OUT OF RUBBLE -- WEREN'T NO FUCKIN' MIRACLE.
NO FUCKIN' MIRACLE AT ALL.
THEY RELEASED A FANTASMA.
LOOKING FOR WHAT GOD OWES.
AND GOD -- HE OWES ME THIS FUCKIN' MAGIC SCORE YOU COOKED UP, GRINGO.
BLAMM
HE OWES ME--
GRAA?
OPTIMISM GETS EAGER.

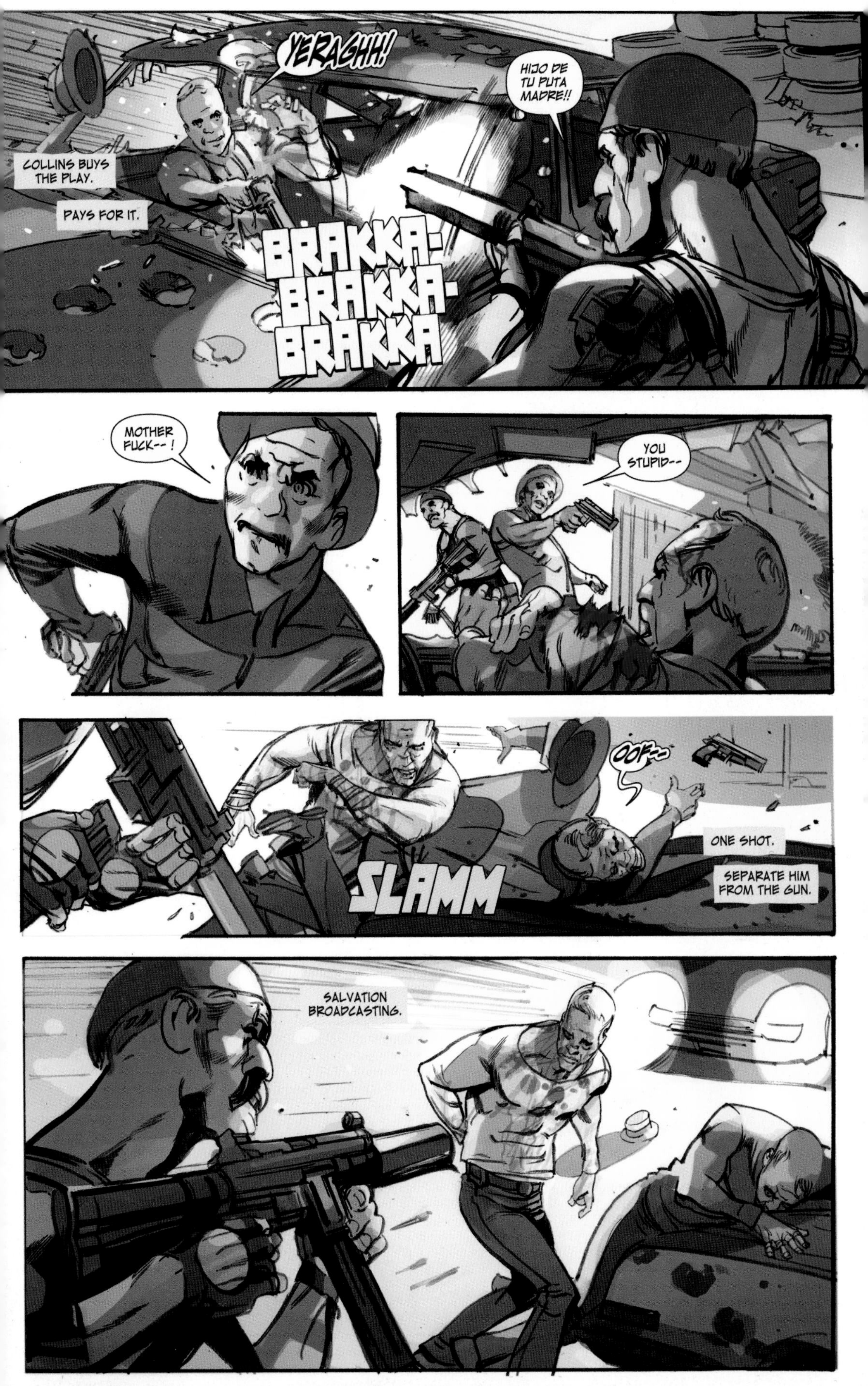
YERAGHH!
HIJO DE TU PUTA MADRE!!
COLLINS BUYS THE PLAY.
PAYS FOR IT.
BRAKKA-BRAKKA-BRAKKA
MOTHER FUCK-- !
YOU STUPID--
OOF--
SLAMM
ONE SHOT.
SEPARATE HIM FROM THE GUN.
SALVATION BROADCASTING.

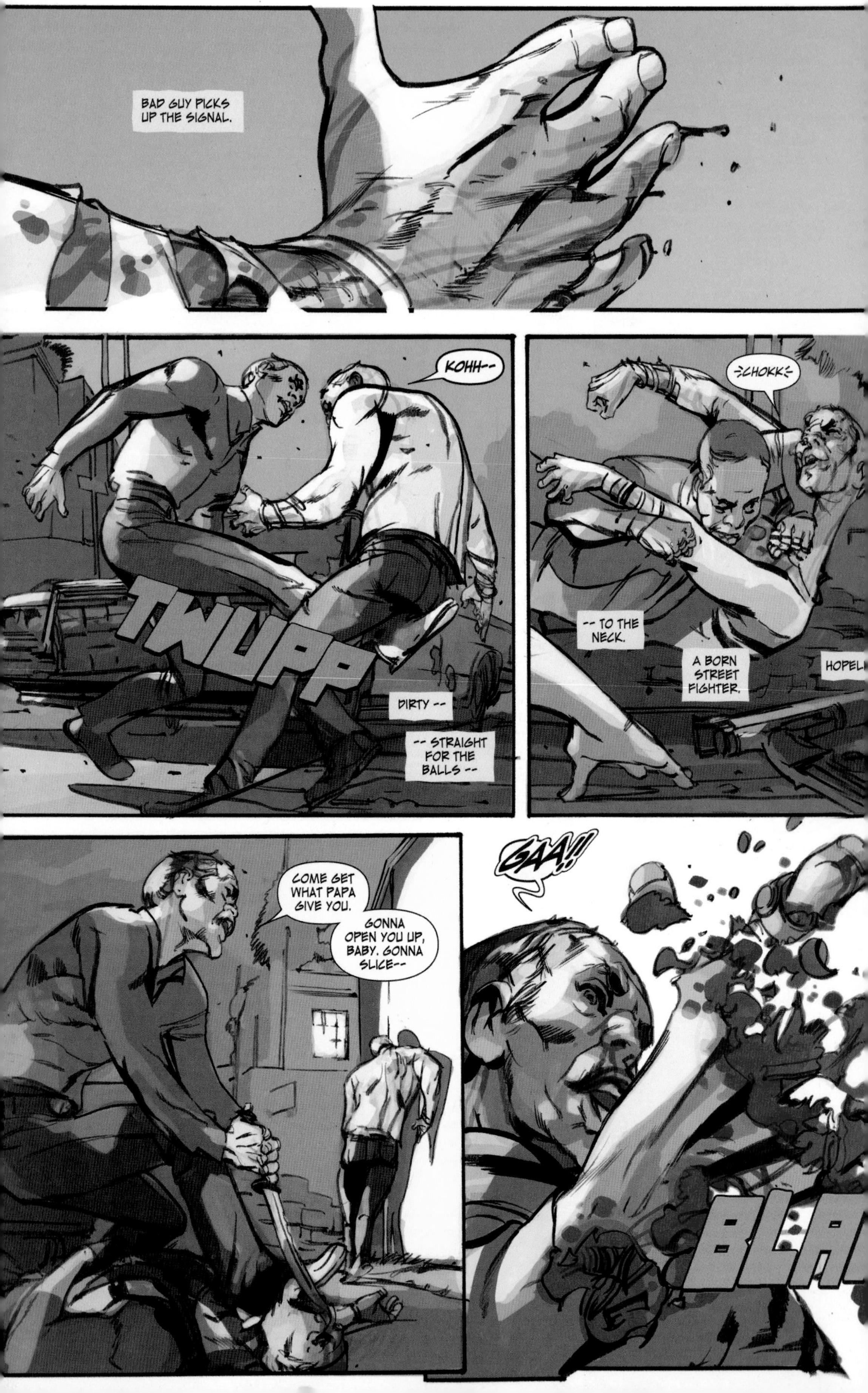
BAD GUY PICKS UP THE SIGNAL.
KOHH--
TWUPP
DIRTY --
-- STRAIGHT FOR THE BALLS --
CHOKK
-- TO THE NECK.
A BORN STREET FIGHTER.
HOPEL
COME GET WHAT PAPA GIVE YOU.
GONNA OPEN YOU UP, BABY. GONNA SLICE--
GAA!!
BLA

SHNKK

ONE LUCKY PUNCH.

ALL I'LL GET.

SPAKK

GET UP.

GET THAT FUCKING GUN.

COME BACK, BABY.

I'M SORRY ABOUT YOUR DAUGHTER.

GAA-- GADAMNIT!!

MOTHER FUCKER!!

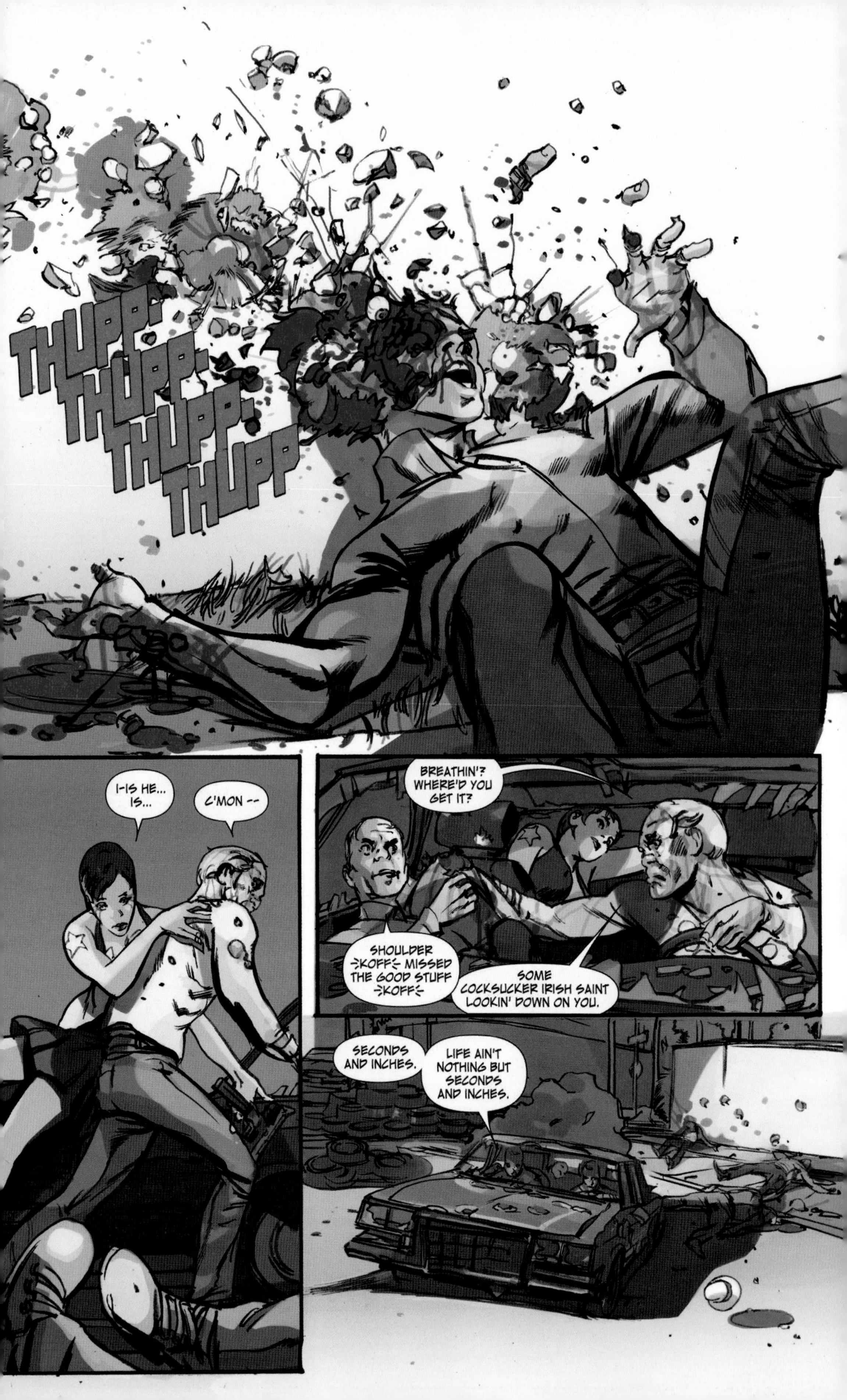
THUPP. THUPP. THUPP. THUPP
I-IS HE... IS...
C'MON --
BREATHIN'? WHERE'D YOU GET IT?
SHOULDER -KOFF- MISSED THE GOOD STUFF -KOFF-
SOME COCKSUCKER IRISH SAINT LOOKIN' DOWN ON YOU.
SECONDS AND INCHES.
LIFE AIN'T NOTHING BUT SECONDS AND INCHES.

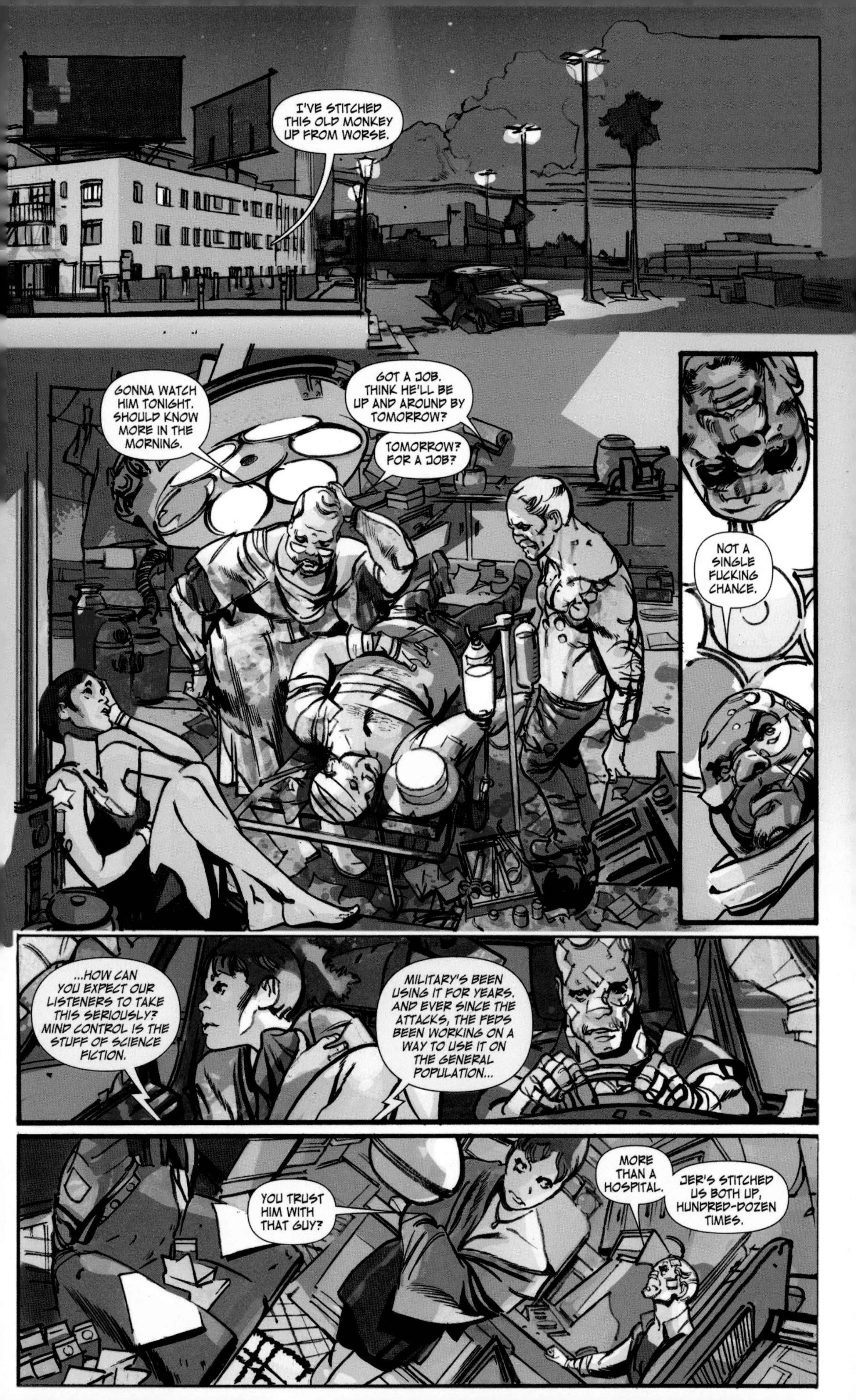
I'VE STITCHED THIS OLD MONKEY UP FROM WORSE.
GONNA WATCH HIM TONIGHT. SHOULD KNOW MORE IN THE MORNING.
GOT A JOB. THINK HE'LL BE UP AND AROUND BY TOMORROW?
TOMORROW? FOR A JOB?
NOT A SINGLE FUCKING CHANCE.
...HOW CAN YOU EXPECT OUR LISTENERS TO TAKE THIS SERIOUSLY? MIND CONTROL IS THE STUFF OF SCIENCE FICTION.
MILITARY'S BEEN USING IT FOR YEARS. AND EVER SINCE THE ATTACKS, THE FEDS BEEN WORKING ON A WAY TO USE IT ON THE GENERAL POPULATION...
YOU TRUST HIM WITH THAT GUY?
MORE THAN A HOSPITAL.
JER'S STITCHED US BOTH UP, HUNDRED-DOZEN TIMES.

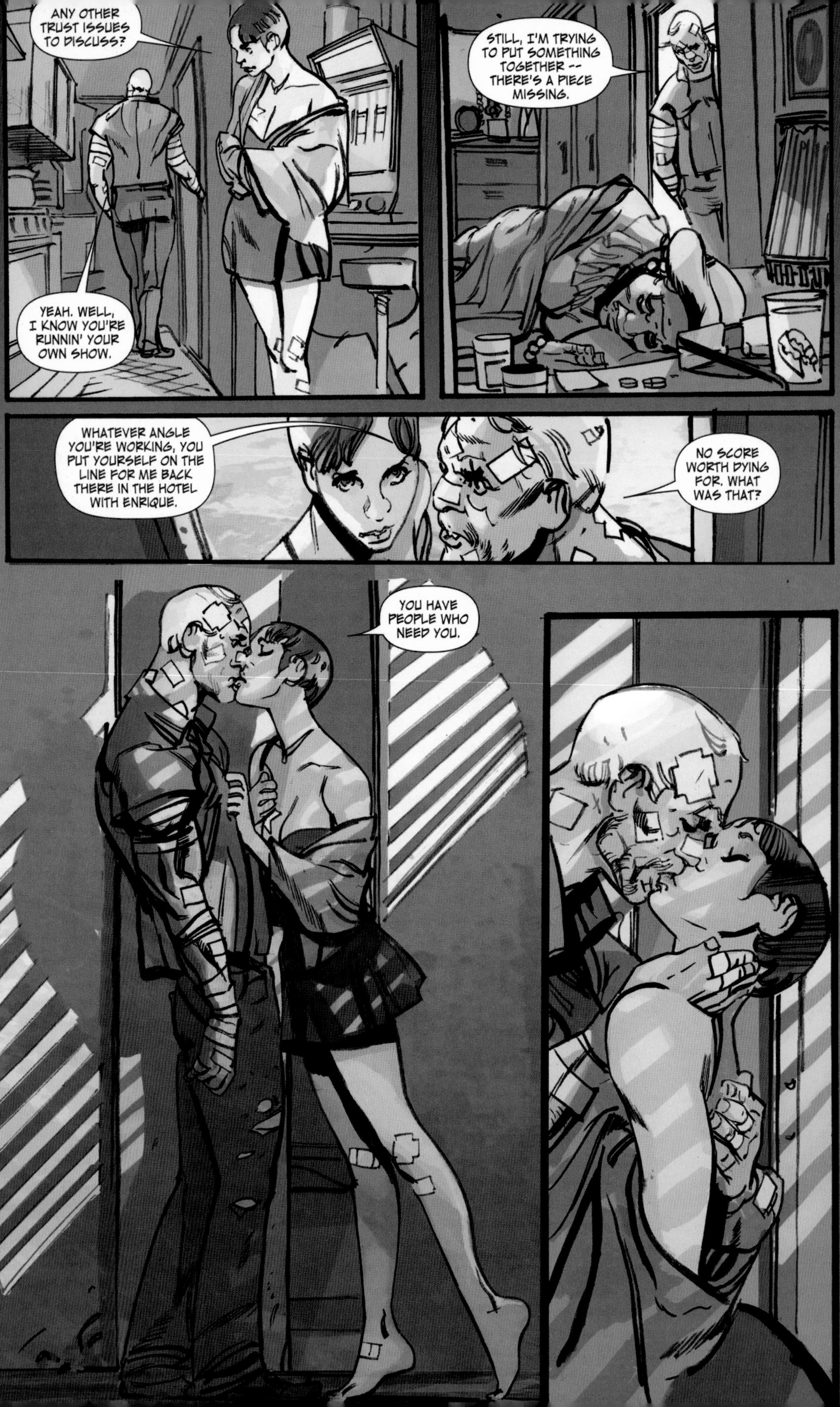
ANY OTHER TRUST ISSUES TO DISCUSS?
YEAH. WELL, I KNOW YOU'RE RUNNIN' YOUR OWN SHOW.
STILL, I'M TRYING TO PUT SOMETHING TOGETHER -- THERE'S A PIECE MISSING.
WHATEVER ANGLE YOU'RE WORKING, YOU PUT YOURSELF ON THE LINE FOR ME BACK THERE IN THE HOTEL WITH ENRIQUE.
NO SCORE WORTH DYING FOR. WHAT WAS THAT?
YOU HAVE PEOPLE WHO NEED YOU.

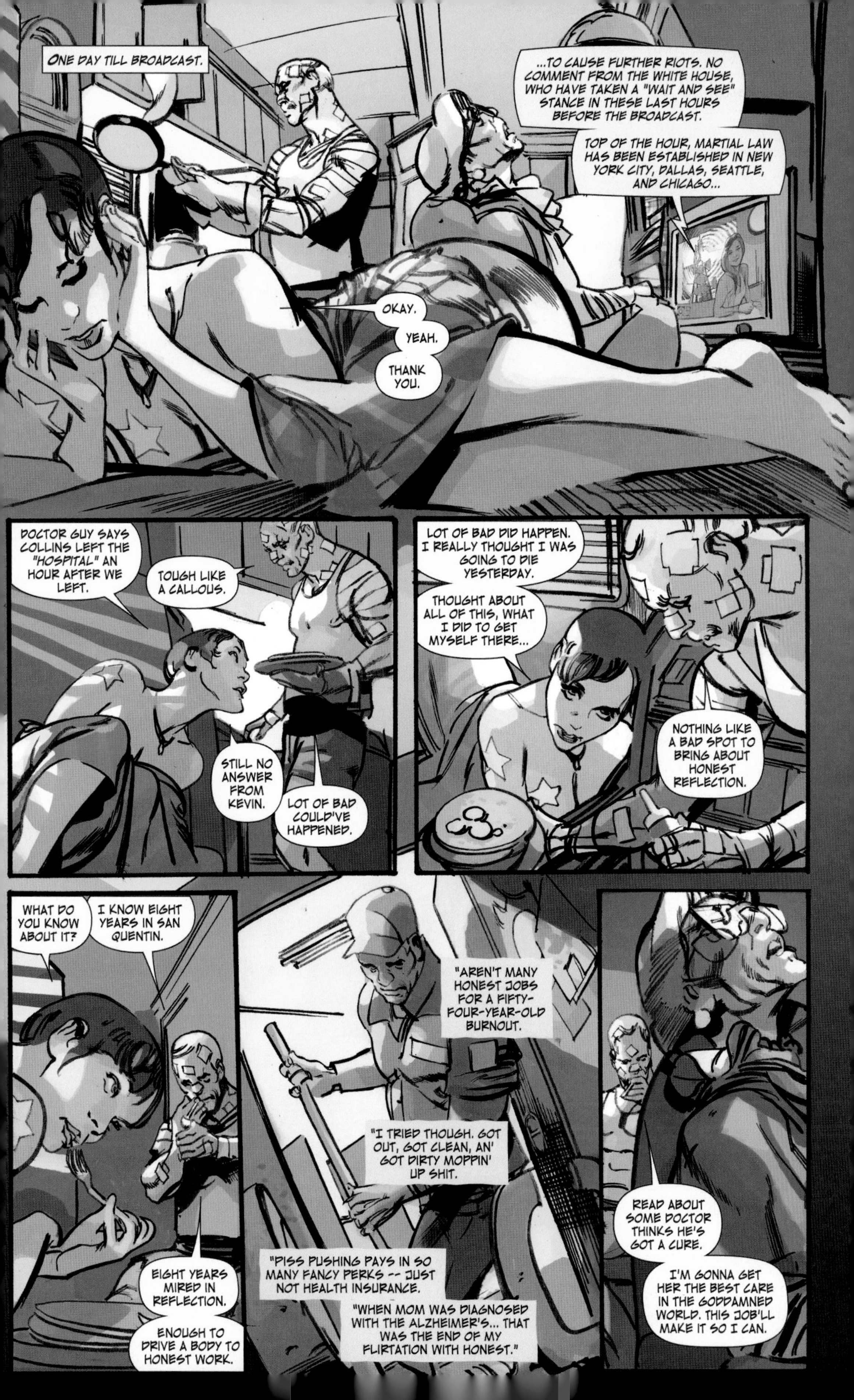
ONE DAY TILL BROADCAST.
...TO CAUSE FURTHER RIOTS. NO COMMENT FROM THE WHITE HOUSE, WHO HAVE TAKEN A "WAIT AND SEE" STANCE IN THESE LAST HOURS BEFORE THE BROADCAST.
TOP OF THE HOUR, MARTIAL LAW HAS BEEN ESTABLISHED IN NEW YORK CITY, DALLAS, SEATTLE, AND CHICAGO...
OKAY.
YEAH.
THANK YOU.
DOCTOR GUY SAYS COLLINS LEFT THE "HOSPITAL" AN HOUR AFTER WE LEFT.
TOUGH LIKE A CALLOUS.
STILL NO ANSWER FROM KEVIN.
LOT OF BAD COULD'VE HAPPENED.
LOT OF BAD DID HAPPEN. I REALLY THOUGHT I WAS GOING TO DIE YESTERDAY.
THOUGHT ABOUT ALL OF THIS, WHAT I DID TO GET MYSELF THERE...
NOTHING LIKE A BAD SPOT TO BRING ABOUT HONEST REFLECTION.
WHAT DO YOU KNOW ABOUT IT?
I KNOW EIGHT YEARS IN SAN QUENTIN.
EIGHT YEARS MIRED IN REFLECTION.
ENOUGH TO DRIVE A BODY TO HONEST WORK.
"AREN'T MANY HONEST JOBS FOR A FIFTY-FOUR-YEAR-OLD BURNOUT.
"I TRIED THOUGH. GOT OUT, GOT CLEAN, AN' GOT DIRTY MOPPIN' UP SHIT.
"PISS PUSHING PAYS IN SO MANY FANCY PERKS -- JUST NOT HEALTH INSURANCE.
"WHEN MOM WAS DIAGNOSED WITH THE ALZHEIMER'S... THAT WAS THE END OF MY FLIRTATION WITH HONEST."
READ ABOUT SOME DOCTOR THINKS HE'S GOT A CURE.
I'M GONNA GET HER THE BEST CARE IN THE GODDAMNED WORLD. THIS JOB'LL MAKE IT SO I CAN.

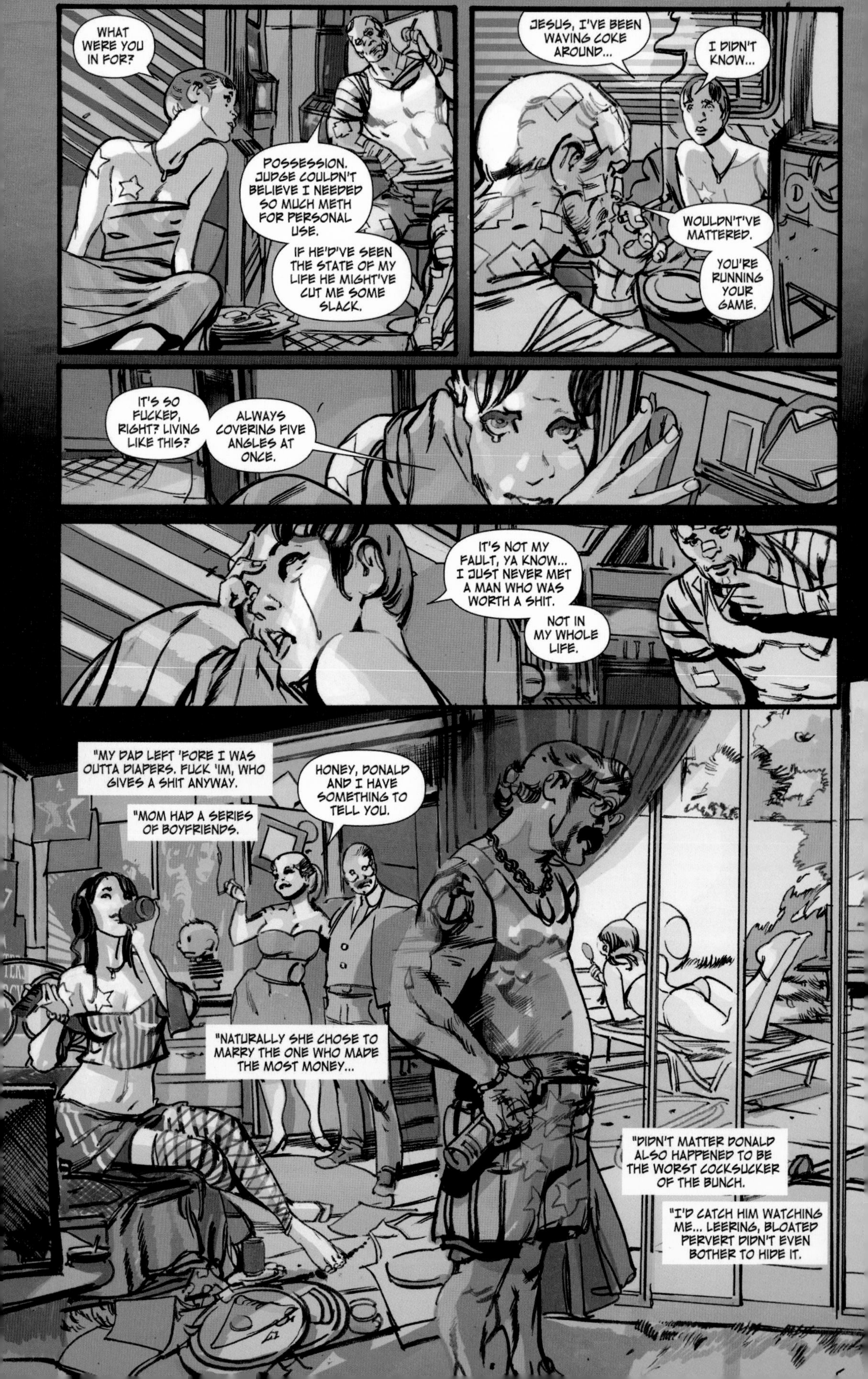
WHAT WERE YOU IN FOR?
POSSESSION. JUDGE COULDN'T BELIEVE I NEEDED SO MUCH METH FOR PERSONAL USE.
IF HE'D'VE SEEN THE STATE OF MY LIFE HE MIGHT'VE CUT ME SOME SLACK.
JESUS, I'VE BEEN WAVING COKE AROUND...
I DIDN'T KNOW...
WOULDN'T'VE MATTERED.
YOU'RE RUNNING YOUR GAME.
IT'S SO FUCKED, RIGHT? LIVING LIKE THIS?
ALWAYS COVERING FIVE ANGLES AT ONCE.
IT'S NOT MY FAULT, YA KNOW... I JUST NEVER MET A MAN WHO WAS WORTH A SHIT.
NOT IN MY WHOLE LIFE.
"MY DAD LEFT 'FORE I WAS OUTTA DIAPERS. FUCK 'IM, WHO GIVES A SHIT ANYWAY.
"MOM HAD A SERIES OF BOYFRIENDS.
HONEY, DONALD AND I HAVE SOMETHING TO TELL YOU.
"NATURALLY SHE CHOSE TO MARRY THE ONE WHO MADE THE MOST MONEY...
"DIDN'T MATTER DONALD ALSO HAPPENED TO BE THE WORST COCKSUCKER OF THE BUNCH.
"I'D CATCH HIM WATCHING ME... LEERING, BLOATED PERVERT DIDN'T EVEN BOTHER TO HIDE IT.

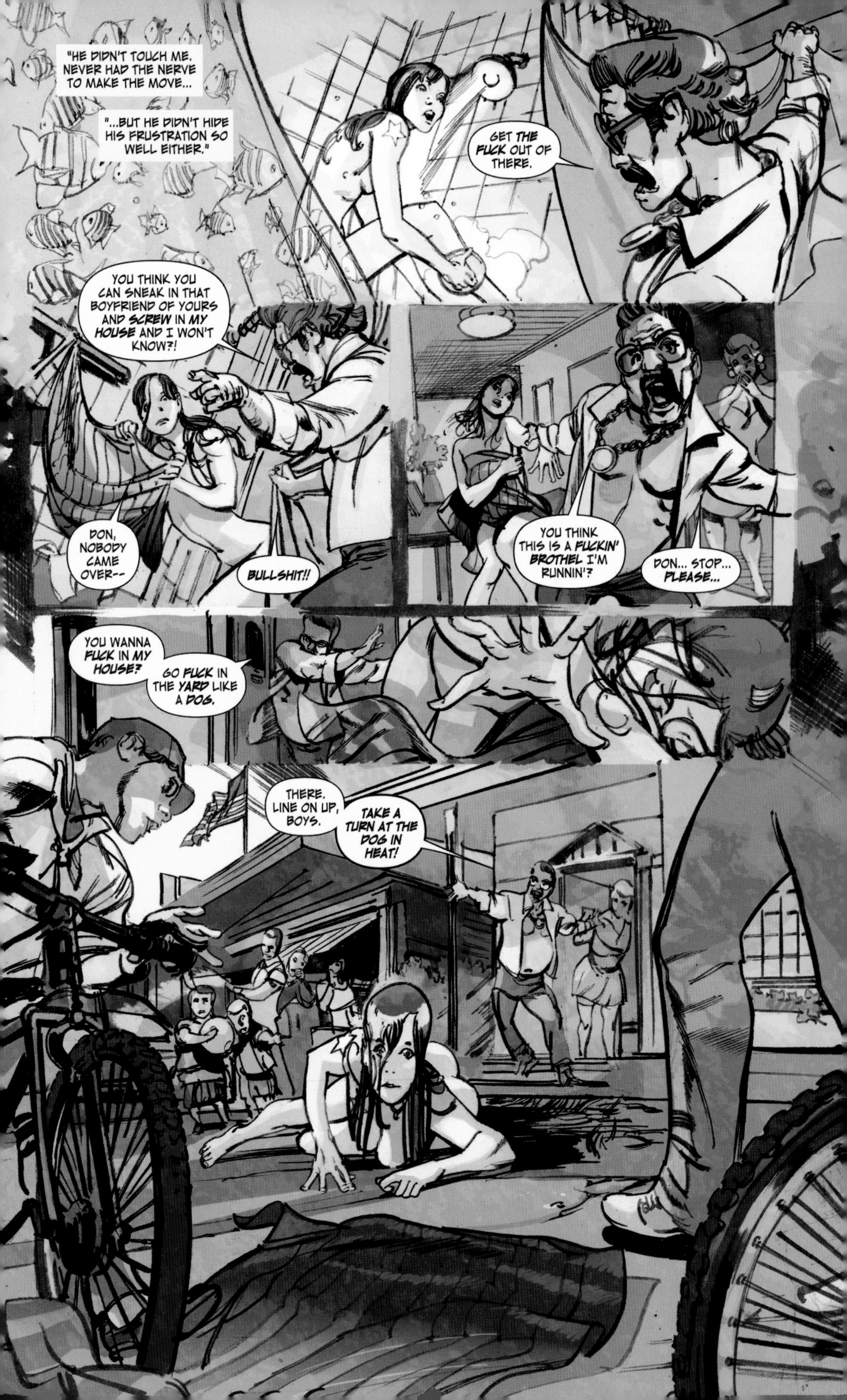
"HE DIDN'T TOUCH ME. NEVER HAD THE NERVE TO MAKE THE MOVE...
"...BUT HE DIDN'T HIDE HIS FRUSTRATION SO WELL EITHER."
GET THE FUCK OUT OF THERE.
YOU THINK YOU CAN SNEAK IN THAT BOYFRIEND OF YOURS AND SCREW IN MY HOUSE AND I WON'T KNOW?!
DON, NOBODY CAME OVER--
BULLSHIT!!
YOU THINK THIS IS A FUCKIN' BROTHEL I'M RUNNIN'?
DON... STOP... PLEASE...
YOU WANNA FUCK IN MY HOUSE?
GO FUCK IN THE YARD LIKE A DOG.
THERE. LINE ON UP, BOYS.
TAKE A TURN AT THE DOG IN HEAT!

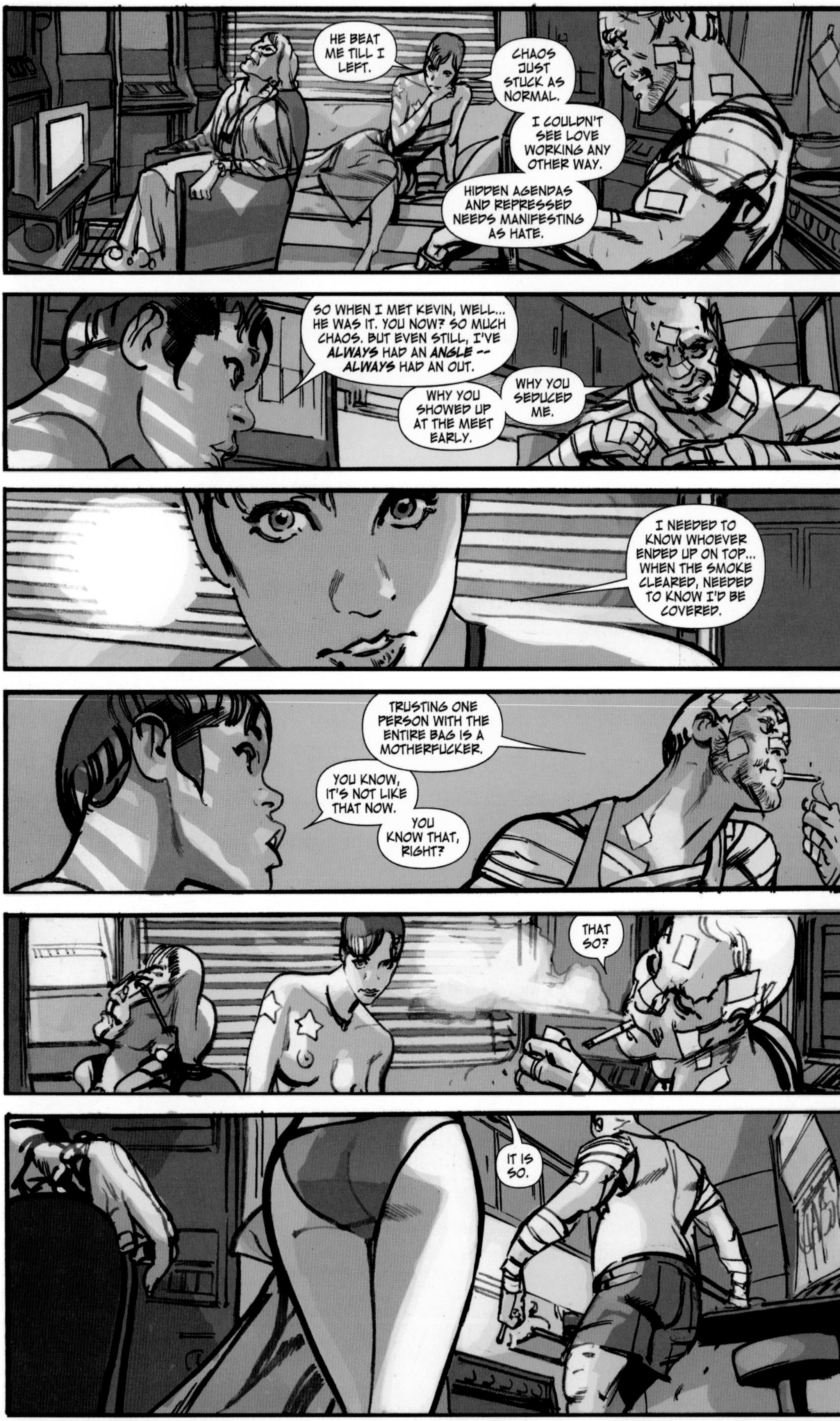
HE BEAT ME TILL I LEFT.
CHAOS JUST STUCK AS NORMAL.
I COULDN'T SEE LOVE WORKING ANY OTHER WAY.
HIDDEN AGENDAS AND REPRESSED NEEDS MANIFESTING AS HATE.
SO WHEN I MET KEVIN, WELL... HE WAS IT. YOU NOW? SO MUCH CHAOS. BUT EVEN STILL, I'VE ALWAYS HAD AN ANGLE -- ALWAYS HAD AN OUT.
WHY YOU SHOWED UP AT THE MEET EARLY.
WHY YOU SEDUCED ME.
I NEEDED TO KNOW WHOEVER ENDED UP ON TOP... WHEN THE SMOKE CLEARED, NEEDED TO KNOW I'D BE COVERED.
TRUSTING ONE PERSON WITH THE ENTIRE BAG IS A MOTHERFUCKER.
YOU KNOW, IT'S NOT LIKE THAT NOW.
YOU KNOW THAT, RIGHT?
THAT SO?
IT IS SO.

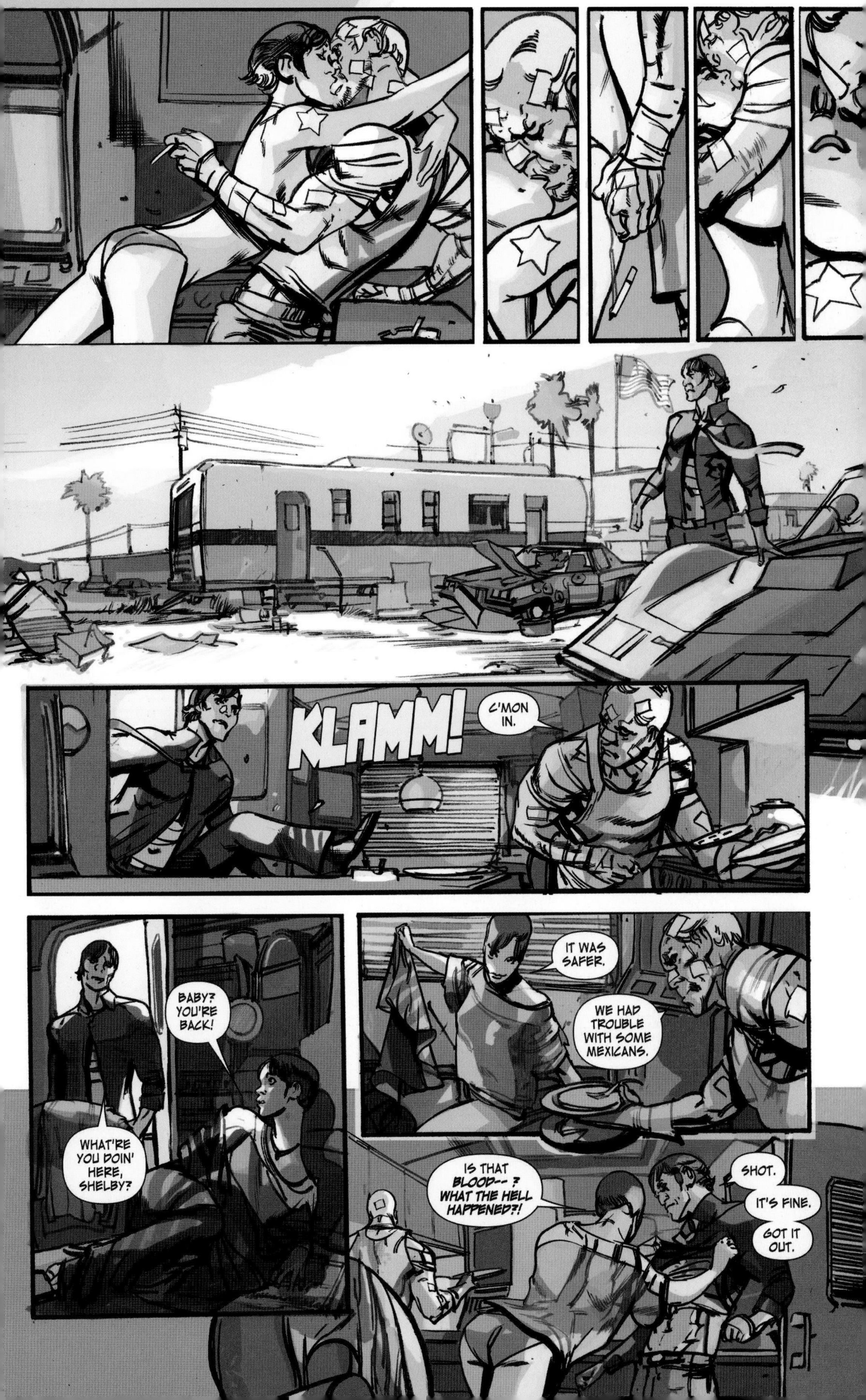
KLAMM!
C'MON IN.
BABY? YOU'RE BACK!
WHAT'RE YOU DOIN' HERE, SHELBY?
IT WAS SAFER.
WE HAD TROUBLE WITH SOME MEXICANS.
IS THAT BLOOD-- ? WHAT THE HELL HAPPENED?!
SHOT.
IT'S FINE.
GOT IT OUT.

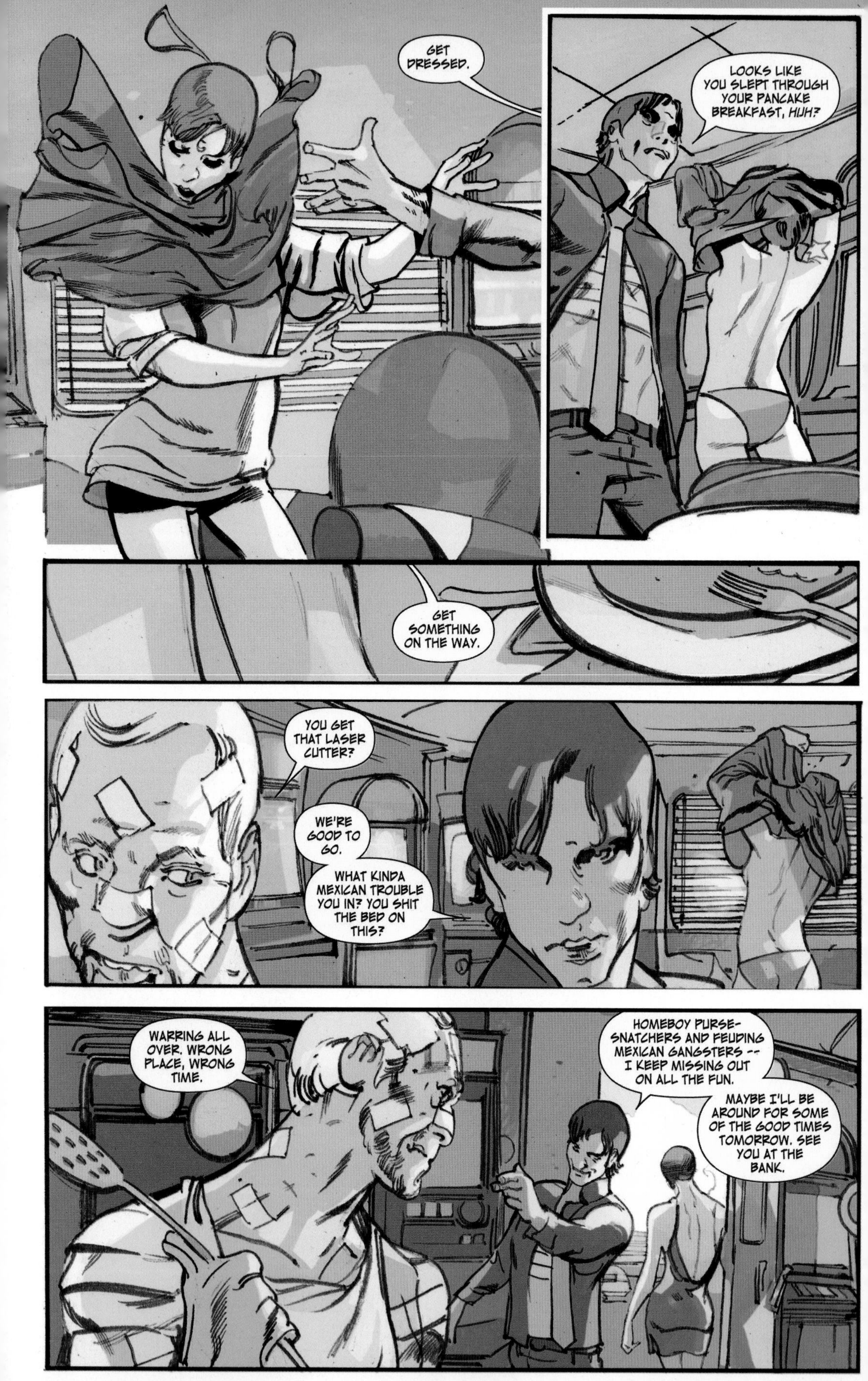
GET DRESSED.
LOOKS LIKE YOU SLEPT THROUGH YOUR PANCAKE BREAKFAST, HUH?
GET SOMETHING ON THE WAY.
YOU GET THAT LASER CUTTER?
WE'RE GOOD TO GO.
WHAT KINDA MEXICAN TROUBLE YOU IN? YOU SHIT THE BED ON THIS?
WARRING ALL OVER. WRONG PLACE, WRONG TIME.
HOMEBOY PURSE-SNATCHERS AND FEUDING MEXICAN GANGSTERS -- I KEEP MISSING OUT ON ALL THE FUN.
MAYBE I'LL BE AROUND FOR SOME OF THE GOOD TIMES TOMORROW. SEE YOU AT THE BANK.

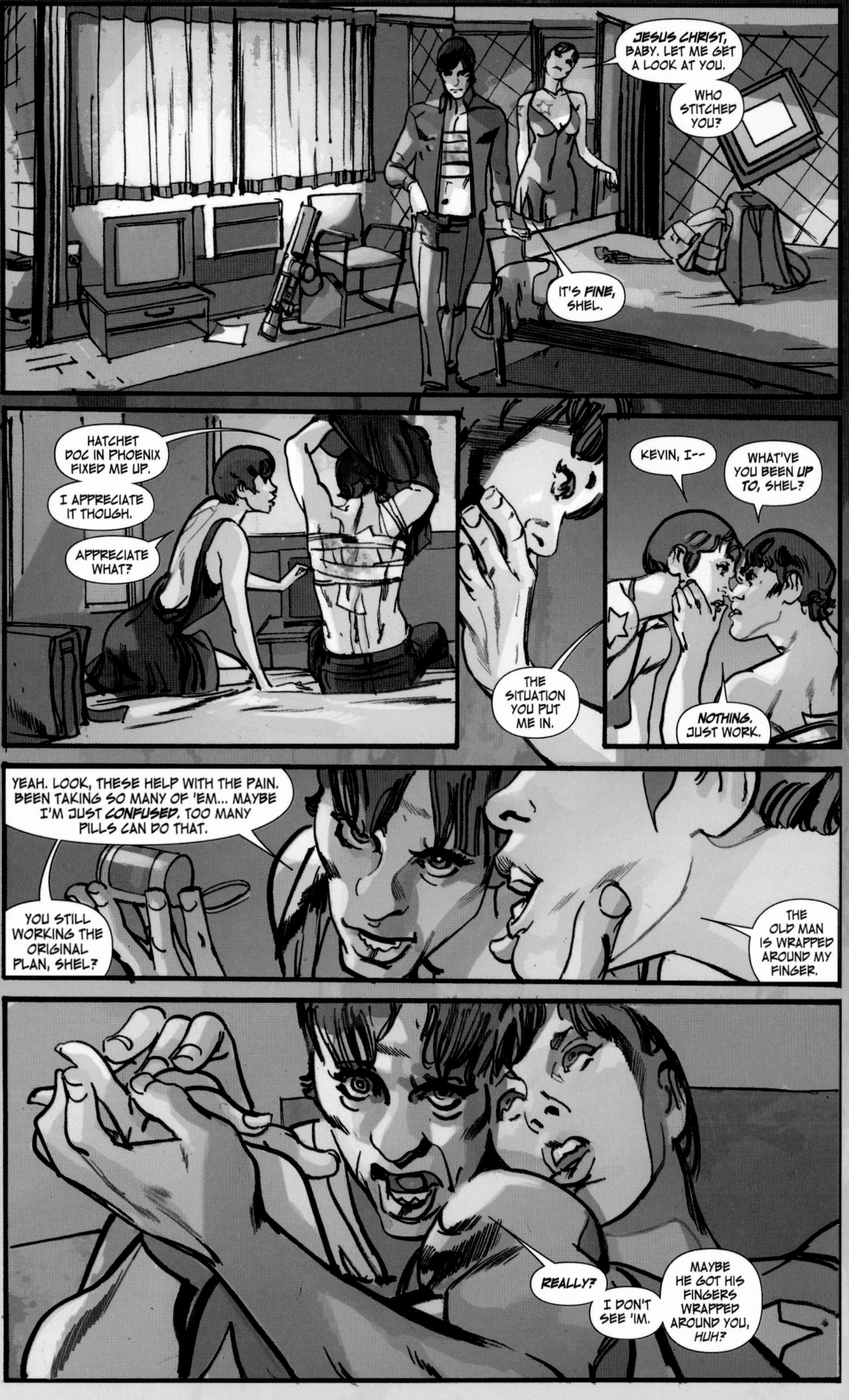
JESUS CHRIST, BABY. LET ME GET A LOOK AT YOU.
WHO STITCHED YOU?
IT'S FINE, SHEL.
HATCHET DOC IN PHOENIX FIXED ME UP.
I APPRECIATE IT THOUGH.
APPRECIATE WHAT?
THE SITUATION YOU PUT ME IN.
KEVIN, I--
WHAT'VE YOU BEEN UP TO, SHEL?
NOTHING. JUST WORK.
YEAH. LOOK, THESE HELP WITH THE PAIN. BEEN TAKING SO MANY OF 'EM... MAYBE I'M JUST CONFUSED. TOO MANY PILLS CAN DO THAT.
YOU STILL WORKING THE ORIGINAL PLAN, SHEL?
THE OLD MAN IS WRAPPED AROUND MY FINGER.
REALLY?
I DON'T SEE 'IM.
MAYBE HE GOT HIS FINGERS WRAPPED AROUND YOU, HUH?

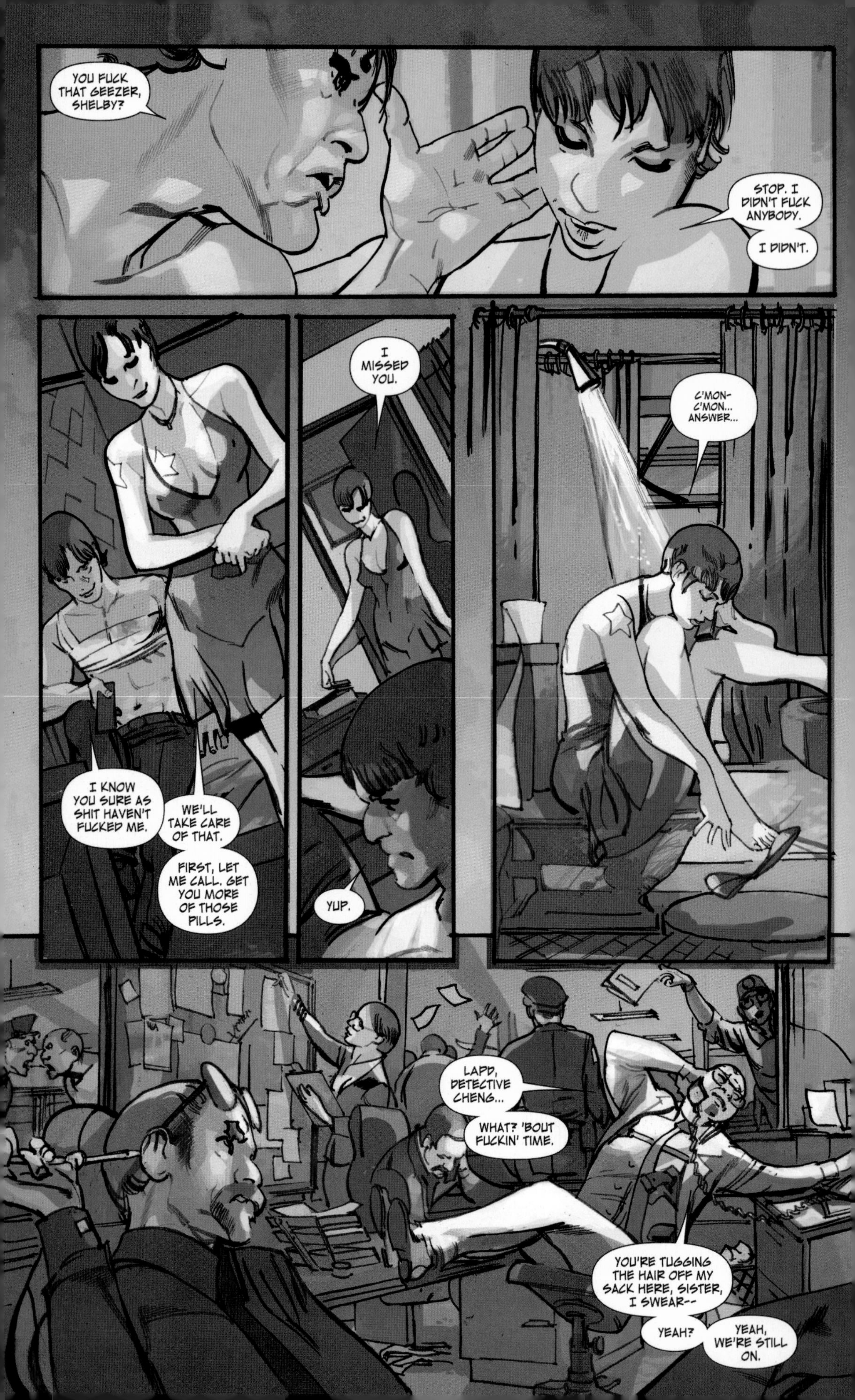

YOU FUCK THAT GEEZER, SHELBY?
STOP. I DIDN'T FUCK ANYBODY.
I DIDN'T.
I KNOW YOU SURE AS SHIT HAVEN'T FUCKED ME.
WE'LL TAKE CARE OF THAT.
FIRST, LET ME CALL. GET YOU MORE OF THOSE PILLS.
I MISSED YOU.
YUP.
C'MON-C'MON... ANSWER...
LAPD, DETECTIVE CHENG...
WHAT? 'BOUT FUCKIN' TIME.
YOU'RE TUGGING THE HAIR OFF MY SACK HERE, SISTER, I SWEAR--
YEAH?
YEAH, WE'RE STILL ON.

EVENING OF THE BROADCAST

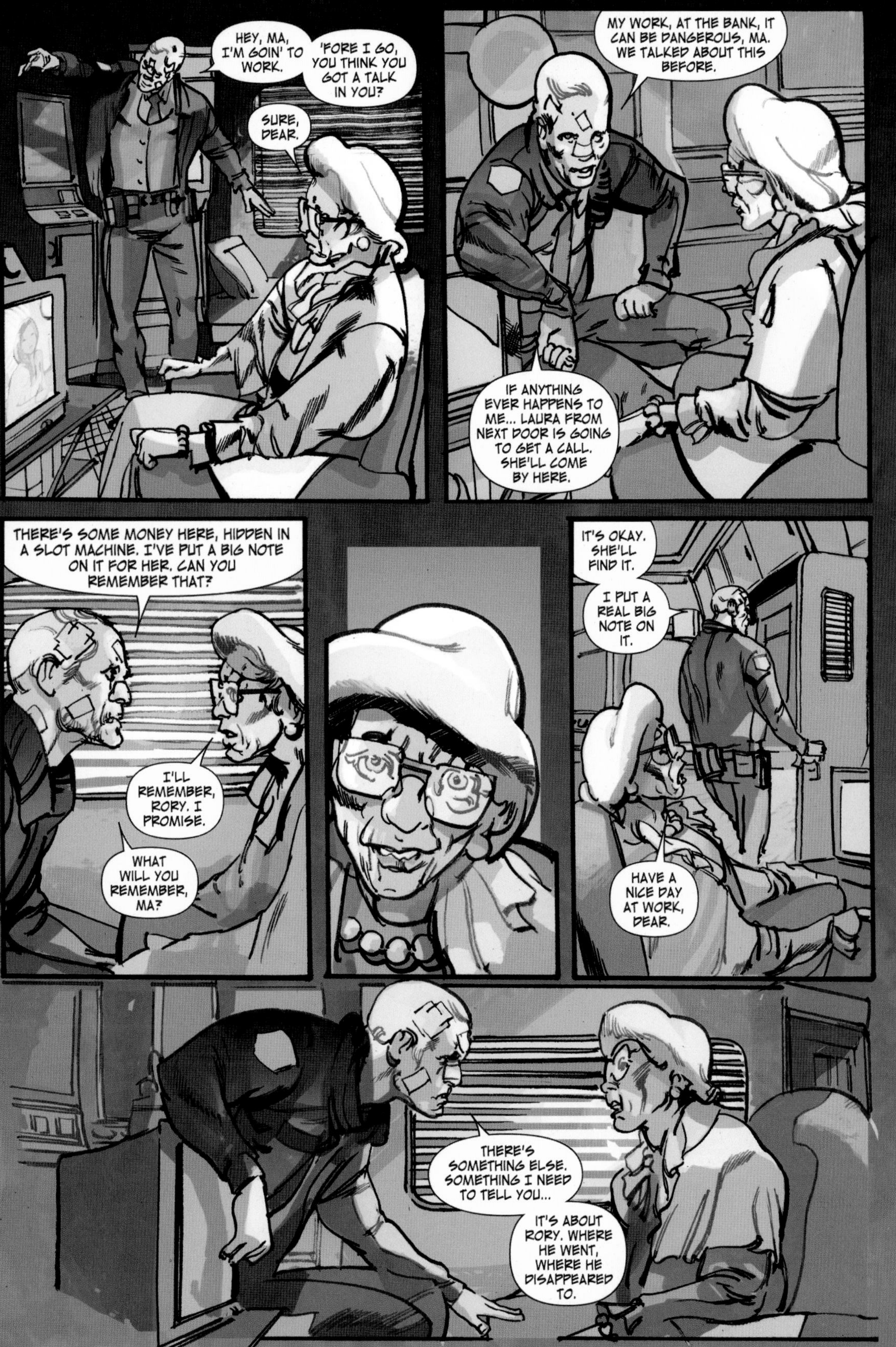
HEY, MA, I'M GOIN' TO WORK.
'FORE I GO, YOU THINK YOU GOT A TALK IN YOU?
SURE, DEAR.
MY WORK, AT THE BANK, IT CAN BE DANGEROUS, MA. WE TALKED ABOUT THIS BEFORE.
IF ANYTHING EVER HAPPENS TO ME... LAURA FROM NEXT DOOR IS GOING TO GET A CALL. SHE'LL COME BY HERE.
THERE'S SOME MONEY HERE, HIDDEN IN A SLOT MACHINE. I'VE PUT A BIG NOTE ON IT FOR HER. CAN YOU REMEMBER THAT?
I'LL REMEMBER, RORY. I PROMISE.
WHAT WILL YOU REMEMBER, MA?
IT'S OKAY. SHE'LL FIND IT.
I PUT A REAL BIG NOTE ON IT.
HAVE A NICE DAY AT WORK, DEAR.
THERE'S SOMETHING ELSE. SOMETHING I NEED TO TELL YOU...
IT'S ABOUT RORY. WHERE HE WENT, WHERE HE DISAPPEARED TO.

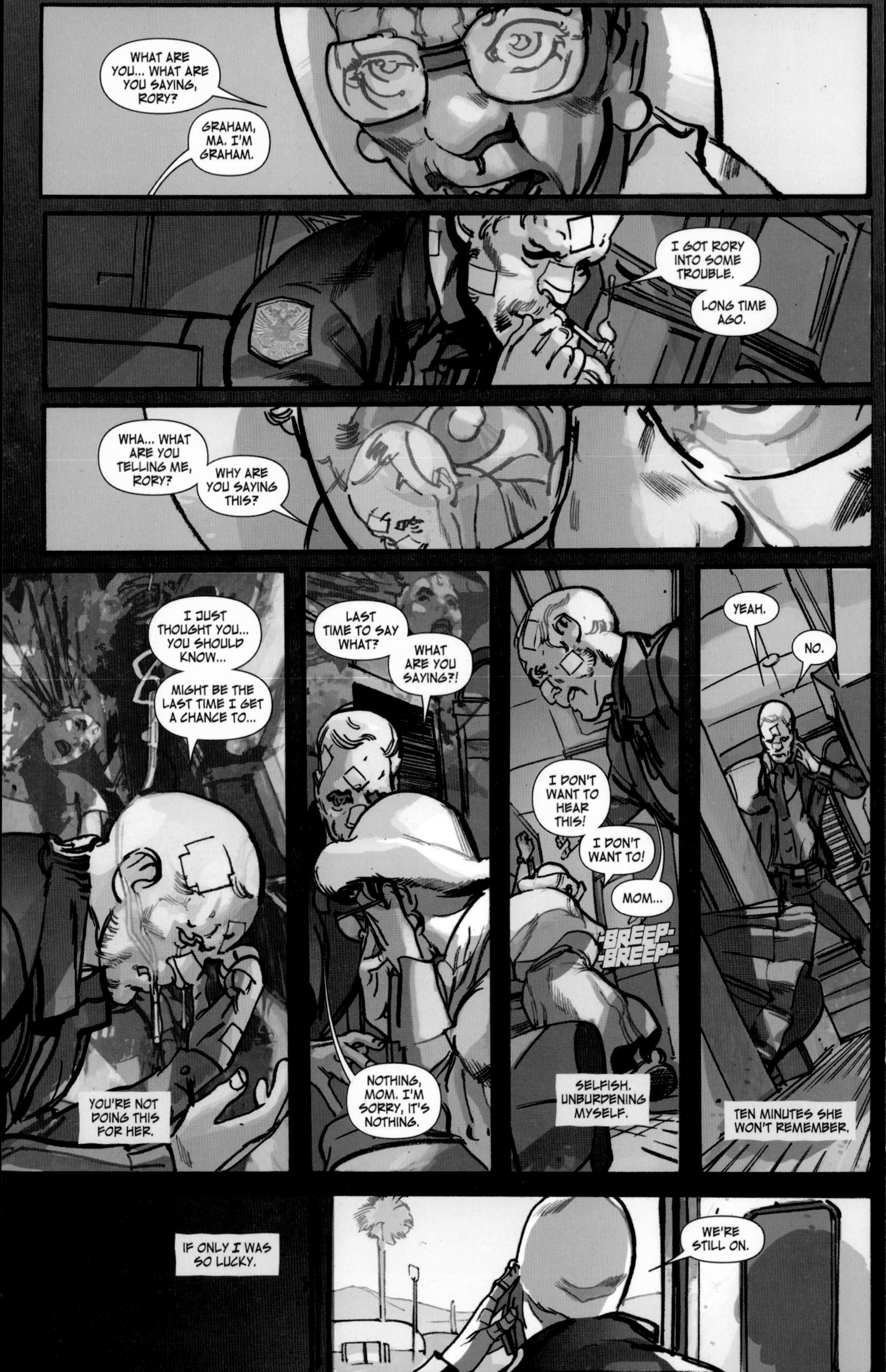
WHAT ARE YOU... WHAT ARE YOU SAYING, RORY?
GRAHAM, MA. I'M GRAHAM.
I GOT RORY INTO SOME TROUBLE.
LONG TIME AGO.
WHA... WHAT ARE YOU TELLING ME, RORY?
WHY ARE YOU SAYING THIS?
I JUST THOUGHT YOU... YOU SHOULD KNOW...
MIGHT BE THE LAST TIME I GET A CHANCE TO...
YOU'RE NOT DOING THIS FOR HER.
LAST TIME TO SAY WHAT?
WHAT ARE YOU SAYING?!
NOTHING, MOM. I'M SORRY, IT'S NOTHING.
I DON'T WANT TO HEAR THIS!
I DON'T WANT TO!
MOM...
-BREEP- -BREEP-
SELFISH. UNBURDENING MYSELF.
YEAH.
NO.
TEN MINUTES SHE WON'T REMEMBER.
IF ONLY I WAS SO LUCKY.
WE'RE STILL ON.

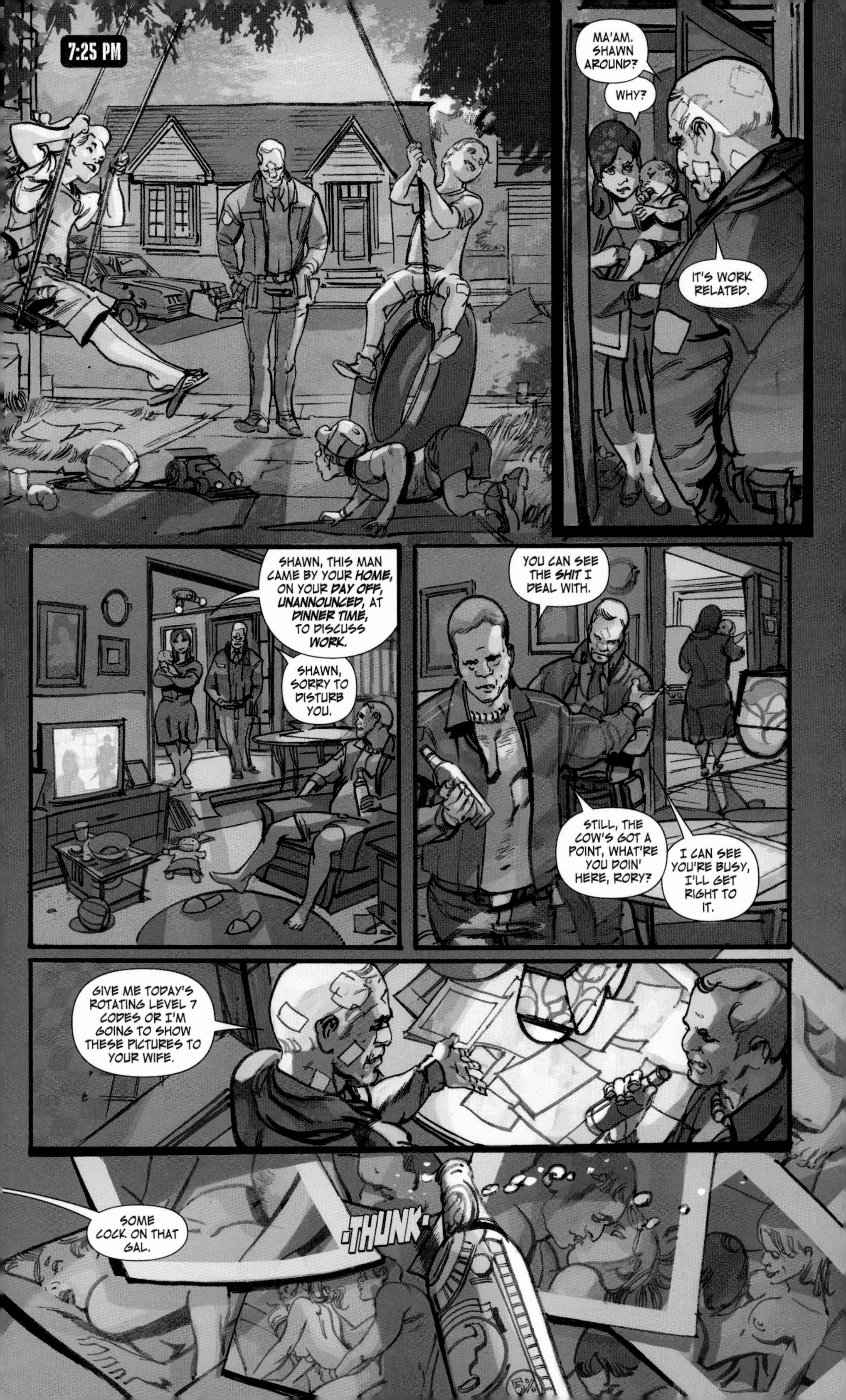
7:25 PM
MA'AM. SHAWN AROUND?
WHY?
IT'S WORK RELATED.
SHAWN, THIS MAN CAME BY YOUR HOME, ON YOUR DAY OFF, UNANNOUNCED, AT DINNER TIME, TO DISCUSS WORK.
SHAWN, SORRY TO DISTURB YOU.
YOU CAN SEE THE SHIT I DEAL WITH.
STILL, THE COW'S GOT A POINT, WHAT'RE YOU DOIN' HERE, RORY?
I CAN SEE YOU'RE BUSY, I'LL GET RIGHT TO IT.
GIVE ME TODAY'S ROTATING LEVEL 7 CODES OR I'M GOING TO SHOW THESE PICTURES TO YOUR WIFE.
SOME COCK ON THAT GAL.
THUNK

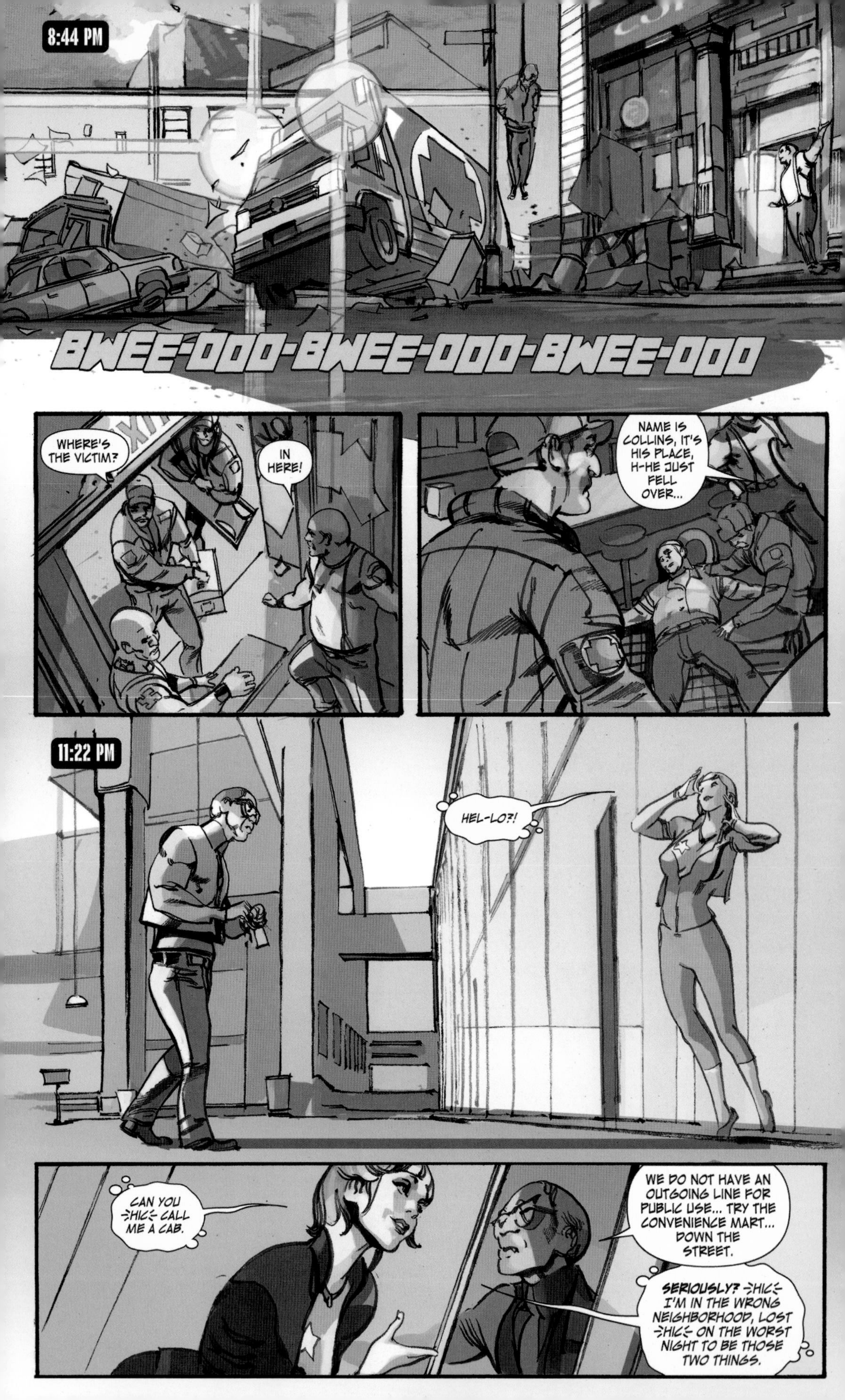
8:44 PM
BWEE-OOO-BWEE-OOO-BWEE-OOO
WHERE'S THE VICTIM?
IN HERE!
NAME IS COLLINS, IT'S HIS PLACE, H-HE JUST FELL OVER...
11:22 PM
HEL-LO?!
CAN YOU -HIC- CALL ME A CAB.
WE DO NOT HAVE AN OUTGOING LINE FOR PUBLIC USE... TRY THE CONVENIENCE MART... DOWN THE STREET.
SERIOUSLY? -HIC- I'M IN THE WRONG NEIGHBORHOOD, LOST -HIC- ON THE WORST NIGHT TO BE THOSE TWO THINGS.

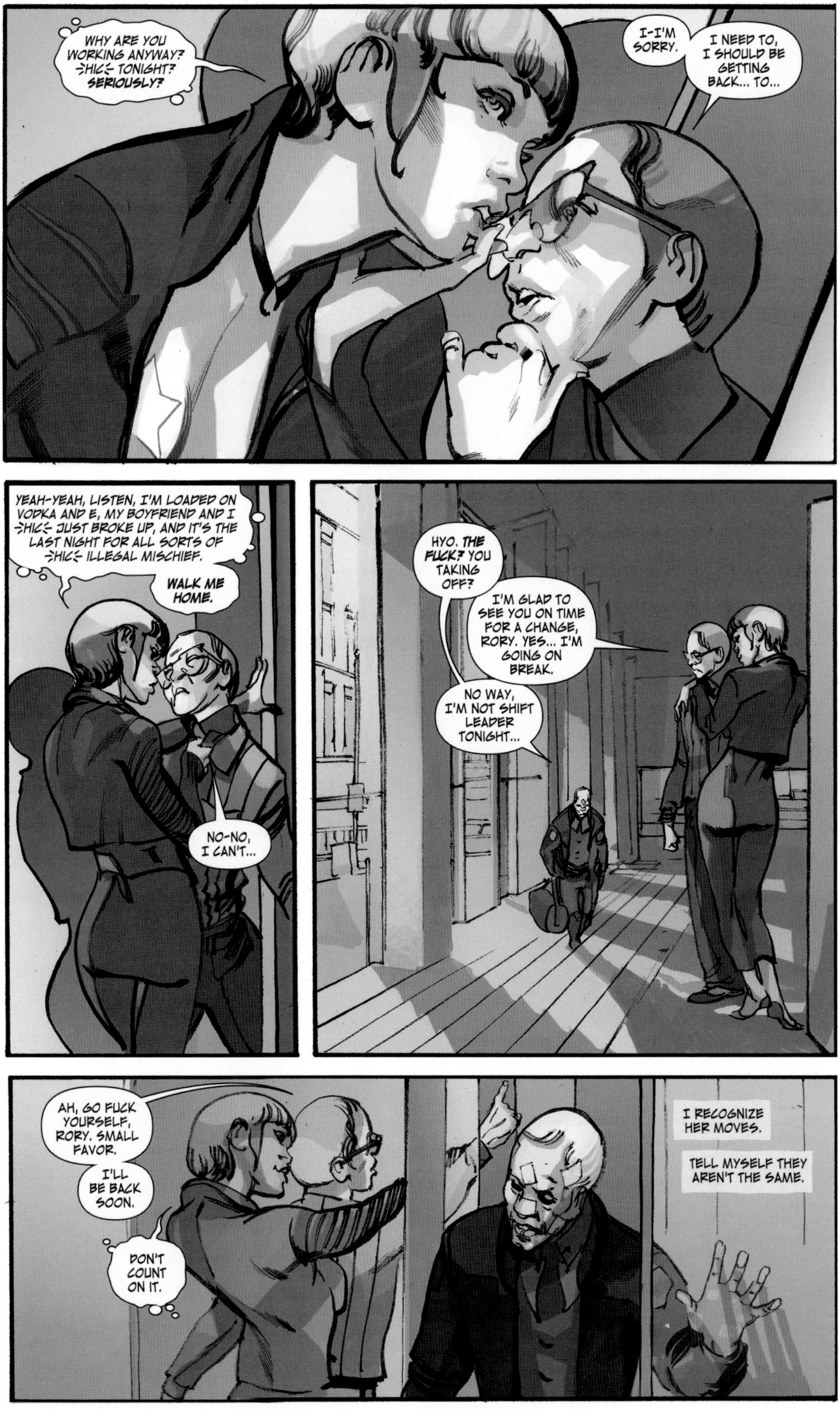

WHY ARE YOU WORKING ANYWAY? =HIC= TONIGHT? SERIOUSLY?
I-I'M SORRY.
I NEED TO, I SHOULD BE GETTING BACK... TO...
YEAH-YEAH, LISTEN, I'M LOADED ON VODKA AND E, MY BOYFRIEND AND I =HIC= JUST BROKE UP, AND IT'S THE LAST NIGHT FOR ALL SORTS OF =HIC= ILLEGAL MISCHIEF.
WALK ME HOME.
NO-NO, I CAN'T...
HYO. THE FUCK? YOU TAKING OFF?
I'M GLAD TO SEE YOU ON TIME FOR A CHANGE, RORY. YES... I'M GOING ON BREAK.
NO WAY, I'M NOT SHIFT LEADER TONIGHT...
AH, GO FUCK YOURSELF, RORY. SMALL FAVOR.
I'LL BE BACK SOON.
DON'T COUNT ON IT.
I RECOGNIZE HER MOVES.
TELL MYSELF THEY AREN'T THE SAME.

TELL MYSELF ALL SORTS OF BULLSHIT.

DID I JUST SEE HYO WITH THAT INCREDIBLE-*FUCKING*-REDHEAD?

TELL ME THAT LITTLE *BOOGER* DIDN'T JUST LEAVE WITH THAT GIRL. TELL ME, RORY.

WISH I COULD.

YOU KNOW, I'M GONNA HAVE A SMOKE BEFORE SHIFT.

FUCK IT. WHY NOT. CAT'S AWAY...

REAL NERVES. BAD INSTINCTS.

ALMOST HOPE THE GEEK GOES COLONEL SANDERS.

JUST CALLS IT OFF. NO SHAME IN IT.

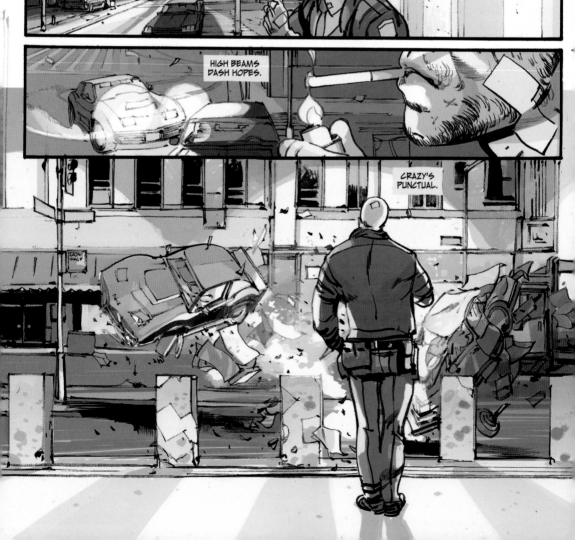

HIGH BEAMS DASH HOPES.

CRAZY'S PUNCTUAL.

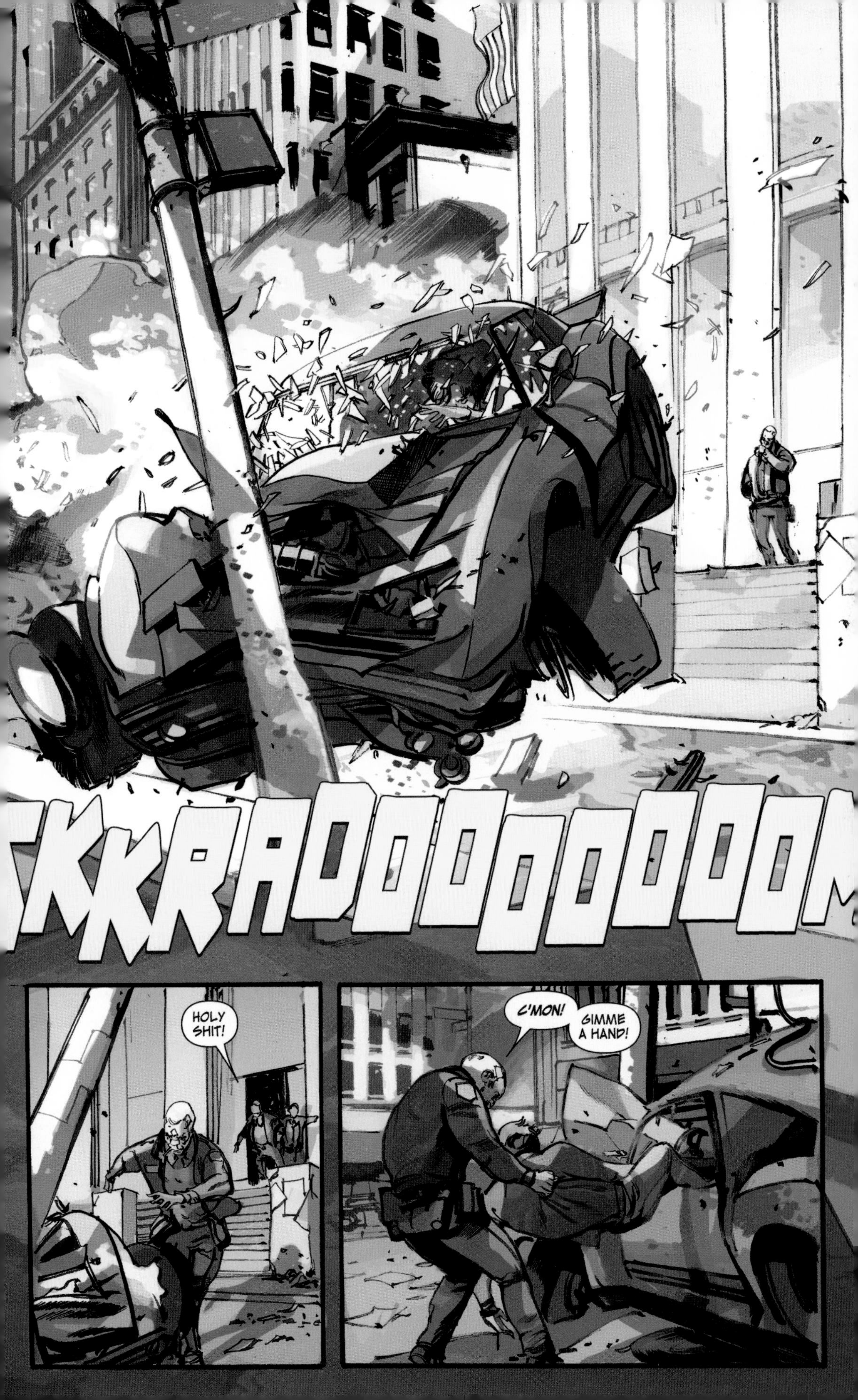
KKRAOOOOOOOOOM
HOLY SHIT!
C'MON!
GIMME A HAND!

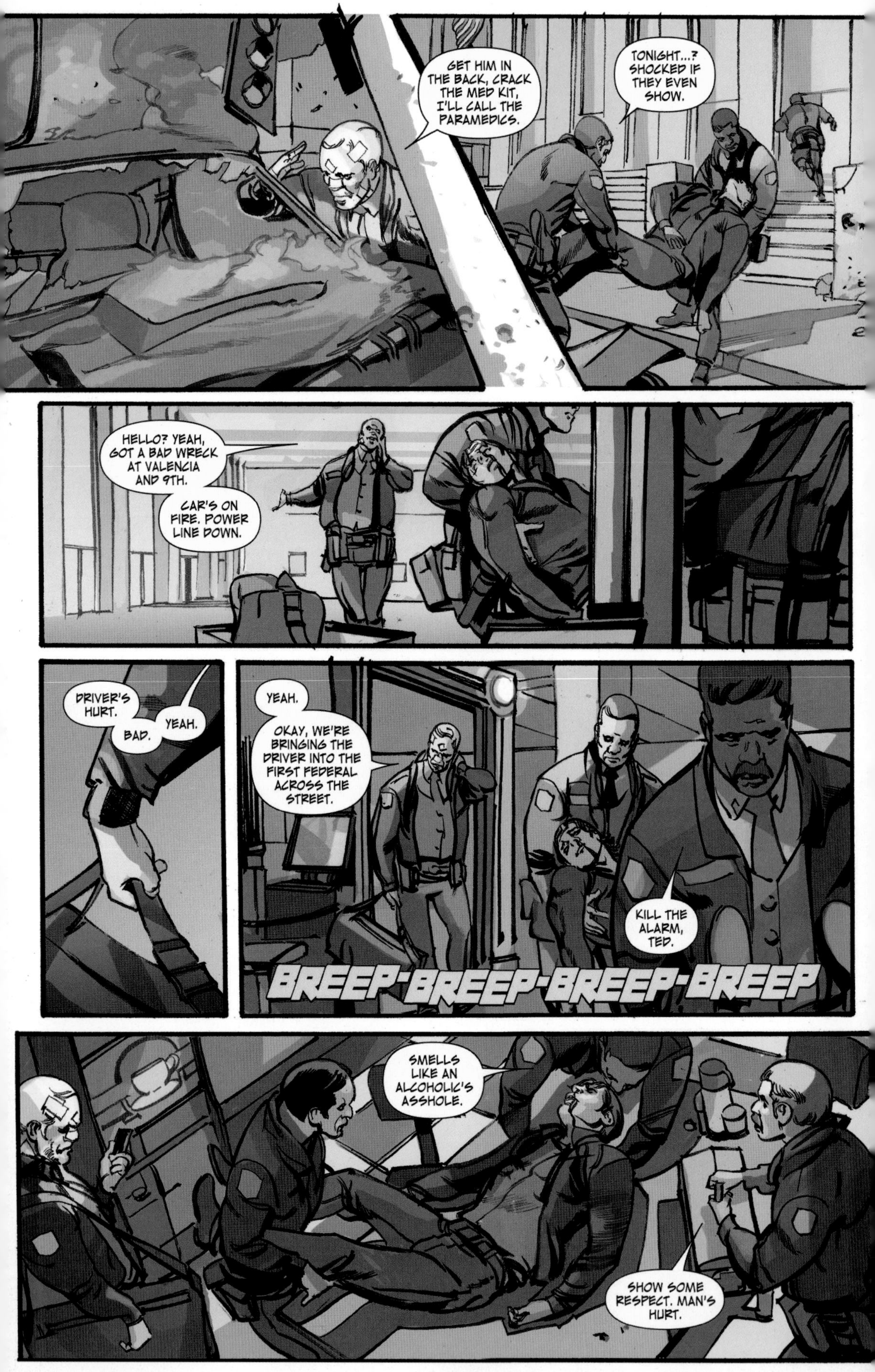
GET HIM IN THE BACK, CRACK THE MED KIT, I'LL CALL THE PARAMEDICS.
TONIGHT...? SHOCKED IF THEY EVEN SHOW.
HELLO? YEAH, GOT A BAD WRECK AT VALENCIA AND 9TH.
CAR'S ON FIRE. POWER LINE DOWN.
DRIVER'S HURT.
BAD.
YEAH.
YEAH.
OKAY, WE'RE BRINGING THE DRIVER INTO THE FIRST FEDERAL ACROSS THE STREET.
KILL THE ALARM, TED.
BREEP-BREEP-BREEP-BREEP
SMELLS LIKE AN ALCOHOLIC'S ASSHOLE.
SHOW SOME RESPECT. MAN'S HURT.

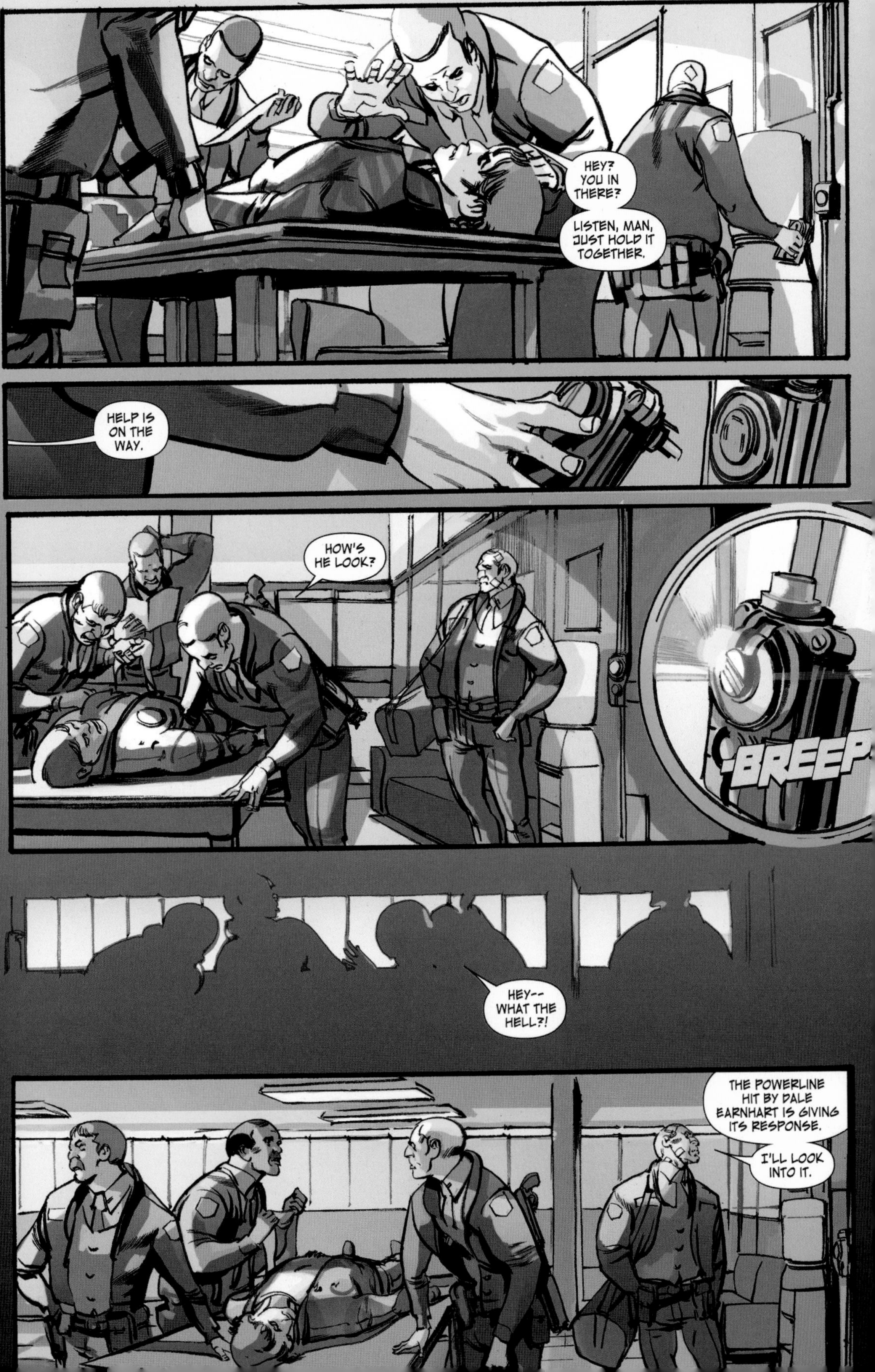
HEY? YOU IN THERE?
LISTEN, MAN, JUST HOLD IT TOGETHER.
HELP IS ON THE WAY.
HOW'S HE LOOK?
BREEP
HEY-- WHAT THE HELL?!
THE POWERLINE HIT BY DALE EARNHART IS GIVING ITS RESPONSE.
I'LL LOOK INTO IT.

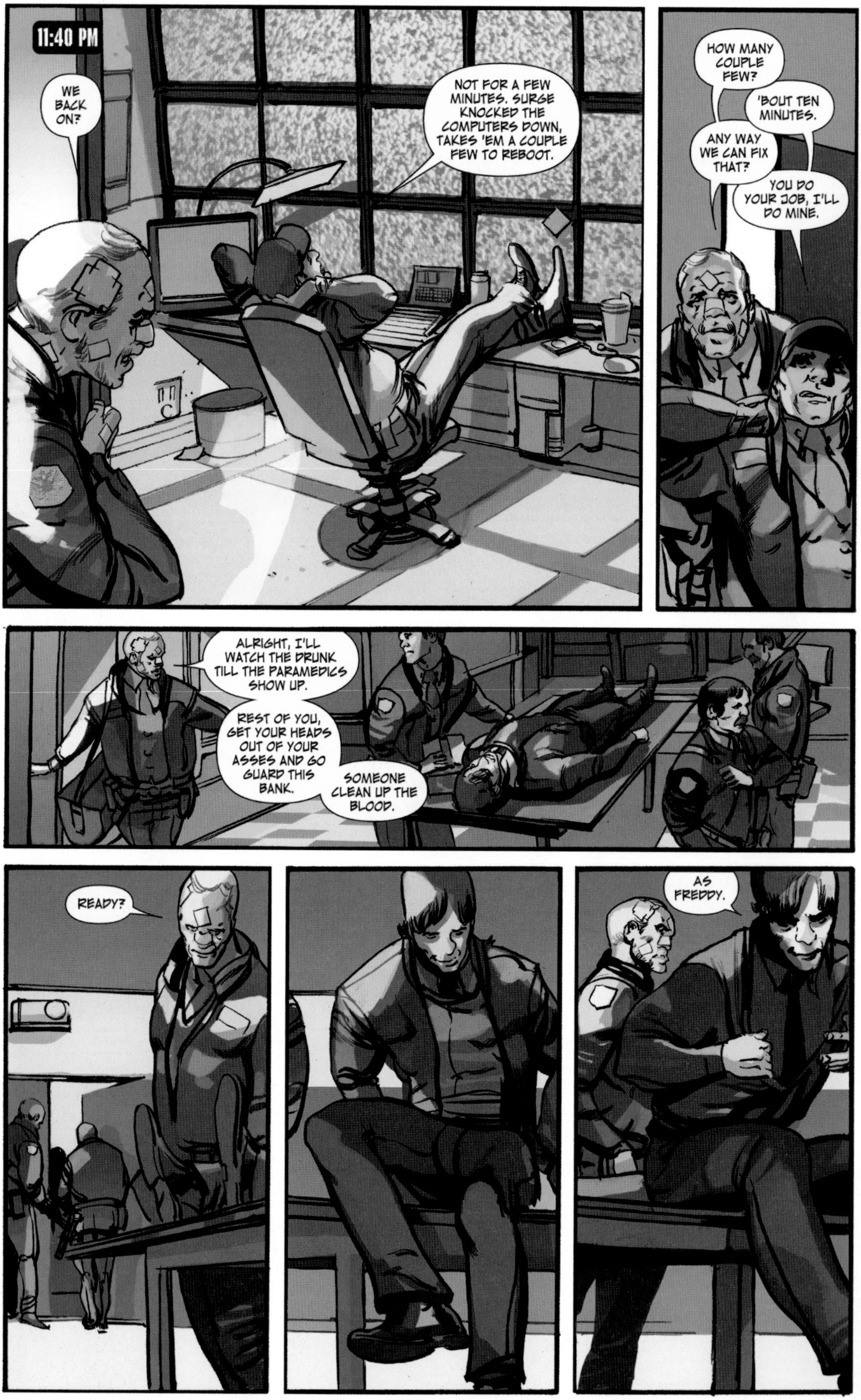
11:40 PM
WE BACK ON?
NOT FOR A FEW MINUTES. SURGE KNOCKED THE COMPUTERS DOWN, TAKES 'EM A COUPLE FEW TO REBOOT.
HOW MANY COUPLE FEW?
'BOUT TEN MINUTES.
ANY WAY WE CAN FIX THAT?
YOU DO YOUR JOB, I'LL DO MINE.
ALRIGHT, I'LL WATCH THE DRUNK TILL THE PARAMEDICS SHOW UP.
REST OF YOU, GET YOUR HEADS OUT OF YOUR ASSES AND GO GUARD THIS BANK.
SOMEONE CLEAN UP THE BLOOD.
READY?
AS FREDDY.

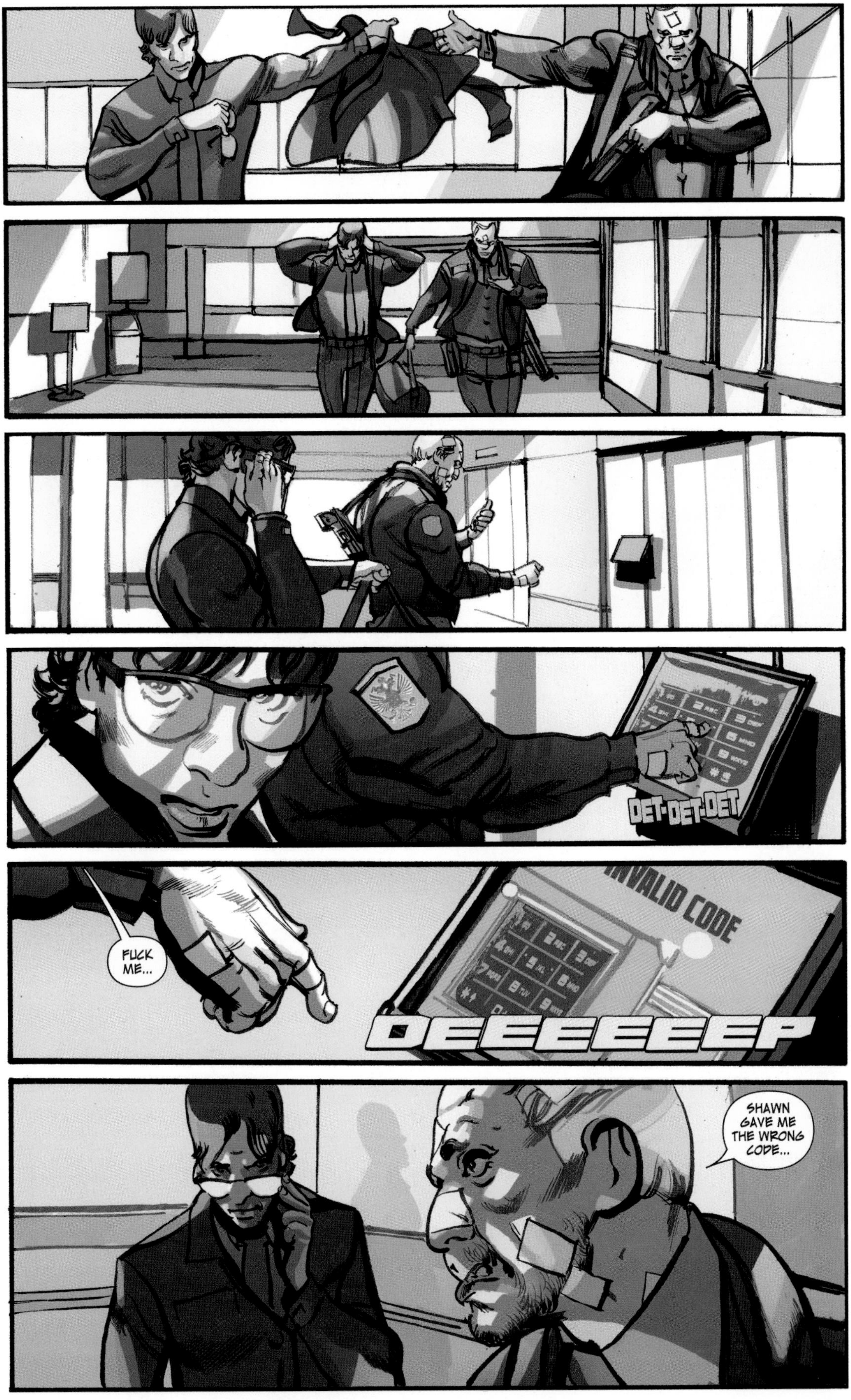
DET-DET-DET
INVALID CODE
FUCK ME...
DEEEEEEEP
SHAWN GAVE ME THE WRONG CODE...

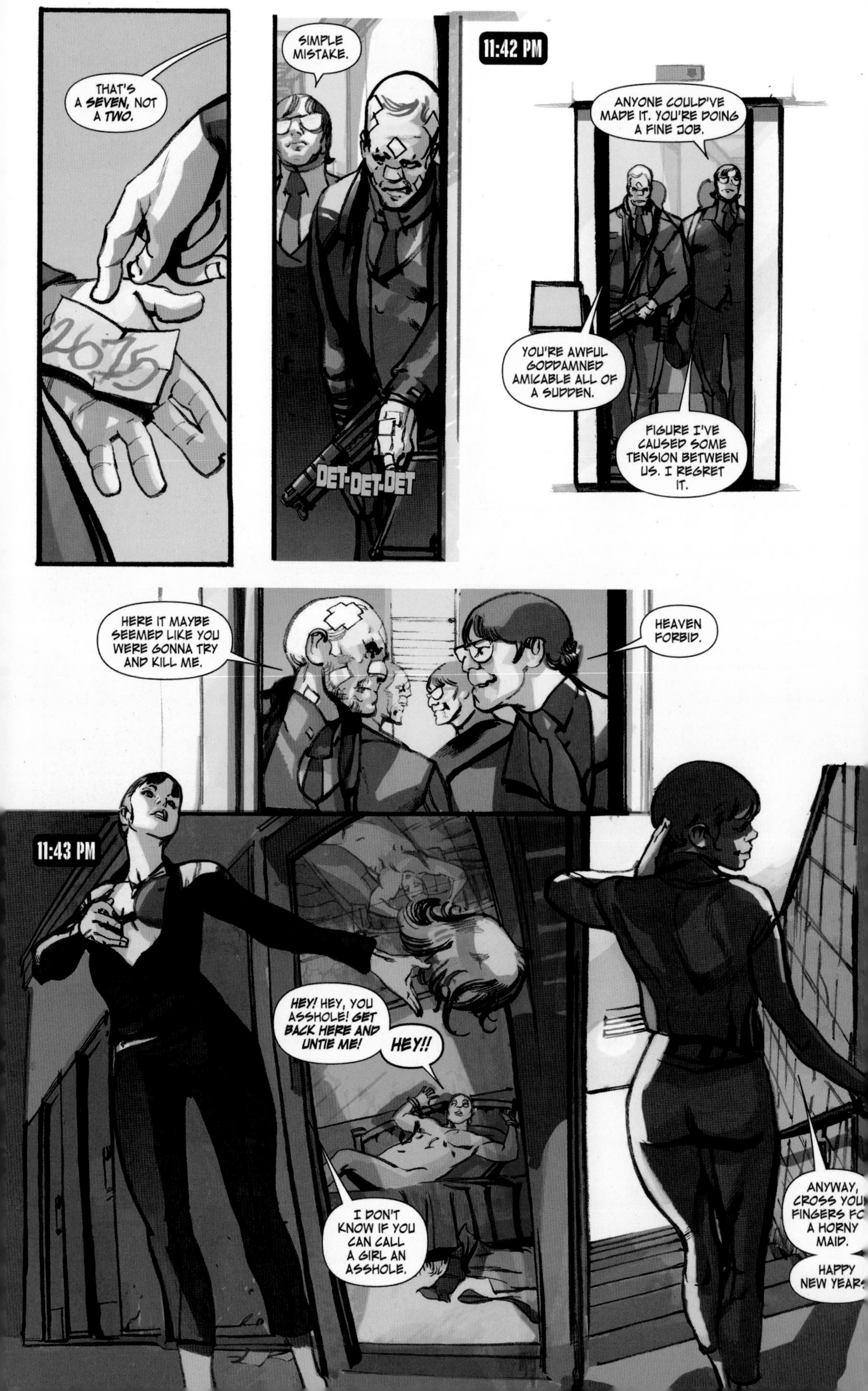
THAT'S A *SEVEN,* NOT A *TWO.*
2615
SIMPLE MISTAKE.
DET-DET-DET
11:42 PM
ANYONE COULD'VE MADE IT. YOU'RE DOING A FINE JOB.
YOU'RE AWFUL GODDAMNED AMICABLE ALL OF A SUDDEN.
FIGURE I'VE CAUSED SOME TENSION BETWEEN US. I REGRET IT.
HERE IT MAYBE SEEMED LIKE YOU WERE GONNA TRY AND KILL ME.
HEAVEN FORBID.
11:43 PM
HEY! HEY, YOU ASSHOLE! *GET BACK HERE AND UNTIE ME!*
HEY!!
I DON'T KNOW IF YOU CAN CALL A GIRL AN ASSHOLE.
ANYWAY, CROSS YOU FINGERS FO A HORNY MAID.
HAPPY NEW YEAR

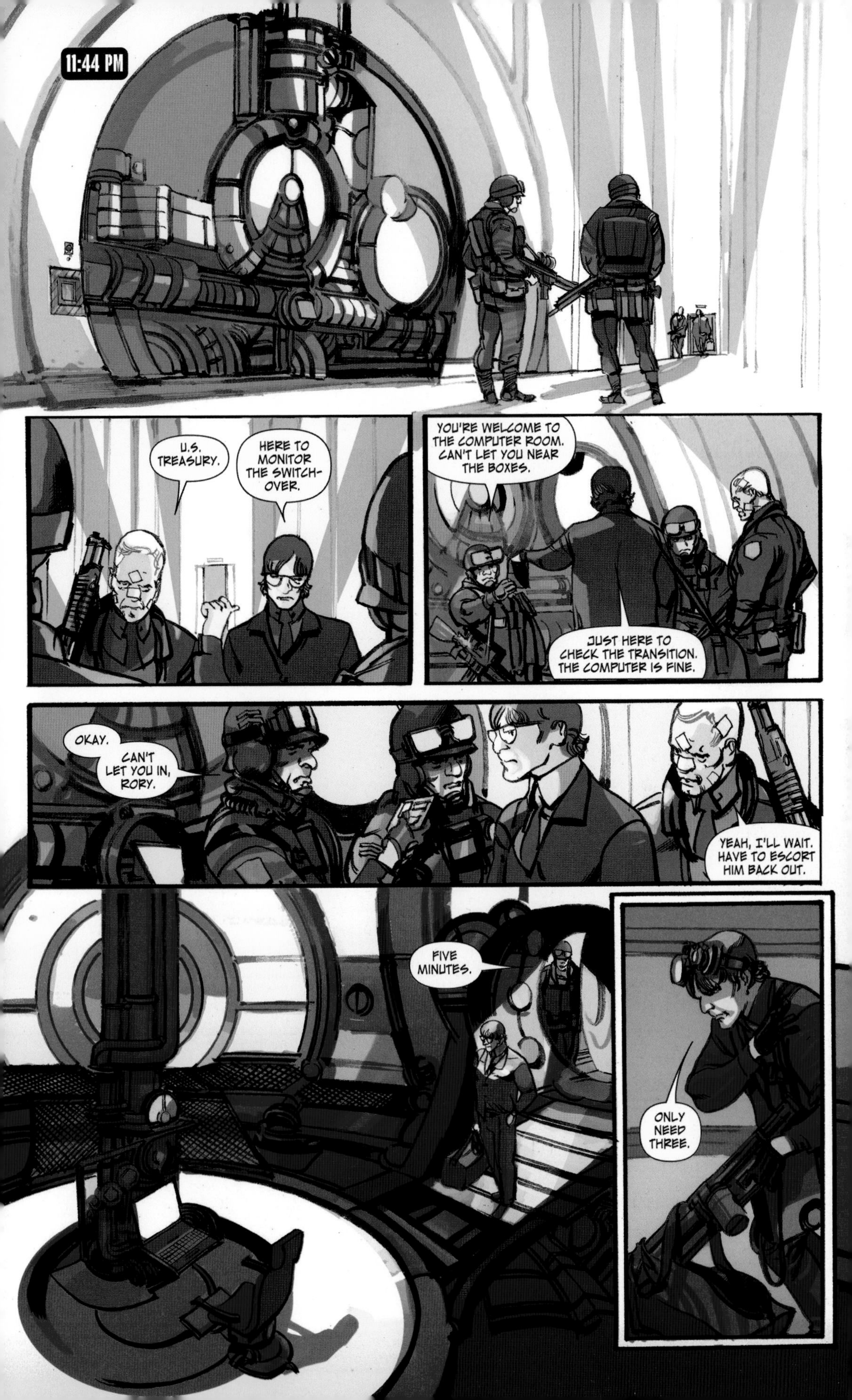
11:44 PM
U.S. TREASURY.
HERE TO MONITOR THE SWITCH-OVER.
YOU'RE WELCOME TO THE COMPUTER ROOM. CAN'T LET YOU NEAR THE BOXES.
JUST HERE TO CHECK THE TRANSITION. THE COMPUTER IS FINE.
OKAY.
CAN'T LET YOU IN, RORY.
YEAH, I'LL WAIT. HAVE TO ESCORT HIM BACK OUT.
FIVE MINUTES.
ONLY NEED THREE.

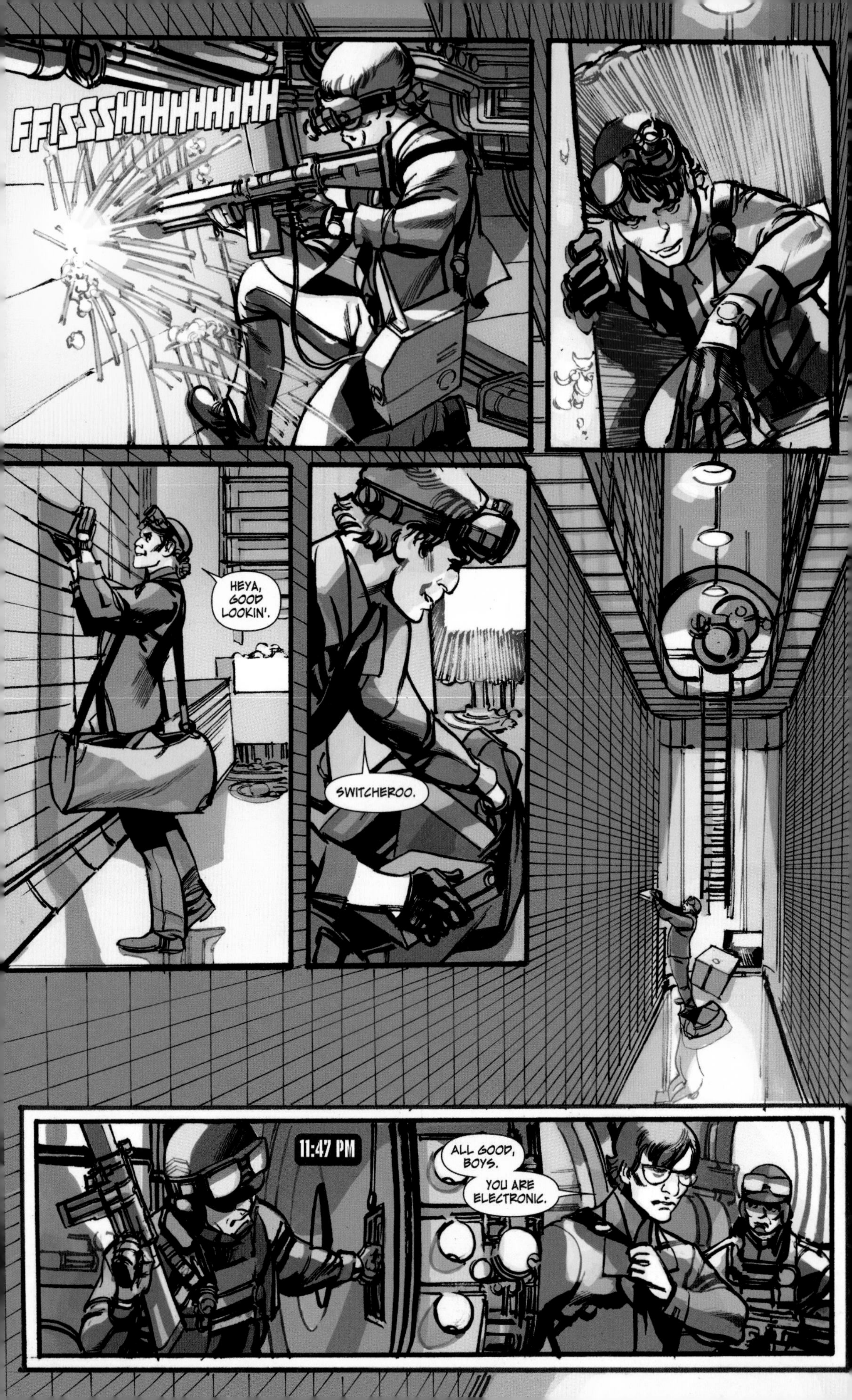
FFISSSHHHHHHHHH
HEYA, GOOD LOOKIN'.
SWITCHEROO.
11:47 PM
ALL GOOD, BOYS.
YOU ARE ELECTRONIC.

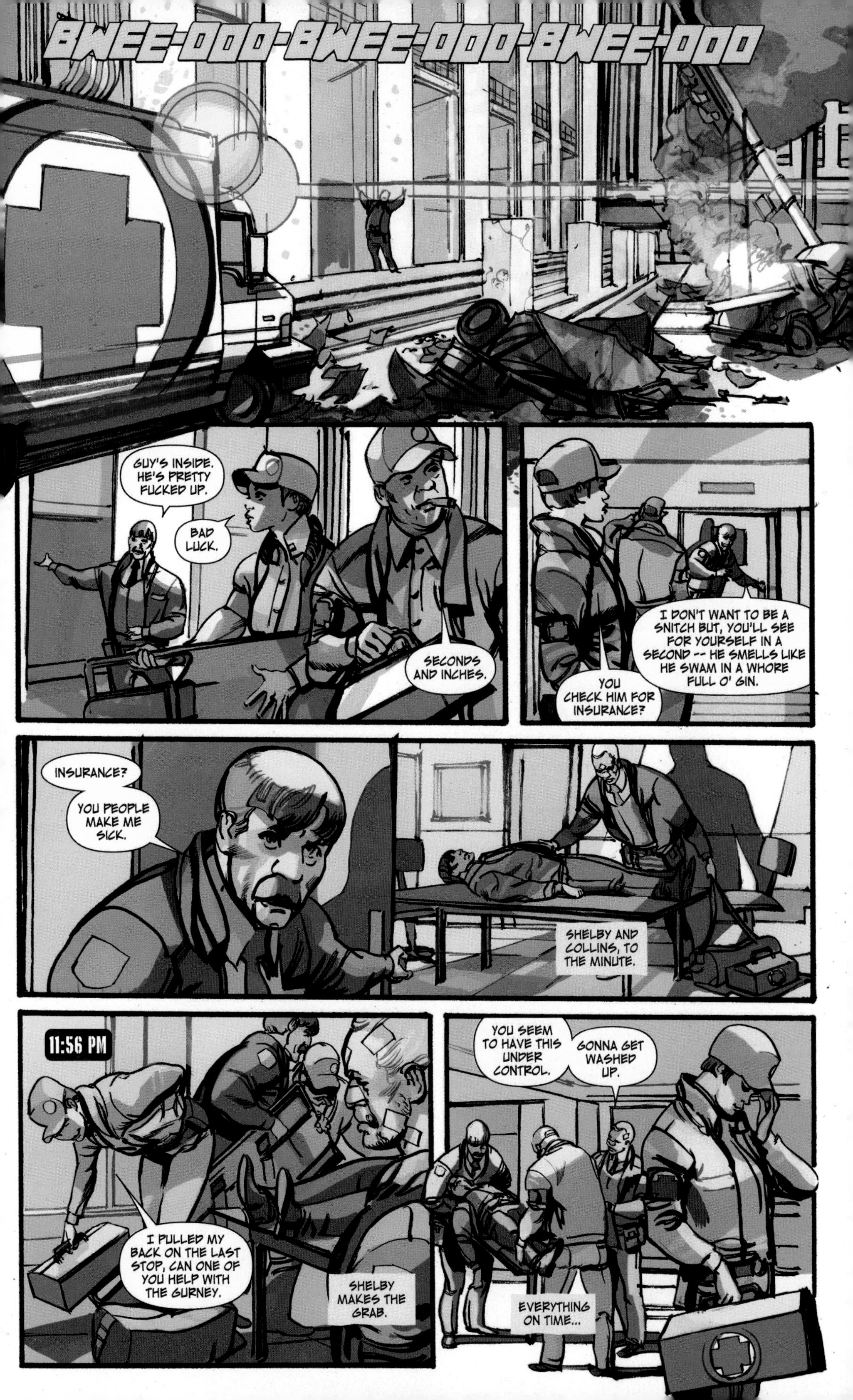
BWEE-OOO-BWEE-OOO-BWEE-OOO
GUY'S INSIDE. HE'S PRETTY FUCKED UP.
BAD LUCK.
SECONDS AND INCHES.
YOU CHECK HIM FOR INSURANCE?
I DON'T WANT TO BE A SNITCH BUT, YOU'LL SEE FOR YOURSELF IN A SECOND -- HE SMELLS LIKE HE SWAM IN A WHORE FULL O' GIN.
INSURANCE?
YOU PEOPLE MAKE ME SICK.
SHELBY AND COLLINS, TO THE MINUTE.
11:56 PM
I PULLED MY BACK ON THE LAST STOP, CAN ONE OF YOU HELP WITH THE GURNEY.
SHELBY MAKES THE GRAB.
YOU SEEM TO HAVE THIS UNDER CONTROL.
GONNA GET WASHED UP.
EVERYTHING ON TIME...

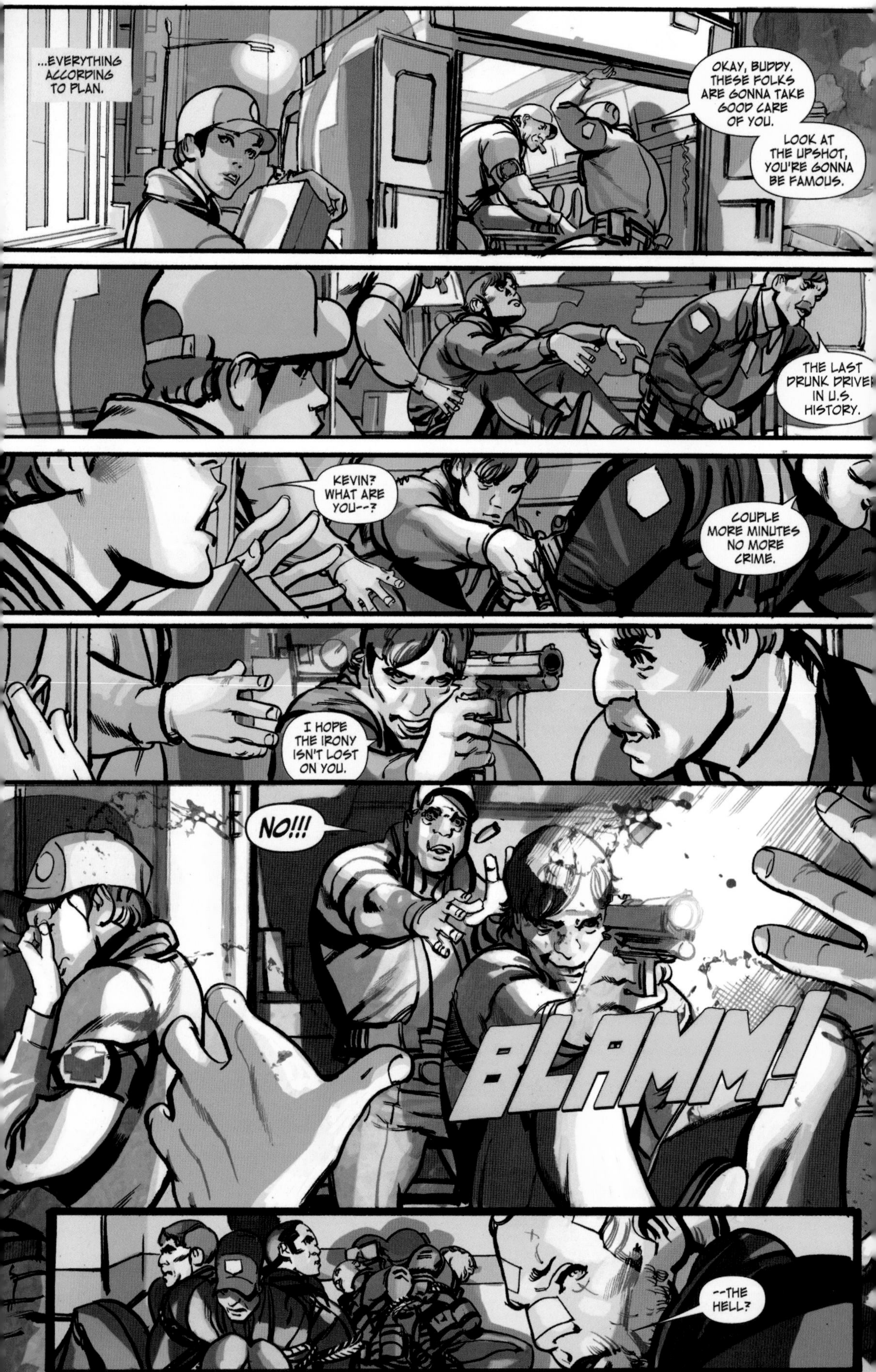
...EVERYTHING ACCORDING TO PLAN.
OKAY, BUDDY. THESE FOLKS ARE GONNA TAKE GOOD CARE OF YOU.
LOOK AT THE UPSHOT, YOU'RE GONNA BE FAMOUS.
THE LAST DRUNK DRIVER IN U.S. HISTORY.
KEVIN? WHAT ARE YOU--?
COUPLE MORE MINUTES NO MORE CRIME.
I HOPE THE IRONY ISN'T LOST ON YOU.
NO!!!
BLAMM!
--THE HELL?

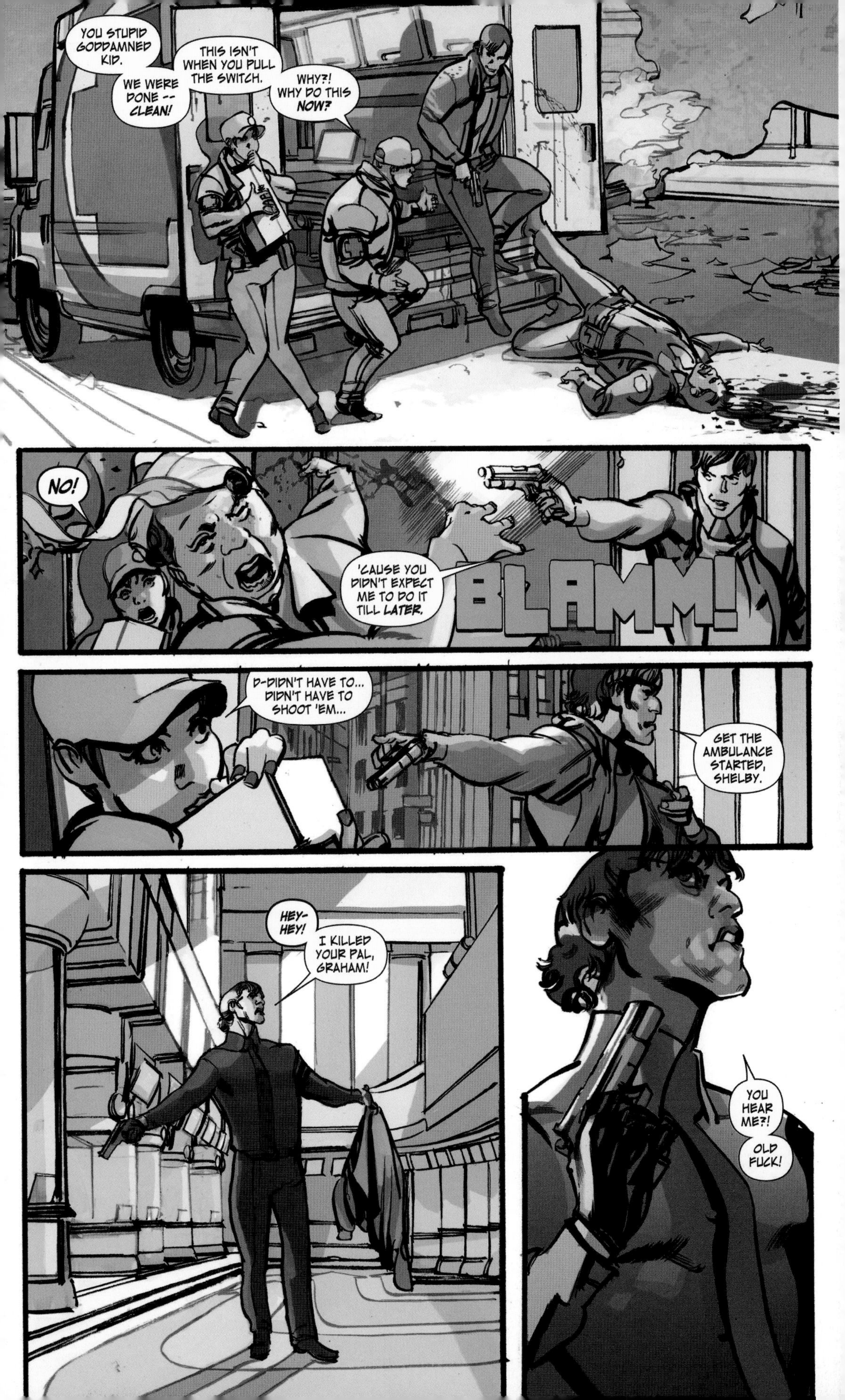
YOU STUPID GODDAMNED KID.
WE WERE DONE -- CLEAN!
THIS ISN'T WHEN YOU PULL THE SWITCH.
WHY?! WHY DO THIS NOW?
NO!
'CAUSE YOU DIDN'T EXPECT ME TO DO IT TILL LATER.
BLAMM!
D-DIDN'T HAVE TO... DIDN'T HAVE TO SHOOT 'EM...
GET THE AMBULANCE STARTED, SHELBY.
HEY-HEY!
I KILLED YOUR PAL, GRAHAM!
YOU HEAR ME?!
OLD FUCK!

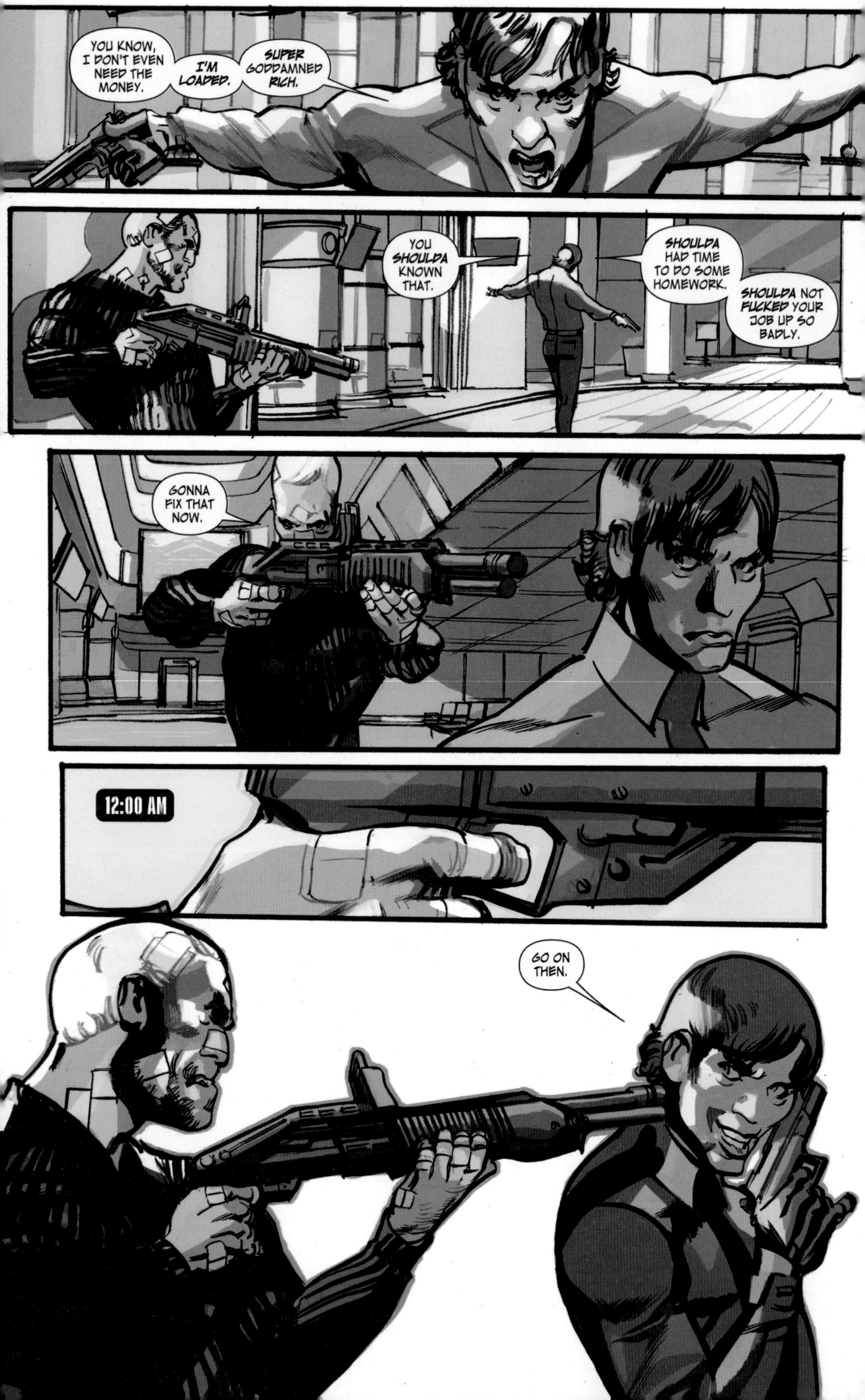
YOU KNOW, I DON'T EVEN NEED THE MONEY.
I'M LOADED.
SUPER GODDAMNED RICH.
YOU SHOULDA KNOWN THAT.
SHOULDA HAD TIME TO DO SOME HOMEWORK.
SHOULDA NOT FUCKED YOUR JOB UP SO BADLY.
GONNA FIX THAT NOW.
12:00 AM
GO ON THEN.

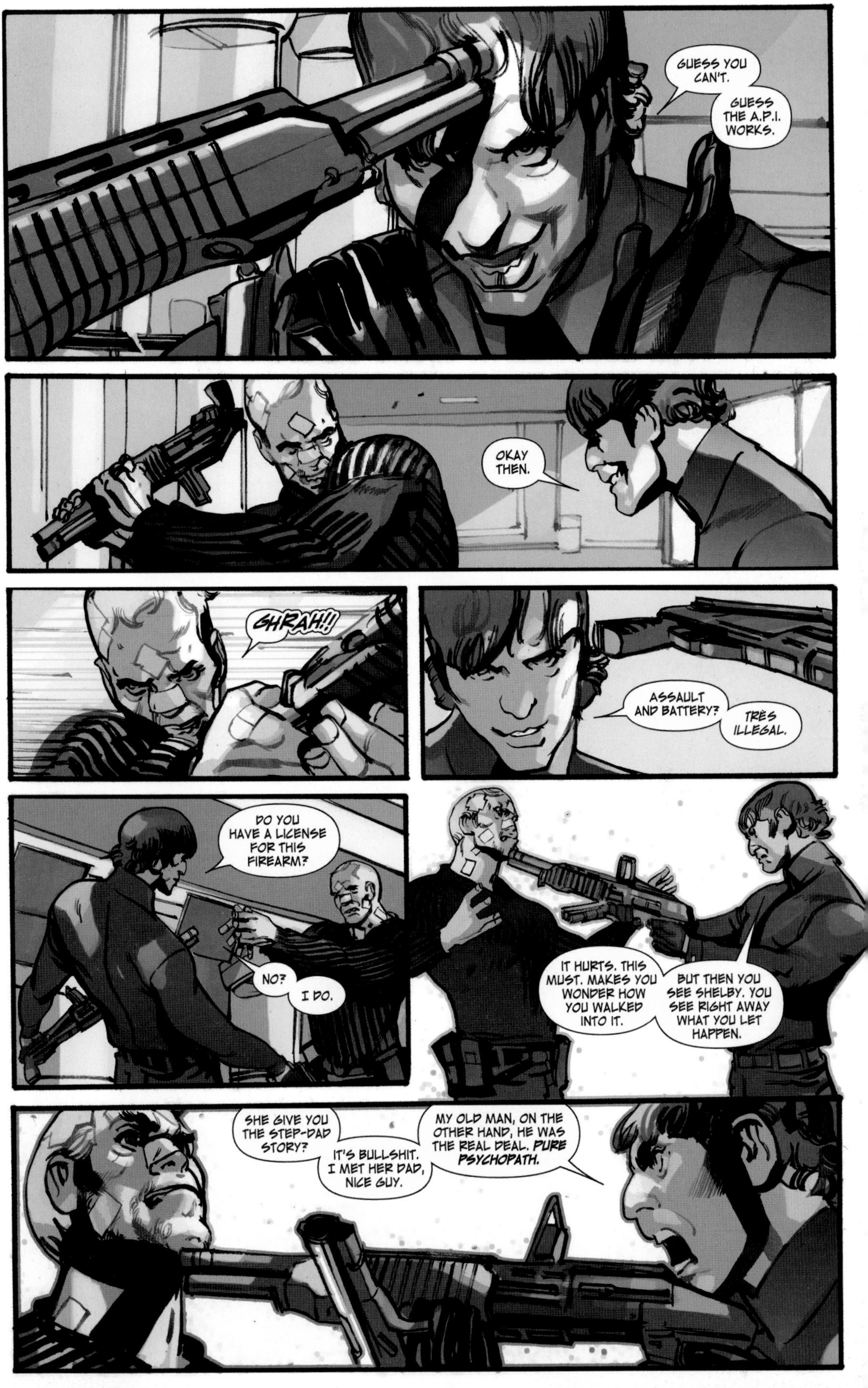
GUESS YOU CAN'T.
GUESS THE A.P.I. WORKS.
OKAY THEN.
GHRAH!!
ASSAULT AND BATTERY?
TRÈS ILLEGAL.
DO YOU HAVE A LICENSE FOR THIS FIREARM?
NO?
I DO.
IT HURTS. THIS MUST. MAKES YOU WONDER HOW YOU WALKED INTO IT.
BUT THEN YOU SEE SHELBY. YOU SEE RIGHT AWAY WHAT YOU LET HAPPEN.
SHE GIVE YOU THE STEP-DAD STORY?
IT'S BULLSHIT. I MET HER DAD, NICE GUY.
MY OLD MAN, ON THE OTHER HAND, HE WAS THE REAL DEAL. *PURE PSYCHOPATH.*

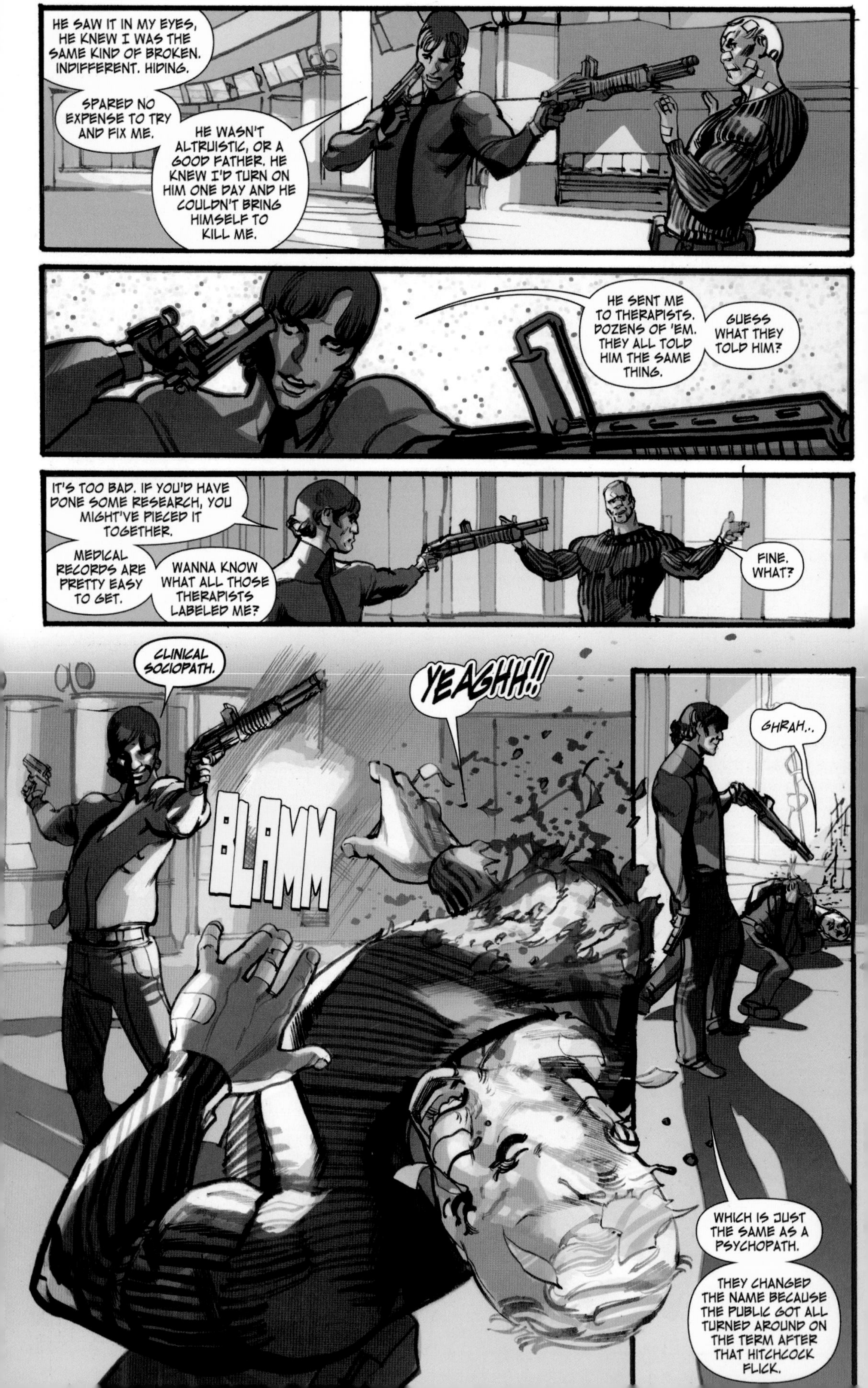
HE SAW IT IN MY EYES, HE KNEW I WAS THE SAME KIND OF BROKEN. INDIFFERENT. HIDING.
SPARED NO EXPENSE TO TRY AND FIX ME.
HE WASN'T ALTRUISTIC, OR A GOOD FATHER. HE KNEW I'D TURN ON HIM ONE DAY AND HE COULDN'T BRING HIMSELF TO KILL ME.
HE SENT ME TO THERAPISTS. DOZENS OF 'EM. THEY ALL TOLD HIM THE SAME THING.
GUESS WHAT THEY TOLD HIM?
IT'S TOO BAD. IF YOU'D HAVE DONE SOME RESEARCH, YOU MIGHT'VE PIECED IT TOGETHER.
MEDICAL RECORDS ARE PRETTY EASY TO GET.
WANNA KNOW WHAT ALL THOSE THERAPISTS LABELED ME?
FINE. WHAT?
CLINICAL SOCIOPATH.
BLAMM
YEAGHH!!
GHRAH...
WHICH IS JUST THE SAME AS A PSYCHOPATH.
THEY CHANGED THE NAME BECAUSE THE PUBLIC GOT ALL TURNED AROUND ON THE TERM AFTER THAT HITCHCOCK FLICK.

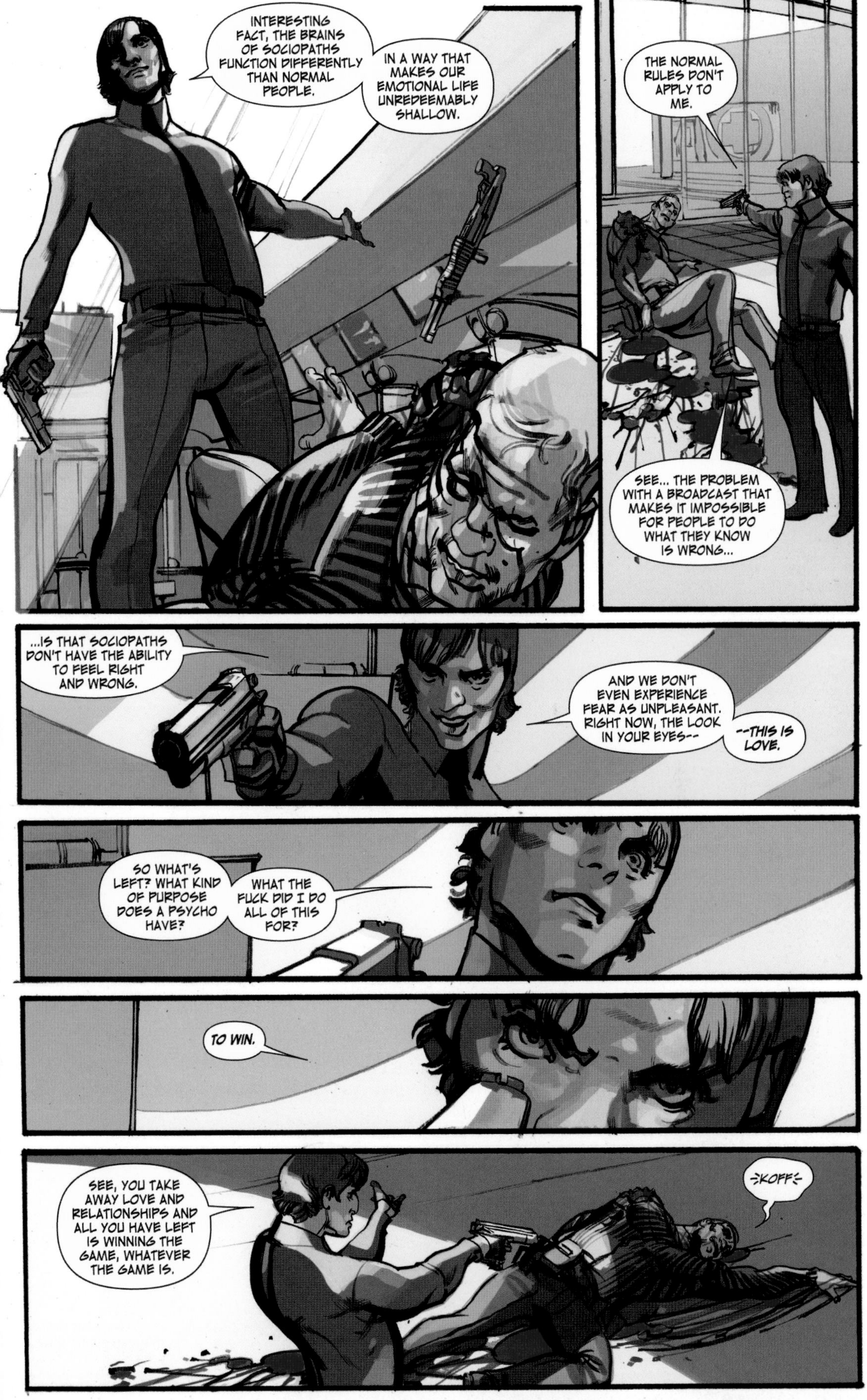
INTERESTING FACT, THE BRAINS OF SOCIOPATHS FUNCTION DIFFERENTLY THAN NORMAL PEOPLE.
IN A WAY THAT MAKES OUR EMOTIONAL LIFE UNREDEEMABLY SHALLOW.
THE NORMAL RULES DON'T APPLY TO ME.
SEE... THE PROBLEM WITH A BROADCAST THAT MAKES IT IMPOSSIBLE FOR PEOPLE TO DO WHAT THEY KNOW IS WRONG...
...IS THAT SOCIOPATHS DON'T HAVE THE ABILITY TO FEEL RIGHT AND WRONG.
AND WE DON'T EVEN EXPERIENCE FEAR AS UNPLEASANT. RIGHT NOW, THE LOOK IN YOUR EYES--
--THIS IS LOVE.
SO WHAT'S LEFT? WHAT KIND OF PURPOSE DOES A PSYCHO HAVE?
WHAT THE FUCK DID I DO ALL OF THIS FOR?
TO WIN.
SEE, YOU TAKE AWAY LOVE AND RELATIONSHIPS AND ALL YOU HAVE LEFT IS WINNING THE GAME, WHATEVER THE GAME IS.
=KOFF=

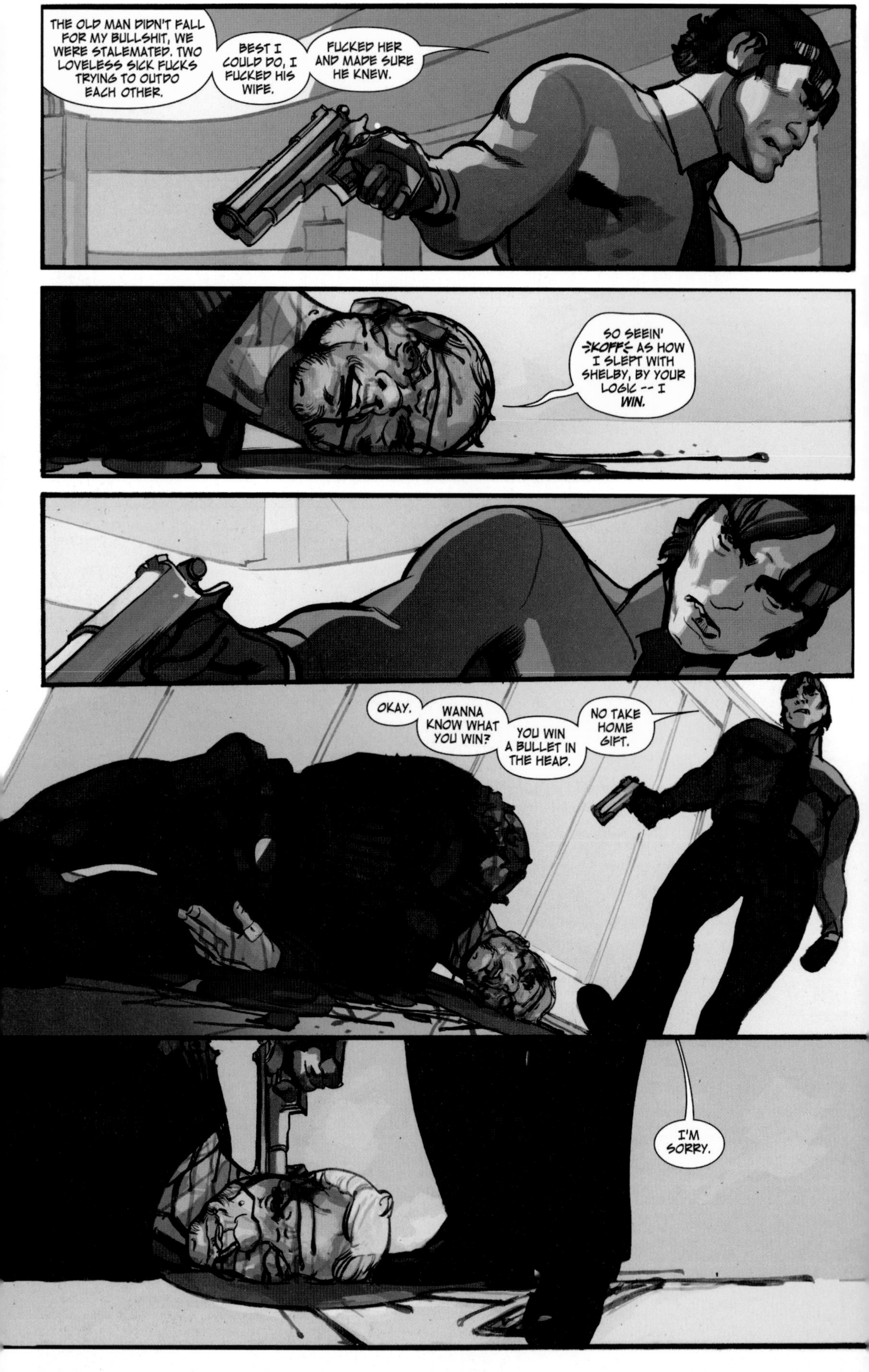
THE OLD MAN DIDN'T FALL FOR MY BULLSHIT, WE WERE STALEMATED. TWO LOVELESS SICK FUCKS TRYING TO OUTDO EACH OTHER.
BEST I COULD DO, I FUCKED HIS WIFE.
FUCKED HER AND MADE SURE HE KNEW.
SO SEEIN' *KOFF* AS HOW I SLEPT WITH SHELBY, BY YOUR LOGIC -- I WIN.
OKAY.
WANNA KNOW WHAT YOU WIN?
YOU WIN A BULLET IN THE HEAD.
NO TAKE HOME GIFT.
I'M SORRY.

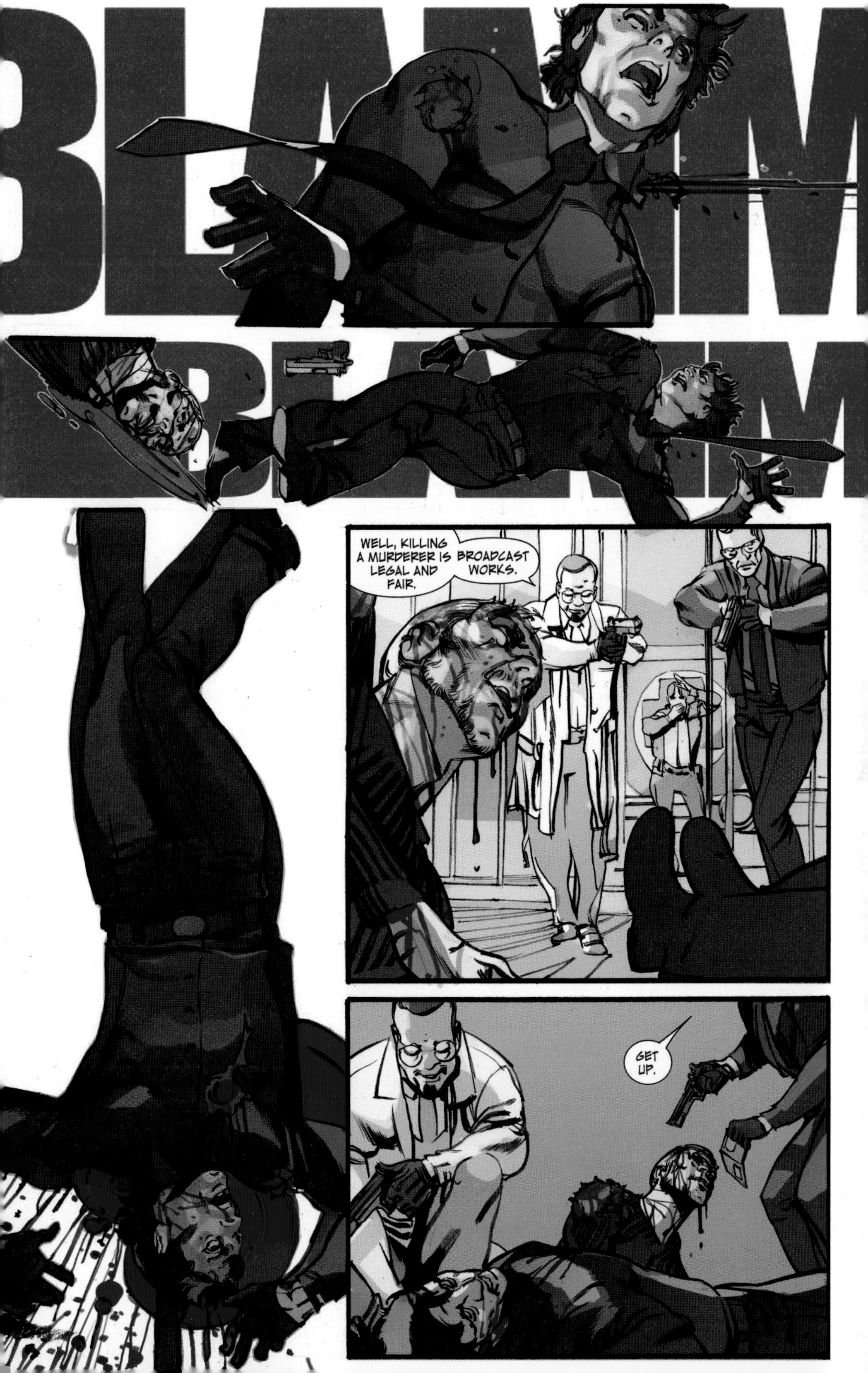
BLAMM
BLAMM
WELL, KILLING A MURDERER IS LEGAL AND FAIR.
BROADCAST WORKS.
GET UP.

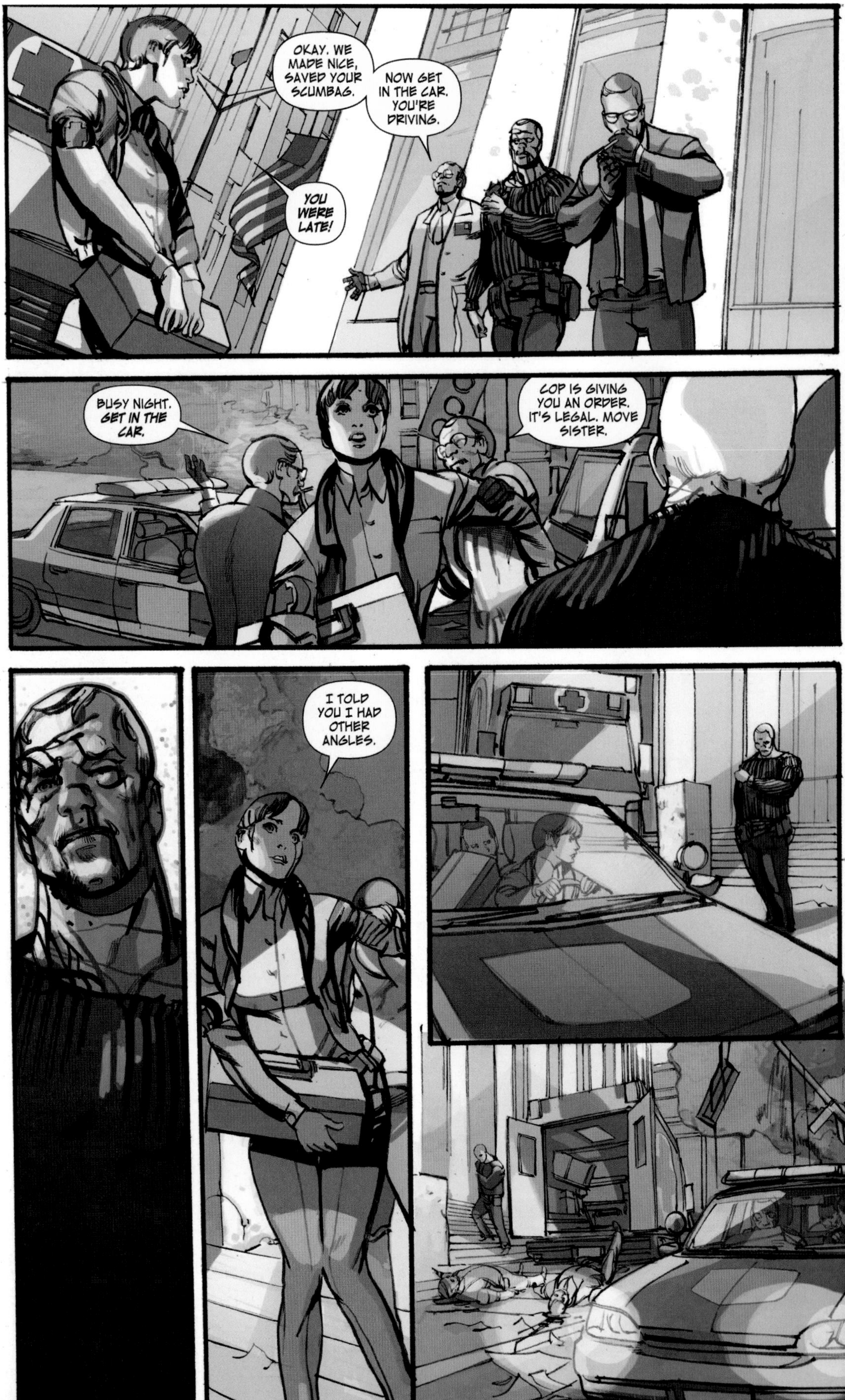
OKAY. WE MADE NICE, SAVED YOUR SCUMBAG.
NOW GET IN THE CAR. YOU'RE DRIVING.
YOU WERE LATE!
BUSY NIGHT. GET IN THE CAR.
COP IS GIVING YOU AN ORDER. IT'S LEGAL. MOVE SISTER.
I TOLD YOU I HAD OTHER ANGLES.

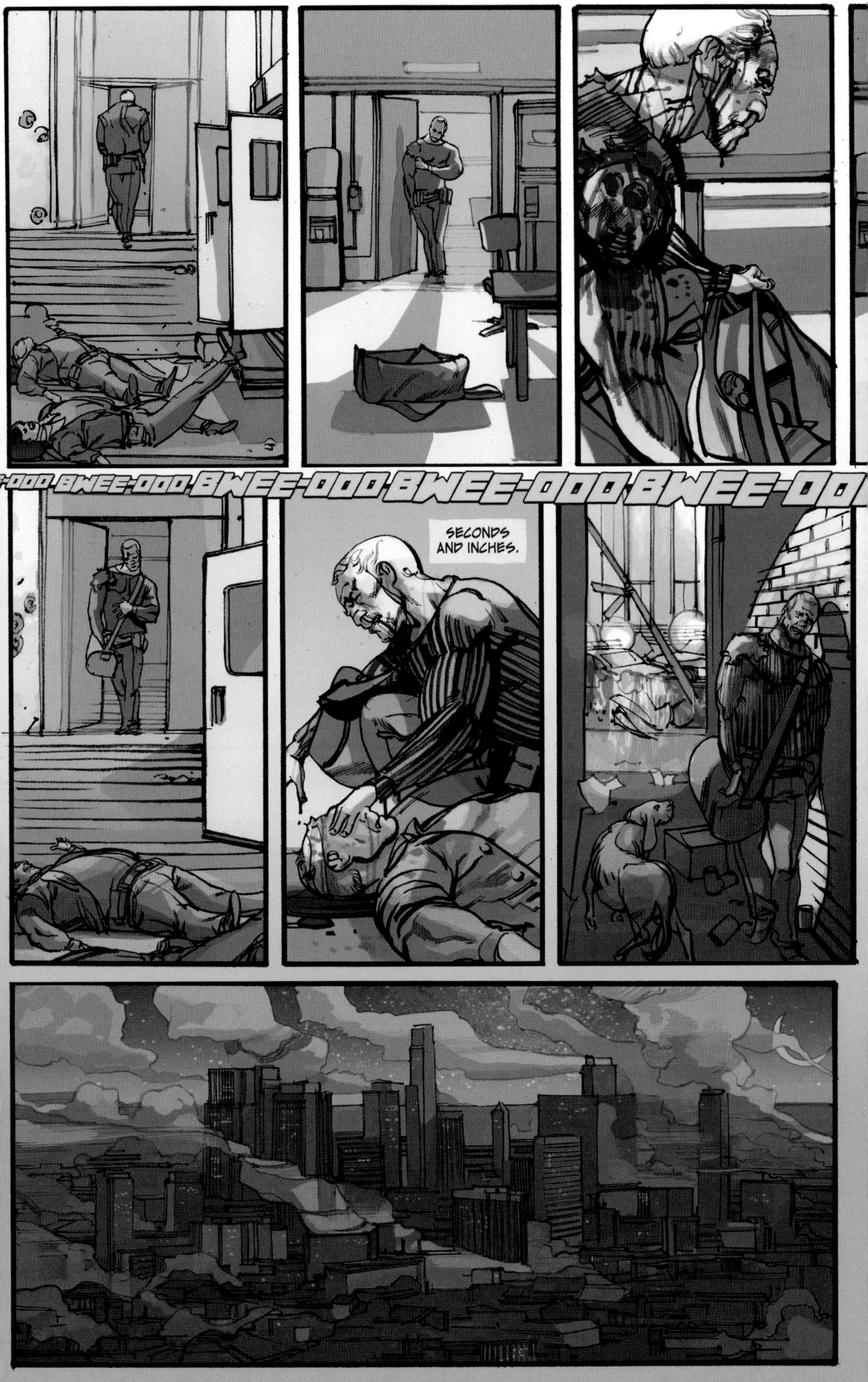

-OOO BWEE-OOO BWEE-OOO BWEE-OOO BWEE-OO
SECONDS AND INCHES.

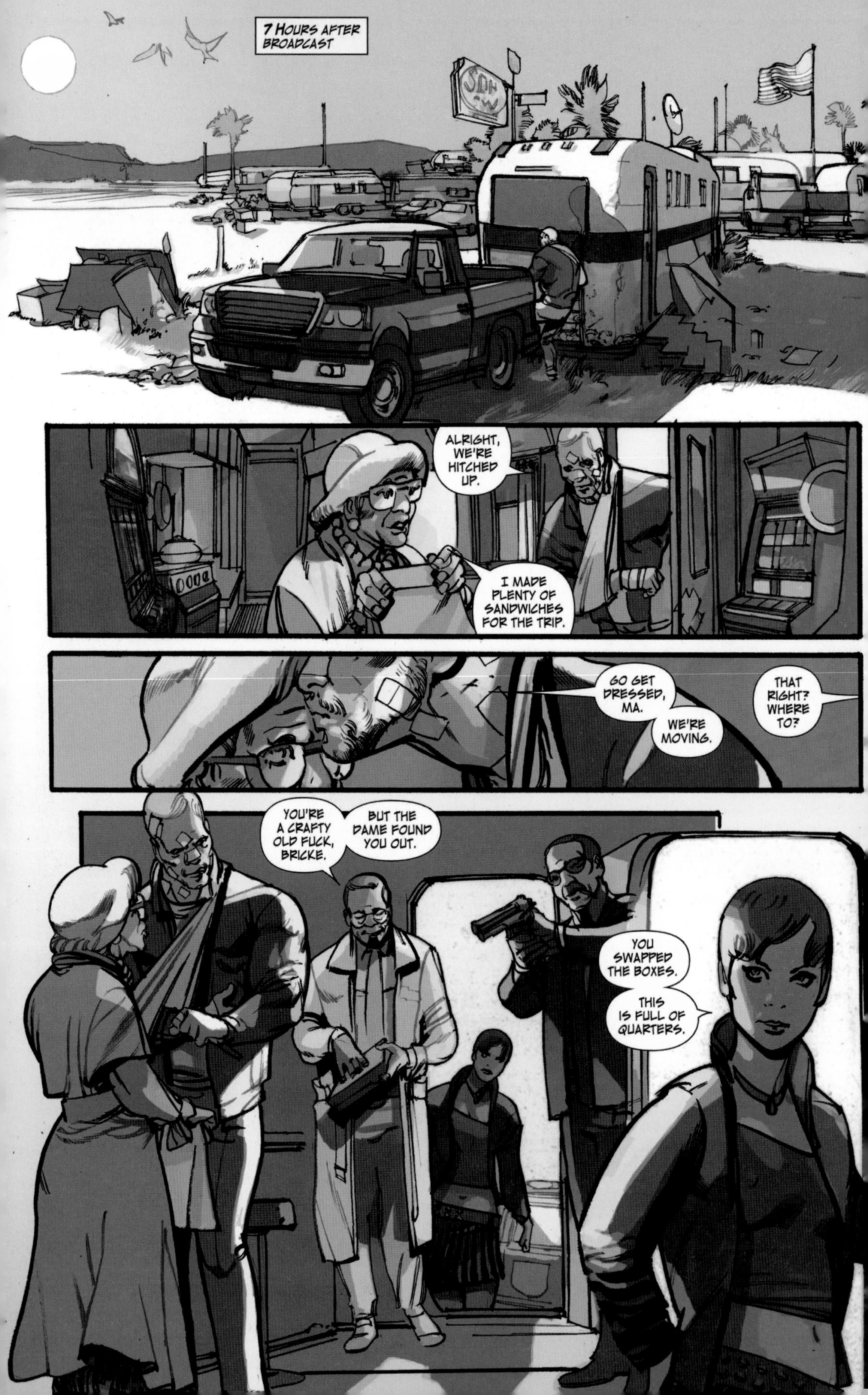
7 HOURS AFTER BROADCAST
ALRIGHT, WE'RE HITCHED UP.
I MADE PLENTY OF SANDWICHES FOR THE TRIP.
GO GET DRESSED, MA.
WE'RE MOVING.
THAT RIGHT? WHERE TO?
YOU'RE A CRAFTY OLD FUCK, BRICKE.
BUT THE DAME FOUND YOU OUT.
YOU SWAPPED THE BOXES.
THIS IS FULL OF QUARTERS.

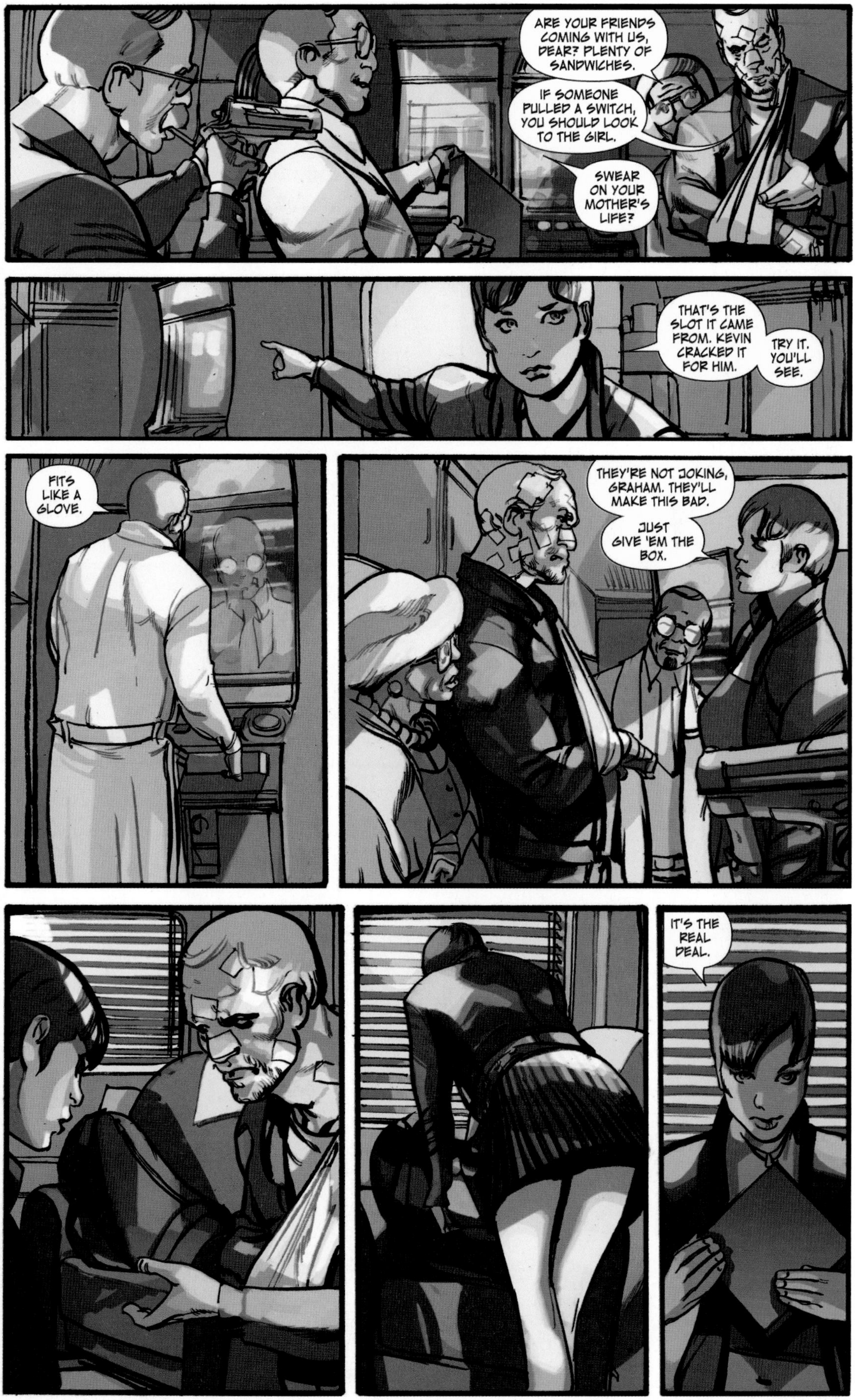
ARE YOUR FRIENDS COMING WITH US, DEAR? PLENTY OF SANDWICHES.
IF SOMEONE PULLED A SWITCH, YOU SHOULD LOOK TO THE GIRL.
SWEAR ON YOUR MOTHER'S LIFE?
THAT'S THE SLOT IT CAME FROM. KEVIN CRACKED IT FOR HIM.
TRY IT. YOU'LL SEE.
FITS LIKE A GLOVE.
THEY'RE NOT JOKING, GRAHAM. THEY'LL MAKE THIS BAD.
JUST GIVE 'EM THE BOX.
IT'S THE REAL DEAL.

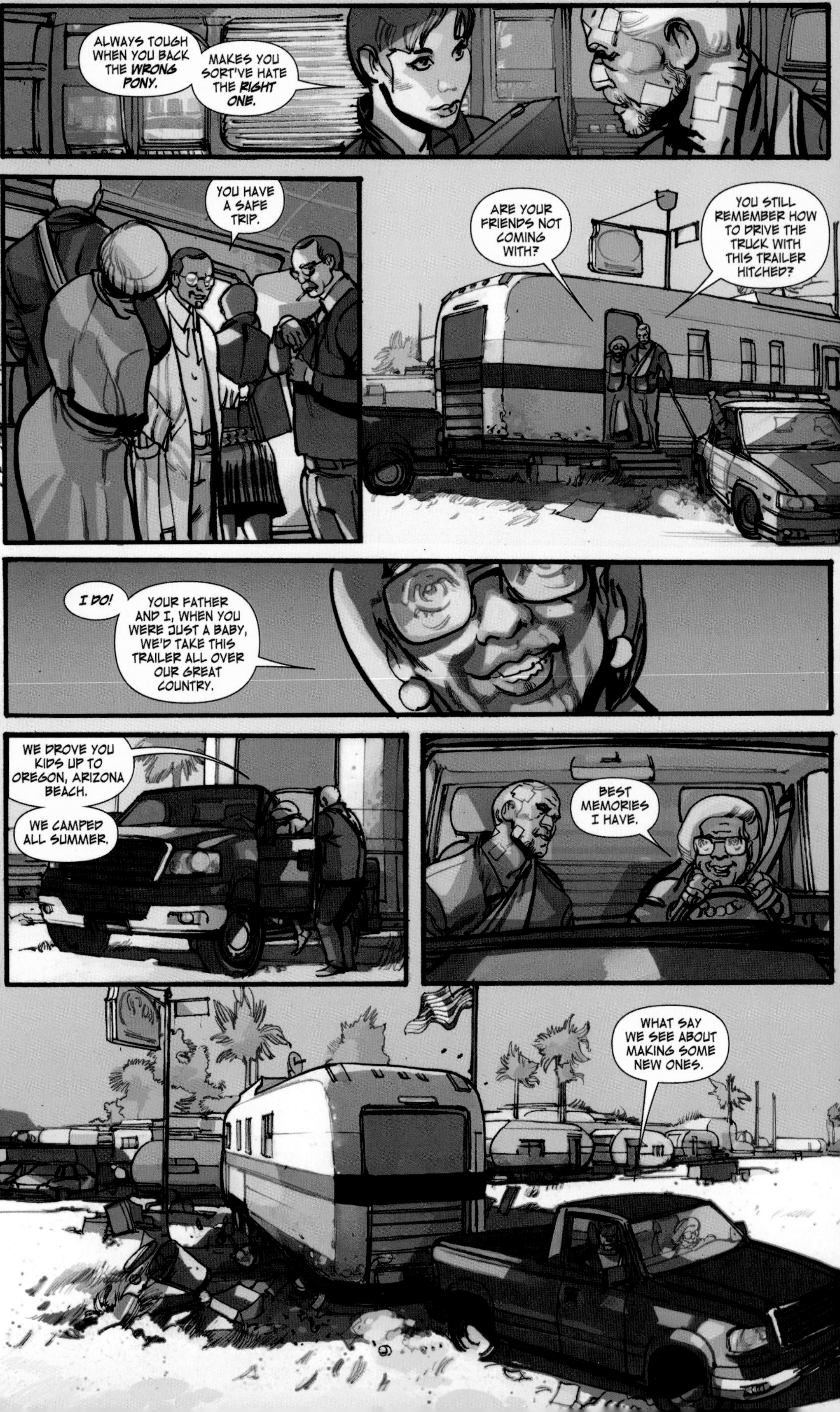
ALWAYS TOUGH WHEN YOU BACK THE WRONG PONY.
MAKES YOU SORT'VE HATE THE RIGHT ONE.
YOU HAVE A SAFE TRIP.
ARE YOUR FRIENDS NOT COMING WITH?
YOU STILL REMEMBER HOW TO DRIVE THE TRUCK WITH THIS TRAILER HITCHED?
I DO!
YOUR FATHER AND I, WHEN YOU WERE JUST A BABY, WE'D TAKE THIS TRAILER ALL OVER OUR GREAT COUNTRY.
WE DROVE YOU KIDS UP TO OREGON, ARIZONA BEACH.
WE CAMPED ALL SUMMER.
BEST MEMORIES I HAVE.
WHAT SAY WE SEE ABOUT MAKING SOME NEW ONES.

MONTHS LATER...

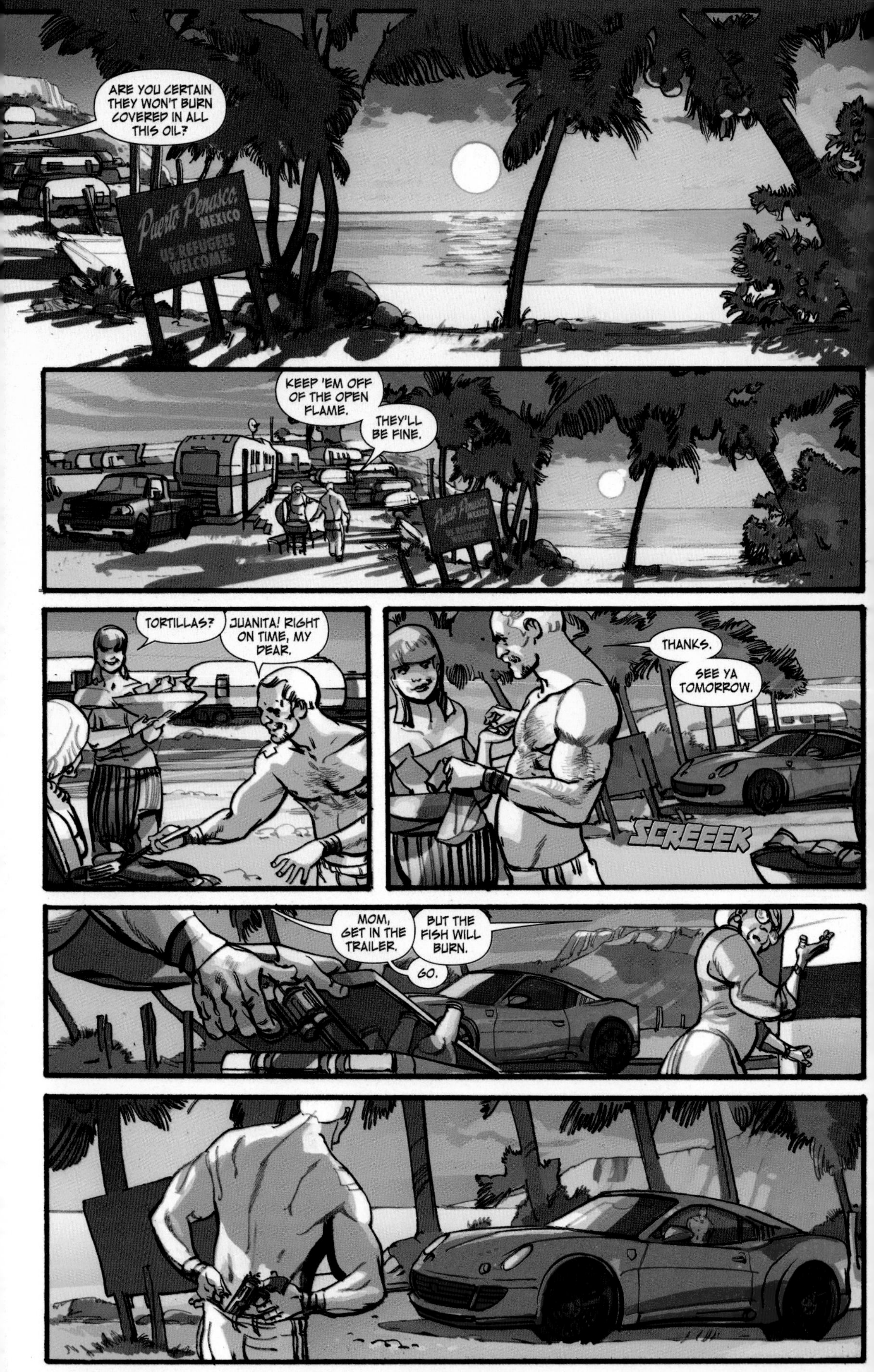
ARE YOU CERTAIN THEY WON'T BURN COVERED IN ALL THIS OIL?
Puerto Penasco. MEXICO
US REFUGEES WELCOME.
KEEP 'EM OFF OF THE OPEN FLAME.
THEY'LL BE FINE.
TORTILLAS?
JUANITA! RIGHT ON TIME, MY DEAR.
THANKS.
SEE YA TOMORROW.
SCREEEK
MOM, GET IN THE TRAILER.
BUT THE FISH WILL BURN.
GO.

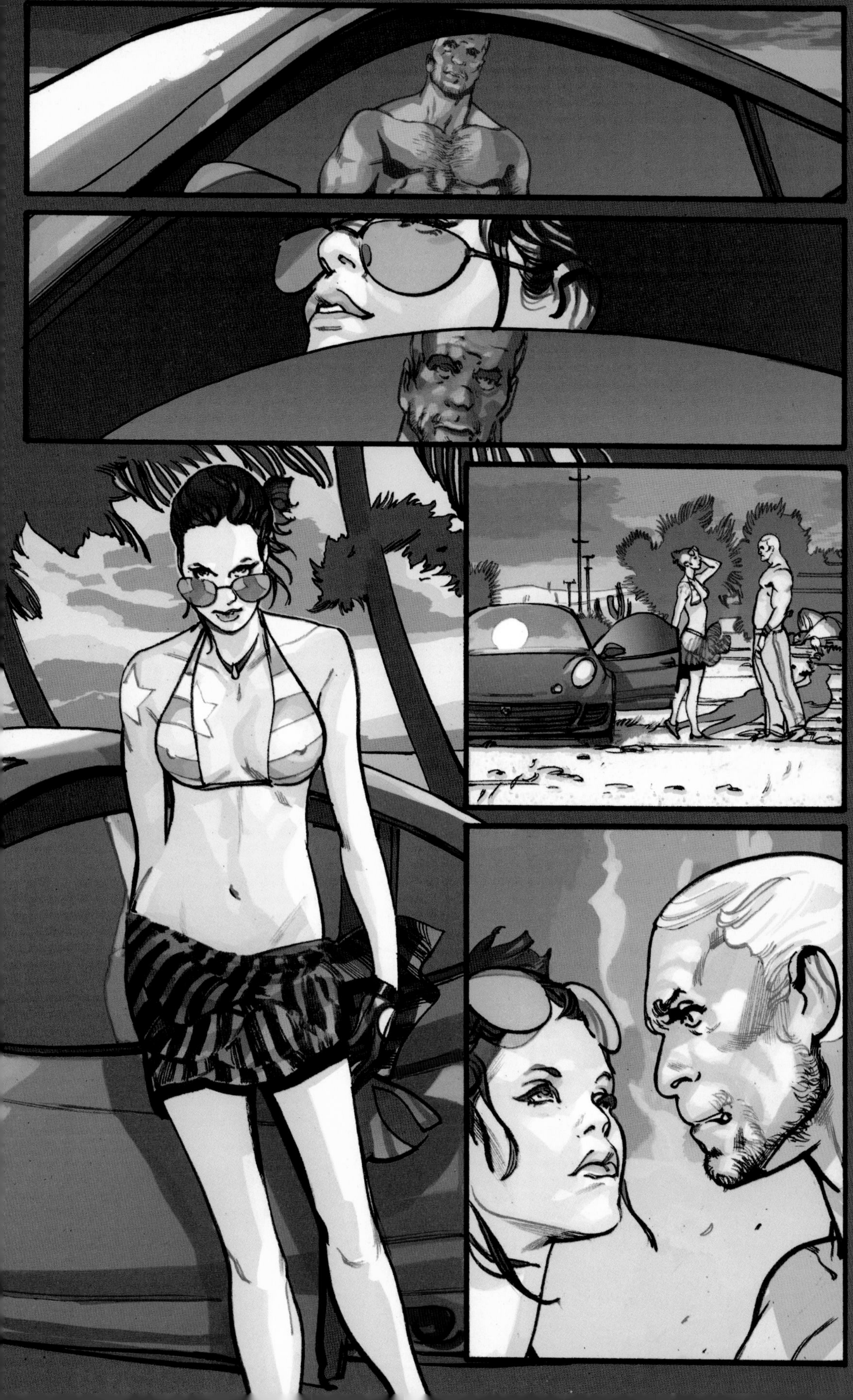

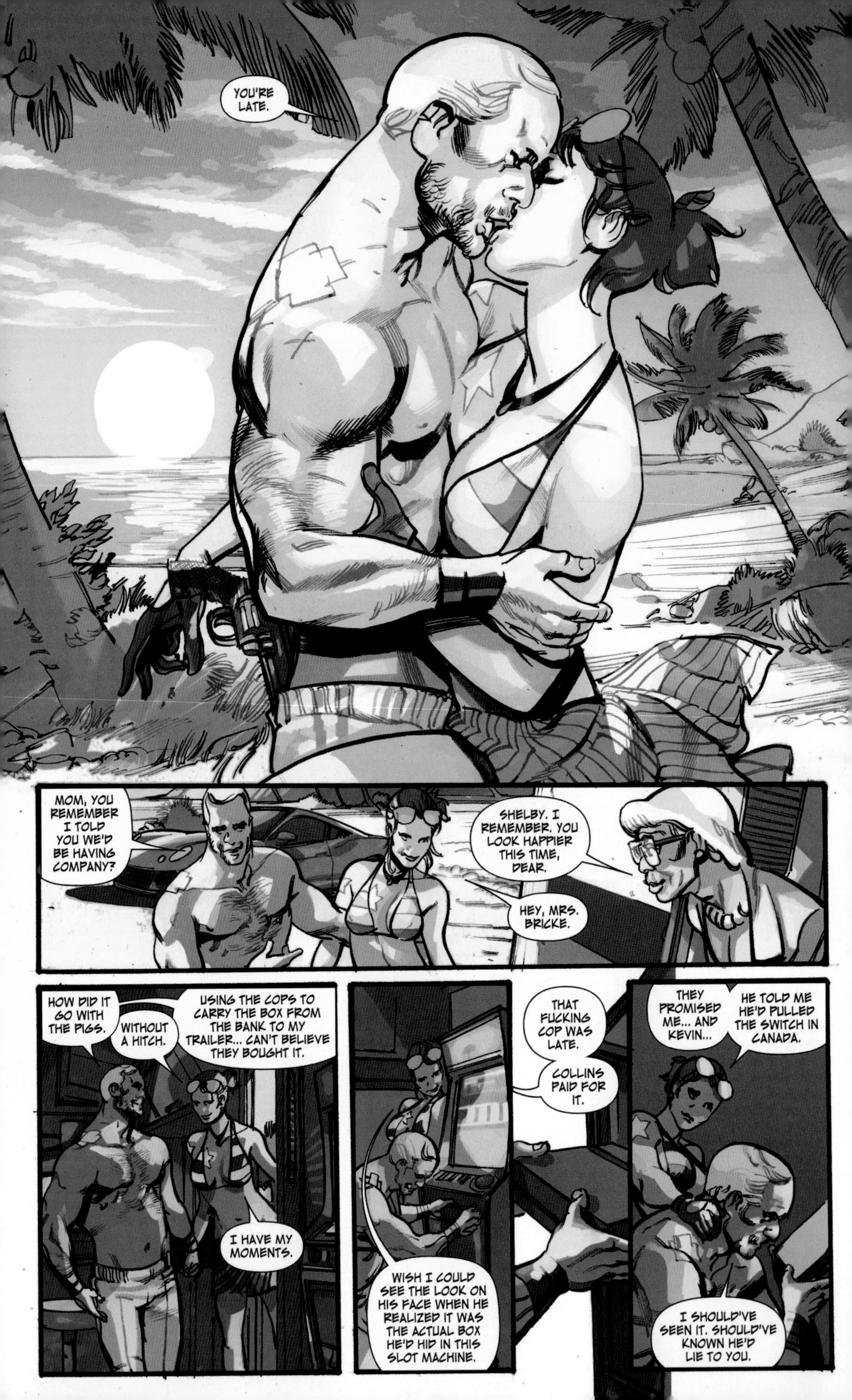

YOU'RE LATE.
MOM, YOU REMEMBER I TOLD YOU WE'D BE HAVING COMPANY?
SHELBY. I REMEMBER. YOU LOOK HAPPIER THIS TIME, DEAR.
HEY, MRS. BRICKE.
HOW DID IT GO WITH THE PIGS.
WITHOUT A HITCH.
USING THE COPS TO CARRY THE BOX FROM THE BANK TO MY TRAILER... CAN'T BELIEVE THEY BOUGHT IT.
I HAVE MY MOMENTS.
THAT FUCKING COP WAS LATE.
COLLINS PAID FOR IT.
WISH I COULD SEE THE LOOK ON HIS FACE WHEN HE REALIZED IT WAS THE ACTUAL BOX HE'D HID IN THIS SLOT MACHINE.
THEY PROMISED ME... AND KEVIN...
HE TOLD ME HE'D PULLED THE SWITCH IN CANADA.
I SHOULD'VE SEEN IT. SHOULD'VE KNOWN HE'D LIE TO YOU.

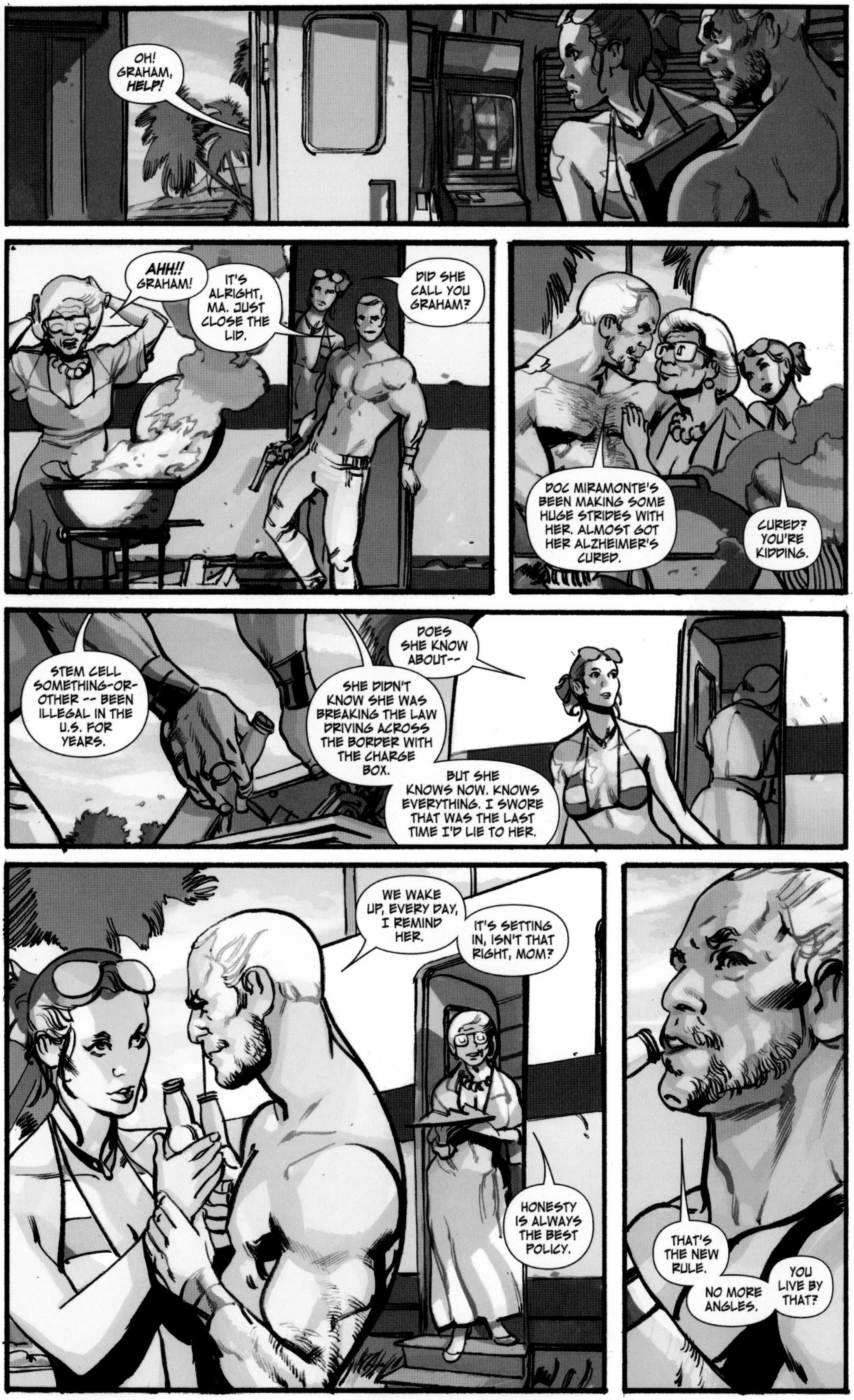
OH! GRAHAM, HELP!
AHH!! GRAHAM!
IT'S ALRIGHT, MA. JUST CLOSE THE LID.
DID SHE CALL YOU GRAHAM?
DOC MIRAMONTE'S BEEN MAKING SOME HUGE STRIDES WITH HER. ALMOST GOT HER ALZHEIMER'S CURED.
CURED? YOU'RE KIDDING.
STEM CELL SOMETHING-OR-OTHER -- BEEN ILLEGAL IN THE U.S. FOR YEARS.
DOES SHE KNOW ABOUT--
SHE DIDN'T KNOW SHE WAS BREAKING THE LAW DRIVING ACROSS THE BORDER WITH THE CHARGE BOX.
BUT SHE KNOWS NOW. KNOWS EVERYTHING. I SWORE THAT WAS THE LAST TIME I'D LIE TO HER.
WE WAKE UP, EVERY DAY, I REMIND HER.
IT'S SETTING IN, ISN'T THAT RIGHT, MOM?
HONESTY IS ALWAYS THE BEST POLICY.
THAT'S THE NEW RULE.
NO MORE ANGLES.
YOU LIVE BY THAT?

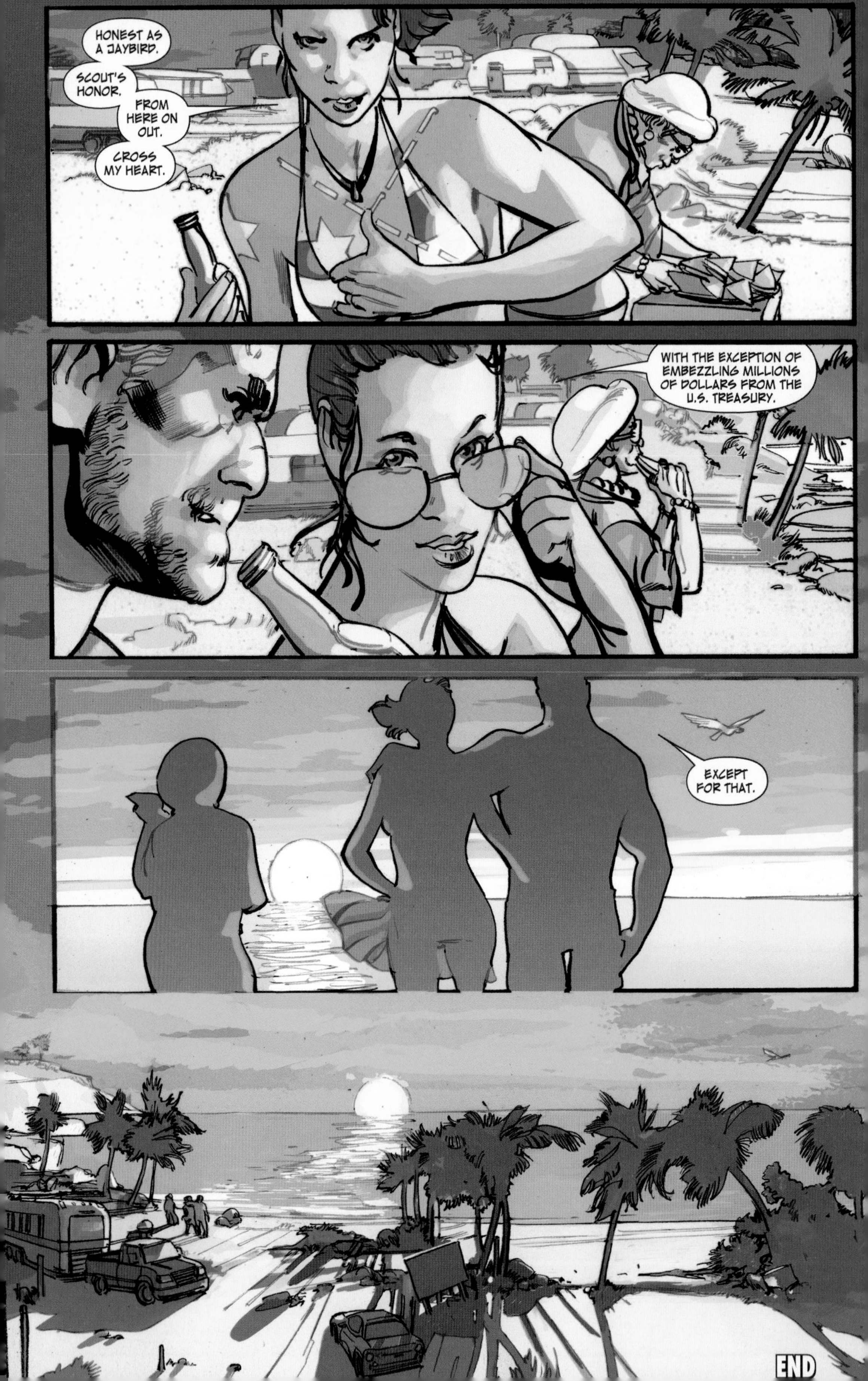
HONEST AS A JAYBIRD.
SCOUT'S HONOR.
FROM HERE ON OUT.
CROSS MY HEART.
WITH THE EXCEPTION OF EMBEZZLING MILLIONS OF DOLLARS FROM THE U.S. TREASURY.
EXCEPT FOR THAT.
END

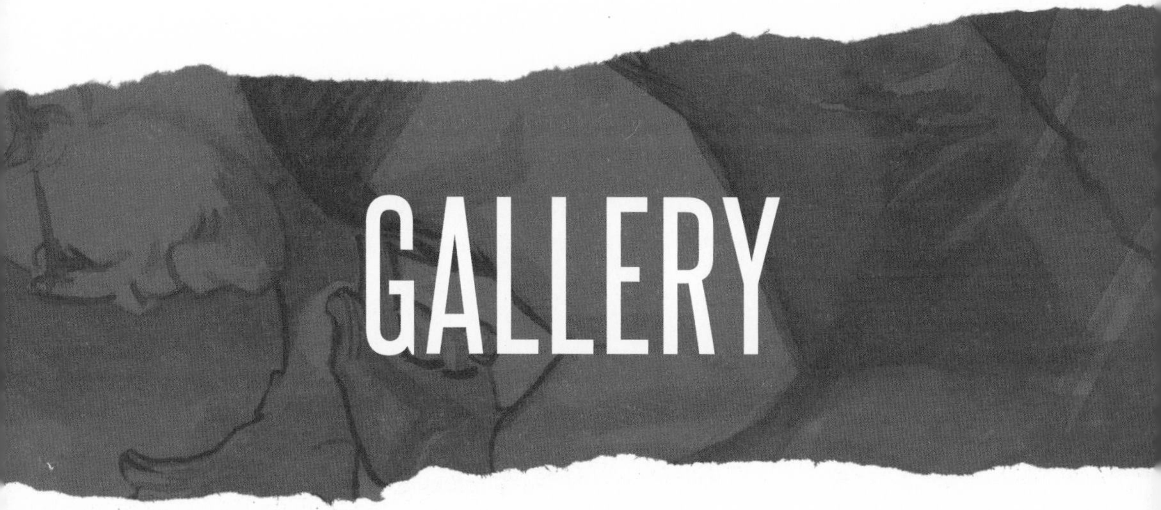

GALLERY

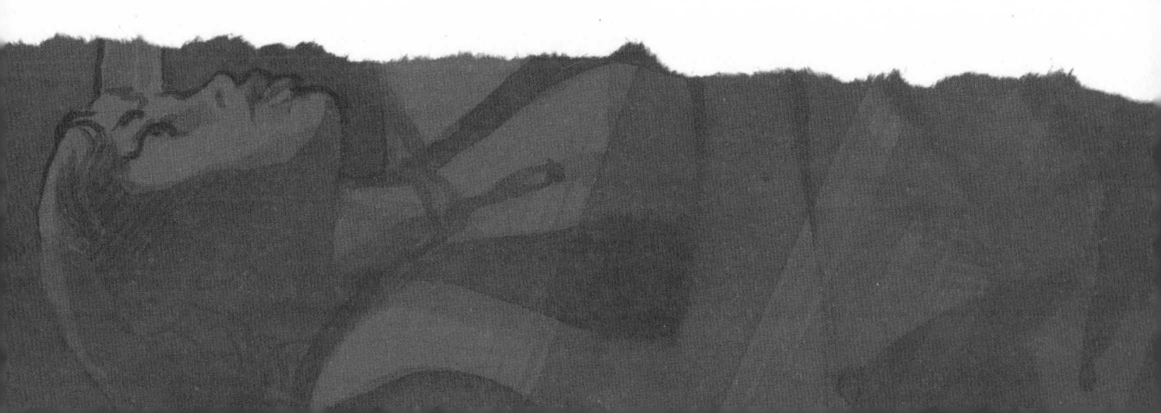

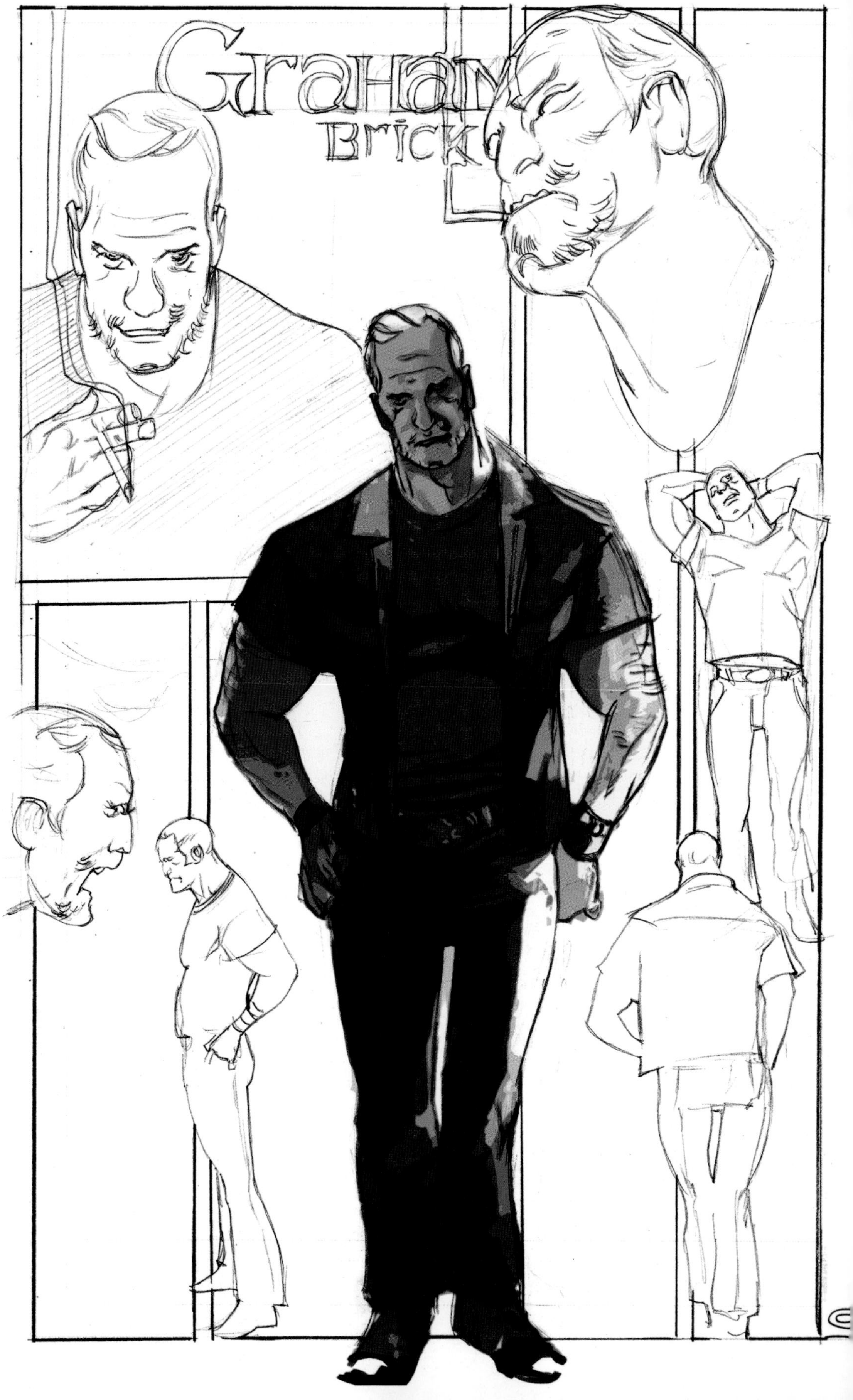
Graham
Brick

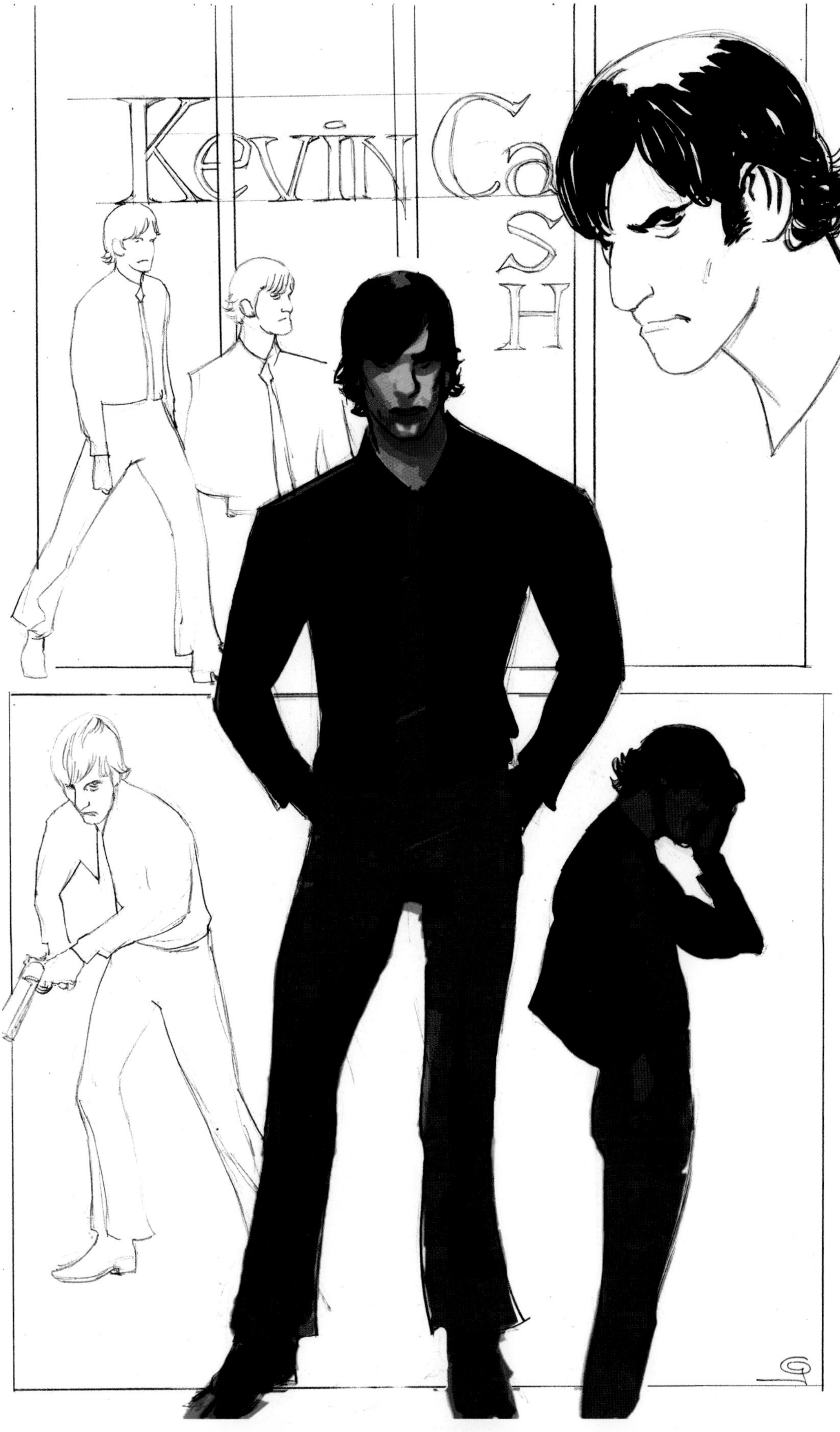
Kevin Ca
S
H

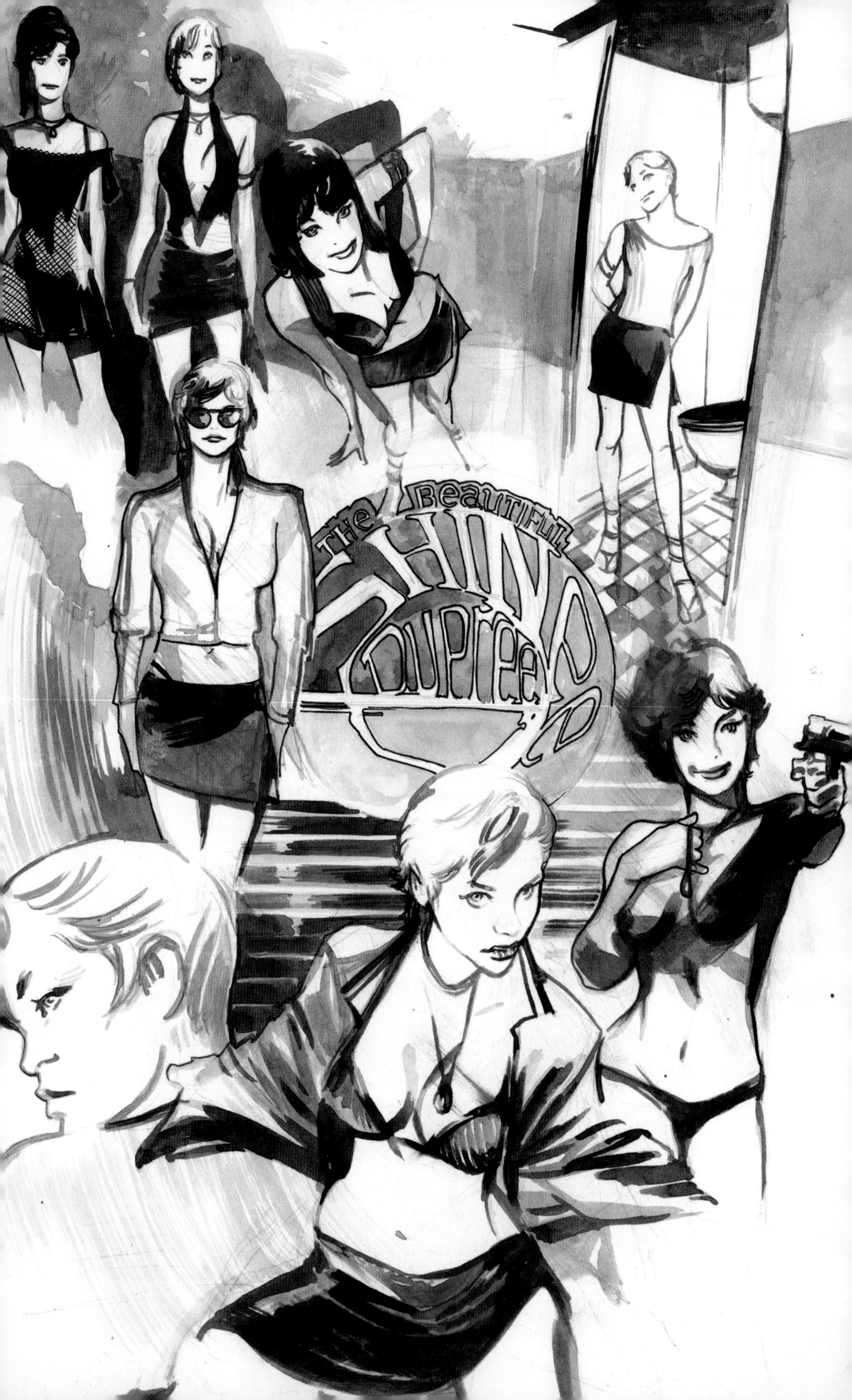
THE BEAUTIFUL
Dupree

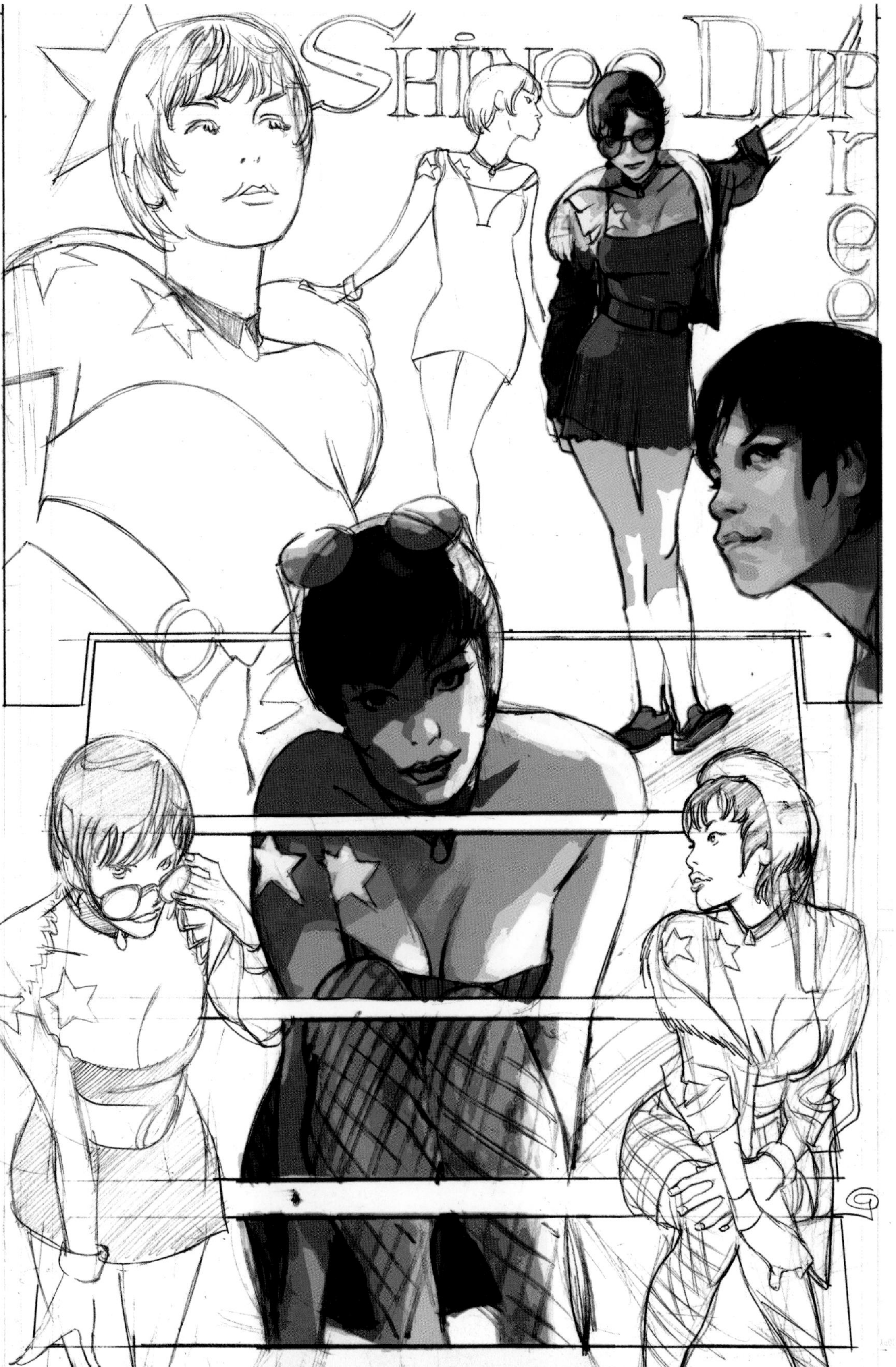

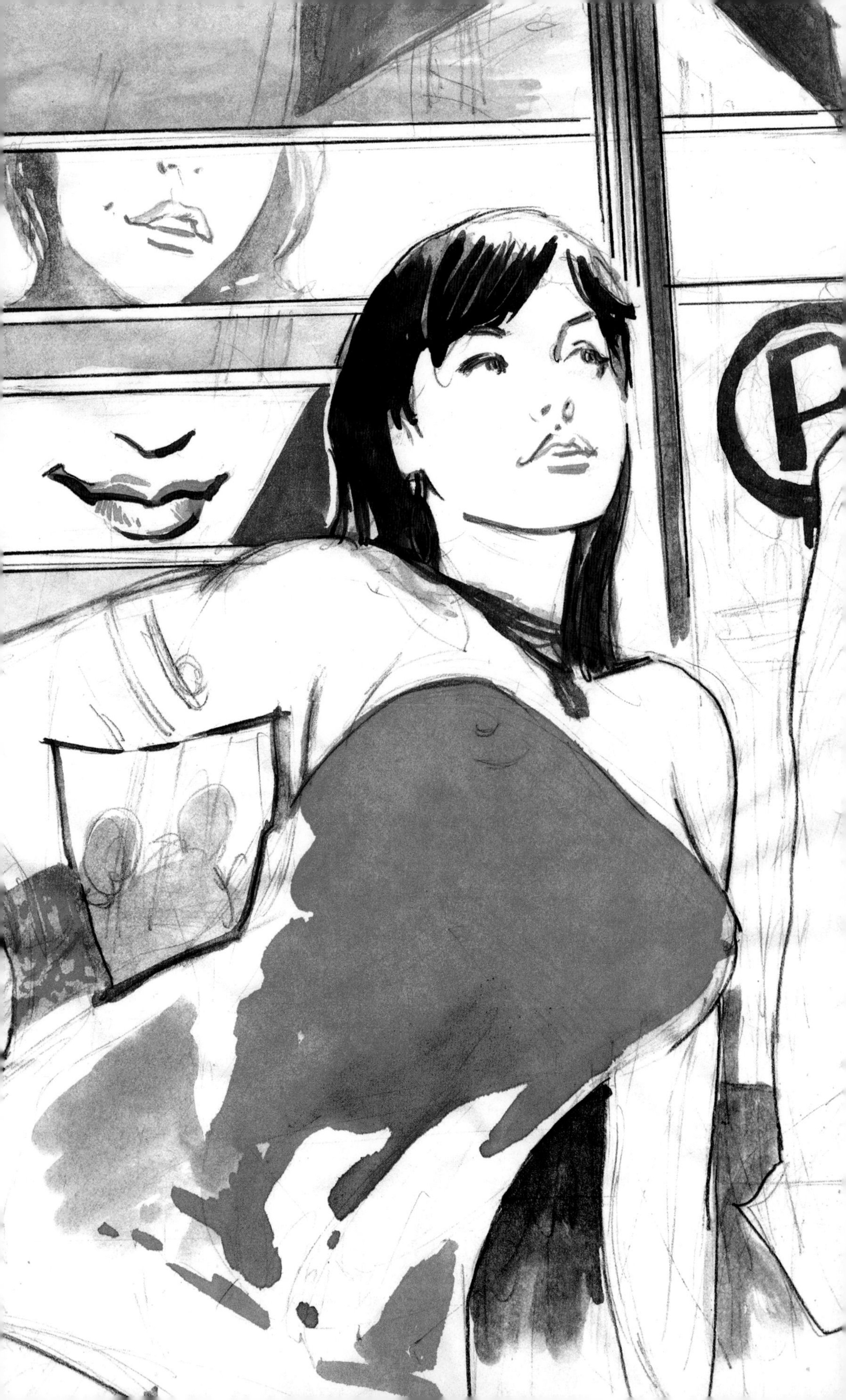
P

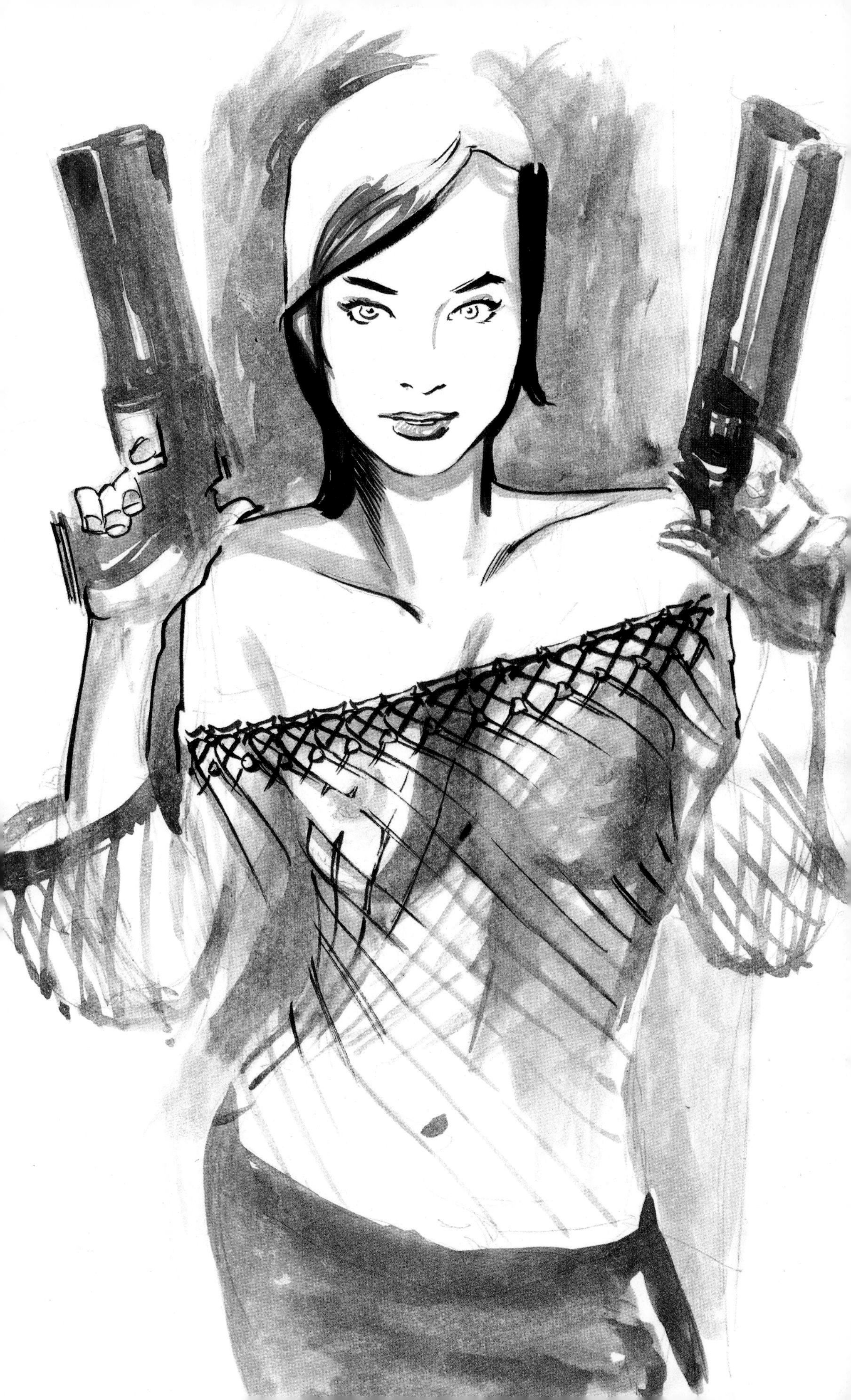

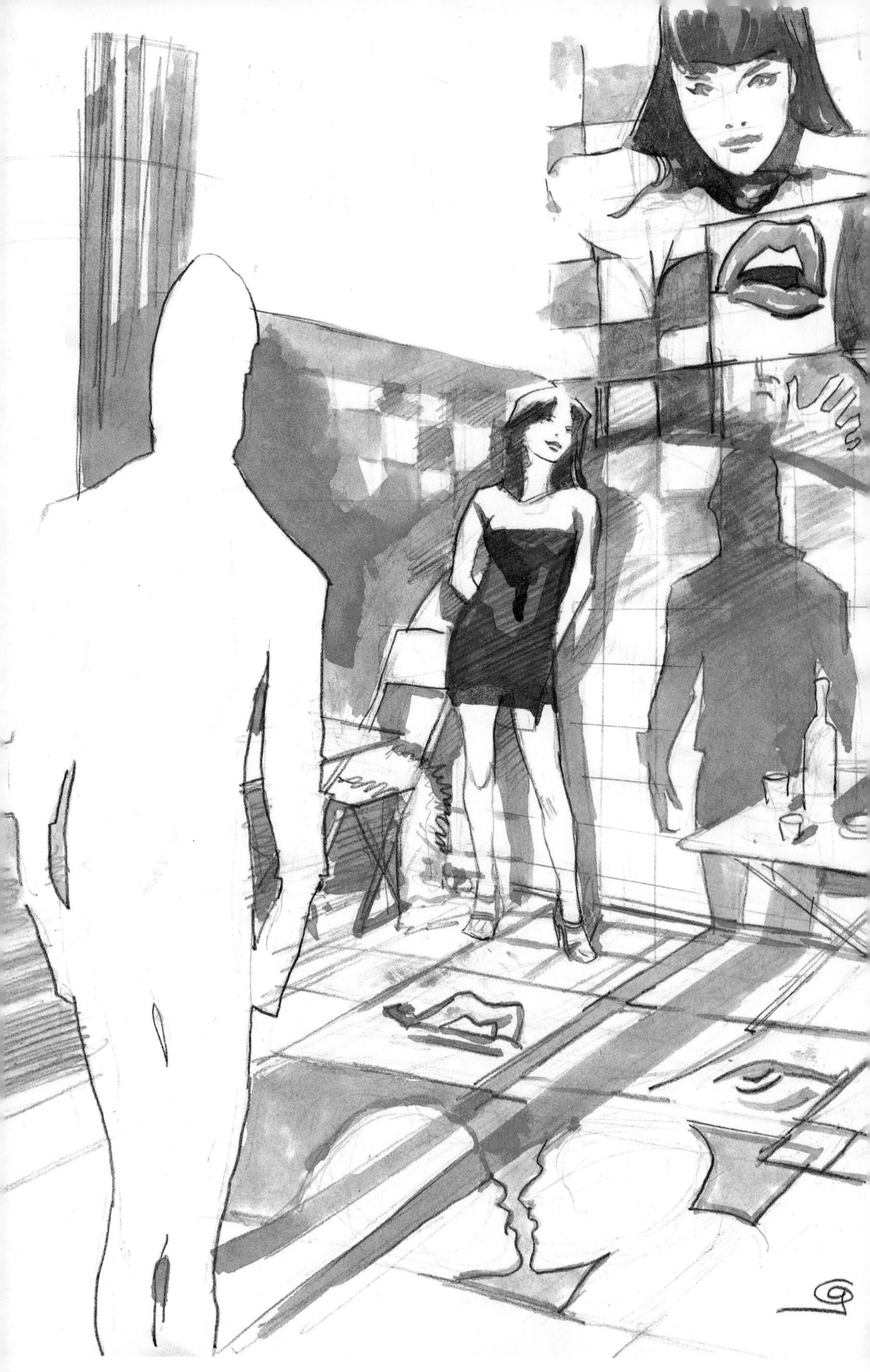

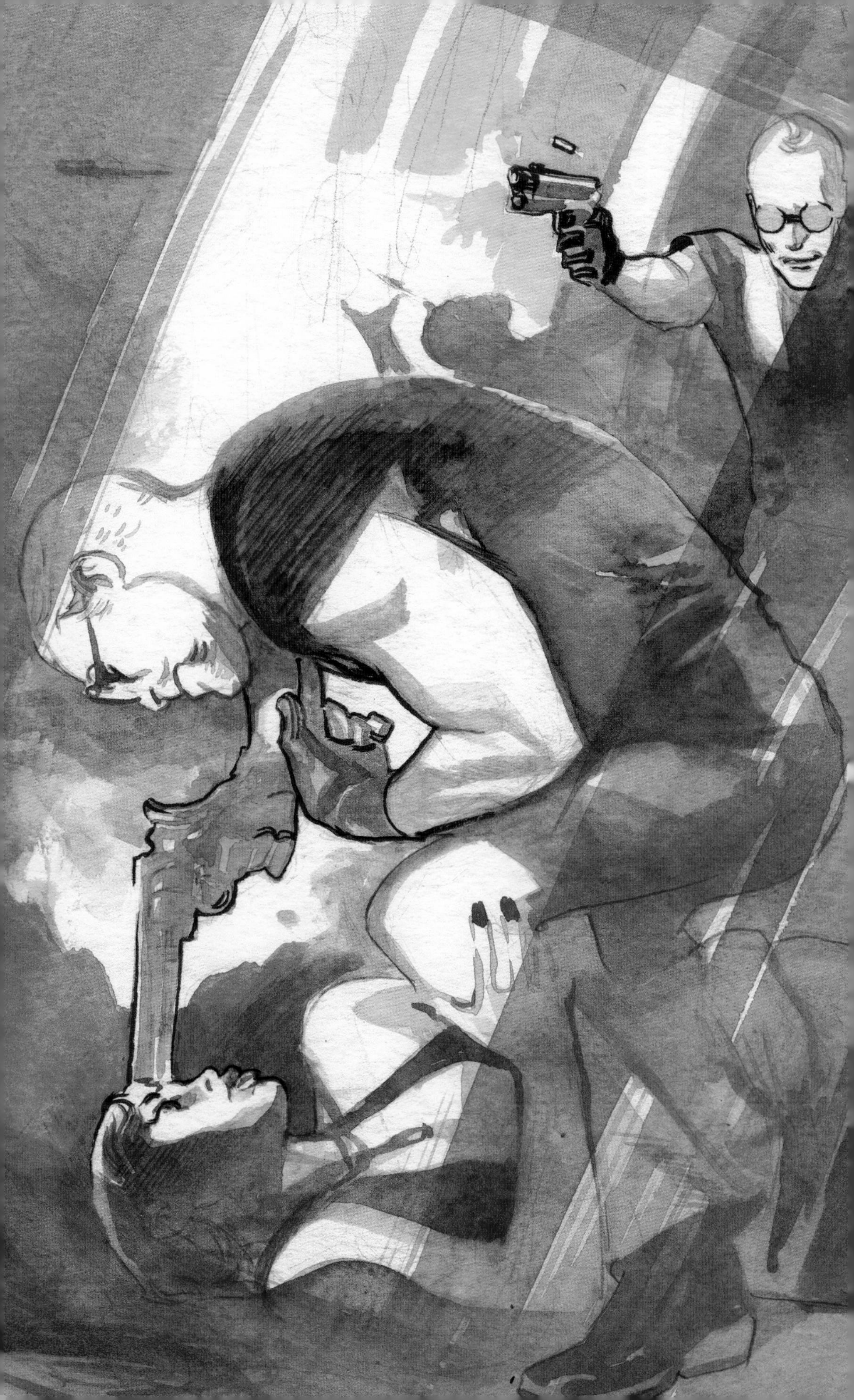

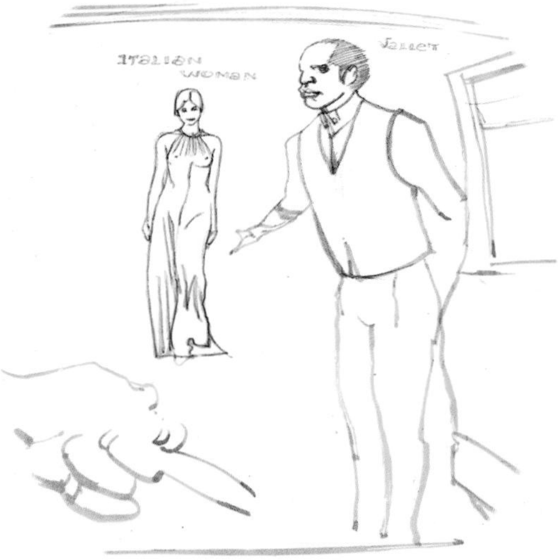
ITALIAN WOMAN
VALLET

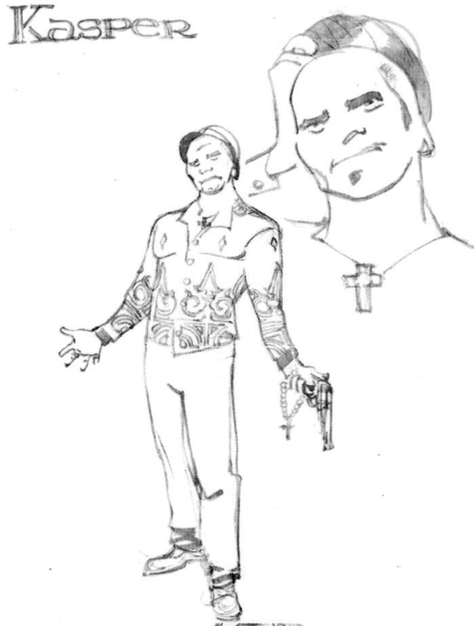
Kasper

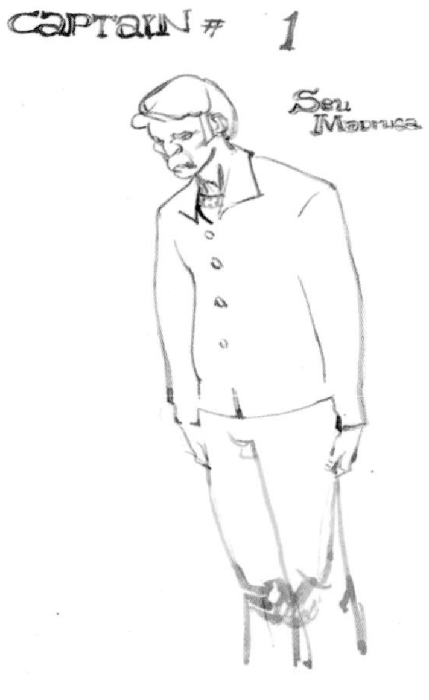
Captain # 1
Seu Madruga

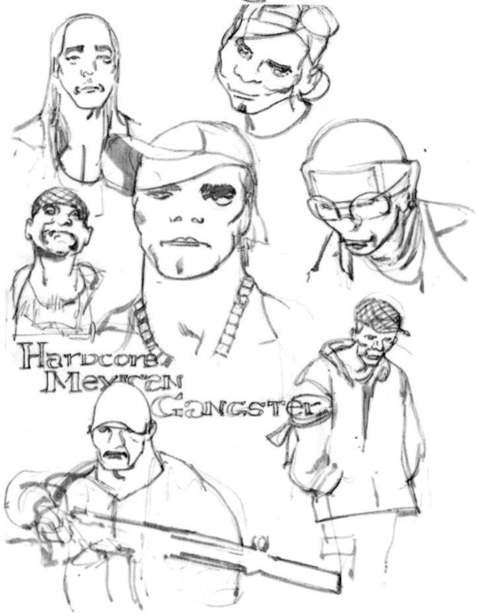
Hardcore Mexican Gangster

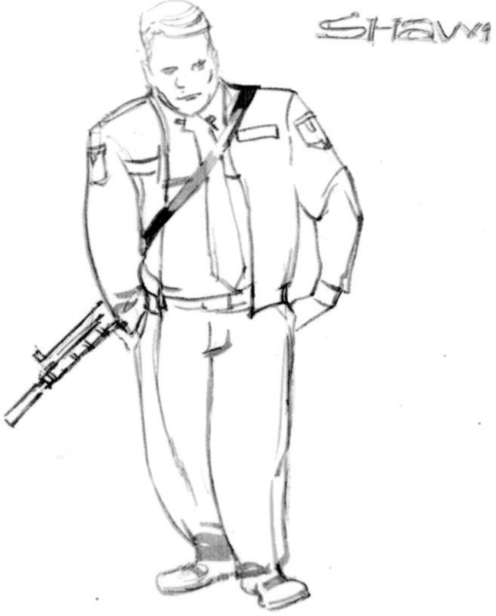
SHAW

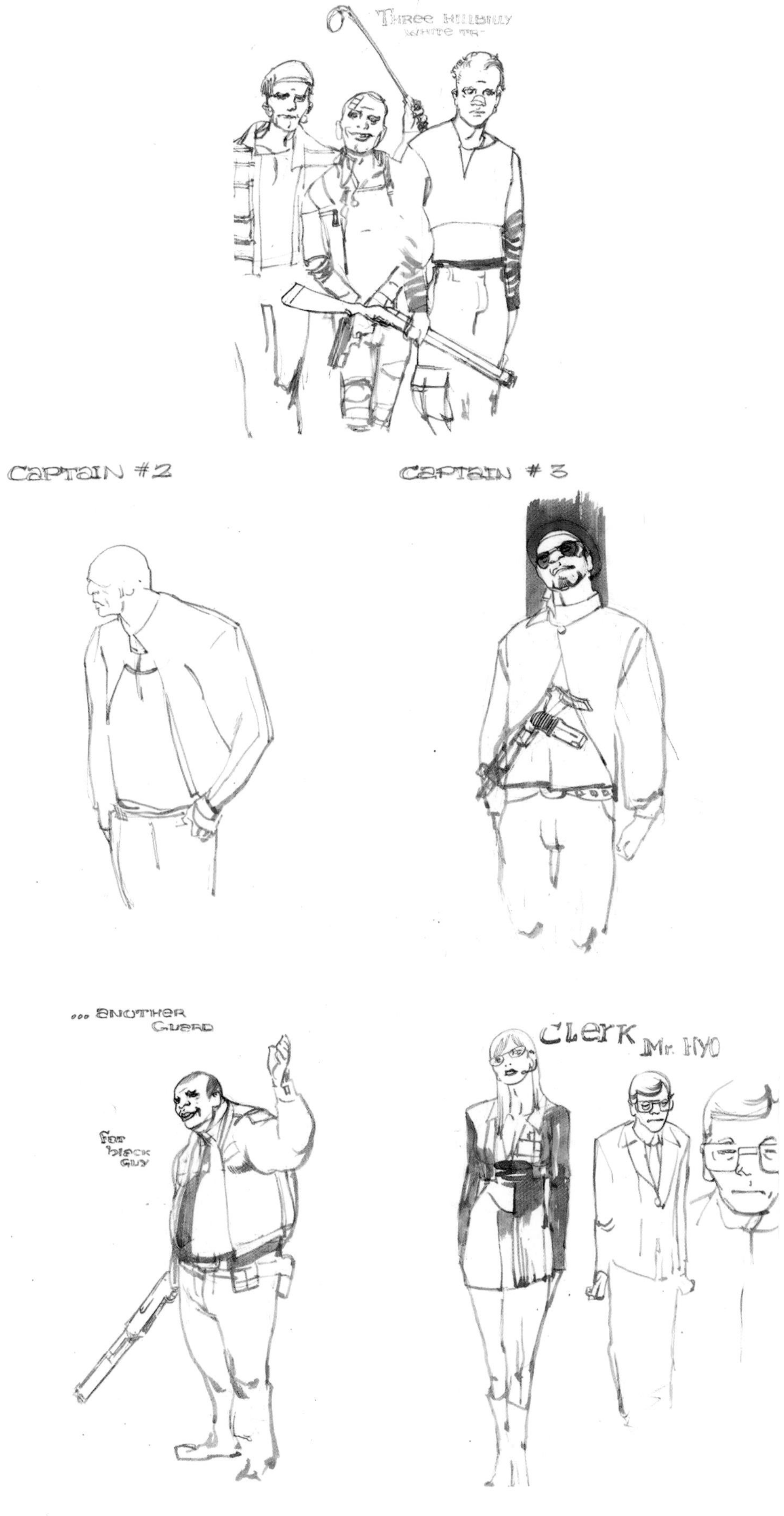
Three Hillbilly
White Tr-
Captain #2
Captain #3
... another
Guard
fat
black
guy
Clerk
Mr. Hyo

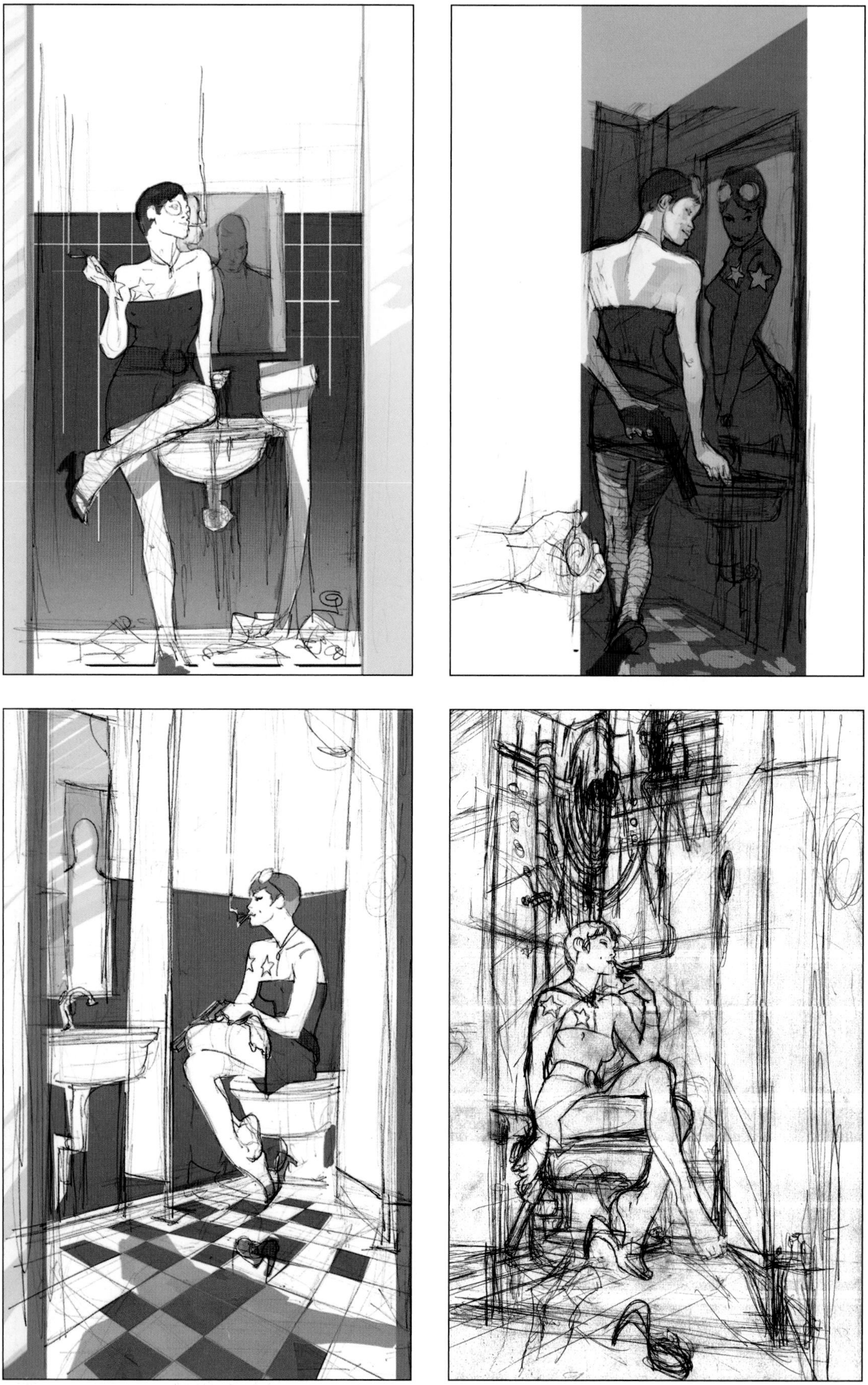

COVER #1 ROUGHS BY **GREG TOCCHINI**

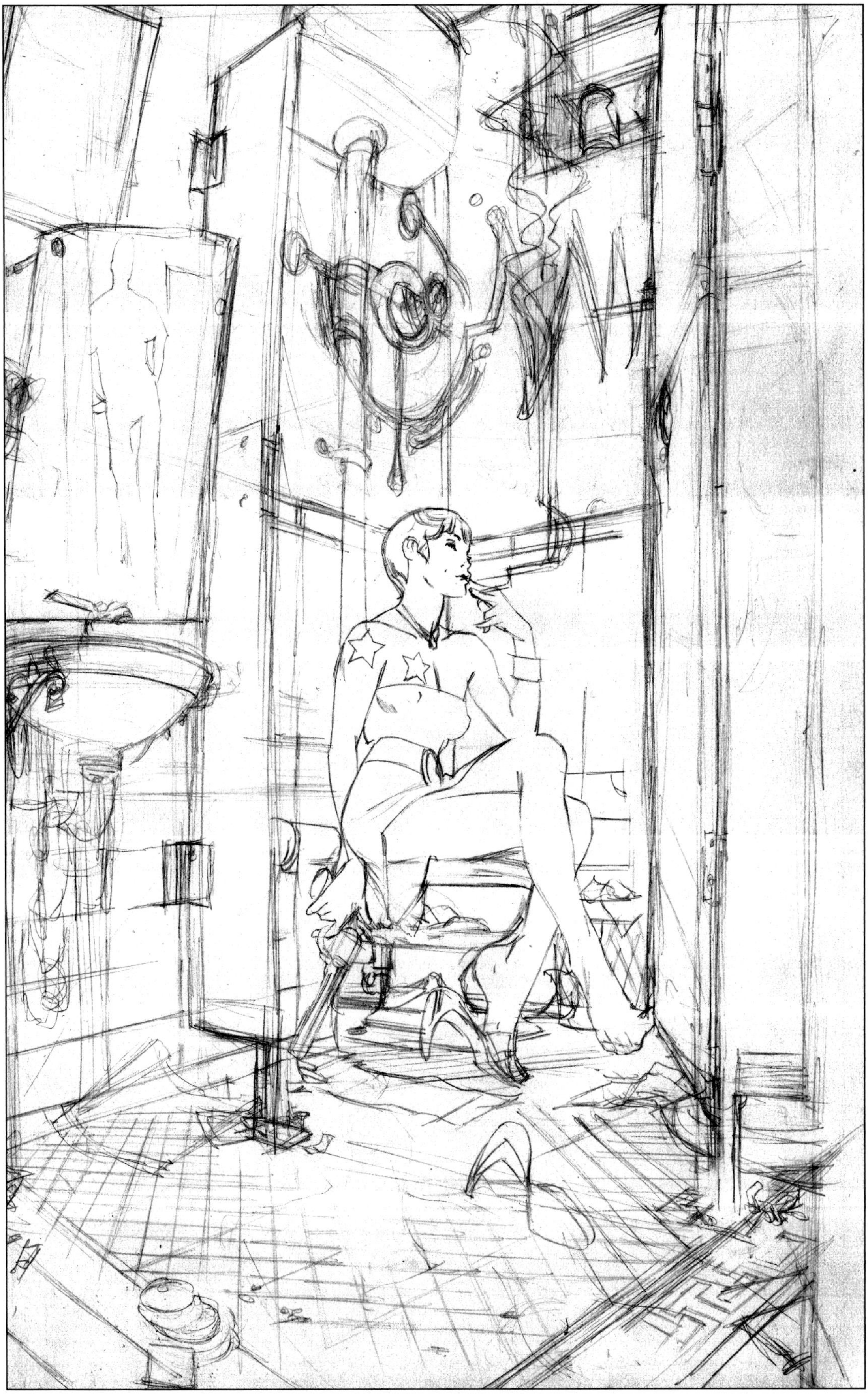

COVER #1 PENCILS BY **GREG TOCCHINI**

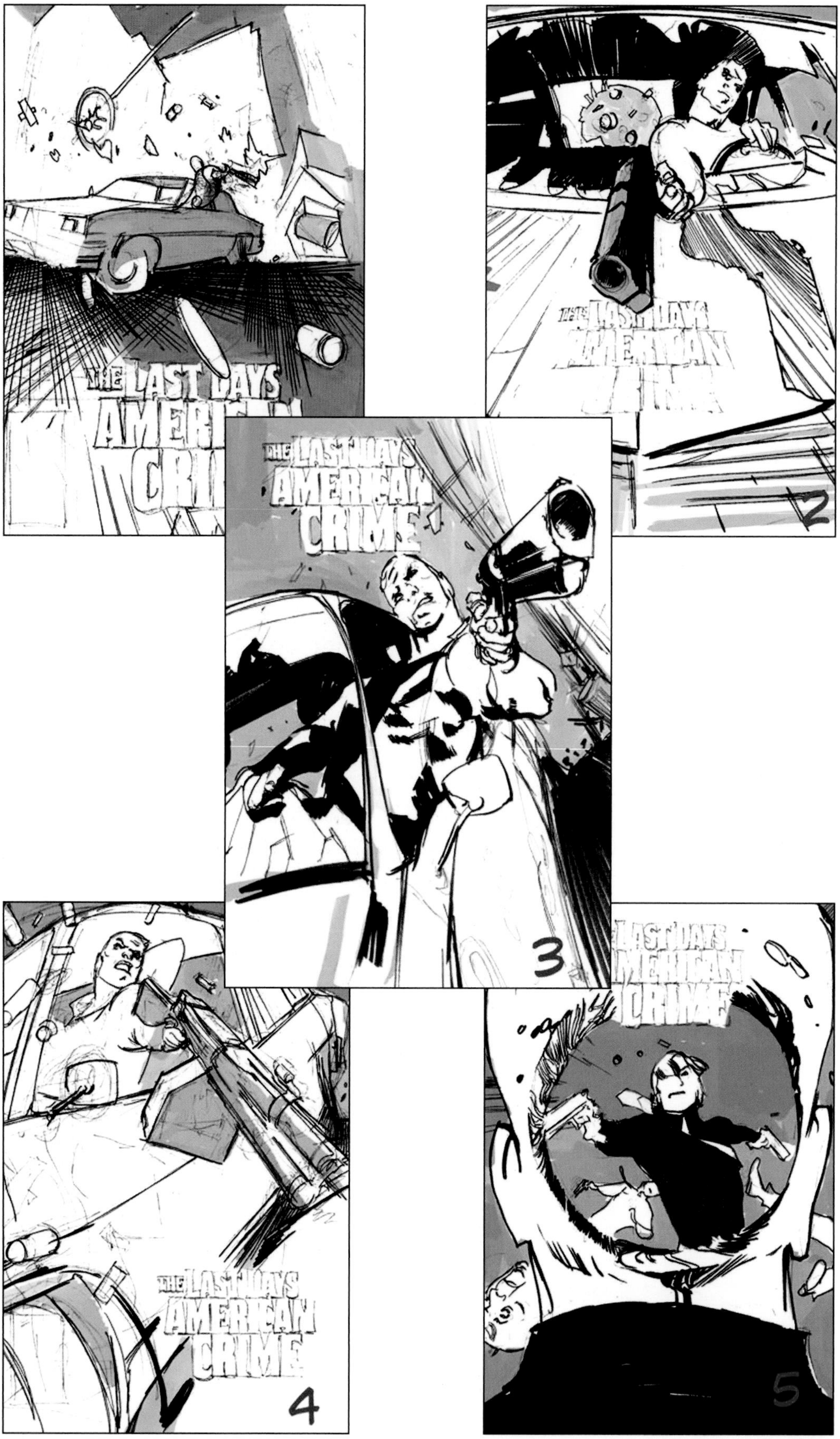
2
THE LAST DAYS AMERICAN CRIME
3
THE LAST DAYS AMERICAN CRIME
4
5

COVER #2 ROUGHS BY **GREG TOCCHINI**

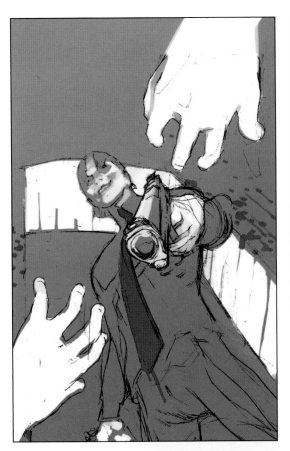

COVER #3 ROUGHS BY **GREG TOCCHINI**

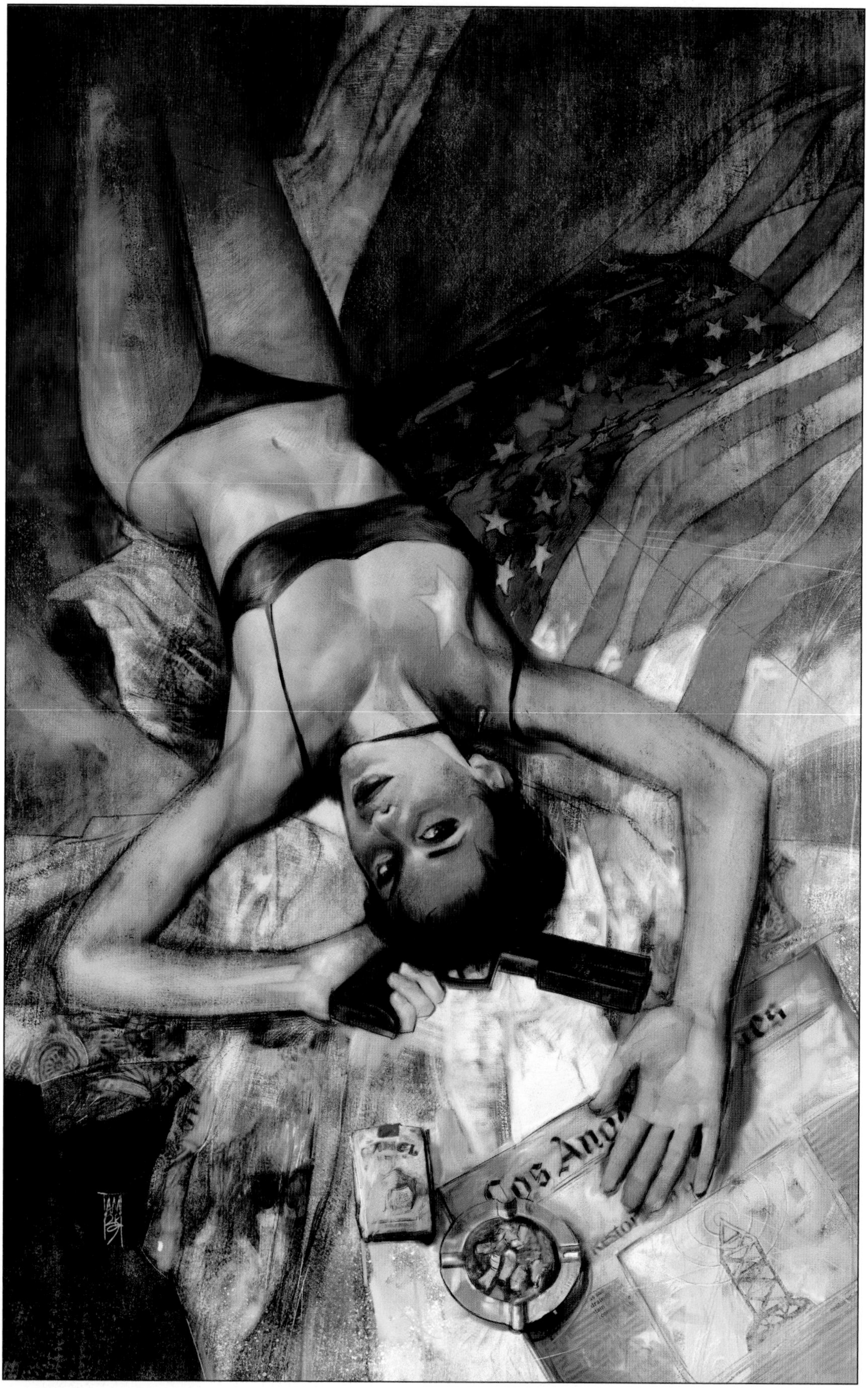

COVER #1 BY **ALEX MALEEV**

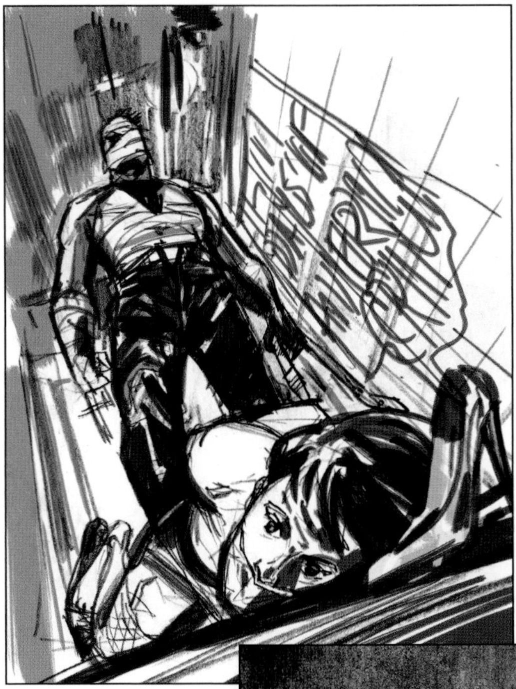

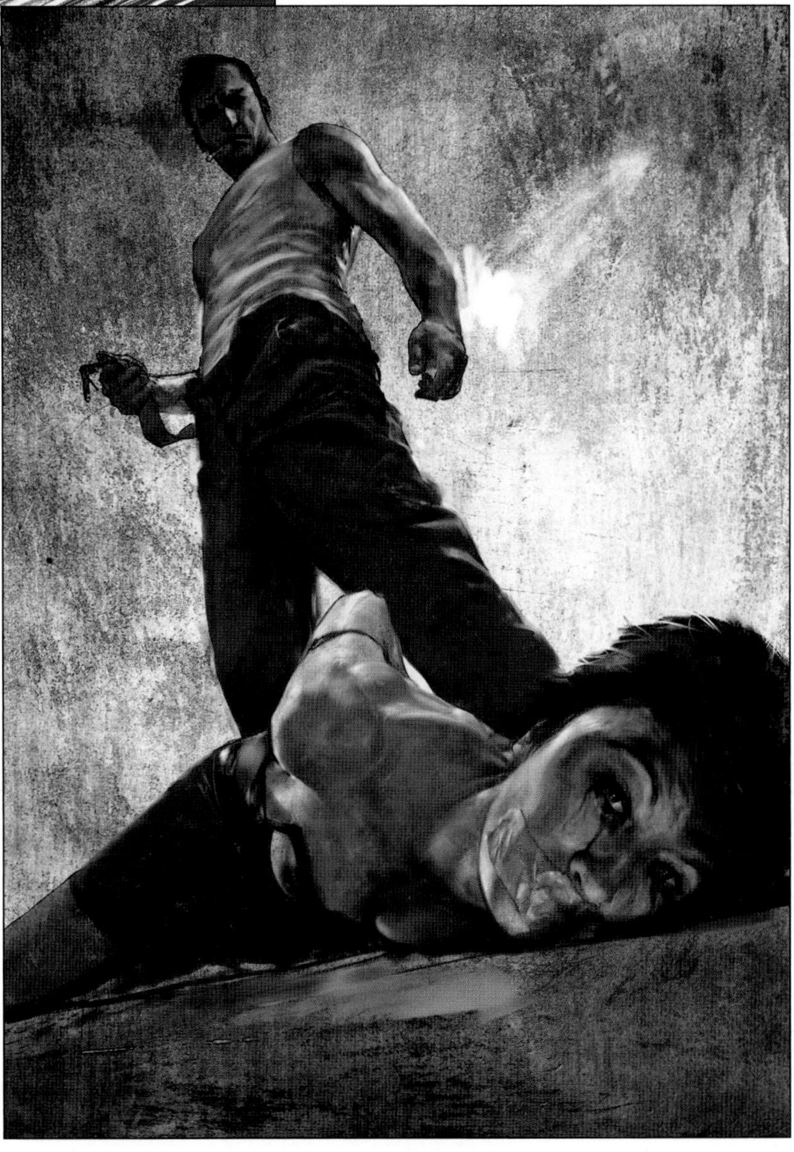

COVER #2 PROCESS BY **ALEX MALEEV**

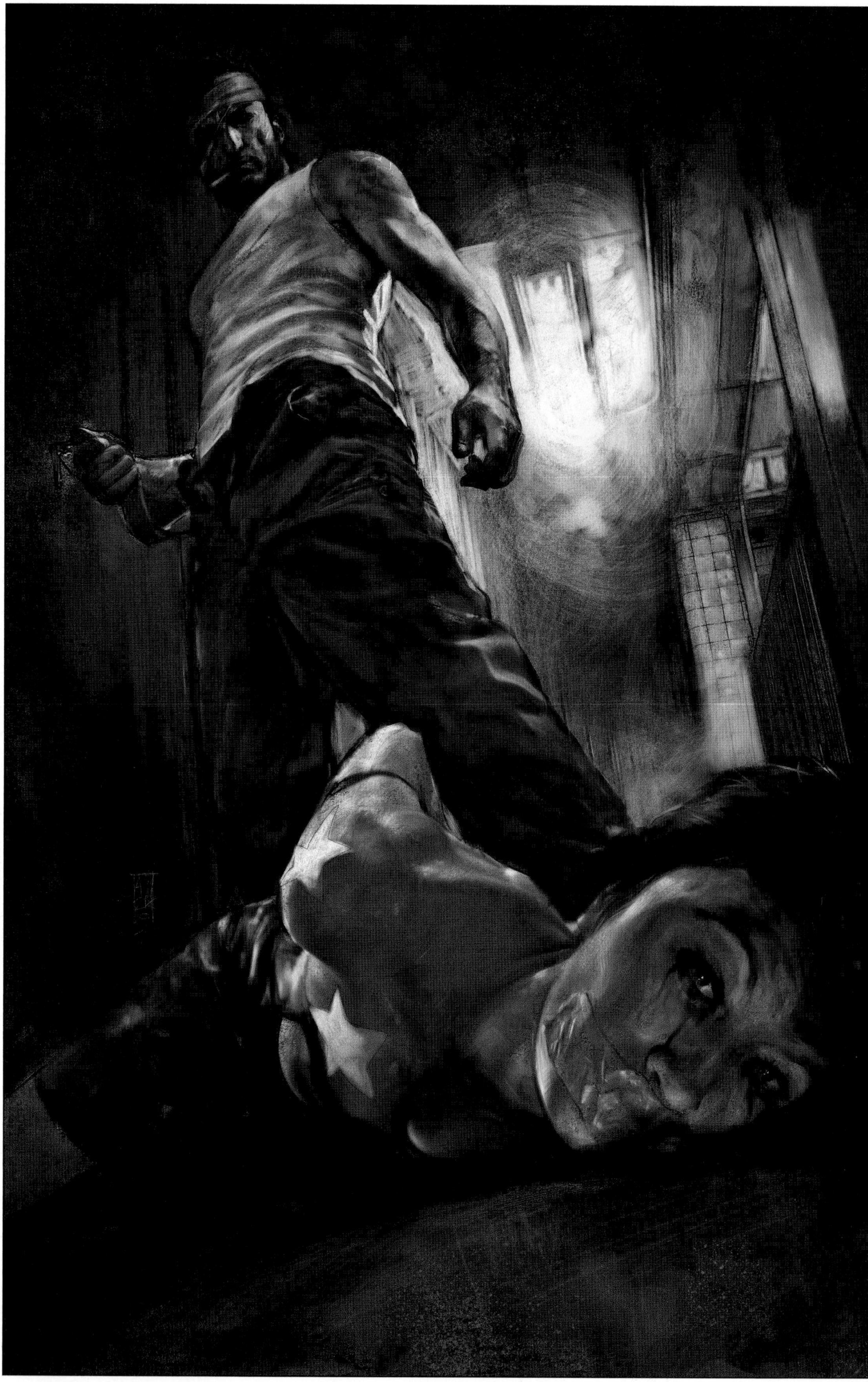

COVER #2 BY **ALEX MALEEV**

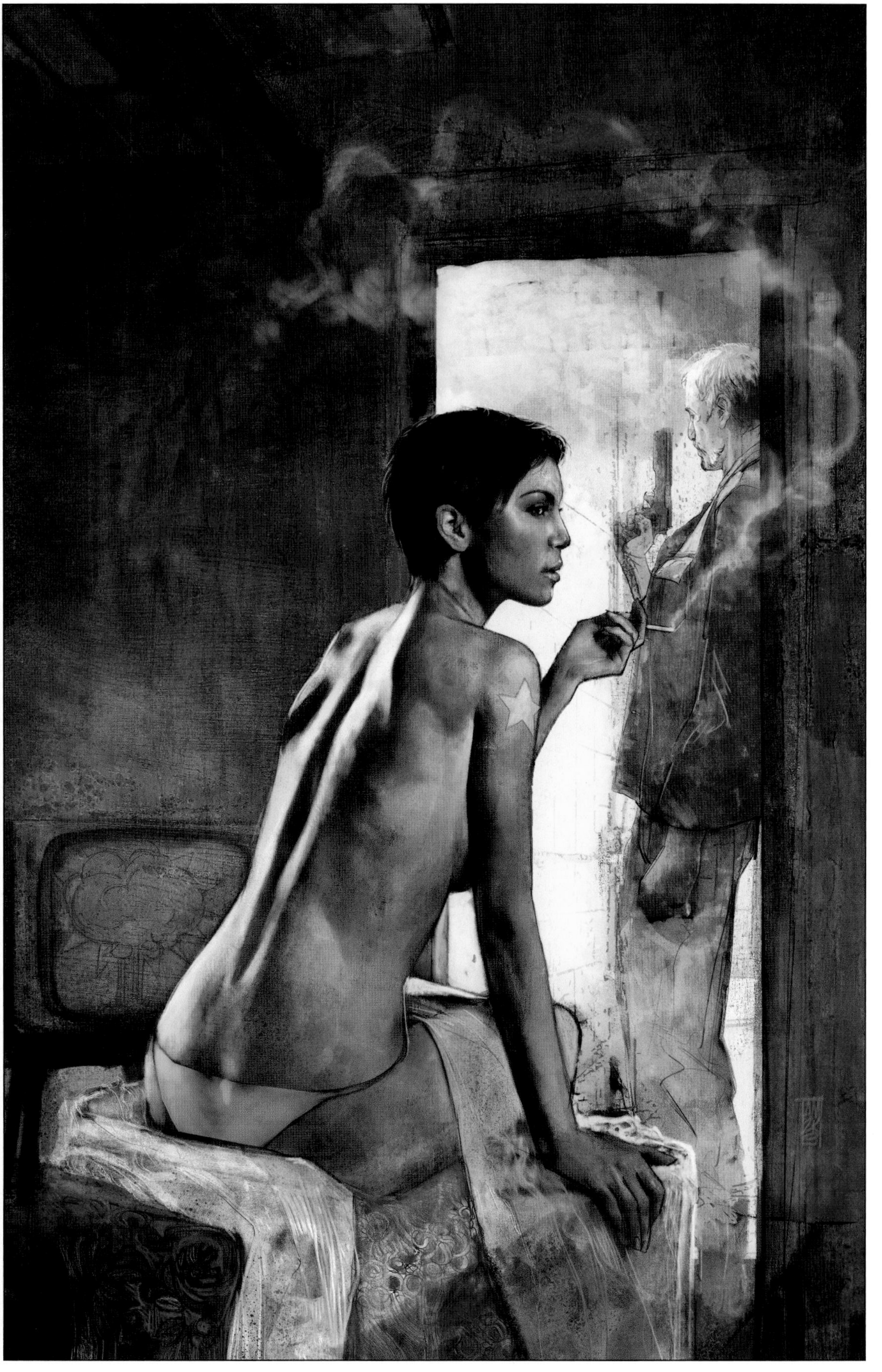

COVER #3 BY **ALEX MALEEV**

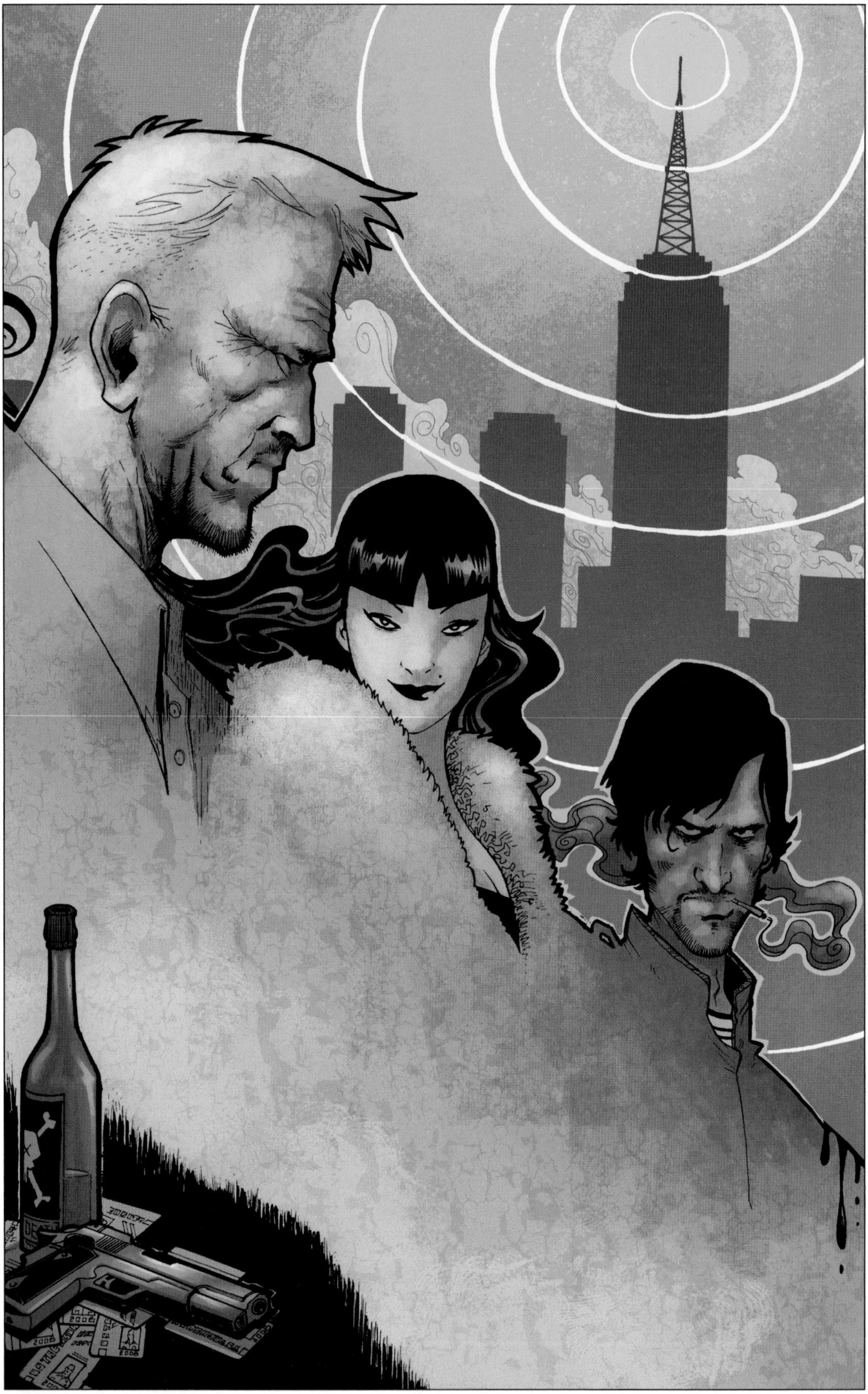

ADDITIONAL COVER ART BY **JEROME OPEÑA** AND **MATT WILSON**

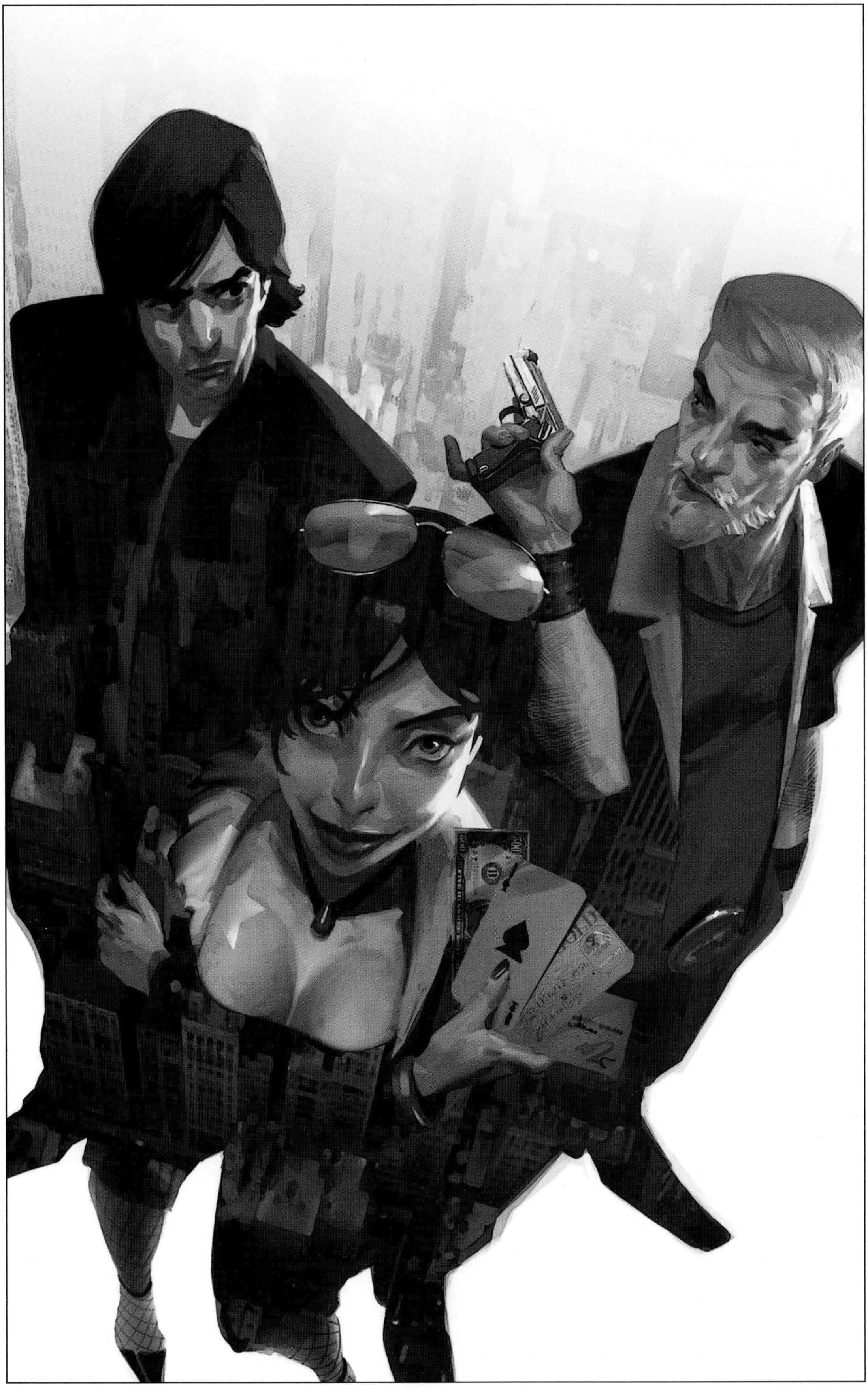

ADDITIONAL COVER ART BY **JOEL DOS REIS VIEGAS**

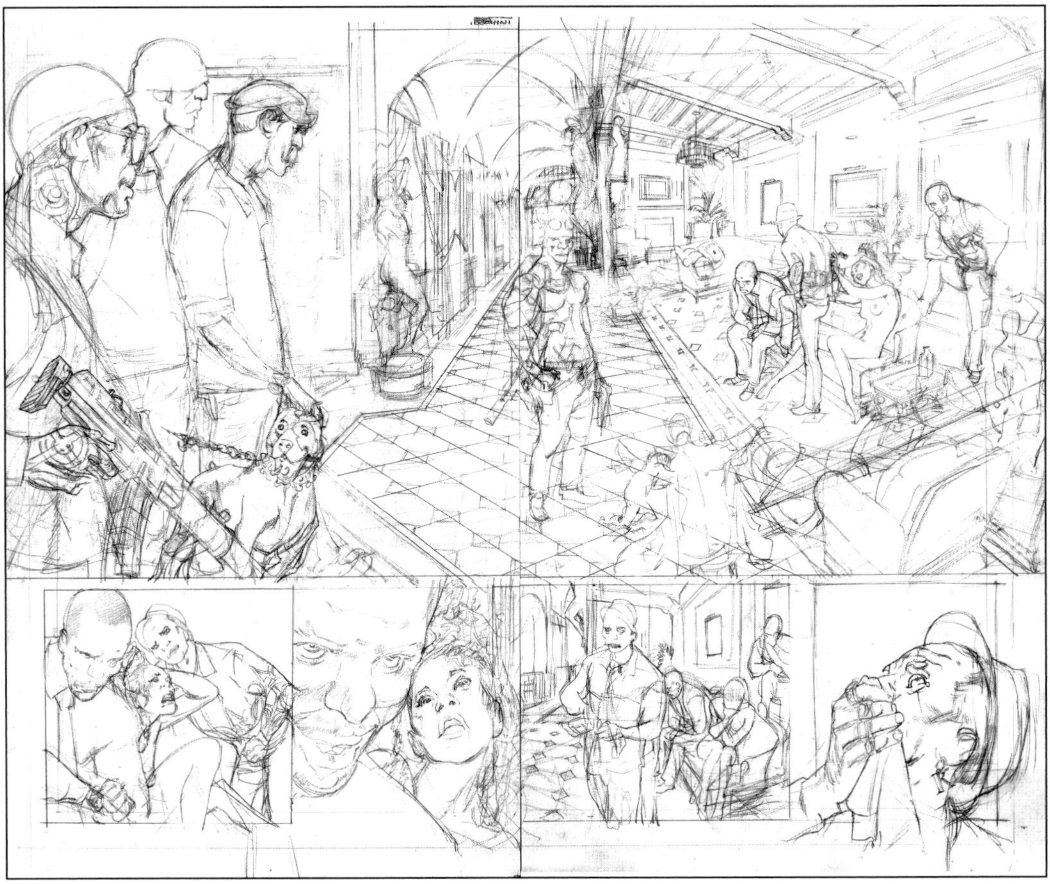

#2 PAGES 2-3 PENCILS

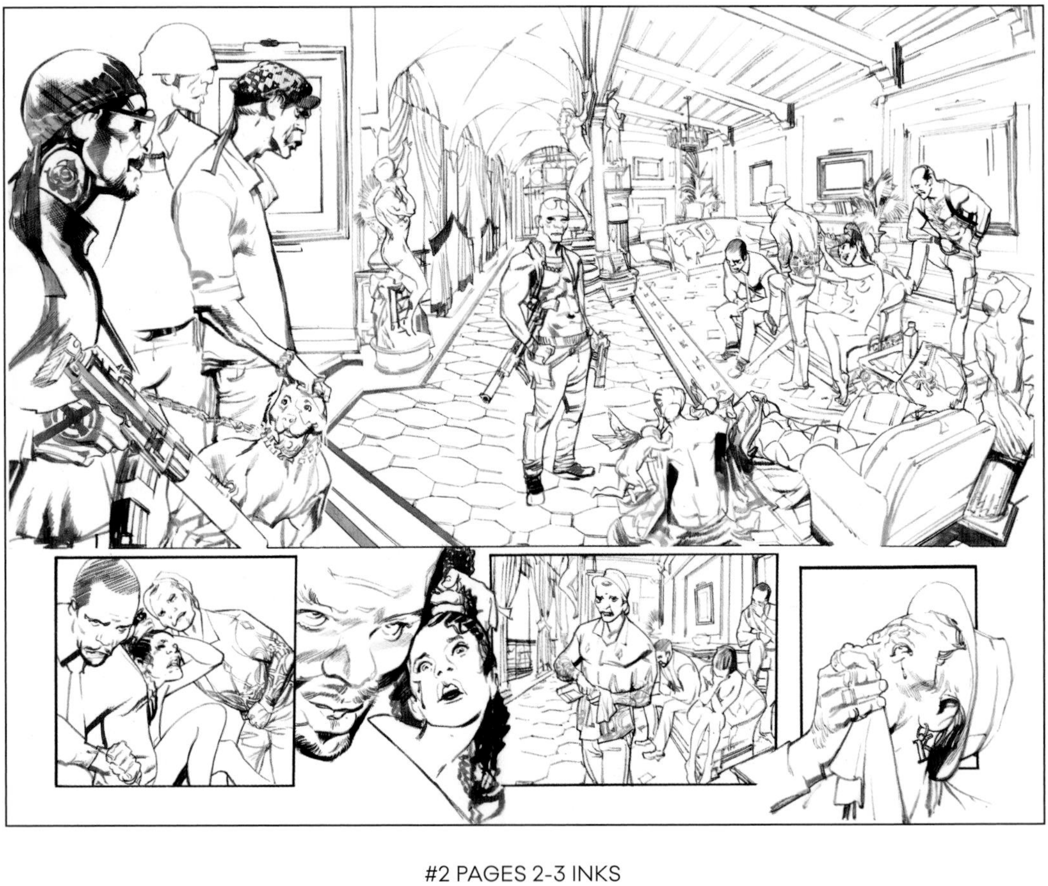

#2 PAGES 2-3 INKS

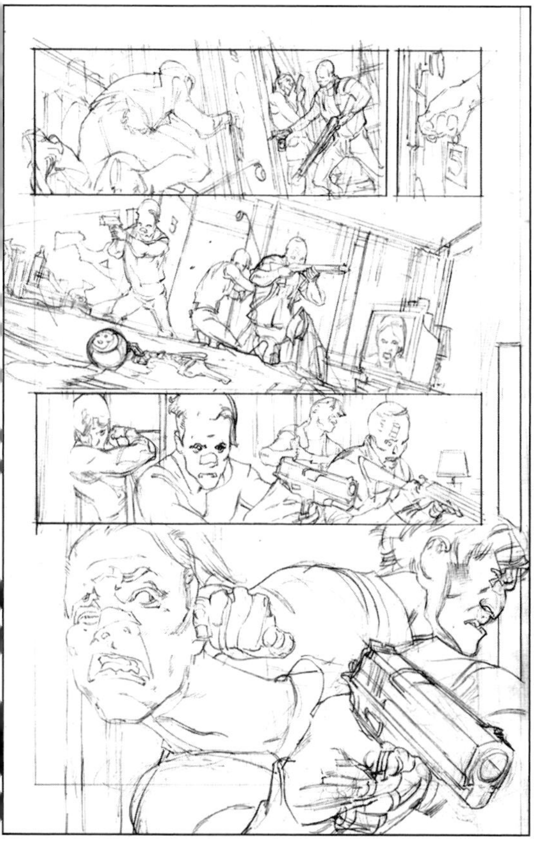

#2 PAGE 16 PENCILS

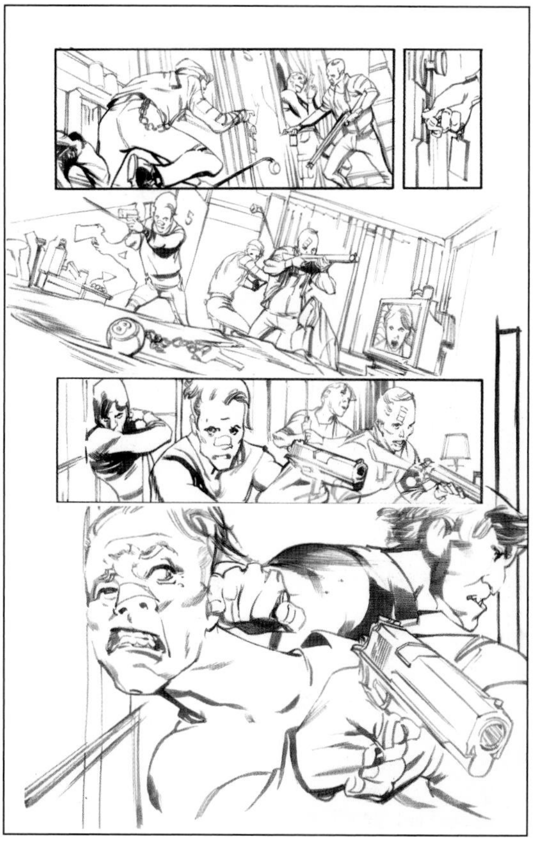

#2 PAGE 16 INKS

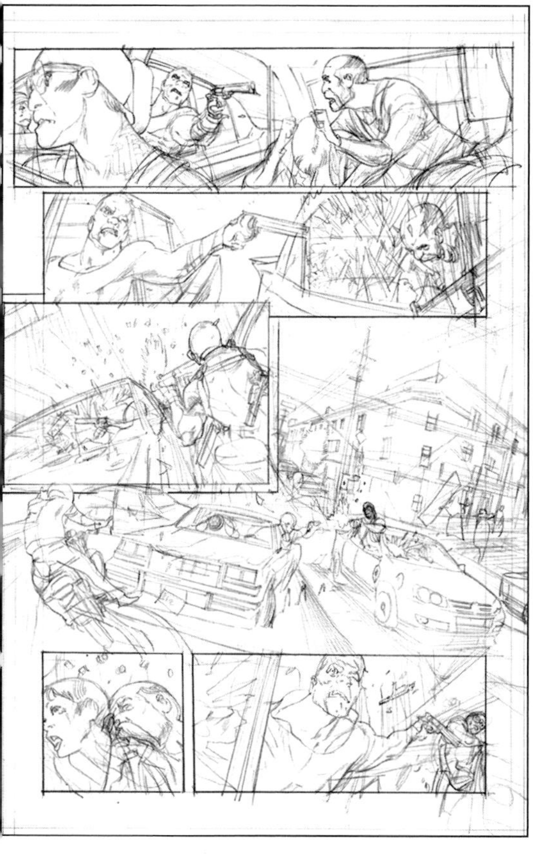

#2 PAGE 42 PENCILS

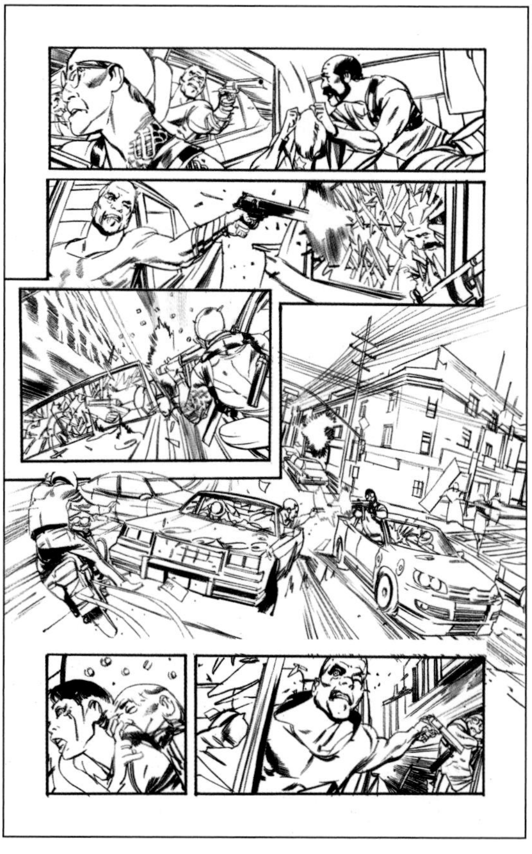

#2 PAGE 42 INKS

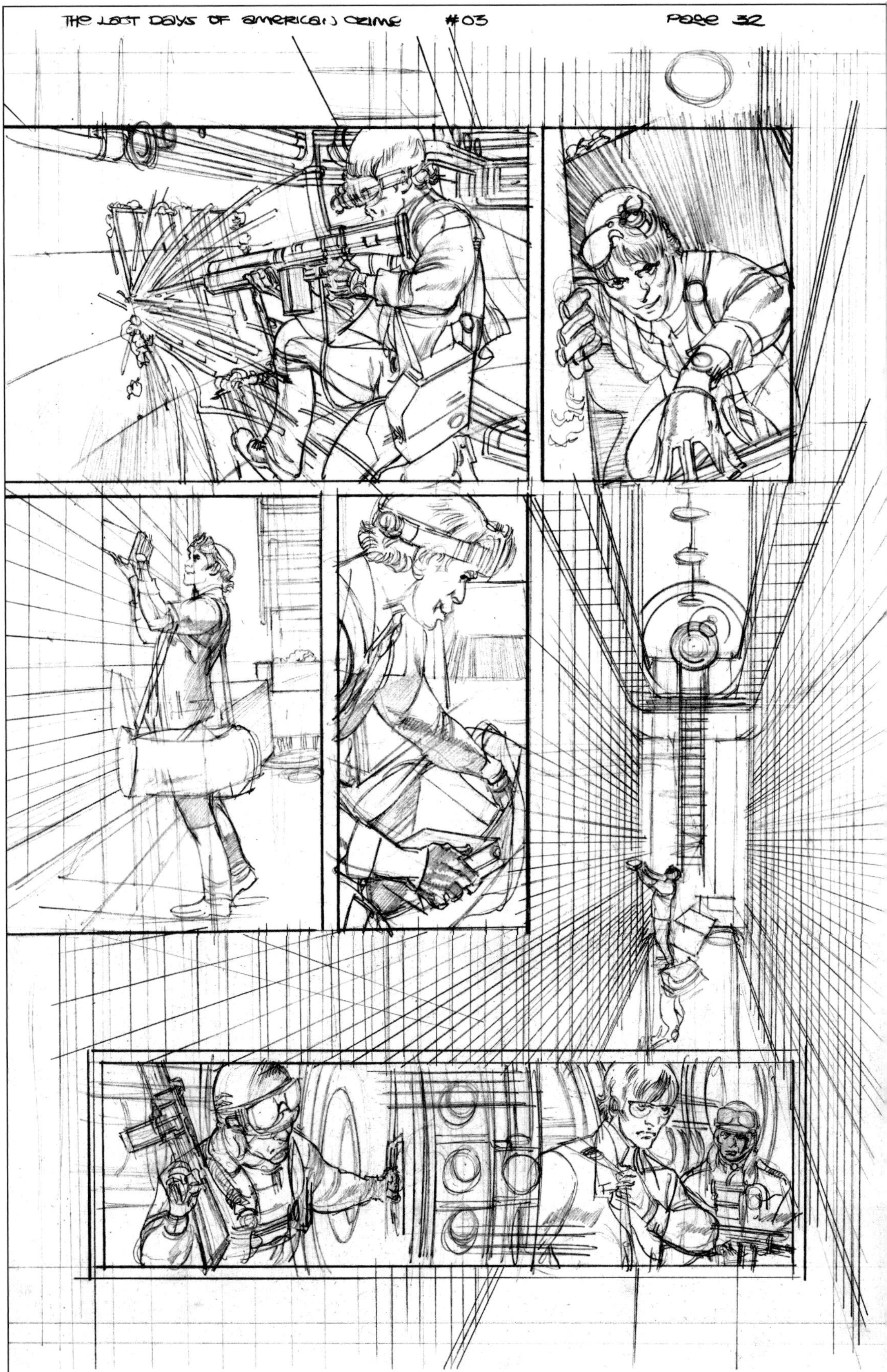
THE LAST DAYS OF AMERICAN CRIME #03 PAGE 32

#3 PAGE 32 PENCILS

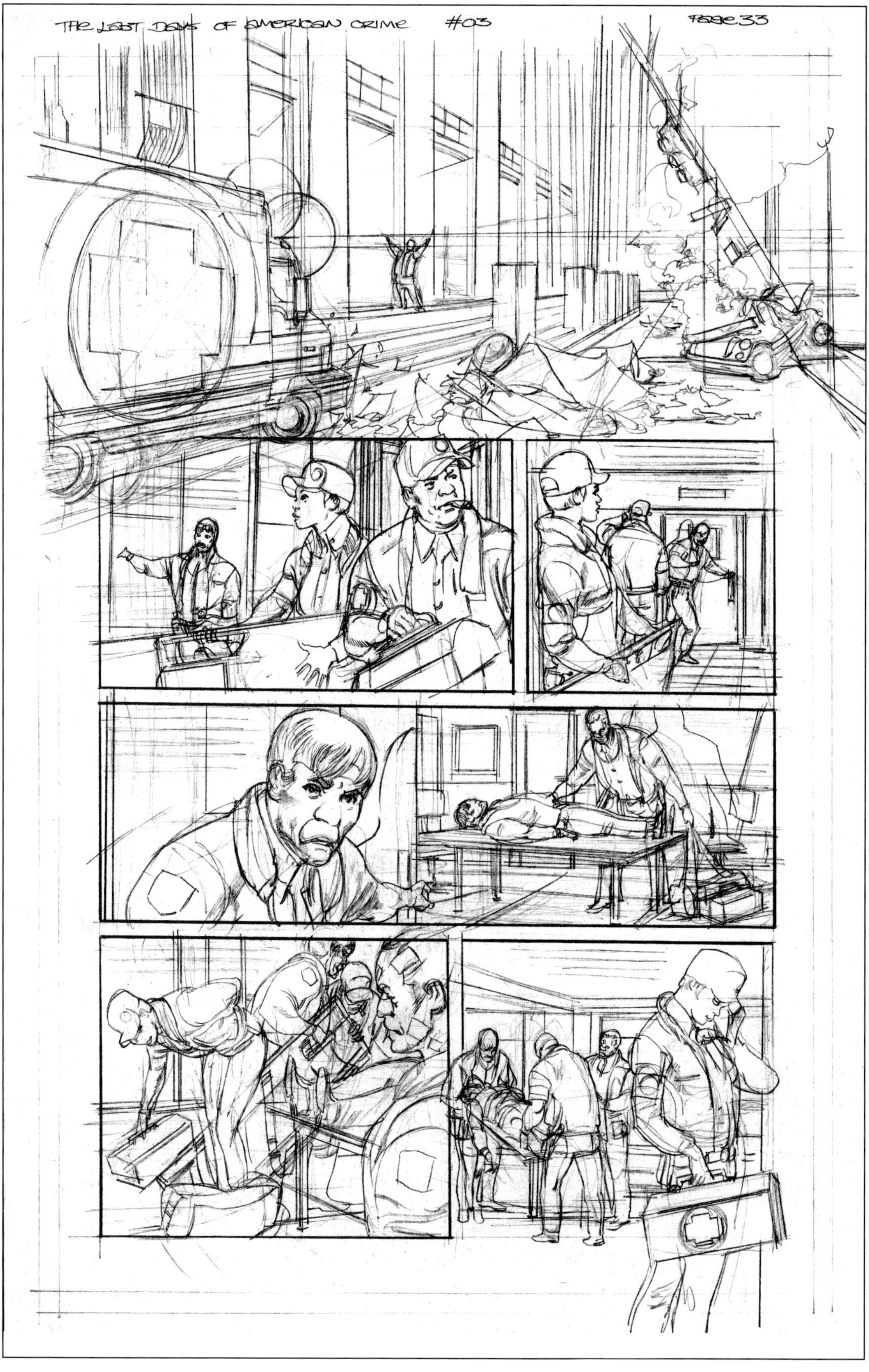
THE LAST DAYS OF AMERICAN CRIME #03
Page 33

#3 PAGE 33 PENCILS

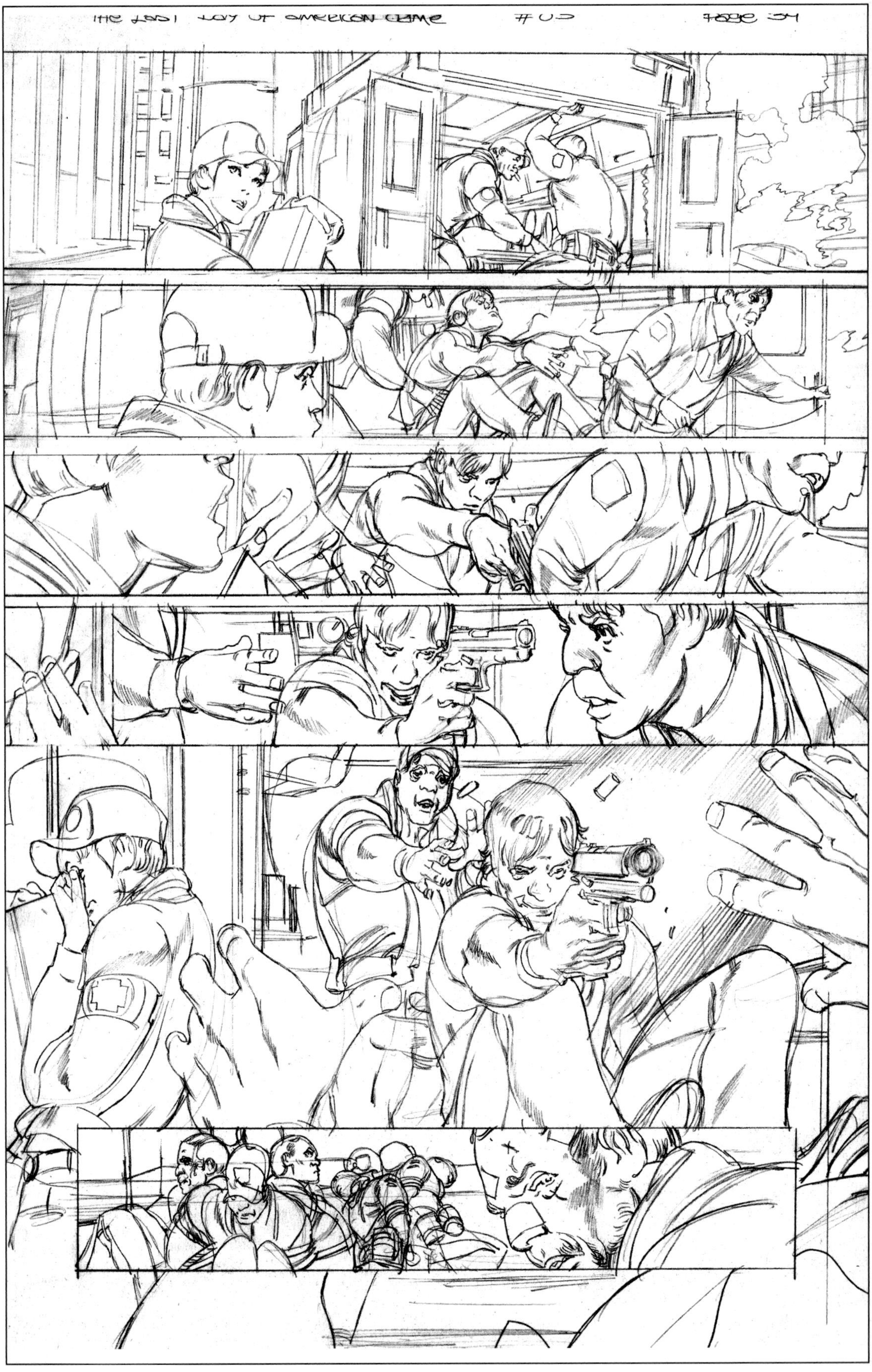

#3 PAGE 34 PENCILS

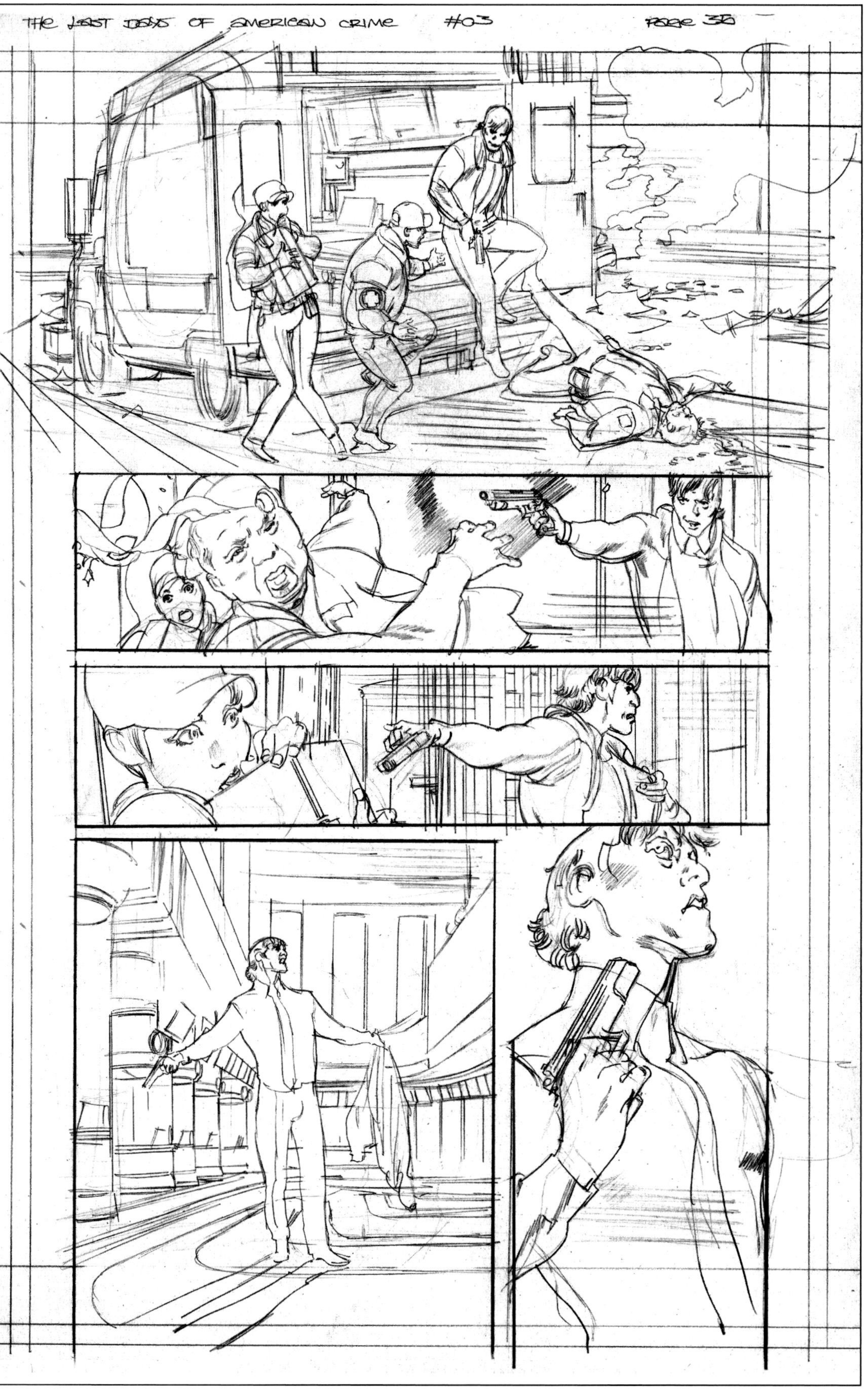
THE LAST DAYS OF AMERICAN CRIME #03 PAGE 35

#3 PAGE 35 PENCILS

THE RESPONSIBLE PARTY

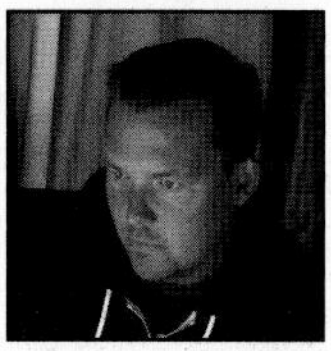

RICK REMENDER is the writer/co-creator of comics such as *LOW*, *Fear Agent*, *Deadly Class*, *Black Science*, and *Strange Girl*. For Marvel he has written titles such as *Uncanny Avengers*, *Captain America*, *Uncanny X-Force*, *Secret Avengers*, *Punisher*, and *Venom*.

Outside of comics he has written video games such as EPIC's *Bulletstorm* game and Electronic Arts' *Dead Space*. Prior to this, Remender served as an animator on films such as *The Iron Giant*, *Anastasia*, and *Titan A.E.*

During his time wrist grinding as an artist, Remender penciled books such as *The Last Christmas*, Bruce Campbell's *Man with the Screaming Brain*, and numerous issues of the *Teenage Mutant Ninja Turtles*, while also inking books such as *The Avengers* and *The Terminator*. He has provided album covers and art for bands such as NOFX, 3 Inches of Blood, Lagwagon, and No Use for a Name.

He taught storyboarding, animation, and comic art at San Francisco's Academy of Art University for many years.

He and his tea-sipping wife, Danni, currently reside in Los Angels raising two beautiful babies.

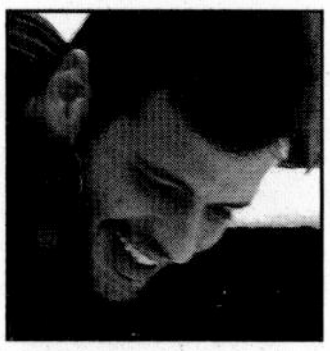

GREG TOCCHINI was born in 1979, in São Paulo, Brazil.

Since 2002 his work has been published internationally by companies such as Marvel and DC Comics (USA) and Le Lombard (France). Some titles include, *The Odyssey*, *Wolverine: Father*, *Fantastic Four*, *Thor: Son of Asgard*, *Captain America*, *Spider-Man*, *1602: A New World*, *ION*, *Batman and Robin*, *Uncanny X-Force*, *Infinity Section* and many others.

He was the artist on the mini-series *The Last Days of American Crime* written by Rick Remender, with whom he recently co-created the science fiction series *LOW*, currently being published by Image Comics. His independent label Dead Hamster Comics published his graphic novel *Sequence Shot* as well as works by various Brazilian artists.

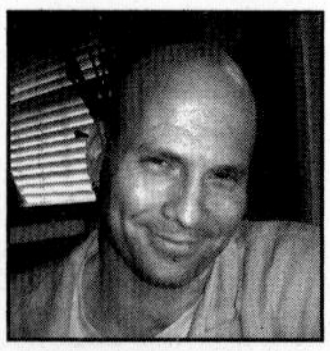

RUS WOOTON has been lettering comics since 2003, mostly Marvel comics until 2011. He now letters a bunch of Image comics including *LOW*, *Black Science*, *Deadly Class*, *The Walking Dead*, *Sex*, and *East of West*. Rus lives in Los Angeles, California and subsists on coffee, spicy Korean noodles, and all the rock music the church warned him about.